A novel by Lucy Ferriss

# THE GATED RIVER

Franklin Watts New York Toronto 1986

Library of Congress Cataloging in Publication Data

Ferriss, Lucy, 1954–
The gated river.

Bibliography: p.
Includes index.
I. Title.

PS3556.E754G3 1986 813'.54 85-29448
ISBN 0-531-15007-0


Printed in the United States of America
6 5 4 3 2 1

*This one is for Carole*

## *Author's note*

This story is set in present-day western Africa, and like all such vaguely located settings for realistic fiction, it begs the question of similitude between the Republic of Yumana, the Lethe and Nebo tribes, and so forth, and the small, turbulent countries that front that coast today. Yumana—along with its peoples and languages—is not a disguise for any country, nor is the fictional role of the United States State Department based on that department's action in any part of the world.

Those familiar with western Africa, however, will recognize certain religious concepts, tribal and racial prejudices, forms of speech, and forms of government, as well as climatic and topographical features. Political divisions in this part of Africa have often been artificial, and many traditions and problems are shared. The attempt in this book has been to draw on those themes that have meaning to the story being told.

Like all the characters in *The Gated River*, Yumana is a creation of the author's imagination, but like all such creation, its roots lie deep in tangible soil.

*The Gated River*

Oh what is this new troubling tide
Of eager waves that pour
Around and over, leaping, parting, recalling?

Elspeth Huxley
*Four Guineas*

# Chapter 1

The night that Biswandi came by, Marika Hooper had been unable to get the girl out of her head since morning. A girl of the Lethe tribe, lying dead under a catalpa tree by the roadside on the way to the Homeland Bridge. The sight would not have been surprising—she herself had seen others, her husband Richard had witnessed dozens by now—had it not been outside the troubled quarter of the city, and had she not at first mistaken what she saw.

As she had approached the spot, early in the day, she had thought the slim, naked object around which the road peddlers clustered to be a branch of the catalpa, fallen in the strong night winds, its polished wood nestled in the long grass. When they saw her, the group of men parted as though she had motioned them to clear a way. Drawing near, she saw the branch transform itself into a girl, and the girl into a corpse, all in the space of time that it took for a broad bluish leaf of the tree to drift from the grass across the body. Then the girl's still grace, the sun on the smooth back and buttocks, struck Marika like a blow. Her hair was gathered into little short braids, the way they arranged it in the country, clasped to her head by plastic bows.

The soles of her feet, pink like the bows, turned upward, their toes pointed in.

There had been no chance to tell Richard yet. He had not returned home from the day's expedition, a trip with Biswandi and outside observers to inspect medical facilities at the huge manmade lake above the city of Revenir. From the dam he had phoned Marika to say he would be stopping off for drinks, which she knew meant he would head due north from the lake to the thickly forested hills where Biswandi could not extend his reach. She couldn't mention the girl on the phone, but when she had hung up she went to find Seki, the housemaid, and asked her what she had seen on the road that morning. Seki had stonewalled: "I'm not seeing anyone when I'm coming straight-on, Missis. It's not liking to be late."

As the light ebbed, Marika sent Seki home. Alone in the hilltop ambassador's villa, she stood on the porch exposed to the early wind of the harmattan and the rising whine of the cicadas. Below, where the trees cleared, a refracted ray fell on the road, and she could just make out Seki's form as the young woman walked fast to beat the curfew home. Seki carried the towels Marika had given her on her head; her arms swung like pistons, moving her away down the wide dirt road.

The girl, from where Marika had stood, had looked untouched. There might have been blood on the other side of the head, near the face, but the deep mahogany-skinned form had lain flawless before the stares of the men and boys who sold ivory and carved trinkets on the way into town.

—*She's no more than a child!* Marika had cried out in her mind.

And, as always, a voice had sounded in her ear to calm her, answering, *Keep a grip on yourself, Rika. Pretend there's a God, and he's showing you this for a purpose. Take in her muscles, the shine of her skin. All that energy. Steal it away like you're saving her life. Cry about her later, when you know why.*

The voice belonged to Justin Kilroy. As she stood near the girl, it ran like an underground stream below Marika's thoughts and mingled with the distant percussion, blown in by the westerly wind, of the Parambo Dam, its thunder muffled by rainforest and by the thick blanket of pollution that hung over the eastern pockets of the city. The warming sun had cooked the yellow haze like a soup, vapors rising in curls against the cloudless dome of the sky.

When Seki was out of sight, Marika crossed the gravel lot to the square, aluminum-roofed garage behind the house, which had been left open in feigned anticipation of Richard's return. Monkeys had been getting into the garbage sacks inside the garage, their shrieks breaking the night silence in the small hours. She closed and latched the sliding door. Back in the house, she poured herself a brandy and took it to the glassed-in patio they called the lesson room, which faced east and was protected from the ocean-borne wind of the harmattan. There were no calendar years here in Yumana, only seasons, wet and dry following one another in unvaried succession. Sixteen seasons, she and Richard had been here—three years before the dam was built, then a respite of three years in Washington, then a second tour to Yumana which was entering its fifth year, its ninth season.

For the last eight of those seasons she had used the lesson room to teach voice and a medley of instruments to daughters and sons of the ruling elite, plus a few pupils of whom the elite were ignorant. Often, on nights like this, she settled herself at the piano and sang, either for Justin or simply to keep in practice; but tonight she took the music stool only to look over the city of Revenir, below. Save for the path of white that led over the inlet to the president's palace, and the red and amber of army vehicles scavenging the streets for curfew violators, its lights were extinguished. Over the rise of the bridge, she could just make out the steel dome of the palace itself, built for its present resident, the republic's president, Amoz Mayume. To the right were silhouetted against the dusky sky the bold new pillars of the downtown area, near the harbor, where the American embassy was. Still farther east came the fishermen's town, the market, and the large, flat tract by the diminished river—all invisible, the moon yet unrisen.

One pair of amber headlights turned off the newly built parkway and, as Marika watched, began the series of switchbacks up the hill that led to the Hoopers'. Marika knew who it was as soon as the high beams swept across the low scrub that began the incline, and she knew he had seen the house lights on.

His full name was James Aholo Biswandi, and he was chief general of the Republican Army of Yumana. It was to him that Amoz Mayume owed his life, and it was on Biswandi's account that Richard had sneaked off tonight like a jackal into the bush. The car's lights approached the house, then disappeared around the back as Biswandi parked. He entered without knocking, though this was the American ambassador's house and American interests were what kept Biswandi in power. Only army personnel could venture abroad after dark, and Biswandi knew how to hold an advantage.

"You are preparing for us a little concert, Mrs. Ambassador?" he said from the other side of the screen.

"Just scraping the rust from my fingers," Marika answered, her back to him. She lifted her hands to the keys, as if Ravel could make the general vanish.

"I must hear your soprano voice one day." The sliding

door to the room swished and clicked, then Biswandi stood next to the piano, his face dark in the backlight from the house. As he struck a match and leaned over to light a votive candle on the console, she smelled the salt of his sweat mingled with the thick oil he used on his hair. "I hear your husband has found a new orchid," he said. He sat down heavily in one of the deck chairs by the window but did not remove his visored general's cap. Marika ran her fingers quickly up and down an arpeggio, the notes slicing into the night.

"I wouldn't know," she said, inventing. "He came straight home and went to bed without eating anything. I'm afraid he's ill." Playing softly on, she avoided Biswandi's eyes as they took in the candlelight without reflecting it back. She glanced only as far as his neck, which bulged over the tight collar of his military jacket, hung heavily with gold-colored ropes and copper medals. "Can I get you a brandy?"

"Don't trouble yourself."

"No trouble."

Lifting her hands from the keys, Marika rose and walked, thinking, *Steady, steady,* to the small bar just inside the main house. Even when Richard was present, James Biswandi frightened her—his liver-brown face unreadable behind its moist folds of fat, his lips bluntly puckered like a fish's mouth. Alone with him, her flesh gelled as if bitten by cold air.

Biswandi was not a Sacatra, like the others who held sway in Yumana, with their fawn-colored skin and the dry humor they had inherited from the British. The Sacatra had been taken from all over the coast as slaves, but when the slave ships were stopped on the sea they had been brought back and set down, dozens of far-flung tribes, in this one place. Here first the French, then the British had taught them colonial rule and bequeathed to them the mannered ethics of a displaced aristocracy. But Biswandi was a Lethe, indigenous. His people had once lived on the banks of Yumana's great Parambo River, the Bird River, so called because its tortuous course had, with some imagination, resembled the wing and beak of a giant stork. Since 1972, when the World Bank had first sent young Richard Hooper here alone to begin negotiations for a dam, experts had known that the lake that would form above it would inundate the forest plain, like a blot of ink spilled on a sketch. Negotiations—loan guarantees, tests of flood levels and bedrock, estimates of fall depth and kilowatt production, the corraling of the IMF—had occupied the three years of Richard's first consulship. By the time the Hoopers returned for a second appointment, the talk had ended; the wing and beak of the river had washed away. Now Pioneer Aluminum of Indiana ran the smelter and hydroelectric plant, worked by the Lethe whom Biswandi's troops had routed from their homes, up at the Parambo Dam.

"So, Mr. Richard is ill from going to see doctors," Biswandi said.

"I heard you checked on the installations at the south shore."

"A sweaty trip—but splendid, this hospital. He told you?"

"Oh, yes, he told me."

Those who still lived by the enormous lake above the dam suffered from schistosomiasis, the "snail fever," and from sleeping sickness; their cattle died of rinderpest and their pigs of the poisonous lilies that bred in the still water. Those who had left had gone mostly to join the *dai*, the guerrillas in the hills—Dai being a Lethe god who roughly symbolized one's own conscience. Tonight Richard was meeting in the hills with *dai*; Biswandi's main job was to hunt the *dai* down.

Marika's hand shook as she poured brandy for her guest. To calm herself, she thought of Justin's hand, pouring, the thick hairs of his forearm. He would not recognize her, afraid this way. He admired her wide-hipped solidity, her Slavic firmness. "I think," she said, "it was the food Richard ate. His stomach."

"He had not complained to me."

"It hit him later, I guess. When he came down from the lake."

Biswandi took the glass she held out. "You should apply this tonic to him," he said, drinking. "Drive out the snail fever!" He laughed, a sound like a bark, then sat forward, his elbows on his knees. "But there sits only the lady's car in the drive."

"The jeep's in the garage. What do you mean?"

"The Land Rover is put away, is it? Richard Hooper is in bed?" The narrow eyes scanned her, noting the soft chin, the thick hair just darker than blond, curling around her neck, the breadth of the upper arms and chest—a singer's chest, slight though she was in the ribcage, the scooped neck of her jersey accenting the broad, freckled collarbone.

Marika nodded, twice. She had an hour at least before Richard would return. "Can I give him a message for you?" she tried.

"A message?" Biswandi seemed to consider the thought as if it were a term to define. "No, no. You must not give Ambassador Richard Hooper, who is sick in bed from inspecting medical facilities, a message. No." He fell silent and after a moment lifted his glass delicately and downed its contents.

Marika, too, raised her brandy to her lips, but she did not taste. She tried to remember how she had acted in the long evenings when Biswandi visited Richard—with others, of course; he'd never come alone before now. They had negotiated American aid, the doe-eyed and torpid President Mayume mouthing friendship and democracy while Biswandi cited rebel installations and Soviet arms. On a lighter note, they stopped to admire Richard's orchids. Marika had served the drinks and entered the conversation only when asked how her music students were coming. President Mayume wanted a national orchestra, the first of its kind in this part of Africa, and he counted on Marika's lessons. Otherwise, she retreated to the closely imagined world she inhabited with Justin Kilroy, her lover—whom she had not seen, save in her mind's eye, for almost fifteen years.

So it was that she had gone to Justin that morning, after seeing the dead girl in her still grace, and conjured him to make love to her. Now, out of the corner of her eye, she could almost see Justin perched on the piano stool behind her.

—*He wants something out of me*, she said to him.

—*What else besides your prize of a husband?*

—*There's a cable inside, from the State Department. I haven't told Richard. They want to send military advisers. They're getting reports of unrest, they say.*

—*You make unrest in my heart.*

—*He'll want to read that cable—Biswandi. He'll worm his way around to it.*

—*I could take you right here, on the bare floor.*

—*Someone must have told him about it. Someone in Richard's office.*

—*Rika, Rika. Give your mind a rest. Feel how tense you are.*

Marika felt Justin's hand, as he leaned over from the piano stool, squeeze the back of her neck. The blood vessels along her spine released, sending a warm rush to her head. Just so, Justin Kilroy had touched her one day in their last week together, walking along Jones Beach in the heat of August's late afternoon, while she had argued herself into marrying Richard Hooper. She could still feel the North Atlantic breeze lifting her hair. The sand under their bare feet was wet from high tide; over their heads, white gulls keened the departed crowds. His hand, suddenly hesitant in a familiar territory, pinched and let go her taut shoulder muscle, then remained there, the fingers rough with salt. *I could take you right here on the beach. Away from the water, in that hollow. No one would see.*

—*See how he rubs the glass between his palms,* she heard Justin say now, bent toward her ear while Biswandi studied his empty snifter. —*It could be a human head, say the head of a child. He's gauging whether he can crush it, or whether he does just as well to drop it onto the hard floor. On the floor it will splinter into a hundred fragments, and in each shard of glass you see a black face shining in the light of the candle. That's what I paint, each face fitting its jagged piece, glimmerous with a film of brandy. I'll paint oil on finished wood, the wood resisting the paint.*

"We tell an old fable here," Biswandi began again, as if he saw the fable in his empty glass. He put the glass down on the low table, where the red light embraced its globe. "It is concerning a man, a scorpion, and a hen. You have heard it?"

Marika shook her head. The Lethe myths she knew came in songs, chants from the hills, ballads of the old Parambo kings.

"Once a man," Biswandi went on, leaning back in the canvas chair, "had a rival in love. He is wanting to rid himself of this rival, of course, and he asks a certain scorpion to do this deed. So the scorpion does the thing, and after that time he and the man, they are big friends. They are sharing a room, it is the man's room, and he is taking care not to step on the scorpion in the dark, while the scorpion is keeping from the man's way and also preying on other insects within the room. But then the man, he decides to marry this same woman he loves."

Biswandi left a dramatic pause while he lit a cigarette. With his face hidden from the candle's glow, his voice floated in the dark. He shook out the match and continued.

"The man worries that his woman will not understand the scorpion's being in the house. When she finds out why this must be, she will know her man to be a killer. Now this woman has a hen, which is to be cooked for the wedding feast. The man goes to it and says, 'Hen, I am sparing you from death if you do a thing for me. Tonight while everyone is asleep you fly through the window to my room. There is a scorpion you see in the corner. Peck it to death, and you will have your life.' The hen is saying all right. But the scorpion also is hearing this talk. That evening when the man is taking off his shoes, the scorpion is creeping up on him. He stings the man in the heel and kills him. Great cries of mourning in the town! But no one can find this scorpion, he has transformed himself."

"And the hen and the girl?" Marika asked.

"The hen is killed for the mourning feast. The girl dies with broken spirit." Biswandi moved his chair forward, into the light. Caught up in his tale, he frowned sadly. On their first tour in Yumana, ten years ago, Marika had seen a headman who had the same aggrieved look: he had sat cross-legged in an embroidered robe, his shaved head swathed in white muslin, and he had tossed colored stones onto the ground to tell how his gods and his people would live with the dam.

"It is not a pretty fairy tale," Biswandi said finally.

"You want me to recite the whole thing to Richard?" Marika sipped her brandy.

"Only the part about the scorpion stinging the man. Let him learn what happened to one who invoked the help of a gabbling hen. Tell him I am hoping his stomach settles." A slice of white glinted in the narrow eyes.

Out of instinct, Marika remembered, she had distrusted the fat, mumbling headman; from experience she knew not to trust Biswandi. The trucks roaming below were his. Seki spat whenever she heard Biswandi's name, and once, when Richard was showing Biswandi the greenhouse, Marika had found Seki on the kitchen floor, muttering a Lethe curse. The bullets that had snuffed the naked girl's brain that morning had been fired by Biswandi's men; the girl to them meant no more than the sleek branch for which Marika had at first mistaken her. The straight back and curved buttocks, caressed by the early sun, turned to meat. Marika brought her eyes level with Biswandi's.

"Tell me," she said. "What girl was that by the road this morning?"

"I know nothing of any girl."

"She was dead."

"Perhaps she was struck by a car?" From his pocket Biswandi had produced a toothpick, and he ran it across his front caps.

Had Richard, the diligent and cautious diplomat, been there, he would have pulled Marika away—to the kitchen, to the greenhouse, anywhere—to keep her from saying more. Richard never showed his hand, a quality Marika forced herself to admire in him. But Richard was with the *dai*, salving his conscience, while Marika's own unruly god made her speak: "She'd been shot. On my way back she was gone."

"Oh. Well." Biswandi thrust the toothpick between his

molars and spread his palms out, helpless. "We cannot be everywhere at once, Mrs. Ambassador. Communist terrorists work at night. They have the old ways of violence. We are after all just out of the tree, isn't that so?"

"She couldn't have been more than fifteen." Marika rose as Biswandi stood up, his mission evidently accomplished.

"I've heard no report, before you tell me this." Something like a smile played over the general's face, but he stood again in darkness, shielded by the visor of his cap. "This girl was not a servant?"

"No. I mean, I don't know."

"You'll tell me if you see any more?"

Marika hesitated at his invitation, like an offhand request for news of a rare orchid. She should have kept still; Richard, as always, was right. "Oh, I doubt I will," she said. "See more, I mean."

"Yes, it is almost under control, now. Almost, almost," Biswandi mused as if to himself. He led the way through the airy space of the sunken and skylit living room, built by Richard's predecessor to resemble a ski house in Colorado. As Marika followed, she switched on the light under the dome, illuminating the oil painting on the opposite wall.

When she left Justin, it had still been unfinished. Hanging like a swirling globe on the right of the canvas was a pearly sphere that Marika knew to represent the moon, or heaven, while from the left corner a charred cone sent smoke upward and across, the blacks and grays forming three faces that seemed the next instant to disappear. The title of the painting was *Apollo*, and Justin had begun it three years earlier, the month when the three astronauts burned to death while still earthbound in their capsule. Marika had gone with him to Florida, where he had tried vainly, posing as a workman, to slip into Pad 34 at Cape Kennedy and view the wreckage the week after the accident. "It's not morbid!" he had shouted when she tried to persuade him to quit. "You have to look at it from a wider angle. What if death is the only avenue to the moon, like the back of the north wind?" The painting had begun in violent reds and oranges, she remembered, and gradually been consumed by smoke and by the black vault of space. The flat surface seemed to recede infinitely, only to loop back and arrive at the swirling moon. "Consider why we're fixed on mortality," Justin had said while they circled the site in a rented car. "Think of Icarus."

Marika had found the finished painting in a gallery three years later, just before she and Richard took their first trip to Africa, and she had bought it with two thousand of Richard's dollars. Other paintings—acquired, as Justin's fame had grown, from the galleries of London or Tangiers—hung in different rooms of their house. Richard didn't like any of them, but he never asked why they hung there. He had never asked anything about Justin at all, not out of jealousy, but because he had pegged Justin as a phase that would pass.

At the door Biswandi stopped and snapped his finger. "Ah," he said, "I *do* have a message for Richard Hooper. Yes." Marika nodded, wanting only for him to leave, now, before the lights of the Land Rover swept up the road. "I regret"—here Biswandi took her hand, which she instinctively withdrew, leaving only her slim fingers in his sticky, honey-colored palm—"I cannot attend this reception the ambassador gives tomorrow night."

"Reception?"

"For the new Pioneer man coming in. I have such

pressing business. The night patrol will know of your guests, however. All is arranged." He let go her fingers.

"Is it?" she asked. Richard had told her nothing, not even when he had called from the dam. He sprang such events on her the morning before, knowing how she'd come to hate them.

"Good, good." Nimble for an obese man, Biswandi hoisted himself over the side door into his jeep. As he glanced toward the garage, Marika was grateful to the monkeys that had forced her to use a padlock on the door. "I shall watch for young girls," Biswandi said, looking up at her.

"Don't," Marika replied, but he had started the engine and pointed its yellow lights down the steep road. She did not watch him descend but shut the front door and leaned back against it, one hand to her forehead.

*—I hate this country*, she said to Justin,*—and all I want is you.*

This time he did not answer her, though she thought she could see his face break into a smile, like the momentary curved ripple a stone will cause in water.

Richard was out until after midnight. Marika watched the jeep climb its way up the last curve of the hill without headlights, following the angled counterglow of the low-slung moon. She kept the lights of the house and porch off until he had uncoiled himself from the jeep, walked across the lot with his jacket slung over one arm and his briefcase in the other, and entered the front hall. Without bending, he dropped the briefcase onto the floor, so that it fell with a thud of finality.

"The lake," he said in the dark before she could ask, "is ghastly. People dropping like flies."

"And the hospitals?" Marika followed him through the sunken living room to the kitchen; he gave off odors of sweat and road dust, palm wine, and the lingering trace of medicinal air.

"Hospitals!" Switching on the light as he entered the kitchen, Richard snorted, tilting his head back. "They've got these tents, from the colonial wars in all likelihood, strung up in the center of the village, and a hose running from the well to a large trough at one end, with a fire burning next to it for when they need to boil water. Cots are full of naked people with their sores streaming, so little kids with river blindness are crawling around on the floor waiting to be kicked or have scalding water spill on them."

"Come on. They must watch for that."

"One got a boiling while I was there. Screamed like a hyena, and all they could do was wrap him in a towel and scramble for ointment. The only difference between now and the last time I went up there is the tents and the cots—they've put the dying in one place."

He loosened his collar and ran his palm over the dirt-caked circle of his neck. As always when he was agitated, Richard scarcely looked at Marika—his pale blue eyes darted from one object to the next, his jaw twitching. It was not the time to tell him about the girl. Marika asked, instead, about doctors.

"That's what they call them," Richard said, heading for the bar. "And Christ, how would I know? Maybe they are trained doctors. They spoke English, they had attendants, they bemoaned the lack of facilities and supplies but were immeasurably grateful to President Mayume and General Biswandi—and, of course, us—for all the money and help. How would I know? They've got maybe one for every two hundred sick."

"You'd better read your cable," Marika said, holding up the blue envelope, "then eat. You must be famished."

Richard had mixed himself a martini and returned to the concentric circles of the kitchen table, fashioned from the trunk of a baobab. Marika had bought the slice of tree from a boy who had sat surrounded by monstrous curios on the road into town from the airport on the day the Hoopers had arrived to take up their second residence in Yumana, five years ago. The scene had charmed her, innocent then and as unfeeling as a tourist; she had stared at the thin naked boy in wonder while he hoisted the dirty trunk onto the top of their car and roped it down.

Richard took the envelope from her and stared at it without reading. His white shirt was rumpled from the long drive, first to the lake and then to the back country of the *dai*. Road dust streaked his face; his hair flew off the back of his head. Reluctantly, he drew his glasses from the pocket of his shirt, wiped them on a napkin, and read.

Marika watched him as he went through the cable, moving his lips as he read, the only trait with any hint of slowness that he possessed. The first thing that had attracted her to Richard was this driving analytic intelligence, and still here, in a ravaged landscape choked with dictatorship, he kept applying it, relentlessly piecing together the chaos that he was powerless to actually alter.

*—He'll drive himself insane,* she said privately to Justin.

*—No. He thrives on it. He will drive you insane.*

Pushing himself up, Richard moved past her to the kitchen sink and scrubbed his hands with the brown soap, as if washing away the black ink of the message. But the water ran reddish and grainy into the drain.

"Is there anything you can do?" Marika asked.

"Oh, there's lots I can *do*. What I can accomplish is another matter." He dried his hands vigorously on a towel, then repeated the performance to get the fingernails. "For now I've got to send them a positive report," he said, returning to his drink.

"Such as?"

"I don't know. Tell them Pioneer's invented a new form of population control, and it's proven more effective than tribal infanticide."

"Why don't you just tell them it's murderous? Pioneer broke its contract when it started importing bauxite into the country, so its nose is hardly clean to start with. The aluminum lobby or whatever it is can't be big enough to send us packing—who'd they replace you with? Anyway, if they did—" She stopped, waving away the rest with her hand.

"If they did, you'd gladly pack in the music lessons and go. You hadn't planned on living in a war zone."

"I hadn't planned on being frightened all the time, no."

He held out his hand; taking it, she came to sit in the low chair, a wood frame slung with oxskin, to his right. The air outside was silent except for the ceaseless chanting of insects and the distant rush of the dam. "Hey, Big Bird," he said. "You've never scared easy."

It was his name for her, because of the slender hook of her nose and the close setting of her round dark eyes, like the bird puppet on *Sesame Street*. He used to say she walked like Big Bird, too, by which he meant she moved precariously on the ground, as if she did not entirely trust her fine-boned legs to balance the generous proportions of her hips and shoulders. Once Marika had liked the name; now she smiled briefly, like a reflex.

As she considered how to answer him, her eyes traveled to the screen door that led through a courtyard to Richard's greenhouse. He had built the greenhouse the year that civil war broke out, and in it he cultivated every variety of orchid he could obtain. He had taken up the hobby the same season that Marika started giving music lessons, a pair of idle occupations focused merely on beauty. By now an entire shelf of Richard's library was filled with books on orchids. Photos of the plants, as if they were children, sat by the lamp on his side of the bed. Twice a week he met with Ichi, a spare Japanese who watered the lawn at the presidential palace and who gave his advice with sharp explosions of the fingers of his hand, stopping to hatchet the palm of his left hand with the side of his right. A blue light emanated from a lamp in the glass house: a growing boost for the *brassavola*, Richard's new orchid, about which Biswandi had heard.

"I saw a girl," she told him slowly, tracing one of the circles of the table, "a dead girl, today. Face down in the grass, about a mile from town. They must've got her during the night."

"Black or Nebo?"

"Lethe. I stopped, but I didn't get close to her. I acted the way you would if you got out to see a dog some car had gotten on the highway. And I didn't even mind seeing the body. I minded—"

She broke off. Picking up her hand, Richard rubbed the knuckles with his thumb. She found herself scanning the rings of the baobab for the exact color of the girl's skin that she had mistaken for catalpa bark. What she had minded was the transformation.

Abruptly she pulled her hand away and stood up. "Biswandi came by this evening," she said.

"Did he now." Richard tapped his fingernail against the side of the table. The refrigerator, an oversized Kenmore that thrummed energetically, like a fat woman sweating in the heat, jerked and settled as she opened the door and pulled out the cold platters that Seki had left them for supper. Bean salad, sliced beef, smoked sardines with curled slices of lemon on top.

"He told a story that he wanted you to hear," said Marika. "About a game of cat and mouse, or rather hen and scorpion."

She summarized the fable, in her mind's eye seeing Biswandi tell it, his mouth moistening the words as if chewing betel nut.

"So I'm the bridegroom," said Richard, combing his thin, unruly hair with his left hand, "and the *dai* are the hen. And James Biswandi thinks Pioneer Aluminum is a virgin who wouldn't like to see what's hiding under the bed, does he? Well, that's his first mistake."

"He sounded ominous about it."

"He must've known I was passing some time with Ngebin."

"Ngebin!" Marika stopped arranging the plates. "I thought he was out of the country."

"He's back."

"You met with him tonight, with the *dai*?"

"I didn't know I would. I knew something was up, that's why I went straight there. His head was shaved in mourning—our friend the general must've struck close to home."

"Well, I told Biswandi you were ill. He practically called me out as a liar. He also told me he wasn't coming to the reception tomorrow night. That's another secret you were keeping, I guess."

"No, no." Richard took the plate she handed him and started on the sardines. "I meant to tell you. We've got twelve for drinks and whatever you can cater that's American-edible. His name is McGrath, and he just confirmed his flight today. There'll also be the president and Bis— no, not Biswandi, you say."

"He had important business."

"I'll bet. Nothing about him smells right these days. He *wanted* this affair, tomorrow, so he could sink his claws into McGrath for weapons aid before they even get to the bauxite thing. You're sure you didn't tell him I was out?"

"Of course not."

"He checked the garage?"

"I'd locked it, he didn't probe."

"Anything else?"

He loaded a cracker with beef and bit down. Marika met his eyes across the table. "What does Ngebin want from you?" she asked.

"We swore a bond," he answered obliquely, his mouth full.

"Like little boys pressing their bloody palms together. What does he want *now*, I mean."

Richard shrugged. "A listening ear. A chance to plead his case to the States before he pleads it to the Soviets."

"You've been through that. The U.S. ambassador is Pioneer's man, and President Mayume is the ambassador's man. That's what you told *me*."

"I have nonetheless been instructed," Richard said slowly, clicking his fingernail with a nervous rhythm on the wood, "to act with some degree of conscience. You didn't see what was crawling around inside those tents today."

"You didn't see what was lying beside the road."

"Yes, I did."

"I thought—"

"Not that one. I see them all, finally. If you think I don't, you're making the same mistake Biswandi's making. Richard Hooper, U.S. ambassador, sees them all." His hand edged across the table as if to take hers again, but he seemed to think better of it and, taking up his fork, he pressed lemon into the fish. "You're not eating, Big Bird."

"Too late at night. I've lost my appetite."

"Well, you go on to bed. I've got to check on the *brassavola* and then work up a report to keep the desk boys quiet at home. No point your losing sleep."

"True," said Marika, rising to clear the plates. Moths, yearning for the electric light, fluttered at the window screen. Outside, an owl hooted, impatient for the rats and gerbils to show themselves. Sixteen seasons ago, there had been a house servant who lived in the basement and who liked to *ping* the rodents with his slingshot. He had gone back to the hills, back to join the *dai*, and Marika had never replaced him, preferring in spite of Richard's concern to keep these evenings to herself.

Pushing back his chair, her husband left the room, and a few seconds later she saw the white lights of the greenhouse come on. His rare *brassavola* had had fungus when it arrived, and he would wipe off every sign with a cotton swab, like a querulous nurse.

She was lying in bed, though far from sleep, when Richard folded up his work and stepped down the long corridor to the back of the house. Through the open door she watched him run a bath then sink into it with a sigh, draping his arms over the side of the tub while steam rose around his thin shoulders. He wiped his face with the cloth and shut his eyes.

Marika had met the *dai* leader, Ngebin, only once, but she remembered him as strikingly tall, large-boned, his hair clipped close to his head; his forehead sloped to a broad nose, and his lips were rimmed with a patchy moustache and goatee. He had worn a turtleneck and had spoken softly but rapidly, mostly of numbers: numbers sick, numbers in prison, numbers dead from Biswandi's squads, numbers in exile and ready to strike. Marika could just see Richard, tonight, trying as always to compromise. He had no doubt told Ngebin to wait, that there remained work to be done with the State Department before they could withdraw support—meaning money—from Mayume's government. He would have cited the hundreds of coups that had only thrown power to the military. Ngebin would have come back, certainly, with more numbers; Richard, with more history.

Shortly after the one time Marika had seen him, in England, Ngebin had returned to Yumana and tried to assassinate President Mayume's predecessor, Otomo—the old Sacatra who had first sold the land for the dam. The plot had been to dynamite the president's car as it wound its way along the Parambo; but General Biswandi, vigilant as always, had sent a servant ahead in the car to be blown up, and had netted the duped, rejoicing *dai*. Ngebin had slipped away to the east—with Richard's help, Marika suspected, though she had never delved further. Still, the old man lost face, and it fell to Richard to find a new president for Yumana. Hence, the elections that had brought in Mayume. Only James Aholo Biswandi had remained right where he was, while Ngebin hovered, invisible, at the edge of the country, sending his *dai* like gnats to sting and distract the government until he was ready.

When the steam had settled, Richard pulled the plug and hauled himself from the bath. Rosy from the hot water, his body against the bright tiles of the bathroom looked pale even for a white man, without so much as a line where a short sleeve would end and a tan begin. He had never liked hot climates, and at the end of their first tour had put his request in for Scandinavia or Eastern Europe, Marika's parents' homeland; he had even persuaded Marika to teach him the rudiments of Serbo-Croatian and a smattering of Ukrainian dialect. Once, long ago, they had taken a trip to Montreal in midwinter, and he had kept saying, "It'll be just like this." But when his time came again there were only African embassies open, and as Richard knew the background of the new dam in Yumana, the post fell again to him. He never complained, but he kept his arms covered and stayed pale as a Swede.

How tired he looked. Marika lay immobile on her side, facing the bathroom, one arm tucked under the pillow, the other on top of the thin sheet so that her hand fell just over the side of the mattress, and from this position she watched through the shield of her eyelashes as Richard toweled dry and, naked, his back to her, brushed his teeth. Camouflaged by her feigned sleep, she might have wanted to witness her husband as he did something startling or merely uncharacteristic; to believe that he could act otherwise than from habit, or to make him reveal the private world he must have—for it seemed impossible that he should not possess one—to counter her conversations with Justin.

As he worked up from his long, bony feet to his thighs and groin, then switched the towel to get the back, side to side, Marika saw that he acted bluntly, from plain fatigue. Still, she lidded her eyes and said nothing to him. Finally he pulled the light cord and, in the dark, shuffled over the rush mat to the other side of the bed. As he slipped under the sheet she moved slightly and sighed, like one in a light sleep. He moved closer, and she felt his thighs cup her buttocks. A hand came to rest on her hip, and after a few moments she felt it move slowly between her arm and ribcage until it found her breast. She sighed again, not unwillingly but as if dreaming, so that all the effort of waking her would fall to him. As he bent to kiss her hair, his sweet breath came over her face, loosening her resistance, and she let her head fall back. When his warm lips found her mouth, they pressed with an urgency that first startled, then alarmed her. That these last minutes, moving through his solitary world, Richard should have been wanting her—and she not know! *But you're his wife*, she said to herself, as his wakening kiss moved deeper.

He knew she was awake now, his hand squeezed her breast; and still a kernel of resistance remained. Let him take it all the way, then. She lay languid, her legs imperceptibly straightening against his. He kissed her mouth again, and his hand slipped to her thigh but stopped there.

"You're so tired," he said, his whisper hoarse. "I won't force you."

"Mm," she said, and touched his neck, but already he had withdrawn. It was too late. He curled his chest around her backside, keeping his hand on her outer thigh.

" 'S okay," he mumbled into her hair. "We've got all the time . . ." His voice faded, and soon afterward his muscles gave an involuntary twitch, yielding to sleep. Still Marika lay awake, her eyes open now, Richard's kiss planted on her lips, listening for the owl and for the faint popping of gunfire that she knew would come when all the other sounds had ceased.

# Chapter 2

Morning broke over the hills in a sudden suffusion of light. Awake before Richard, Marika cupped a mug of thick coffee before the dark picture window, watching for the wash of salmon pink over the gray stones as if awaiting a birth.

It was, in fact, such brief, still moments that caused her sometimes to hear the imaginary sing-song babble of a child. Rarely now, but more frequently years ago, when she would run scales early in the morning in the kitchen of Richard's New York apartment, the swinging door shut to hold in the sound and the pale light streaming through the high east window, she would hear the childish melody as an undercurrent to her own voice. That was the time when she had made the chorus at City Opera, and she had rehearsed fiendishly, Richard indulging her late nights and applauding her indiscernible performances at the opera house. At first they had thought of everything but a child, so that the voice she heard weaving into her own came as an unexpected visitor. Later, it seemed she had sought out that voice with every hope she held, and still no child had arrived to embody it.

Richard would sleep through the day's lesson, the early one she gave twice a week to the stocky, serious boy who was even now seated in the back of the black limousine that snaked its way up the hill. The boy, Constantin, was the president's son, and Mayume insisted he should take his violin lessons before school, when he was alert and fresh. The Nebo driver parked and went around to open the back door. Yawning, Constantin stepped out in his square, pressed suit, then advanced through the foyer like a pint-sized diplomat.

"Brought your music?" Marika asked.

"Oh yes, Madame!" the boy said, going ahead of her. "Though I should say I shouldn't need it. I've got the Bach memorized, you know. My father listened to me do it last night!"

"Did he enjoy it?"

"I don't think so," said Constantin without the trace of a joke. His legs pumped beneath him, and when he had reached the piano he waited impatiently for her. Looking over the Revenir harbor, the glassed-in lesson room soaked up the sun as it struck the western peninsula, which swept around like a long comma, separating the city from the open Atlantic. Marika had set up Constantin's short music stand, and already he had the instrument out of its small case and was tuning it. She hit the A on the piano.

"Do you like this piece, Constantin?"

"I like it, yes, Madame."

"But?"

"I want to play Brahms, Madame."

"His violin works are too difficult for you yet. Let's loosen your E string, it's sharp."

"My father says he will ask for you to let me play Brahms."

"And I'll tell him no. I will tell him, 'Next year.' "

"He won't listen to you."

"But you will. Now, let's hear the first movement."

The concerto was Bach's Fifth Brandenburg. She had a flutist studying it, too—a Nebo boy, son of one of Mayume's ministers who cared nothing for music but much for his standing in the government. Others could be recruited from the small university and from resident Europeans. Some of the Yumanans had learned all they knew from Marika; others had learned in the bush from missionaries; and still others, children of the wealthier Sacatra, had gone to Europe to study and had picked up its music there. But she took the rest and was glad for the distraction and the reminder that she had been a performer once, a lover of pitch and melody.

*—Is that so?* said a voice in her ear as the boy struck his first entrance. *—Let me hear "The Very Thought of You." Billie Holiday. Knock my socks off.*

*—Lord, Justin, I don't remember the words.*

*—Sure you do. "I'm livin' in a kinda daydream, I'm happy as a queen, and foolish as it may seem, to me that's everything—"*

"Madame!" Constantin scowled.

"I'm sorry. Bar sixty. In four."

The boy had the first movement down perfectly. His arm held like a hummingbird over the trills and undulated across the theme. There was none of the screeching and sawing that marred others' early efforts—his notes were as true as a lark's first song.

And yet she wished he would not love his music so much. If he were her child, she had sometimes thought, she would take him to the shore, free him of all his man-tailored clothing, and give him different music to hear—

the echoes of shell and surf. She would teach him jokes, and if he failed to laugh, it would be that failure, not a missed note or an awkward phrase, that would worry her.

But Constantin Mayume was not her child, and to adopt him or any of them in her heart could lead only to pain. The doctors had never pinpointed where the fault lay for her and Richard. At first they had paid scant attention, children being difficult baggage for diplomats, but little by little their desire had increased, Richard's surpassing Marika's one day, then Marika's stronger than Richard's. There had followed night after night of anxious lovemaking in Richard's apartment, series upon series of tests with results as ambiguous as the half-lit New York dawn. It seemed they gave up the same year that Marika canceled her contract with the opera and embraced the move to Africa.

But they had never really given up. Here, where history moved in seasons, it had become clear that the will for birth, as for life and death, was universal. Marika heard the sing-song child's voice as something she carried with her: high-pitched, soft, and slow, hers to attend to in the hours before Richard woke and began with her this life in which they both wore their lack like a shared cloak, gone thin and past mending. She heard the voice over the screech of wild parrots on the hill, over the echo of early-morning construction in the city below, through the pounding rain of the monsoon. With Constantin Mayume, she heard it in the pure notes he played, unaware of his own exploitation.

The second movement was less perfect. "That should be *affettuoso*," Marika said, holding up her right hand to beat time. "Take it slow. Play through the long notes."

Constantin relaxed the tempo, and a trace of feeling crept through—but it was a sentiment so far from the music as to leave only a haunting sense of emotion brushed against and let go.

"Listen a minute," Marika said, and tried the passage on the piano. In her own notes the imagined child lived as a wanting, a cloudy thing caught in the lifting pause of Bach's triplet.

"I don't think I can play it like that, Madame."

"Play it your way. But let it build in you. It's the long notes that sit flat."

The boy had emotions stored in him, she knew. Ever since he was born he had had an armed guard with him always—the chauffeur was a lieutenant—to prevent kidnappings. Shortly after Marika had given him his first lesson, when he was five, he had run from home, and for a tense two days the president had had every member or sympathizer of the *dai* rounded up to be interrogated. Constantin was Mayume's only son. Before the boy ran off they were never seen together; in fact, Mayume spent his free time mostly alone in the presidential tier at boxing matches held in the palace stadium, or at receptions abroad with one of his wives discreetly in the background while he posed, smiling broadly, with the administrators and generals of that country. After the boy was found, hiding by himself in an abandoned boat in the harbor, waiting to scuttle aboard a ship, they were seen often as a family, close-knit and waving their identical plump palms at the people.

When they found the boy, the reports said, there were bruises all over his body, some made with a metal stick and others with hands. Mayume had let most of the *dai* go, but he had shot five of them in the public square, one for each year of his son's life. Constantin had not returned to his lessons for a year. When he did, it was with this fanatic determination that he still displayed, and what had been a flowering talent became a massive obsession. Before, he had wept when he made too many mistakes, and Marika had wanted to hold him to her. Now he bit his lip and knotted his face, and she held off and thought again of the child she could not have, who sang off key to her in the early mornings.

The kitchen door banged shut. Richard was up, out tending his orchids. Marika gave Constantin a new piece, a Haydn sonata, and made him promise to work only on the first movement for next time. "You'll neglect your schoolwork otherwise," she told him.

"It doesn't matter. My father says I shall be going away to school next year, and everything I learn will be better."

"Do you want to go away?"

"I don't know, Madame." The boy's flat nose wrinkled, the nostrils flaring wide. His mother had oiled his hair and worked it into a mist of curls, so that he looked like an African Little Lord Fauntleroy. "If I go," he said matter-of-factly, "they might kill my father before I can come back."

"No one's trying to kill your father, Constantin!"

"Oh, yes, all the time. They hate us all, the *dai* do."

The limousine driver appeared at the door, his officer's cap in his hand. Marika helped Constantin pack his violin and music into the case and watched them wheel out of the drive. Then she went to join Richard.

The greenhouse was no more than a glass dome over the existing bricked garden, where the same enthusiast who had built the sunken living room had installed a center fountain surrounded by pots of gardenias. Richard had replaced the fountain with an atmosphere-sensitive humidifier, and the gardenia pots with aerated beds of soil specially developed for orchids. By now he barely had room to step between the crowded rows of tables to water and feed each plant. Before the recent outbreak of schistosomiasis had pillaged his time, he had been planning an extension of the greenhouse to reach as far as the garage.

It was, Marika had observed, a tailor-made passion. Trained to an even temper and the uninspired logic of the diplomat, Richard raved and despaired like a poet over the plants. When one was ill, he went sick with worry. He came in from currying them, spent and recharged as an athlete coming from a workout. The orchids allowed him to function, in all other ways, as an effective ambassador to the so-called Republic of Yumana—so it was that they had gone beyond being an idle occupation with beauty.

As Marika unlatched the louvered door to the greenhouse, Justin spoke in her ear:

*—You should admit you hate these plants.*

*—Nonsense. They're breathtaking.*

*—They're his drug. He's an orchid junkie. One quick hurricane, and he'd have to quit cold turkey.*

*—He'd leave Yumana if that happened.*

*—So? Have you considered arson? Herbicide?* He was gesturing as he grinned, his arms wide, devilish.

Without turning her head, Marika could see how Justin must look now: his black hair peppered with gray, the thick muscles of his upper arms and chest gone rock-hard, like a longshoreman's. He had aged at the same rate as Richard—though, of course, differently: Justin's face, to her, had fleshed out, the pull of gravity working on his broad cheeks, while Richard's sharp chin and long neck had grown leaner over the years, his high forehead extending upward first into the temples, then over the balding crown.

She pushed the door open, leaving Justin behind. She mustn't hate Richard's orchids. Whatever Justin might think, Yumana was not the suburbs. Escape from life here made life possible.

"How's the little prince?" Richard asked when she found him among the sick plants in his "infirmary corner."

"Prodigal as always. He thinks his father's going to be assassinated."

"He is not a stupid lad." Richard squeezed a teaspoon of blue liquid from a dropper into the soil of the *brassavola*.

"He has the makings of a brilliant violinist. I hope Ngebin doesn't mean him any harm."

"I don't think Ngebin's outfit works that way. There, that's done."

He had tied the weak stalk of the *brassavola*, and smiled at his work. His face, alert and placid, betrayed none of last night's enervation. Under the cold-water tap in the kitchen, he scrubbed the same hands that had groped for her breast. Again she thought, *Such control*. He removed his white gardener's apron, and underneath wore a light gray suit—like the British in the bush, Marika always thought, with their starched cravats.

"No time for breakfast," he said lightly. He poured black coffee into a mug and dropped in three white cubes of sugar without stirring. They would sink to the bottom, she knew, and melt into the sweet syrup he always left behind. "I've got to get this report typed and sent from the office, then there's this McGrath guy to pick up at the airport. Spend the afternoon showing him the sights." He pursed his lips at the hot coffee, then added water and gulped it down. "So it's off to the gristmill. Bye-bye, Marika." Pecking the top of her head, he left her sitting in the kitchen as he strode out the back door to the garage. She didn't like his kissing her head, like an uncle. She didn't like his using her name like that, as if he were picking her out of a crowd when there were just the two of them there. She didn't like his plants and the way they calmed him down. His sweet coffee, his tailored suits, his shrewd assessments, she didn't like any of them.

Rinsing the mugs, she thought of Ngebin's head, shaved. In eastern tribes she had seen the women shave, running straight iron razors over their scalps and then oiling the smooth skin, but here they braided their hair and pulled it over the crown to the nape of the neck. The dead girl had worn bright plastic barrettes in the shape of bows. Marika sat down and shut her eyes. Sinking her head on the table, she held in her breath, then released it as she heard her name.

*—Rika. Rika, wake up. If we get to the market by six they'll still have oysters. Think of the tomatoes. Shake a leg.*

Marika groaned and stretched, the pale rays from the skylight washing over her shoulders and breasts. Justin pulled at her ankles. The room smelled of turpentine and clove. Justin tossed clothes at her. *—Put this on, and this. There's a cool breeze outside.* He tossed her a T-shirt, a pair of white painter's pants.

*—Justin, I can't wear these.*

*—You can't wear last night's dress, it's still wet. Here's a rope to tie the pants. Hurry, hurry!*

He stood with his back to her, facing the mirror over his one sink. His knit shirt stopped just above the neat tuck of his buttocks and the coarse black hair of his legs. She jumped from the bed. *—I'll have to call my mother, she'll be sick.*

*—Don't wake her up, we'll phone her when we get back.*

*—Are you always up this early?*

*—Always Saturdays, that's the market. Blue-point oysters, shrimp, mangoes, asparagus. Shad roe, maybe, by now. Basil, garlic, plantains. Cauliflower big as a basketball.*

*—Who's eating all this stuff?*

*—People can come by tonight. I like to cook for my friends.*

*(And I, Justin? Am I your friend? Will you feed me?)* Marika knotted the rope belt and crossed the broad-planked floor. Paint dust caked her feet.

*—When we get back,* he was saying, *—I'll make eggs Florentine. There's nothing so fine as spinach first thing in the morning. Pumps that iron into you, turns your shit black.* His hands describing an arc around her sharp shoulders and upper arms. *—I want flesh on you like a Raphael nude. Substance, here.*

Marika lifted her head from the table. Seki was coming soon, and there was a menu to plan. An order remained to each day, even here. Blinking her eyes as from sleep, she rose to shower and dress.

When Seki arrived, Marika asked her to stay late for the reception. "A military man will take you home," she said. "It will be all right."

"Not to worry from the curfew-time, then?"

"Not at all. And I'll pay you extra for the late hour."

Seki shrugged assent, then brightened with a thought. "You'll be asking me, Missis, then to fetch from the market?"

"Well, I—" Marika looked askance at the girl. *—Always Saturdays. Blue-point oysters, mangoes, plantains.* "I may just go down myself, Seki. I'll see what's there, what's fresh. I can always get a caterer to put it together."

"No, Missis." Seki drew herself up, looked stern. "You not be so wise, going down there. Not safe for you, na, Missis, in such a place."

"In broad daylight? There aren't riots anymore, Seki. The worst that'll happen is that I'll get cheated."

Seki shook her head, balanced on her long ebony neck.

"These market women, worse from riots. Diseased. They be selling you rotten stuff. You'll not be seeing, na, Missis, any one of your people there, at that place."

She meant any white people, any Europeans, any sheltered diplomats' wives. *Here's a rope to tie the pants. Hurry, hurry!*

"So I'll break one of the rules," she said defiantly. "If Richard calls, Seki, you just tell him I've gone for a drive. Tell him I'm visiting an old friend."

Seki blew out her breath. "You say, Missis. But is not for you a friend, this marketplace."

Outside, the wind had picked up, scattering white frangipani blossoms over the black gravel. Marika's Renault was a station wagon leased by the embassy, replaced each year by a new model shipped from France. Coaxing it into reverse, she swung around and down the hill. Other foreigners had had similar cars, dotting the western hills along with their whitewashed villas and Tudor houses, their swimming pools like blue oval eyes staring up from the land. Most had left six months or more ago. The four young people who carried on the major functions of the embassy all lived in town, in one of three tall self-contained apartment buildings near the harbor, with bars and discos that had been installed in the basement when the curfew went into effect. These young people had all read Yumana's foreign-educated writers, Achiye and Towola and Ngebin himself, before coming here, and they had learned Nebo and French, and some even Lethe. They could grasp, they told Marika, "the situation." Bodies on roads and in alleyways did not surprise them, and they had grown quickly accustomed to the curfew, the trucks, the gunshots.

Descending the hill, the front wheels of the car knocking fallen coconuts from the road with slight dull thuds, Marika passed two houses that had emptied only in the past month. One had belonged to an Englishwoman, Denise, whose family had harvested cocoa since the time when Yumana was a Crown colony. Denise had been collecting Lethe songs; she had translated them and pasted them into a fat black binder that she left with Marika when she sold the farm and moved to Monaco. The other house, bright green and slate-roofed, belonged to Pioneer Aluminum, and from time to time they would install an engineer or minerals expert in it, until he had completed a study of the Parambo or of the mines in the neighboring country from which Pioneer still bought its bauxite.

The trouble with the Yumana mines, the experts always concluded, was first, their physical distance from the dam. The northern plateau barred a direct line and meant that the minerals would have to reach the plant by sea. A second complaint was the longer monsoon in Yumana, which shut down the mines for five rather than three months out of the year. The experts recommended that Pioneer's contract with the Republic of Yumana be amended or abrogated or simply forestalled, and their reports were sent to Yumana's president along with a generous personal check. After one Pioneer man had drawn up his conclusions, the green house would stand empty until the next arrived. The last one, Marika remembered, had had a perky wife who wore dresses the color of the house and who volunteered at the city hospital when a mine collapsed. In two days the wards had filled with victims, not only from the tunnels but also from the broad city square, where a sudden crowd of demonstrators had appeared and had been just as suddenly mown down by the city guard, leaving eighteen dead and ten to die later in the hospital. Marika had seen the wife only once after that. She had been dressed as brightly as ever, her blond hair pulled back with a neat gold headband; but she had sat on the Hoopers' patio alternating between quick pulls on a French cigarette and short sips of Scotch, until she spilled the Scotch on her green dress and her husband took her home. They were gone soon after.

Turning right at the fork, Marika followed an army limousine that streaked down the parkway from Mayume's palace. As it passed the scattered crowd of roadside merchants, one old man spat after it, his saliva an iridescent stream shot over the road. He spat again when Marika stopped to get out where she had seen the girl, and with deliberation he moved his rugs away from the car.

The stands were no more than crates set up on end, with faded cloths draped over them and objects for sale piled on top. They hoped for tourists, mostly, who took this road from the main causeway to get a better glimpse of the presidential palace or to ride through the tamed and richly landscaped western hills where the colonials had had their villas and foreign emissaries still held sway. Most of the merchants were Nebo, Muslims who had drifted south from the desert generations ago—a short, sharp-faced people who still kept their women at home and covered their heads. These men wore turbans that were little more than knotted rags; their boys, who ran out to the cars, their arms loaded with scarves and their hands with figurines, were clothed only in rope-tied shorts of sackcloth, their feet and legs red with road dust.

But this time, as she got out of the car, none approached her. Passing between one stand loaded with carved elephants and another draped with necklaces strung of teeth and feathers, she stepped through the tall grass toward the catalpa that yesterday seemed to have dropped the girl on the ground below. The winds had stirred up the grass, and no indentation remained. Nor, as she bent low and pulled back the stiff growth, could she distinguish blood on the damp red earth.

*—I just drove on,* she found herself saying to Justin. He shrugged, his thick eyebrows lifting.

*—You think if you'd stayed here she'd have come to life?*

As she turned back to the car, three boys broke away to circle her, holding out statues and bracelets of elephant bone. "Please, Miss!" they shouted. "Hand-carve!"

"Gold, five rupa only!"

"You like blue stone?"

"I give you two-for-one!"

They held the things above their heads for her to see. Bloated, their stomachs hung over their short pants. One wore a hammered aluminum cross around his neck. The old man shouted at them in Nebo, but they ignored him. Shaking her head, holding them at bay with her arms, Marika got back into the Renault. They backed away as her turning wheels sent off a spray of mud from a drying puddle. She saw in the rearview mirror that they had latched onto the next car, offering what they held as if the trinkets were babies to be taken up and fed.

The river trickled to the sea at one-tenth its ancient power. One would think that the water could be held back, at the start, for a week or two, then left to run at the same force as before, the dam's gates filling and emptying at once, just a wedge of time behind schedule. But it didn't work that way.

When Marika was a child in New York, there had been a broken-down walk that ran by the East River near Twelfth Street. Late in the day her mother, Katya, would take her there to watch the barges shovel in against the tide, and in the stinging salt air she would point out the dead fishes and debris that washed up against the white boulders of the embankment. Katya would compare the river to the Dnieper in the Ukraine, which ran deep and clear to the Black

Sea. The East River, by contrast, floated a yellow foam of waste collected from the boats and the city's pipes, and gases rose and floated over the embankment as if the river were a living bilious creature. Yet as soon as Marika was close enough to get a whiff of salt or see the first gray line of the river or the rare mast of a reefed sailboat, her heart rose several notches and rested there, on a high plane of expectancy. As the rivery surface surged below their feet, she had asked like any child where the water went. Instead of saying "to the ocean," Katya had squinted up her eyes as if this were a question she had put to herself a long while. "It turns and comes back, my darling girl. They say it turns at the tide, but I think it's a mistake, for a river to run the wrong way."

The Dnieper, Marika had calculated, ran straight out and never washed back. Later, on the other side of the island, she would hear Justin compare the Hudson to the magnificent Rio Grande; and in his turn Richard, faithful to New York's waterways, would bemoan the killing pollution that made the Hudson rank as far north as Poughkeepsie and that fouled the East River as it silted past the mayor's mansion.

To Marika they were all river, the wide dark Hudson on a par with the blue ribbons of New England that flashed by once on her way to Maine with Justin. It was not until she arrived in Revenir with Richard and saw the Parambo cleaving the city that she felt the water's current tug at her. Somewhere in the ink-green hills lay the source and heart of this river that sent its thundering water headlong through the thronged African city to the sea, and it was that fountainhead that pulled her and tethered her fast.

Even then, powerful interests had been planning the dam. The *dai* at that time were a small tribal group in the hills with a gripe against the government for depriving their chief of his power. Pioneer Aluminum was uninvolved except for strip mining, which it practiced in the north and about which one occasionally received literature from human-rights groups; the majority in Yumana were too busy farming or too much in need of their mining jobs to protest. Before dawn there teemed over the Homeland Bridge to the city all its commerce—on foot, on bicycle, in slow-moving, clumsy cars. Even government officials used the Homeland, there being no suspension bridge to the presidential palace then. Late in the evening, when the merchants had passed again with their baskets and truckloads empty, Marika would walk down to the bridge entrance and wait for Richard there. In those days there was no curfew, and the sun trickled across the flat ocean like syrup, while the river ran like molten iron under the bridge's girders. From far off, past the new highway and the hills, came the muffled sounds of drums. Marika used to think back on the day, or farther back, to days in New York with Justin, and staring into the fast, silent river, she would sing snatches of arias, or old love songs, or in rhythm with the drums a bit of jazz. The Parambo neither swallowed nor reflected her voice; it carried the notes palpitating on the threads of its current like dragonflies. Richard was often late, and she sang for hours, because the river never tired.

When they built the dam, the Homeland Bridge came to arch mostly over dry land, with a narrow, lazy flow running through the center of the riverbed. It was no longer the most direct route, as Mayume had created his suspension bridge and the new highway looped over the neglected streets of the eastern part of the city. Though the plan was to tear down the Homeland, it somehow stayed erect, the fishy things that had clung to its girders drying up and at last falling off, exposing the rust underneath.

But Marika still took it, parking her car, as now, out of sight of the road vendors and unfolding her metal cart to roll behind her as she walked. The footbridge avoided the clogged lanes of cars and bicycles along the superhighway, though the sleepy river far below, the trickle from the dam, gave her scant cause anymore to tremble or sing. Her voice in any case would have carried too far over the bleached riverbed to the shantytown that had quickly grown up where the shallower water used to run. At the center she paused and looked far to the east, where just the pencil-line of the dam's high ridge was visible behind an outcropping in the foothills. If she could blow a trumpet, Jericho style, and bring the thing down, she used to think, she would.

Now she only bore witness, as at the cenotaph of a friend sharply remembered but long absent, and with a dull pang like that of a tooth, she went on.

As she neared the market, buyers and sellers funneled into the main street, their bright *dashiki* and sweat-stained undershirts brushing her bare arms. Ahead of her, a tall woman wore a long Lethe dress with a portrait of President Mayume, his stenciled Sacatra features smiling generously, superimposed on the geometric print that zigzagged across her back. Others sported buttons and caps, or western shirts with the same portrait in miniature, stamped repeatedly front and back. Before Mayume, Marika remembered, it had been the wrinkled face of Otomo. The people wore the portraits easily, as if they were birds or constellations or any other symbol of good luck.

The January sun beat down, reflecting off the corrugated iron roofs that slanted over the city hutches, their rain-drenched wattle walls shored up with lumber and sacking. The sun pulled out the buried smells of feces, rotted meat, mash fermenting for beer, and mingled them with the varied odors of men and women, the dirt-coated yams, the heavy fish-smell of the morning bonga catch. A number of mud houses stood empty and gutted, flabby old women sleeping in their doorways. Abandoned cars, also gutted of their radios and upholstery, listed sideways on the heat-buckled sidewalk. Six months ago there had been death here, too, Biswandi's men loading the bodies conspicously onto truck beds as the market gathered. The buyers and sellers had clucked and mumbled; the bereaved, standing alone, had howled, moaned, and then stared dumbly at the ticket the driver gave them so they could collect the remains. So they had learned to stay in at night, to hang the yellow and black flag of the republic by their doorways, and the trucks rumbled through the district silently and did not return by day.

Even now after harvest there was little fresh in the market. The small farmers had gone back to trading mostly in the villages, while the big ones opted for cash crops—cocoa, palm nuts, cassava. Still there were more sellers than buyers—most of the black mass that carried Marika toward the stalls were wandering through, laid off from the mines or drifting south from countries where there was even less work. The cries rose in Lethe, English, French: "Lentils! Hot chilies! *Fèves de Calaban!* Fresh, *tout frais!* Sweet chili! Tobac'! Sardinella! *Viande!*"

Under canvas umbrellas, canned lychees, mangoes, fish, and mixed curries lined up on the rusting metal tables, with a special area for unmarked cans that sold cheaper. Most were Turkish or Moroccan brands, with some American labels and a few unrecognizable tins from Hong Kong. Baskets held relief supplies of powdered milk, beans, mushrooms, wheat flour.

"*Moutarde!*"

"Sugar, lady, sugar!"

"Bonga!"

Marika wove between the stalls. The sellers were mostly Lethe women, with a few transplanted Nebo pushing tobacco wrapped in moist leaves, or long brick-red chili pods. Sun had bleached the can labels; their tops were rimmed with corrosion. Voices rose, hammering out the price. Here and there, a sulky big-lipped Lethe farmer stood before his remaining plantains and mangoes or bags of rice, fanning off the flies and watching for thieves.

"Goat meat, lady! So tender!"

"Yams! Yams!"

"Florence," said Marika when she had reached the last stand, its faded yellow umbrella flapping in the dry wind.

"Missis Hooper. Na, how are you keeping?" Turning to face Marika, Florence hitched up her skirt and left one hand fisted against her broad hip. "It is a long time. You look fine." Flicking her eyes over Marika, she nodded, satisfied.

Florence Raleigh had been the night nurse at Revenir Hospital eight years ago, when Marika was admitted for what they thought was malaria but turned out to be a simple staph infection. Like Justin, Florence had wanted Marika to put on weight and would step uninvited into the room to tempt her with sweet biscuits and hard candies. She stayed until Marika swallowed something and kept it down, and she spent the time teaching Marika Lethe phrases and the history of her tribe, the great Kikuyu of eastern Africa, some of whom had fled here during Mau Mau. Florence's ancestor had been christened Walter Raleigh by the Methodists, and at the time when they sat together at night in the dimly lit, echoing hospital, Florence told Marika she took pride in her Christian name and in the monogamy her family had practiced since that first baptism. Since then, the Parambo Dam had been completed, Pioneer had broken its contract, and the scattered *dai* had found their figurehead in Ngebin. Implicated in the attempt on Otomo's life, Florence's husband had been arrested, tried, and shot within the space of one hour just before dawn.

Florence had never come back to the hospital. On her return to Yumana, Marika could discover nothing of her. Then one day, still in the days when the market was a piece of local color to show one's guests, Florence had appeared under her yellow umbrella. Wandering the marketplace with the Englishwoman Denise, Marika had found her selling yams and telling fortunes, her abundant breasts and hips wrapped tightly in traditional dress, her head shaved and swaddled. She had changed her last name, she told Marika, to 'wa Mthongo, "born in betrayal."

"Give me your hand," she said to Marika now. Obediently, Marika sat in the metal chair by Florence's table and opened her palm. Leaning over it gravely, Florence traced the lines with her broad index finger. It was in exile, she had claimed, that she had learned to see beyond the tangible, to find the subtle crossings that twisted into future trouble. "I see," she said now, "this hand broken by glass. And soon after that you are going away from us, which is not a good thing for you, even though you are thinking it is a good thing. But you turn round, right here, at the broken glass again." She pointed to a V in the hollow of Marika's hand, then closed it up and sat silent.

It was perhaps the hundredth fortune, though the first in several months, that Marika had heard from Florence. For a short time they used to meet in Florence's bungalow, where Marika had given sporadic lessons on the cello to Florence's shy daughter. Then Marika had sought Florence out here, at the open market. Now unrest cordoned this place off, too.

"Well, I can't go away anytime soon," Marika said uneasily. "Richard wants a party tonight, and I don't think Seki will stay, though she said she would. And I got here too late to find any fresh food. I'll have to rely on the embassy caterers."

"Na, I know of this party." Florence's smooth alto voice cut through the babble of the market. As they talked, people were stopping to buy yams, and she made the transactions wordlessly, with no bartering. Her eyes did not flit around like the other sellers', watching for thieves, because no one darted in toward her table or shoved her umbrella, as they did to the others.

"What do you mean?" said Marika. "*I* just found out this morning. There's some new man for Pioneer, and—"

Florence put up a ringed hand. "Missis Hooper." A wedge of light, like a tribal scar, shone on her cheek through the torn umbrella. "You are being blind from many things. Inside of your kitchen somewhere is hiding this small black box. This is hearing you speaking, your husband too."

She looked patiently at Marika, like a teacher going over an old lesson. Marika drew in her breath. "We're bugged."

"Yes, yes, this is a microphone. And he is listening—" she jerked her head in the direction of the palace where Mayume lived—"so we also have to do, to listen to him. So we are hearing of your party in any respect. Like so, in passing."

"Where have they got it hidden?" Marika asked. She thought of Biswandi, saying, *The jeep is put away. Richard Hooper is in bed.* He'd known all along where Richard was. What else had she and Richard said to each other? Why hadn't Richard thought?

Florence turned up her palms in ignorance. "But I will send some person to remove it, this device. Still, na, another appears when this one goes. So," she said, abruptly raising her voice, "you are wanting a fine chef and serving boy for the boss's dinner? Florence is cooking a fine goat curry, not too many chilies for the American boss. Count on it, Missis."

Florence's right hand, in the folds of cotton between her legs, was making shooing motions. Marika yawned in order to look up and saw a tall Sacatra lounging against the utility pole between Florence's stand and the next one. "I can expect you about six, then?" she said, standing.

"Count on it. We are bringing it all, what you need for food. No single thing will be missing." She nodded and smiled like a simpleton. Reluctantly, Marika turned away into the stream of people. A few seconds later she glanced back, but the man had disappeared, and Florence stood disputing with a customer, her white turban bobbing over her yams, her thick arms flapping like wings.

# Chapter 3

The part of town that housed the American embassy had grown in quick, fitful layers just after the Hoopers returned to Yumana. Marika used to watch the construction from the house on the hill, and it was as if some occasional artist were sketching in yet another grid, yet another few stories, yet another and taller obelisk on the flat plain near the slim harbor that crooked its way into Revenir. Long after the building work had finished, she kept scanning the cityscape for a new member in the cluster of steel and glass oblongs, but there were no more businesses or universities to invent.

Mayume kept the streets clean in this part of the city—there were parking meters, traffic lights, mailboxes, phone booths, divider strips, cement sidewalks, newsstands, trash bins. In contrast to the press of the market, so little business remained to be conducted here that the sidewalks stood white and empty while a smattering of cars paused at the lights. Any day of the week might have been mistaken for a holiday, save for the acute emptiness of Republic Square, the broad grassy park next to the embassy, where on a real holiday people would have ringed the obsidian statue of the first ruler to take over from the British.

Marika had taken a taxi from the market—a rusted Fiat with doors roped shut and aroma of beer and *kif*. It swept around the traffic circle and parked, like landing a plane on a clear airstrip.

A guardsman for the Yumana Republic stood by the elevator. Above were the French, Russian, and British embassies and, seated heavily on the top three floors, the American diplomatic mission. Years ago, Marika used to meet Richard for lunch in another building, squat and pillared, by the piers, where the guards had sat lazily below the flag and waved her in. Here, a few natty Oxonian Africans hurried through the air-conditioned lobby, and as the elevator doors opened, a flock of young women poured out, chattering in a babel of languages. Frowning, the guard examined Marika's pass card and pocketbook, reached inside the elevator to unlock the top floor, then stood outside like a sentinel while the doors slid shut. At the nineteenth floor the consular secretary got on, smiled nervously—"Oh, Mrs. Hooper! Here for lunch?"—unlocked the twentieth floor, and stepped out into the labor office, where Marika could see Curtis Lovell, Pioneer's local government liaison, on the other side of the glass doors. His back to her, Lovell was pumping the hand of the slight, effeminate labor officer who had arrived in Yumana just last month.

And on top of this beehive sat Richard, the biggest drone. Blue carpeting and chandeliers bedizened the hallway that led to two marines posted at the gold doors of the embassy reception. Pushing himself off the wall, one of them called Marika in over the intercom, then went back to arguing baseball. A third marine, tall, helmeted, and as black as the Hausa mineworkers who came up to Yumana from the south, approached the wide doors from the other side and wordlessly let her in. As the entrance sucked closed behind her, Marika let out a sigh, like one seeking asylum.

Fluorescent-lit, humming with the building's cooling system, the embassy's central office refuted its impressive exterior. It was easy enough to stride past Suzanne, the receptionist—who in the midst of polishing her fingernails had just started on a surprised greeting—and continue down the narrow hall to Richard's office. No one else was about to stop her.

Richard had been recording on his cassette player, a neat black box he kept stationed on the side of his desk. As Marika shut the door behind her, he clicked it off. Before she could get out a word of Florence's warning, he crossed his long arms behind his back, cracking the knuckles, and said, "Good timing, Big Bird. I've got some news about your girl."

"What girl?"

"The one by the road. The dead one."

"My God. I'd put her out of my mind. I hate to think I'm getting used to it."

"You're not. When you don't even see them, then you're used to it. Anyway, it seems it wasn't a curfew shooting."

"I saw her early in the morning, though."

"Oh, they got her at night. Took her from her mother's hut, raped her, shot her point-blank in the forehead, and dumped her out on that road. It is my private opinion that they left her where the ambassador's wife might just find her, but I didn't broach that with Ngebin."

"Ngebin told you all these things?"

Richard nodded at the telephone. "First thing this morning. Rare for him to take the chance. But it seems she was his sister."

"You mean by blood?"

"As in having the same parents, yes. That was his mourning, last night. I didn't ask, then. Taboo. But I sent out a feeler on the body you saw, and I got a stinger back."

"I don't get it." Marika groped for a chair, a bitter saliva in her mouth. "They must have known he was in the country, that this would inflame him. Was she plotting something, or what? She looked so young." Her bare legs like ripe shoots.

"Innocent as the snow." Richard held out his white hands, palms forward, as if to prove it. "They know, first, that Ngebin won't wait much longer. They want to send him a message that they'll stop at nothing to push him back. Plus, this business with the dam and the aluminum plant is getting bad press, for those who read the press on little African nations, and they need a stunt to show Pioneer's new foreign man that his enemy is also the government's enemy is also the people's enemy. They bank on someone—my bet, since you did see her, is that they hoped for you—to go to the authorities and report the dead girl, because she was so far from the bazaar or any part of town where the army patrols. And Ngebin believes they've got a pair of suicides ready to confess as *dai* to the murder and to claim he ordered it because the girl slept with one of Biswandi's men. Killing within family for that reason is an old tribal custom. It's plausible enough."

Biswandi. Marika's stomach dropped like a lead anchor. She had already fallen into the trap. "Did she?"

"Yes, in fact, and they'll drag the soldier out, too." Richard came back to a sitting position and took up his pen. Shuffling one pile of papers onto another, he found a stack to sign.

"How does Ngebin know all this?"

"I don't ask." Richard's signature was large but exact, the *o*'s like the slit irises of a cat. "My guess is that he's planning something to discredit Mayume before Mayume even comes up with a statement on it. But he wouldn't give me a hint. Just asked that we be discreet and stopper the State Department until he'd had a chance to play his card. I might add he was pretty distraught."

"Was she his only sister?" A Lethe woman's worth was still measured in bride price: goats, chickens, paper money.

Glancing up from his desk, Richard nodded. "But they're dead wrong if they think this'll weaken him. Just makes him want blood. Christ, they all want blood."

Rising, Marika walked slowly to the picture window behind Richard's wide desk. It looked out over the harbor, the gray gunwales of freighters and the light brown sails of fishing boats. "Our blood, too," she said.

"If we get in the way, sure."

"I think we're in the way. Richard, our house is bugged."

"That's impossible," he said quietly, as if it really were. He had come over to where she stood; in the translucent reflection of the window she saw his face floating just above hers, his aquiline nose level with the top of her head.

From the other side of the door, she could hear the voice of Lisbeth, who with two other subalterns shared the top floor with Richard. Lisbeth prepared releases on Yumana for the International Communications Agency, and she was shouting to her secretary to copy Richard's report on conditions above the dam. The secretary shouted back that she'd done it. The copier whirred and snapped.

"Florence told me," Marika said, feeling the cool air rise from the vent flush with the window. "She said there was a machine hearing us speak. About Ngebin, for instance. About your going to the hills. You remember Florence."

"How did you find Florence?"

"At the market. Her usual spot."

"What the hell"—Richard turned her around to face him—"are you doing at that marketplace? At the least you could've gotten one of the boys here—"

"I wanted to see some things by myself. The city's been quiet. Let go of my arm, Richard."

He dropped his hand to her wrist. "Don't act like a *naïf*, Big Bird. People know who you are. I'm talking kidnap."

"Well, I'm talking eavesdrop. And Florence doesn't usually tell tales."

"Up to now." Richard left her side and paced the room, his steps muffled by the nubby brown carpet. "It's possible, of course. Though I shouldn't think they'd bother. If the hand that feeds you is giving scraps away somewhere else, you go after the scrap-nabber, not the hand."

"It would explain Biswandi, last night."

"So would the general's sheer chicanery. Look. I haven't got any CIA detectors to sniff out pin-sized microphones. I'm a diplomat. And I've got to meet McGrath's flight."

A knock came at the door, and a young male voice. "Richard? The driver's ready."

"On my way, Jeremy," Richard called. Officially in charge of economic assistance, Jeremy had taken over the office from his arrival—hoping, Marika suspected, for the deputy chief position that had been vacant, along with their neighboring villa, since they had taken up their second tour in Yumana. "Go on home," Richard said to her. "Take some vodka with you for tonight—Suzanne'll help you load it. Where are you parked?"

"By the Homeland Bridge, on the other side. I walked to the market."

"Walked." He pressed his fingers to his forehead. "Well, get one of the guards to take you back. Jesus."

"When will you be home?"

"In time for the reception."

"Anything you want me to say if I see Biswandi?"

"Sure. Tell him we've got xylocaine now."

"Why?"

"For scorpion stings. And if I know Ngebin, he's one smart black hen. But you won't see Biswandi. And about the girl—just let it lie low, can you, Big Bird?"

"Not to myself, I can't." She blocked Biswandi from her mind.

"She's not the first you've seen."

"No," said Marika. "Nor the last."

She bent her head to his shoulder, and for a moment, in the rarefied atmosphere of the fluorescent-lit, air-conditioned office high above the city, there was almost that sensation between them that she had let slip the night before. But then Suzanne knocked again, and taking Marika's shoulders, Richard squeezed them as one might a growing child's, before he stepped away.

Marika followed Suzanne down the bright corridor past the file room, where she could see Tom, the A.I.D. researcher, bent earnestly over a stack of papers, his collar loose around his broad neck. Tom was from Mississippi and sweated as naturally as others drew breath.

"Suzanne," Marika asked, "they ever teach you anything about eavesdropping?"

"Sure. 'Don't do it; you'll get caught.' "

"I mean about watching for it yourself. For a bug."

"Oh, that." Suzanne tried one key, then another, in the fat lock of the storeroom door. Swinging her straight brown hair behind her shoulders, she smiled wide, showing her even teeth. "Some countries you have to watch for that." Suzanne wore a loose, smocked Indian dress that fell over her knees as she finally pushed open the door and bent down to pull out a case of vodka.

"Not here?"

"Here they can hear whatever they want. We're their sugar daddy. And the other side's up in the hills trying to keep from starving—they're too busy to plant bugs."

"That's plenty." Marika took two bottles of vodka along with one of bourbon. "They must tell you some things to look for, though."

"Well, bumps in wallpaper, oddly placed electrical outlets. But you've seen our security—all those *soldatike*! Why, did Richard say something to freak you out? I mean Mr. Hooper."

"No." Marika led the way back down the corridor. "But I get the sense something's brewing. More than the usual."

"I got a spell of that. Last year, when I first came here. Thought there was going to be a coup any second and they'd charge in, quoting Marx, and kidnap us."

"I first came here eleven years ago," Marika said. She loaded the bottles into her metal cart. Her sleeveless shift felt rumpled, dirty from the market.

"I forget that." Suzanne shook her sleek head. "Must be old stuff for you. I'll do two years, then it's back to Washington for me."

Marika curved her lips to return Suzanne's broad smile, then ducked out. The humming elevator took her down to the unsmiling guards and the street, its nigrosine asphalt baking in the midday sun.

*—I hate this country, Justin. And all I want is you.*

*—When we get back I'll make eggs Florentine, then we'll fuck all morning. My hands are aching for that ass of yours. Do you mind?*

—*Do I look*—pushing the sensation of expectancy, breaking the surface of the suffocating street, the impassive statue—*do I look like I mind?*

The house looked no different from the way it had when she left. She started to phone Claire Lovell, one of the few who remained, a mile down the road, but she found herself staring at the receiver as it droned the dial tone. Fetching a pocket knife from Richard's study, she unscrewed the bottom of the phone's casing and then both ends of the receiver. All she found were colored wires and metal fasteners, no foreign device.

She put the phone back together and started on the kitchen. "What for are you looking?" Seki asked as she ran her hands over the wallpaper.

"A button," Marika said.

It could have been Seki, even, who planted it. The girl stood in the center of the room, her brown hands twisting in front of her. Seki had come to the Hoopers through Ichi, the Japanese who helped Richard with his orchids. She had left her family in the hills, Ichi had said—all her brothers had the snail fever, and there were no young men to pay a bride price for her.

But Ichi worked at Mayume's palace, Marika remembered, then as now. "Go wash down the patio," she said to Seki. "We'll want to use it tonight."

"Yes, about tonight, Missis. I'm not liking to stay, really. As I am at the house since morning, I—"

"It's all right, Seki," Marika said, taking clay pots from the open shelf to check behind them. "I've got other help coming. You can go home when you always do."

The girl scooted from the room. Marika stole a glance at her, out on the patio; she was polishing the table, making slow circular motions with her hand, like a moth. Last year, Marika had helped Seki get an abortion and had kept her at the house the days following. She had never asked Seki who the man was. Behind the impassive domino of Seki's face lurked at least acknowledgment of that. And Seki spat when Biswandi entered the house—she brought down curses on him. And any device would be Biswandi's.

The kitchen yielded nothing. Slowly Marika replaced the plates and glasses, the foodstuffs. Maybe Florence was wrong about the location. Maybe Richard was right and there was no bug anywhere, and at the palace they had no idea what he was up to. She, his wife, had little more than an inkling. Maybe—but here she stopped, Justin's hand stealing unexpectedly around her middle. Maybe the microphone, hearing nothing, could wait.

Leaning out toward the patio, she told Seki that she was taking a nap. When she had locked the bedroom door, she peeled off her light cotton dress. From high on the walls, Justin's paintings called down to her, shimmering with light. She sank onto the white sheet of the bed and shut her eyes.

For once he did not talk. He entered the room softly, mutely, and touched her first with his lips, grazing the tip of her nose, then hesitating, extending the long wait by just a fraction before he took her mouth and urged it open. His tongue flickered and thrust like a small animal. Still he had not touched her with his hands when he descended, the same mouth working the small nipples erect, sliding over the belly. Only as he paused between her legs did his hands reach up and under her thighs to ease them back and apart. She felt his rough beard against her pubic hair, then again his tongue, which drew forth and tasted her moisture as if there never could be enough of it. His long arm stretched up taut and molded her breast while he worked his way deeper, her pelvis rocking slowly with him. Bombs could have gone off, and they not know.

From the crack in the wood door, Seki watched her mistress on the wide bed. Her knees up and her hand thrust between, she was rolling from side to side. Her moans were held in by clenched teeth that kept her pleasure from shattering the quiet of the house.

Some time after the heat of the day had passed, a motorcycle slalomed noisily up the hill, and as Marika watched from the back door, a young man dismounted and hoisted two brown paper sacks, one in the crook of each arm, like babies. Carrying them toward the house, he announced that Florence 'wa Mthongo had sent him with the goat meat and cheeses—more food would arrive in an hour, when the meat had stewed.

"It is all cut to the proper shape," he said, radiating heat as he stepped inside. "I'm to boil water and drop in this meat. About two hours it's simmering."

As he lifted his sunglasses to read the knobs on the stove, Marika gave a start of recognition. She had seen this man before he was fully grown, the first year she arrived in Yumana with Richard. Otomo had just come into power, and Biswandi was carrying out the cleanup of those who had ruled before. Every day there were new trials, new executions. This boy, Marika remembered, came to Richard because his father had disappeared and he wanted to gain asylum in the small carpeted offices of the American embassy. His face, then as now, bore the marks of aristocracy, the high cheekbones and unusual aquiline nose forming a cross of bone on his face, below which his small roselike mouth turned downward, almost in a pout. Richard had told him to think hard before emigrating, suggesting it might prove more worthy to stay in one's own country and work for better things. He had taken the advice but retreated to the hills. Now he stood a head taller, the muscles of his copper-skinned arms like ropes as he lifted the bags of food onto the counter. He was one of Ngebin's *dai*, Marika thought. He had to be.

"It has been given me to understand," the man said when he had set the meat to boil, "that you have a fixture that needs adjustment. It is such chance that I am handy in these ways." The corners of his eyes behind his dark glasses gave the suggestion of a smile.

"I haven't been able to find the problem," Marika said carefully. "It's a leak somewhere, perhaps, but not in the kitchen."

"Oh yes, I think so, that it is."

Motioning her silent, the young man looked around the room, then reached unhesitatingly for Justin's charcoal sketch. "But I've already—" Marika started. He put his fingers to his lips. Taking a paring knife from the sink, he slit open the back panel, then reached in and peeled away a thin black disk. Noiselessly he took it over to the stove and dropped it in with the meat.

"I am not thinking it will flavor the curry," he said.

He tossed Justin's sketch onto the counter, and Marika picked it up. Where the thick paper had been glued to the microphone it had peeled away and now hung from the rest of the frame like a flap. "Thank you," she managed to say, "for finding that thing."

"Listen to me now," he said, taking off his glasses as if the microphone could have seen as well as heard him. "My name is Amet. Florence sent me here to tell you as how your husband is not safe at this time."

"With that thing listening, how could he be?"

"Florence is saying he ought not be in town anytime tonight, or it will be bad for him."

"We're having this reception here tonight," Marika said, gesturing toward the goat meat as she followed Amet out to the living room. "There isn't a chance he would be in town. Why? What's going to happen?"

"Too much will happen that we cannot watch for him."

"You know my husband, don't you?" Marika ventured. Amet had started pacing, restless, surveying first the city from the east window, then the back hills from the north. "I saw you with him, years ago."

"Not possible. We aren't acquainted."

"I'd swear it was your face. Your father—"

"I am stranger here in Revenir. I know only Florence." Pronouncing the name as if it were French, he glanced at Marika sharply, and she recognized the wide, almond-shaped eyes, the high arched brows. "Florence is requiring assurance that you and your husband be at home this night."

"I told you, we have guests. Anyway, there's the curfew."

"I am aware." Amet leaned briefly against the wicker frame of the couch, his long fingers drumming its arm. "But many aren't abiding the curfew."

"They're the ones who get shot," said Marika.

"Or shoot back." He uncoiled from the couch like a spring. "We have your assurance, then. Because we cannot watch, and your man, he is on quicksand."

"Yes, yes. Florence will be here, won't she? She'll see him herself."

"Not Florence. Two others that are coming, girls, they can cook and serve fine." He had put on his dark glasses again and headed for the door. "It will be fine for you," he said. He seemed to have forgotten her already, but when he reached the motorcycle he turned back. "You tell Richard Hooper from me," he called as he started the motor, "Amet stayed!"

"You *do* know him," Marika called back, but he had waved and wheeled away. Back inside, she fished the disk from the pot of boiling meat and, taking it to the patio, flung it down the hill. The ripped charcoal drawing she took back to the bedroom and stored behind a pile of old music scores, lacy with dust, high up in her closet.

It was then that Marika realized Seki was gone. She ran through the living room out to the garden, called Seki's name, and then returned to the hallway to find her basket and walking shoes missing. Nothing else was gone, nothing stolen.

So Seki had been the one. Had Biswandi for all her curses gotten to her? Or had she been his already, before she even began cursing him? Marika remembered how she had lain doubled over with cramps in the spare room, the day following the abortion. When Marika had brought her a brandy, she had kissed Marika's hand, like some mute and grateful slave, and Marika had snatched the hand away.

From the gravel drive, Marika looked down the hill for a trace of Seki, walking or running away. Instead she saw two young women trudging up, baskets on their heads: Florence's replacements. Already the sun was low among the western hills, casting a burnish on the haze that hung over the smoke-colored outline of the city center. Still Marika continued to search, past the fork at the bottom of the hill through the flat brush, for a slight black figure hurrying away, but Seki was gone completely.

# Chapter 4

McGrath was like all the others from Pioneer who had come to Yumana—meaty and jovial, plainly amused at a country run by black men. Richard had steered him away from the burned-out parts of the city with their boarded shops and stalls, their stream of the wounded and the vagrant. They had lunched at the top of Revenir's newest skyscraper, the Pioneer office building, and McGrath's large nose was still cheerfully pink. He had worn his safari suit for this reception because, he said, it looked as though he wasn't going to get a crack at any bigger game than President Mayume. His arms filled the short khaki sleeves, while at the wrist his gold digital watch shone city-smart.

Florence's girls had not let her down. The sweet curry, its meat cut the size of dice, was preceded by a mash of eggplant and lentils—Marika had not seen a fresh eggplant in over a year. Wearing long printed *kanga*, the girls moved gracefully and silently among the guests with Scotch and vodka, their eyes lowered like Muslim Nebo women. Richard had rounded up a dozen of the embassy staff, as well as Curtis Lovell, his wife Claire, and the Yumanan

Peter Abeche, who worked up at the Pioneer plant. Mayume would bring his own retinue.

The youngest group from the mission—Suzanne, Tom, Lisbeth, and Jeremy—arrived first, the others following in a steady flow. Marika signaled to Richard, caught up in a circle with the labor officer and the consul, and he followed her down the hall.

"You may need," she said, pulling him with one hand into the bedroom and shutting the door with the other, "your xylocaine."

"Biswandi hasn't been here again!"

"No, but his ears have. Florence sent that boy Amet up here. He found the device."

"Nonsense. Where is this thing?"

"I threw it out."

"Then how can you say? Who is this Amet?"

Richard's face had a blurred look; he had been drinking with McGrath.

"I'm trying to tell you," Marika said slowly, holding both his wrists, "that you're in over your head. Maybe you've been planning something wild and noble. I don't know. But these people you deal with are on to you. I'm the one who gets the warnings. They think that because you're my husband, I'll react. But all I know is someone's been listening to us, and you have to stay out of town tonight."

"Or what?"

"Or you'll be killed."

Behind his glasses, Richard rolled his eyes. "Did somebody tell you that?"

"Well, not in so many words. . . ."

"Listen, Big Bird." Richard loosed his wrists and patted her shoulders. Against the background buzz of conversation coming from the other room, he seemed genial and wise, like a professor at a conference. "We all know there's a war here. There are the ones who butcher, and the ones who get butchered, and then there's this third party who move their mouths. That's me. And they don't touch the mouth-movers. Okay?" He tilted up her chin and touched her lips lightly with his.

"What about the microphone?" she asked as he opened the door to leave.

"Well, that's a new development." He paused and looked absently at the door handle. "We'll have to work around that one. I didn't know I supplied them with evidence."

Brushing back his thin hair, he returned to his guests. Marika could hear Claire Lovell's wavering, high-pitched greeting, her husband's raspy monotone.

—*He's so damn moody,* she said to Justin, her eyes shut to conjure him up.

—*You used to praise him for being so consistent. You said I was the moody one.*

—*But you had moods where I couldn't resist you. He—*

—*He hasn't got moods,* said Justin, his rough beard against her temple. —*He's got thoughts. He'll think himself into dust.*

Marika opened her eyes onto the painting that hung opposite the door to the bedroom—a portrait of the ancient flounder, slicked blue-black with oil and broken into pieces on a deserted beach, his prophecies like flotsam brought in by the tide. From the west, she felt the dry night wind of the harmattan. Over the next several weeks it would blow everything into dust—the roadside dead, the soldiers, Richard, Ngebin, even the Lethe driven mad with river blindness.

—*I want to sit for you,* she said to Justin.

—*You never would before.*

—*I was afraid for you to look at me so long.*

*—And now?*

*—Now I want there to be some part of me left.*

"Marika Hoo-o-o-per!" Claire Lovell was calling from the living room. Marika left Justin to rejoin her party. Claire was wearing a halter top that showed mostly the angularity of her shoulder blades, and shiny black pants that stopped at midshin. A spare, once-delicate beauty, she had fallen for Curtis on the rebound, she had told Marika several times, from a French movie director. "You are going to kill me," she said, spreading the fingers of one hand apologetically across her chest, "but I simply can*not* make it to the hospital tomorrow. I threw my elbow out playing squash, of all silly things, and—oh wait, here he comes."

Yumana's president stood in the foyer, his company of four spread like a fan behind him. "Does that man give you goosebumps, or *what*?" Claire whispered to Marika as he approached the living room.

Mayume was an impressive middle-aged Sacatra, typically light-skinned, with thin lips and a high forehead that, apart from his springy, close-cropped mat of hair, would have let him pass for a dark Indian. One would have said that his musically gifted son had his broad Negroid looks from the French-born mother now at Mayume's left. Mayume's watchful, emotionless eyes and erect shoulders were what impressed Claire, though Marika knew the effect was gained from the tailoring of his white summer suit, which camouflaged the small pot-curve of his belly below a sagging chest. Still, he spoke well, with a lilting Oxford accent, and photographed well for the press and the buttons people wore, so he had been a good choice.

But Marika thought of Constantin, of the boy's conceit and his dogged talent. "He gives me," she said, glancing at the presidential father then smiling down at the diminutive Claire, "the creeps."

"*Oh,*" said Claire, and reached for a drink from the platter the girls were carrying around. When the Lovells had arrived six months before, Claire had told Marika that she had read all of Isak Dinesen and intended to minister to the natives just like Karen Blixen. Since then, she had read Robert Ruark and intended, she had told Marika last week, to try some of this savage sensuality first hand. Marika did not suppose that Claire planned to experiment with the president, but still she made her remark, smiled, and took a drink herself before coming forward to greet Mayume.

Trailing behind Mayume came his sister as well as his wife and two bodyguards, large, thick-lipped, and slow-moving soldiers who installed themselves silently at either end of the sunken living room. "Such a charming space," said the president as the small group parted for him. "Have you ever considered, Mrs. Hooper, pulling up this fine rug and filling the oval with water? A California hot tub!"

The wife and sister tittered; Claire Lovell's laugh descended like a waterfall. Mayume looked around approvingly.

The ice broken, their voices rose and hummed in the room. "I don't know if you realize this," McGrath said to Marika as he tried the curry, "but the pin-sized articles they tuck into the newspapers about countries like this all say that there's a revolution going on."

"No, really?"

"You wouldn't believe it! They've got poor Mayume here murdering his old army buddies and eating peasants for breakfast. The *Times* says your lovely city"—he gestured toward the row of presidential lights that had just come on with the reddening twilight—"is gutted. They say people who go out at night get shot. People like us, having a little party! Believe me, I read up on this place, and if I hadn't gotten the real scoop from the fellow who came over last year, I wouldn't have stepped on that plane."

"Well, there *is* a curfew," Marika said.

"Sure, sure. Probably keeps the drinking problem down."

"I wouldn't count on that!" said Lisbeth, her ears pricked for public relations as she joined them by the doors to the patio. Lisbeth claimed Lethe heritage, and when she started as a Peace Corps volunteer she had asked for this part of Africa. Marika suspected that she had seen the effect of the Parambo Dam on the population and had drawn her own conclusions about Pioneer Aluminum and the Yumana government. But Lisbeth was learning from Richard Hooper: she believed in circumspection, in diplomacy. Propaganda was her job. Her round tortoise-shell glasses sat on the small bridge of her nose, as perfectly symmetric as the halo of black hair that framed her face and made her look, still, like a fresh Barnard graduate. It was her first visit to the house. "What's this painting, Marika?" she asked. "Is this a real Kilroy you've got here?"

Marika followed her gaze to *Apollo*. "Y-yes," she said. "Just an early one. You know his work?"

"Man, people I know *memorize* his work! You do realize this is worth a hefty insurance policy, don't you?"

"It's just a little sketch." Marika knew better than to tell her about the others.

"I never can figure out what makes these guys worth bucks," said Bud McGrath, joining them. "You mind if I'm blunt, Marika?"

"Please."

"You could put a nice print there, and it'd all be the same to most people. And if it was a picture they knew what *of*, it'd be a lot better."

"But then, Mr. McGrath—" Marika began.

"You call me Bud." He wiped eggplant from his mouth.

"Bud, if everyone did that, we'd run out of new pictures, wouldn't we?"

"No big loss, far as I'm concerned. 'Course, if he's making green stuff, hey, I'm not one to knock the *painter.*"

"It's not just worth money," Lisbeth started in, laying propaganda aside. "This painting happens to be by a *genius.* The Raphael of our time, man."

"Look, you can drop names all you want, I got my opinion—"

—*How's it feel to be Raphael reincarnate?* Marika asked as she left her guests to argue it out.

—*Messy. All these ruffled collars, I keep getting turpentine on them.*

Justin's grin revealed the slight space between his two front teeth that seemed to disarm his most sober critics when they met him. He wasn't painting for disciples like Lisbeth or for the art moguls who, stripped down, resembled McGrath. Marika had seen him approaching his canvas with a dripping brush, like a priest approaching the altar with a chalice or a cowboy approaching his horse with a bridle. She had seen him in vexation kick wooden frames into kindling, and she had seen him sit weeping with exhaustion when the last stroke had gone on.

He used to say that the only way off the ledge of fame was to stretch your work until you fell again into the grand excitement of obscurity. Thousands of miles away from the city that was the source of his fame, Marika was waiting with a queer hope for him to fall.

Moving out of the living room, she managed for a brief moment to pull Richard into the kitchen. "Remember that charcoal over the cutting board?" she said, pointing to the blank wall. "That's where they had the bug."

"Where is it now?"

"I tossed it down the hill. That boy, Amet, *boiled* it, but for all I knew it still worked. Richard, what is Ngebin doing tonight?"

"I don't know." He looked from her to the empty space on the wall, then back again. For once he seemed to be listening, if not to her, then to a voice in himself. "He said only that they'd give her a Lethe burial. Which they can't do without the body. Apart from that, no clues. I wonder why Biswandi isn't here."

"He said he couldn't make it."

"I know. But I expected him just the same. Especially when you told me about the microphone. I should've known, of course. I heard an old saying from a worker up by the dam—'Watch the one who points your path—see which way *he* goes.' "

"I wish you'd be frightened, Richard."

"I am frightened." His blue eyes glinted, annoyed with her. "But don't ask me to lose control."

"Well! The lovebirds in the scullery!" McGrath's head appeared through the open doorway. "Your husband, Mrs. Hooper, promised me a sniff of some of these rare orchids he's world famous for."

"No, no. Marika's got to play for us before anyone wanders off!" cried Claire behind him.

"I don't know, Claire, everyone seems happy just talking—"

"They are *not*. Richard, tell her she's got to give us a song."

"I am not my wife's *maestro*. If she wants to entertain us for a few minutes, I'd be happier than anyone." He smiled diffidently.

"Hey, a talent show! I love it," said McGrath.

Marika hesitated. She had given little performances at Justin's loft parties, when Justin had pushed her into it, showing her off. Here, Richard never pushed, but she gave in easily to requests like Claire's, partly to remind Richard that she could sing and partly because, so far from theaters and concert halls, people hungered for something so simple as live music. But McGrath rubbed her wrong.

"I could do a couple of Schubert *Lieder*," she said reluctantly. "But go on out to the flowers, I'll take a minute to set up."

"There's my woman." Richard touched her cheek with a long, cool finger. "Always on your toes."

*But I'm not your woman*, Marika thought as the two men headed out the screened door. The greenhouse, filled with its lush, exotic scents, its glass dome perfectly circular, harbored Richard's wild affections more than she had or would. It constituted that private universe for which she had watched the night before. Even for her, and despite what Justin claimed for her, it was impossible to resist the fireworks that seemed to pour from his *pleione* orchid, or the head-spinning aroma of the *cattleya*. The greenhouse was Richard's woman.

She saw McGrath bend and sniff as instructed, then she turned to weave her way among the guests to the gratifying cool of the lesson room. Catching one of the serving girls with a tray, she asked, "Where is Florence tonight?"

"Sorry, Missis, I'm not knowing," the girl answered. "She's come to me maybe around three o'clock, and telling me only to bring the fruits and things for the curry. Then off she goes."

"How do you know Florence?"

The girl looked surprised. "Why, she's my mother," she said.

Marika caught the girl's elbow and stared into her face. Four years ago, she had taught cello to Florence's only daughter—then a thin, awkward adolescent with small breasts and slumping shoulders. The girl's face, at that time, had not achieved enough clarity even to say that she looked like Florence. Florence had sent her back to Kenya, to school, and had always gone to visit her rather than bringing her to Revenir. Grown, the daughter resembled her mother markedly—the wide lips, the square cut to her chin. Marika did not remember the girl's name, but before she could ask, the girl had smiled nervously and slipped away to the kitchen.

Marika resolved to talk more to her when the guests had gone. Continuing into the glassed porch, she began to sort through the sheet music piled on the baby grand. She had just located the *Lieder* when first Lisbeth, then the rest of the guests, streamed out in a pack from the living room. At first Marika looked back to see what they were running from, but the living room was empty and they had all stopped dead by the cluster of music stands. She turned her head and saw, far below the house, to the north, a bright swath of orange that cut through the bazaar section of town.

"Christ almighty," said Curtis Lovell. As at a signal they crowded toward the glass and stared down. Enormous flames rushed like a current of gold toward the modern buildings by the harbor. The wail of sirens floated up the hill, followed by the report of gunfire. While the ambassador's guests watched, speechless, the headlights of cruising army trucks converged on the area below as if drawn by a magnet, leaving the rest of the city in total darkness.

They had all seen other fires, but none had been so sudden or sweeping. When the sirens grew to a constant pitch, Tom from the embassy broke the silence in the room. "They must've used a truckload of gasoline," he said.

"Who?" asked Lisbeth.

Standing slightly behind the others, President Mayume answered quietly, as if naming an act of God, "*Dai.*"

Someone suggested they hear the radio, and stepping inside, Marika went to the kitchen to turn it on. Florence's girls, too, had left the food to watch, their faces pressed against the window of the lesson room. Unable to pull in anything but static, Marika fiddled with the radio knob, oddly relieved that Ngebin should have chosen a simple conflagration to avenge his sister. As she lowered the whining pitch of the broadcast, suddenly she heard the splinter and crash of glass.

"What?" said Lisbeth, joining her.

The glass shattered again, followed by a brief sputtering explosion and a heavy crash. Marika tore out of the house, leaped to the greenhouse door, and flung it open. "Richard!"

He lay sprawled against a fallen table, the orchids in broken pots all around him. McGrath had collapsed against the back wall. For a split moment, as Marika looked up from her husband to the gaping hole in the glass wall of the greenhouse, the light overhead fell on two sinewy blacks, their heads made faceless by stockings, the yellow band of the *dai* ringing their upper arms. As soon as they had been seen, they backed off into the night.

Claire Lovell screamed. "Holy God! Hooper!" said her husband. While Mayume's guards stood still on either side of the president, Peter Abeche pushed past Marika, glass crunching under his heavy feet as he ran after the men.

Kneeling over her husband, Marika straightened his neck where it had twisted against a table leg, and held his head. Blood flowed from his temple, as well as from his shoulder and somewhere farther down. His eyes blinked once at her, then remained open, the black pupils startled wide, reflecting twice the thin tube of fluorescent light and the glass roof. "Oh, Richard," Marika said. Shaking her head, she stroked the spattered dirt and blood from his cheeks, first right, then left. "Oh, poor Richard."

McGrath was still alive. "Get an ambulance, somebody!" said Lisbeth, then ran to call it herself. No one else moved in the greenhouse until Florence's daughter and the other girl came in with a blanket and got McGrath to lie down. One loosened his collar and pants; they exchanged words in Lethe. Then Florence's daughter crawled over to where Marika knelt.

"Have you alcohol?"

Marika narrowed her eyes at her. "Your people did this," she said, her voice throaty.

The girl repeated, "Have you alcohol?" Her hair was braided in the traditional way but was covered with a blue scarf that framed the features of her face, the eyes prominent like Florence's, with flecks of gold in the brown irises.

Marika looked down and spat. The girl left, returning after some minutes with disinfectant and a clean cloth. Marika heard the tearing of McGrath's shirt, the quiet swabbing of wounds. Suzanne had come into the greenhouse and knelt to put her hand on Marika's shoulder. Marika could feel Suzanne's sobs shaking through the hand.

*—Justin. Justin, talk to me. Richard's been shot.*

*—The first thing to do is breathe. In, then out. Slowly. In. Out. There, that's good.*

*—He was just a mouth-mover. He said they'd never touch a mouth-mover.*

*—Listen to me, Marika. Shut his eyes. Think of how you have been loved.*

Carefully, Marika placed her fingers on Richard's eyelids and lowered them. Her gaze drifted over his damaged face, from the close-shaved follicles of his beard around his short, dented chin, up to the great red gash that had torn the hair from that side of the head. She had nothing to stop the blood. Instinctively, her hand moved up to the one on her shoulder, and she gave a little start to find it was not Justin there but Suzanne still, whose sobs had abated to whimpers. "I can't believe this," Suzanne said. "Can't we try something? Give him a shock, or something? I know he's not gone yet."

"He's gone," said Marika.

"Let me just try. Let me help him breathe. Can't you feel his pulse?" Suzanne crouched over Marika, trying to reach Richard's body through the legs of the table and the broken pots. Catching her by the wrist, Marika pulled her down to the floor and held her there. Suzanne burst again into wails. Guiding her hand to Richard's wrist, Marika too felt for the pulse, but the only heartbeat the women discerned, as they gripped the dead limb, was each other's.

Peter Abeche returned alone. The assassins had run toward the hills, he reported, and disappeared into the thick growth. He was breathing heavily; as he rejoined Mayume and the guards, they all backed away, through the garden into the house. Curtis Lovell came over to Marika. "Can I do anything?" he asked.

"A towel," she said, "for his face."

He returned with one and then stood there, leaning against one of the orchid tables. "Fucking pigs," he said. "Savages. We never should've let them rule themselves. Christ, Richard was *good* to these people. Thought they didn't need the military cracking down on them. Ought to have the fucking marines crack down on them, you ask me."

"Just so I have been saying, Mr. Lovell." Marika looked up. Peering through the broken glass of the greenhouse was James Biswandi, hatless, his face shiny with sweat. He shook his head. "I've been warning. These people are communists, they are killers. Our lives are filled with these tragedies. Mrs. Hooper, I am desolated." He stretched forth his hands as if to show them empty, then clenched his fists. "The ones who do this will be brought down!"

"How do you even know who did it?" Lovell exploded. "These people kill and steal and run right back to their village fires! So you round up the village and shoot the whole bunch! But you never catch them!"

A sound came from the corner. It was McGrath, retching onto the floor while one of the black girls held his shoulders. The vomit, liquid and bloody, ran down the slope of the cement onto the petals of the fallen orchids. McGrath groaned. "Where's he hit?" Suzanne asked, rousing herself and pulling away from Marika.

"I think the lung, from the back," said Florence's daughter. "His arm also, but not so bad."

"Can you get the bullet?"

"It is too far implanted."

"There is only one to catch," Biswandi said, leaning as well as he could on the shelf of broken glass. "He burns his city, below"—he jerked his head—"and he murders his friends. When Ngebin goes, then will the people have peace."

Slowly, in the brief silence, Marika looked up. She had wiped Richard's face clean; she held the damp towel against the blasted temple to stop the blood flow. "What about your scorpion, Mr. Biswandi?" she asked, unable to steady the quaver in her voice. "What about your fat hen?"

He shook his head; the top of the skull was unexpectedly low and flat, like an anvil. "Mrs. Hooper, you are grieving. Look, there, at your hand. You must care for yourself, too."

Glancing down, Marika saw the clean gash that a shard of glass had made in her palm as she wiped Richard's face. The blood welled up from it, deep red like the juice of a guava. She touched her lips to the small pool of blood, the cut Florence had foreseen for her, then she lifted her stained face to Biswandi.

"We cannot," he was saying, "be everywhere at once."

"Can't you?" she whispered. Her vision was blocked by the rows of orchids, their colors blending into a pastel sea between where she sat on the floor and where Biswandi stood outside. Above the distant crackling of fire and gunfire in the city below, they heard the scream of the ambulance siren as it mounted the steep hill. Flanked by both bodyguards, President Mayume made his first entrance into the greenhouse with a pronouncement that Marika did not hear. Turned back to Richard, she was repeating to herself the words that Justin had given her, *Think how you have been loved*, and through the words wound the current of the Schubert she had been going to sing. *Wenn in das Abend*,

> . . . in the moonlight's pallid lustre,
> Your dream becomes more fair . . .
> As your vision grows more clear
> It will be I, who hover near . . .

The melody bore her away from the floor of the greenhouse, from the dying orchids and the strangers who rushed back in, now that help had arrived. Thinking how she had been loved, Marika sang Schubert's *Lied* silently to her husband. His sharp shoulderblades rested against her thighs, his smoothly woven jacket fallen open at the front to the cleanly pressed blue shirt. His eyelids sealed his features, but his tie looked painfully tight; she loosened it carefully, as if not to disturb him. The heat of his flesh then flowed to her fingers, and with it his spirit ebbed, like the tide vanishing from shore. She sang as if to call him back, while her fingers spread farther and farther over the shirt, seizing glimpses.

# *Chapter* 5

The fire set by the *dai* drove through almost to the harbor. Among the buildings it engulfed were the jail and morgue, where Ngebin's sister lay. In the foreign press, Ngebin (photographed blurrily, his head still shaved, cone-shaped) took responsibility for the fire, but nothing was said of his sister's death. Unable to move from the heavily guarded house, Marika had learned from James Biswandi that three men, escaping the jail, had been caught and executed for conspiring with arsonists.

By the time the police had gathered up those they suspected of Richard's death, five days later, the city had become impossible to navigate. In the marketplace and again downtown, where the embassy was, barricades obstructed every corner, and the green trucks slalomed past them to roll through the empty streets. Most shopowners had closed up and hidden away whatever goods had not been stolen or destroyed in the fire. When Peter Abeche came to pick Marika up and drive her to the place where they had lined up the men, he explained that they would take the long way around, through the fishing village.

"But these stores are closed, too," Marika said as they passed the boarded buildings, untouched by fire, in the old town.

"Na, it is Tuesday, Mrs. Hooper," Peter said gently. "You know they are always closed, so."

"Tuesday," Marika repeated, as if making sense of it. "I had lost track." She gave her head a slight shake, loosening the pinned curls, as if shaking herself awake. She had slept little, the nights like long tunnels to be got through.

"Do you know," Peter went on, his hands stroking the steering wheel, "why it is that we rest, so, on these Tuesdays after the high noon?"

"No."

"It is coming from the day the Afoni Kon, the Lethe leader in this fight we are having then with the Nebo. The day he is seeing the battle lost, and he paints his body half with white clay, the other half with charcoal. He say, 'If I fall with white side up, we win together. I fall with black side uppermost, we are fighting within ourselves, and we lose.' Then it was that, seated in his tent, he shot himself in the heart, the Afoni Kon, with all his ministers, na, looking on."

"And which way did he fall?" asked Marika. She watched a Sacatra boy, bronze with sweat, his muscles flowing like mercury, dash in front of the car and disappear behind a flap of cotton protecting a side yard. All Yumana's stories, it seemed, flirted with death. From the stoops where they sat drinking or mending nets, the fishermen eyed them with lazy suspicion.

"Black side uppermost. So it was the Nebo held our people, na, hundred year or more. They are saying this happened on a Tuesday, and that is why we rest. To reflect."

"But you're Sacatra, Peter."

"Father, yes. Mother Lethe. Very problematic."

He pulled the car into the reserved spot outside the courts building, down the street from the embassy offices. Across the wide, untrafficked boulevard, the green Republic Square shimmered in the fulgent sun, the early haze burnt away. The black statue sucked in the heat. The fire had been quickly smothered in this area, left to rage around the market and the hastily constructed apartment buildings that reached like corrugated fingers into the foothills to the north. With its trees moist and swollen from spring rains, the park had held its own.

Peter came around to help Marika from the car. She let him ease her up, as she had let the others who stepped in with their small kindnesses. As if they know how, at every other moment, she could hear glass shattering and smell the bloody, broken pots of earth, how flesh appeared to her a thing to be ripped away. Inside the air-conditioned building, she followed Peter down the corridor to where the three State Department officials sent by Charles Hallerin waited with the chief of police—a dull, unctuous man—and Biswandi.

The usual chorus of condolences fell tidily on Marika's ears. The men were grievously sorry and terribly disturbed. They hated putting her through this, the way she must feel. What a great statesman Richard had been. Nodding, murmuring, Marika said yes, thank you, so kind. She tucked the comments into place like stray winsome locks of hair, then the party proceeded to the room where Biswandi had lined up his nine suspects.

From the moment the white-smocked ambulance men had arrived at the house, she had known what the officials would want from her. Florence's daughter and the other girl had disappeared as soon as the hoarsely breathing McGrath had been lifted onto a stretcher. Their ministrations, the Sacatra doctor said later, had saved McGrath's life; where had they come from, those girls? And the State Department people had already asked who else had been at the house that day, where had Richard gone the night before, had he mentioned any worries he had?

If she had wanted to, Marika could have located Florence, who had made so very certain that Marika keep her husband at home to be murdered. She could have found Seki, too, if Seki were still in the Lethe quarter of the city, ringed now by Biswandi's men. Biswandi himself had come by the house daily with his well-oiled attentions to report the clues they had picked up and gently to pump Marika for names associated with the spectre of Ngebin. Gone were the sarcasm and elliptical suspicions; Biswandi removed his cap and bobbed his low forehead respectfully as he spoke of her husband's good faith, of the betrayal he had suffered. Of how he, Biswandi, had feared this from the start and had tried to warn Richard that day they went together to the Parambo.

No, Marika had answered his and the others' questions. She had noticed no one strange visiting the house—the general himself could remember stopping by the night before to find her alone. Richard had talked that day of his report on the health situation, the arrival of McGrath, and of course his orchids. As for the girls at the house that night, they were town girls that all the white families had used—they were good girls and she would not give the officials their names.

Thus, up to now, she had lied, not to protect Ngebin or the *dai* but because she wanted Florence to come to her—to sweep away the damning evidence or, more logically, to silence Marika before Marika told Biswandi of

Florence's urging her to keep Richard at the house. Of her sending the young man, Amet, with the pretext of removing a hidden microphone, to confirm that Richard would be there that night. Of her not dropping so much as a hint of what Richard had done to deserve death.

From the small, dark room into which they crowded—she and Peter Abeche and the heavyset officials—she stared through the camouflaged glass at the men standing in a line at the back of the next room. They were all Lethe. With the image of the Afoni Kon in her mind, she saw them all as if divided left from right, half charcoal black and half chalk white, wondering which way they would land when she pointed to each in turn and each fell dead. She passed over their faces until she reached the last on the right—the young man Amet, naked to the waist, his strong chest red as copper, his eyes trained on her as if he could see through the one-way glass. Carefully she composed her features. If she started or took a sharp breath, the boy would die, and if she knew anything, it was that he had not stood outside the greenhouse that night. Ngebin had sent others, nondescript men.

"I don't recognize anyone here," she said.

"Are you sure?" one of the Americans urged. "Look again. I know it's hard to tell them apart—I mean with it having been night and all—but—"

"I may recognize one," said Peter. "In the middle, there, the short one."

"You never saw their faces, Peter," said Marika. "How can you tell?"

"I am seeing something, maybe, in the shape of the head."

"Have these men done anything? Something else, I mean," Marika asked the police chief.

He rubbed his hands together. "All bad elements,

Madame. Subversives. No one to explain, na, where these all be that terrible night."

"Maybe there, on the left, too," said Peter. "With the scars on his chest, I am thinking he's one of them."

"No," said Marika quietly. She was conscious, as she had been the five days since they had covered Richard with a white sheet, of a great canyon into which everything around her was falling. "Whatever Peter says, these aren't the men. I can't tell you what they looked like, but I know they aren't in that room."

"Not even there," said Biswandi, pointing toward the right, at Amet, "the young one there?"

"I never saw him before in my life."

Early the next morning Marika descended again—this time on foot—to the place where she had seen the dead girl. The roadside merchants had vanished, and the dry wind had whipped the vegetation to a prickly brown mass.

In the midst of his condolences, Biswandi by now had reported on the body that Mrs. Hooper had seen that other morning. There was a girl killed, it seemed, by the *dai*. Their leader's sister, she had taken a young Sacatra soldier for a lover and so broken the oldest tribal rule. Those people lived by blood and died by it. He had the confession of two *dai* thugs who had done the deed, but the cause, Mrs. Hooper had to understand, lay with their leaders, far back in the jungle.

Across the river, the city was quiet. Cars rumbled peaceably over the causeway. Marika had walked down to escape the State Department and embassy people, who met now at her home as if it were a public place—as indeed it was, United States property. They suspected something wrong in her poverty of grief. They desired a distraught wife, a widow spilling over with clues tucked between her demands for retribution, clues that would allow them to wrap the matter up.

Richard had died almost instantly of a massive brain hemmorhage, the doctor had told Marika. If his eyes had actually blinked, it had been no more than a reflex, an aberration. He had suffered little pain. Both President Mayume and the State Department people had proposed flying Richard's body back to Port Henry, New York, the old trappers' haven in the Adirondacks where his father Morton mended broken limbs and delivered babies. They had offered to pay for a dignified and costly funeral, but after calling Morton and hearing what he had to say, Marika had demurred.

His first question, crackling over the line in the middle of the night, had been how it happened. He had known already the cause of her call. At his voice, for the first time, Marika had begun to cry, not for herself but for him to whom Richard had been the last and the only.

"Last night," she had said. "Some gunmen, they don't know who."

"You bringing the body home?"

"I thought I'd ask you. The government people here are offering—"

"To hell with it! I am a doctor, Marika. I don't have to look death in the face to know it. You collect my boy's ashes there and then come on home yourself."

"I'm sorry, Morton."

"There's nothing to be sorry for. There's only bad luck and evil men. My Richard, my boy. Let an old man go weep, Marika."

Above the silence of the city floated the white noise of the Parambo Dam. Yesterday Bud McGrath had flown back to the States, boasting of a punctured lung and vowing to stop smoking. But nothing stopped the smelter, its fumes knit up by the morning winds and brought down to the city to rest, a fuliginous layer, until they rose again with the sun's heat.

Justin, she thought, would have liked to paint this, the lifting of the pressure as the golden ozone took off for the stratosphere. He'd want to capture those noxious colors, show off their beauty. In chalks, maybe, on a linen canvas imbued with oil.

But Justin failed to speak to her. Since that night, he had been silent, leaving her to face the lineup of men, the unctuous officials, the shell of a house on the hill, alone. She barely whispered his name, as if the louder she called to him the greater would be the void when no answer came. As if Richard's death had felled him, too, in one stroke.

A pale blue Fiat sent up a cloud of dust as it rolled down the hill toward Marika. Suzanne. They had arranged to go together to the undertaker. It hadn't been Marika's idea; Suzanne's, then? No, Claire's. Claire had thought she would need a companion when she went to pick out an urn—someone, Marika supposed wryly, to prop her up if she were to faint, the scene painted in Claire's vivid imagination.

Suzanne pushed open the passenger door. "There's a boy at the house, in a limousine," she said. "He wanted to wait for you, but I told him you had gone shopping. I actually think he came for a music lesson, can you believe it? He gave me this."

Marika took the thick, gray envelope. She had not had to close her school of vocal and instrumental training. All twelve students had simply failed to show up, beginning with the talentless Nebo flutist whose father was ambitious in the government and whose lesson fell on the morning after the reception. But she knew whose flat, square handwriting it would be before she read the note: TO MRS. HOOPER, MY SINCERE CONDOLANCES, SINCERELY CONSTANTIN MAYUME.

Marika had seen pictures of Mayume, his right hand extended upward in gestures of peace, in the newspapers that blared reports of the assassination and the riots. Next to him stood his son, the heir, serious and darker than most Sacatras, his eyes like laminated buttons in the round face. One American paper, which arrived by diplomatic pouch, had shown as well a blurrily photographed Ngebin, his head shaved and cone-shaped, but it had made no mention of his sister's death.

"The boy knows," Marika said. "There won't be any more lessons."

Suzanne spun the wheel with one finger as she drove, as if they were taking the freeways of California. "We don't have to go there today," she said as she swung onto the causeway.

"Sure we do. I leave the country day after tomorrow."

"I mean, the embassy could take care of it. Which reminds me." She reached a slender arm under the car seat and brought out a bottle of Cardhu. "Secretary Hallerin wired for flowers, but Lisbeth and I thought this'd be better. I mean, you've got all those orchids—"

"Thank you," said Marika. She turned the trapezoidal bottle over in her hands, the glass cool and heavy.

The somber Nebo undertaker pointed out the urn he had already selected for Richard's remains, but stubbornly, while Suzanne pouted, Marika insisted on another, one smaller and rounder, less like Richard. As the women left the Byzantine white building, Suzanne held Marika's arm at the elbow, as if she had planned this and must carry it through, however superfluous the support might be.

But when they reached the car Suzanne sat behind the

wheel, her key poised by the ignition. "Well?" said Marika. Richard had used to do this, to pause in the midst of an action and dredge up some long-dead event. It had always irritated her—now, in the thick of his absence, even more. "What's wrong?"

"I shouldn't tell you this," Suzanne said, her voice weak as she started the car, "you being his wife. But I was crazy about him." She put both her hands on the steering wheel but still the car idled. "I used to wait for him—at the corner near the palace—just so I could pretend to bump into him and walk by his side the rest of the way. He must've known. I didn't have to come from that direction."

From the side, Suzanne's eyes seemed to sharpen to triangles of water. Her upper lip was rimmed with sweat; in the heat, the car swelled like a balloon.

"He liked you," Marika said, reaching a hand to Suzanne's shoulder but stopping short, a cushion of air between them. "I know he liked you."

"What an honor, living every day with a man like that." Suzanne turned to look at Marika as if seeing her for the first time. "He always called you at lunchtime, too. The jealousy killed me. Oh, I didn't mean that."

Back at the house, in the sea of boxes, Marika poured Suzanne and herself double Scotches, from the embassy's gift bottle. Out in the greenhouse, Ichi was packing plants; otherwise the house was quiet. There had been a brief invasion of newspaper reporters, but they had moved off as quickly as bees pollinating one flower to the next. Suzanne poured herself another drink and asked if she could look at pictures of Richard. Her face, pinched between the narrow fall of her hair, had blanched to alabaster. Uneasy, Marika fished a photo album out of the packed box and, handing it to Suzanne, slipped from the room.

"Can you save them?" she asked Ichi as he knelt on the greenhouse floor, packaging the undamaged orchids. Someone had thought to clean the cement. There lingered no trace of blood. All around her, people were tending to these things. She saw the orchids as if for the first time, huddled in the boxes, their pale thick petals like ears, listening.

"Oh yes, yes indeed. Velly strong prants." But Ichi shook his head doubtfully. "You sure you no keep this one or that one? Two or thlee?"

"No. He'd want you to have them. They'd just wither away, with me."

Marika started back to the house, then stopped. "Ichi," she said. "You remember Seki, the girl you sent to us?"

"Ah, yes, *Okusama*. That one velly bad gill."

"Do you know where she's gone?"

"That gill traitor." Ichi stood up and wiped his hands on his wide apron. "She run off to go with *dai*. Bad gill, wicked."

"You think she had something to do with—?" Marika gestured indeterminately at the wrecked flowers, the jagged hole in the greenhouse wall.

"Evelyone," said Ichi, looking at her under heavy, flaring brows, "has to do. *Okusama* going home, yes? Back to U.S.?"

"Soon as I'm packed."

"Is good. You stay gone. You neveh come back to Yumana. You forget Yumana, is betteh."

"And Seki?"

"Her, too. You forget. These"—Ichi finished, stooping to cradle the bulbs broken from their pots when Richard fell—"the best of all."

Back in the living room, Suzanne had fallen asleep and

Claire had shown up, perched on the arm of the couch, flipping through the photo album. She had walked from her house. Worse than the men from Washington, she could not keep away.

"I have nightmares," she told Marika when she was settled with a Scotch. "They've lined us all up against a wall, and I just know they're going to shoot us all dead. Then just as I hear them fire, I wake up. But I'm covered with sweat."

"Who's 'they'?"

"Those blacks. The ones we're living with."

On Marika's lips there came a softness, the indulgence with which Richard used to smile. "This is a black country, Claire. It's black against black. We only get caught in the middle."

"You're wrong." As she leaned against the sofa back, Suzanne curled up below her, Claire's smooth, tanned face twitched around the mouth and eyes. "This is a Pioneer country. Oh, a little British oil, maybe, and an Italian copper mine. But any way you look at it, the place is kept going by whites. Curtis explained it to me. The president's just the houseboy. And those"—she glanced around the room; only the Nebo who helped clean up at the embassy was there, wrapping Justin's paintings—"those bush niggers know the story. They're out for white blood, just the way they were in the colonies. They won't be happy until this whole continent is pitch black, communist, and back in the jungle. I say that's what they want let them have it."

"I remember one year," Marika said unexpectedly, "when there wasn't any fighting. It was during our first tour, before the dam. Richard actually got a vacation, and we decided not to fly back—to spend the time here. A fellow from the embassy building took us to visit his family, up north, near the source of the river. There were trout running in the river that time of year, and the whole village spent the day on the banks, catching them with their hands. Richard said it reminded him of the alewives running on Cape Cod. That night we roasted trout and ate them with new beer. The women danced, so I danced with them. It was the first time I felt at home." She shook her head. "I don't know what made me think of it."

"Your husband," Claire said, "died like a hero in a war. And all I want Curtis to do is get us back home."

The harmattan had run to earth, leaving an oppressive heat. When the house had emptied of Suzanne and Claire and the rest, and night settled in, Marika switched on the light over the bathroom washbasin. "You're in shock," she told her pale, oval face in the mirror. Beneath the dry tissue of skin, the puffy area below her eyes was translucent as egg white. In shock, like the orchids Ichi would transplant, caught for a time between death and growth. At night she lay still, unvisited by Justin, untouched as a statue. *Richard*, she had tried to think once or twice, but the sound rang as hollow, as smoothly enameled inside and out, as the urn she had chosen.

Now she laid herself carefully on the bed, as if she were china that might crack, or as if, having painted one side of her body white and the other black, she were unwilling to list toward either for fear of either consequence. Straining to hear the distant pounding of the Parambo Dam, she willed it louder, to bring to the dry air of the room a sound that might slake her thirst.

"Ano, that they call the goddess of the river, will not be loving the men who destroy her this way," one of the village elders had told her the time that she and Richard visited the north country. "She will make their women barren and the work of their hands to wither in their hands."

They had slept that night in hammocks covered with mosquito netting, and sometime after midnight Marika had been awakened by an overwhelming perfume—coming, as she could just make out through the net, from the nearest cassia tree, where a vine of moon flowers embraced the trunk. Their heavy waxen blooms bled into the night, releasing all their life's scent into the hours alotted to them. By morning they would shrivel to damp tissue, the vine gone hard and hollow. She had lain back, the hammock rocking, and breathed the attar deep until she, like Richard in his netting a few yards away, slept soundlessly, the riffle of water running through their separate dreams.

Close to a hundred times, mostly in the last five years, but even before acknowledging her motive, Marika had driven to the Revenir airport over dusty or mud-hollowed roads and had sat in her car watching the small jets land and take off again for Madrid and the West. In the dry heat their metal had shimmered, miragelike; but through the heavy rains the noisy liftoff had actually appeared a miracle, defying not only gravity and the sucking mud of the runway but also the relentless torrents lashing everything else back to earth. It was then that Justin began speaking to her, not out of the past, but in the present, in Yumana.

—*There's the moment of risk, Rika,* he had said as a plane shuddered up from the runway, lights blinking through the rain. —*That's why we fly. You could say that's why we do anything. Look at you, in this place.*

But on the day she left Revenir, Marika saw little risk in it: the flat-roofed cement terminal, the wide airstrip flanked by tangled forest, the five battered gray planes, Yumana's air force, like cows nosing in the same direction on a barren field.

"No one," Lisbeth kept saying, blinking her brown eyes behind her large glasses, "could handle this place like you and Richard. We're gonna *founder.*"

Among the forty or fifty passengers milling through the terminal, Marika thought she saw the young man Amet. He was leaning against a pillar by the men's room, wearing a bush hat, a cigarette drooping from his mouth. Only his height and the strong bones of his face, half hidden by dark glasses, gave him away. But Marika had to present her ticket to a plump, official agent, and when she turned again to where Amet had stood he was gone. "You okay?" Lisbeth asked her. "You look queasy."

"It's the heat," said Marika, wiping her forehead with the back of her hand. Anticipating New York's January, she had worn a wool suit, and in fact she could feel the warmth of her torso rising like steam through her clothes and up her neck. "Maybe I should lighten up a little."

Removing her jacket in the narrow women's room, Marika caught sight of herself in the oval mirror that hung over the cracked procelain sink, a mirror just like the one in Richard's old office in Revenir, where he used to stand behind her while she put on lipstick or combed her hair before they went out to lunch. In the wavy surface of the airport mirror she could trace where his features would be reflected, his neck bending so that his eyes could meet hers, his nose level with the top of her head. He would be speaking to her, reflection to reflection, as he had often liked to do. They had not gone out together for lunch since he had moved to the new building, but early on, in their first tour, they would walk from the embassy to the harbor and sit at the little café, eating couscous and drinking local beer. As the mirror distilled the shadow of Richard's face, Marika's mouth filled with saliva, as if hungering for the hot pork and rice, and within her dropped a round, hollow ball of regret. Turning away from the mirror, she hurried back out to the bright terminal.

On the plane Marika sat next to a handsome young man, a Sacatra, dressed smartly in a spotless cotton shirt and silk tie, his loafers polished and smelling faintly of fish oil. His eyes had the soft, ivory-hued white of his race; his cheekbones, flat and symmetrical, might have been pressed from wax. As the plane lifted easily above the dense patch of trees, Lisbeth and Jeremy waving their arms like flags and dropping farther back until they fell out of view, Marika heard a shuffle of papers and for distraction turned from the window to see the young man pull out a small leather briefcase and extract a brochure and leaflets. The cover of his brochure showed a white couple walking beneath a canopy of cherry trees, the white blossoms swirling around their feet. They hugged books to their chests and smiled at each other; above the tree branches, the text dropped out in white: "George Washington University: A Place to Grow."

"You're going to school in America?" Marika asked.

"Yes, Miss, that's right." He opened the brochure to a listing of courses.

"Nervous?"

"I think not so much." He spread his coppery hand on the page and looked at her. "I have only myself to worry for. When I come back this way again—to my country, I mean—then I will be nervous. Oh, sure."

"Your family must be proud."

The young man laughed, shaking his head as if he had heard an old joke. "My apologies," he said when he stopped. "But white people are always thinking like that, that my family should be proud since I am going to this U.S. school to study. But my father, you see, is right now covering his head with shame. My brothers are saying I am not their brother."

"What would they want you to do?" Marika frowned.

"Work at the bauxite mines. Marry this fat strong girl in our village. Make many sons. My father is still chief, you see. He is hoping after many things that are many years dead."

He chuckled again, but bitterly. Marika thought of Amet, if it had been he, in the airport. He had come to watch her leave. He might have killed her husband. She looked out the window at the dark green rainforest below, the sparkling edge of the ocean. Eight years of Yumana. Fifteen years of Richard Hooper. She felt them like a kaleidoscope that had passed before her eyes, like the scenery dropping away behind the wings of the plane.

"And you?" the young man was asking her. "You are going home for holiday?"

"Not really." She turned back to him, his smooth eager face. "I'm going home as you will from college, years from now. I've finished my education."

"And what will you do?"

"Do?" Marika took a deep breath of the rich oxygenated air filtering through the cabin. "I guess," she said, "I am like your father. I'm hoping after many things that are many years dead."

The young man's name was Paul Ophalete. He planned to study United States economics, in order to spring his people from the trap of foreign obligations. Neither he nor Marika mentioned the murdered American ambassador, though he seemed pained that she should not have married and borne children. At Madrid, he rushed to the next concourse to catch his flight to Washington.

Missing his company, Marika wandered through the airport shops like a starfish suspended, until her flight was called. Choosing three adjoining seats in the half-empty plane, she stretched her legs across. As they took off, from the tiny oval window she watched the steel blue of the ocean darken to mauve and finally disappear in the black night. The lights of the cabin soon snuffed out.

She was cut free. From the week of events, from the odor of death, a brief blameless respite awaited her in the cocoon of the plane. As the in-flight movie caught the attention of the other passengers, Marika slowly lifted the lid of her memory. Slowly, she delved, so that whatever crawled out would not make too loud a sound, so that not everything she had trapped within would jump out at once. Thousands of feet up in the air, she was safe. The images moved on the floor of the dark sea, too far below to drown her.

The first thing she remembered was Justin's loft. They had reached it through a wide corridor of cheese and dairy wholesalers, the sickly-sweet smell of fermenting milk filling the air. Loading docks faced each other across the street; above, the shaftways yawned dark and hollow as caves. She had come with Justin from a party at the Ukrainian Institute in honor of emigré painters, but Justin's only connection to the party had been that he liked to drink beer with the Pole who had framed most of the pictures.

Marika's mother, Katya, had invited the Pole, not to be rude, and the Pole had invited Justin. They had both arrived just as the awards had been given and the small band at the end of the gallery had launched into a *hopak*. Justin—clean-shaven then, his jaw short and square, like his hands—had thrown off his coat and grabbed Marika by the elbow.

"I can't dance," she said. "I'm serving punch."

"Here, then," he said, downing one cup, then another. "You've served it."

"But the others—"

"Anybody want punch?" Justin had cried out, holding the ladle aloft. Joining in the circle, they had all glanced over, then ignored him. "See, no one's thirsty. Come on." He had pulled her by both hands around the long table and onto the floor. "I have absolutely no idea how to do this, incidentally," he said as the figure began.

"You take me by the waist, here, and we turn a circle." She had been serious about all things then, at twenty-one, her dark blond hair pulled back and up, her mother's gold cross gracing the dip of her collarbone. "No, not so fast! Now you hold my shoulder, the way I'm holding yours. Follow the people in front of us. That's good."

He had caught on quickly, especially for one who acted so ungainly, his blue workshirt hanging over his bluejeans, his large feet hesitating in their steps. "I don't know your name," he said as they spun off into pairs.

"You haven't asked it."

"I'm asking it now."

"Marika Rybak. You ought to tuck in your shirt."

He did so as best he could, keeping one arm around Marika's waist. "Well, you sure belong here, with a name like that," he said.

"And with an accent like that you don't, whatever your name's like."

"Justin Kilroy," he said, the shirt mostly tucked in. "And I don't belong most places."

Marika remembered her mother's eyes on them as they finished the dance and Justin descended once again on the punch. "What's in this?"

"Vodka, mostly."

"So, Marika Rybak," he said, dropping pieces of cake into his mouth after the punch, "where do you go to look for meaning?"

"To the opera."

"Uh-uh. *Nobody* does that, unless they want to sing in it."

"*I* do."

"Do what? Sing, my pretty?"

She saw his chin thrust forward and knew not to give too much away. Serious as she was, she could be coy with this one. "No," she lied calmly. "I go to the *opera*. For meaning."

She remembered how much she had liked his hair, wavy and coarse as it was on his head as well as his forearms, bared by the rolled sleeves of his shirt. His eyebrows, too, were dark and tangled over deepset eyes that wouldn't let go. "Stop looking at me like that," she said later in the evening, when he had let her alone awhile and then had come back to finish the dregs of the punch.

"It's the only way I can look at you."

"I don't want to flirt." She reached for plastic cups, napkins, paper plates to clean up. "So go away."

"Come outside with me," he said, taking her hand.

She never knew why she did what he told her. Obedience had never been in her nature. But he walked her across the street to the stone wall by Central Park and then stepped back. "Underneath that ridiculous outfit," he said, "you have the hips of a madonna."

"It's starting to rain, Justin Kilroy."

"Turn around."

"I won't."

He approached and took her by the hips. She was wearing a Ukrainian *platye*, starched petticoats puffing out the skirt, the waist cinched with a wide cummerbund. Marika thought her body was shaped like a pear and disliked it. "When can I paint you?" Justin asked.

"You can't. I don't know you."

"Come see my paintings. Once you see them, you'll beg me to paint you. Hey, Milos!" he called to the Pole. "I'm going to paint this girl! She lucky, or what?"

"Not as lucky as she'll be when I frame her!" Milos called back, and they both guffawed.

"Come on, I'll show you my place," Justin said. His hand grazed her upper shoulder, where the dress was cut low. Marika swallowed.

"I can't. I'm with my mother. She has to clean up."

"Hey, Milos!" Justin shouted again. "Tell—what's her name—Mrs. Rybak, her daughter's with me. Tell her what a great guy I am! And hey, Milos?" The Pole had started to go back inside, but turned around. "Help Mrs. Rybak clean up, would you? I'll get you some framing jobs!"

"Is no problem!" Justin's friend called back, hopping inside from the rain, which had begun in earnest.

"Hurry," Justin said to Marika. "Here's the bus. I can't afford a taxi, can you?" She shook her head. When they had boarded and taken seats at the back, he turned to her, sober, and she met his eyes, though her neck pricked as it flushed slowly red. "You've spent nights away from home before, haven't you?" he asked her, his voice soft and heavy, like flannel.

"Yes."

"It's all right, then."

"It's all right."

So he had led her through the steaming rain, past the pungent loading docks to the red-painted steel door with a wood carton nailed into the cement for a mailbox, and up the three straight flights of broad, slanting stairs to which her legs would grow accustomed over time.

At first all she saw was a square, barren, high-ceilinged room, with long narrow windows covering one wall, the others stripped in most places to the bare wood or brick.

Here and there patches of printed wallpaper, its flowers faded to obscurity, had stuck to what remained of the plaster. High above, the pattering rain struck a domed skylight. Justin switched on his lighting, a row of track lamps made from black-painted coffee cans that trained the light onto the far wall, where he had stretched a canvas and covered it with short, thick strokes of green and brown, over which he seemed to have begun the pale body of a nude woman, though all Marika could make out was a pair of limbs. Near the canvas, stacked against the same wall, stood a dozen other paintings and a squat black garbage bag, which Marika later learned was filled with cuttings—paper, twine, metal strips, glass, shells—for collage.

"But where do you live?" she asked, shivering unexpectedly in her wet dress.

"Oh, that. This way." He led her past the only piece of furniture in the open space, a round oak table covered with bills, letters, and statements, littered with Styrofoam cups, orange rinds, apple cores. She saw that what she had thought to be a wall was only a partition, and reaching the other side, Justin turned on a table lamp. "Here's where I live," he said.

Under her feet, instead of the hard floor of the rest of the loft, lay a thick wool rug, its edges tightly braided. Justin's furniture was all pale oak—the small table in the center, the high-backed rocker, the wall of shelving where he kept his books and tapes. Above the deep porcelain sink were rows of spices, some of them hanging fresh—the room smelled distinctly of clove—and below it, wine bottles nestled in a wood frame. A ladder by the far window led up to a high bed. "It's another world," Marika said, "this side of the wall."

Leaning against the partition, which was covered on this side with polished wainscoting, Justin grinned like a boy and stroked his chin. "I made it all myself," he said. "Part of me wanted a home."

Dropping her handbag and wet sweater onto the smooth seat of the rocking chair, she slipped off her rain-soaked shoes and walked over to him, almost formally, as if he were hosting a dinner party and she were a late guest. He stood still by the wainscoting until she touched him. Then, just as formally, he bent down and kissed her lips.

# Chapter 6

The plane touched down and came to the gate in a steady drizzle, the gray fog a balm after the dry scourge of the harmattan. Marika's legs had fallen asleep. They carried her like wooden pegs through the exit tunnel and into the bright lights of the terminal, where she saw her mother's frantic arm waving and waving over the taller heads crowding the waiting area.

"Mama!" she cried, bending to embrace her. Small-boned, smelling of loose powder and sweet perfume, Katya clasped her daughter's neck and began to cry. "Stop that, Mama, I'll think you're not glad to see me."

"I can't help it, my poor baby. I keep thinking what a good man, what a good husband he was to you. And they cut him down like that."

"Mama, please, I'm sad enough. Tell me you're happy to see me, tell me the news."

"Of course, of course I'm happy. You have to come rest. Here, give me that bag."

"No, Mama, I have it." With sharp shoots of pain, Marika's legs came back to life as they waited for the baggage and hailed a cab. Traveling with Richard, she had always taken the helicopter, their heads too jarred from sixteen hours' travel to cope with the traffic and potholes on the way to the city. But now she was alone with her mother, and the taxis were safe and easy to understand.

"Since I got your telegram, I've been crying," Katya said as they reached the old neighborhood, the shop with its icons, and finally the red-tiled vestibule and the flight of carpeted stairs, smelling still of yeast and sugar from the bakery. "I wake in the middle of the night and can't stop. The neighbors say I look bad, I don't know."

"You look fine," said Marika, though as always she had been taken aback by the curve in her mother's spine, by her thin hair and pinched face. "You still getting up to the Institute?"

"Every day, just like always. I told them all there about your coming and the tragedy. I passed around the newspaper clippings. You've got cards, here inside, to read."

In the apartment where she had grown up, Marika dropped her two suitcases to the floor. She had brought only the clothes she needed and a few books; the rest would arrive by slow boat in a few months, and by then she would know where she was going, how she would live. Because she could not stay here.

The living room, kitchen, bedrooms might have made up a museum, each article clamored so for attention. The living room ached with furniture. Two upholstered couches, each of crushed velvet with embossed leafy patterns, faced each other in the narrow space with a low wooden table between. On either side of both couches, heavier tables carried small figurines of peasants and saints, silver ashtrays, and cylindrical lamps bearing shades like upturned wastecans. Deeper in the recesses of the room, three armchairs shared two velvet footstools, and lining the alcove were glassed-in cases holding more precious knicknacks, glass and pewter miniatures that had arrived stuffed in pockets and the recesses of bags during the war. Marika's mother had replaced the carpet two years ago with a deep maroon pile, but the same embossed wallpaper, unnoticed behind framed squares of lace and dark oily still lifes, graced the walls. The only other addition besides the new rug was a compact color television, set up next to one of the lamps on a slender stand, its antennae scratching the wallpaper.

"I cooked a roast," Katya was saying, disappearing into the kitchen. "But I didn't invite anyone. You don't want excitement."

"No," said Marika. She brought one of the suitcases into the bedroom that had been hers, where her mother had turned the walls into a memorial of diplomas and photographs. There had been three wedding pictures, in heavy gilt frames, but they had been tactfully removed from the wall, leaving bright squares in the wallpaper that attested to the years of marriage gone by. She and Richard had never stayed a night here. For a long while they had tried to persuade her mother to move, not far away but only to one of the new buildings in the neighborhood with a doorman and an elevator. But for the first few years Marika's father had been slowly dying, and afterward Katya had settled in even further, like a piece of furniture laying claim to its place. She said her legs would miss the steps, if she were to move.

In Marika's mouth, as she pulled off her wrinkled blouse and with relief unhooked her brassiere, was the faint taste of revulsion at these close, carpeted rooms, the narrow closets and arched doorways, the steam heat that banged through the radiators, their valves rusted open. The smells and sounds of her childhood. But her head swam with fatigue, and she was content to peel off her clothes and sink into the deep porcelain tub of her mother's cleanly scrubbed bathroom. Lying immersed in the hot, oil-scented water, she thought of nothing until her mother knocked softly on the door; then she wrapped herself in the plush oversized towels that had always been Katya's indulgence. At the table, laid with linen damask and sparkling china, Katya sliced the roast meat, pink and nourishing. Marika ate what she could, then she slept.

The morning mail held a pouch from Washington, full of cards from those emissaries and heads of state who had failed to send their condolences to Revenir. These were handwritten, on white vellum stationery, and spoke of Richard's dedication, his loyalty. On the front of one, forwarded from Yumana, was an India-ink drawing of one man carrying another, with the message inside, "His friends will not forget." It was signed simply Ngebin. Marika crumpled the card and dropped it into the trash.

"Bastard," she said aloud.

"That you, Marika Theresa?" called a shrill voice from the kitchen. "We've been waiting for you to come down, you know, from the clouds!"

"It's me, Aunt Sacza," Marika said, stacking the cards on her bedside table.

"Well, come on out before it's night again! This is no tropics here, you know!"

Facing one another across the square table, the two women had changed neither their positions nor their temperaments since Marika was a small girl. Sacza sat splay-legged, her beefy face pocked with age spots, her breasts filling the front of her wool jumper, while Katya, porcelain-skinned, sipped her coffee like a squirrel, her knit jacket hugging her compact body.

Always there had been for Marika these relatives, like Sacza, who were completely unconnected by blood. So few had brought more than the nucleus of their family with them when they came over that they had adopted their neighbors and neighbors' children. They came for holidays and funerals; they had attended Marika's voice recitals en masse, and some had even made it to the opera house. Piled next to the notes from Washington in her room were the velvet-papered and gold-embossed cards they had sent, with standardized messages of comfort, as if she had been the one shot and had survived. *They hurt Richard*, was all she had thought last night as she leafed through them. *Not me.*

"And no children to comfort you, either," Sacza said at one point as Marika sat with them, taking the small chair as she always had.

"With a divorce people are always happy if there aren't children," Marika answered calmly. "With a death they think it makes it worse."

"That's a difference, between a divorce and a death," Katya put in. She pointed her finger at her daughter as if already chiding.

But then Katya had loved Richard more than anyone, Marika reminded herself as she retreated from the room. Stamped forever with the world war, with flight, with the felt strangeness of language and ways, she had praised Richard's height, his taste in clothes, his marvelous capacity for listening to her, in the long evenings in the dark living room of this same apartment. She had found Richard's Russian adorable. When Marika had announced a protracted engagement, Katya had pulled her aside and asked, "What's this two years? You're making no sense. Do you love him or no?"

"Mama," Marika had said, "I'll be traveling all summer with the opera. And Richard has no idea where he'll be assigned next year. This is just kind of a symbol."

"A wedding ring is a symbol. If you're not sure, I'm

not pushing. But if you're going to do it, I don't see why not now. A wonderful man, you shouldn't take chances."

*Justin*, Marika had wanted to say; but his very name betrayed her. She had given Justin up. He didn't need her. He could do anything, everything. Brilliant people worshiped his vision, his passion—even his excesses, the bouts and tirades. She had told herself she wanted children, comforts her parents had lacked, time for her music, things she could control.

Justin hadn't guessed she was simply afraid, and so he too had said, Go—go to Richard, who can make you happy.

So she had gone. And now as her punishment, Marika stood alone, childless, in the very place from which she had flown, with two old women waiting to judge what she did next. Because she still believed in the god of her childhood, who so fascinated Richard, and who would not tolerate betrayal.

That afternoon more relatives came—summoned, Marika guessed, by Katya—each protesting that they happened to be near the building. The landlord, a Jewish doctor named Dniprovsky who had been on the boat with Marika's father, brought flowers for Marika and a box of nougat for Katya.

"So. It has not struck you yet," he said to Marika.

"What hasn't struck me?"

"The loss of him. It is like an adrenaline, you know, this shell that goes up—immediately!—round us." He hit his palm with his fist. "We don't feel the agony until the drug wears off."

"Reuben, you are cruel to the girl," Katya said, taking a nougat, but she watched him as if waiting for more.

"Not at all! What destroys us is the later time, when this loss finally digs through to us. Then what? We don't annoy anyone, we are friendless and miserable. So I say to

Marika Theresa"—he patted her knee—"your mama and I, we'll still be here."

How little he understood. Dr. Dniprovsky had a bald head the shape of kiwi fruit, with the same thin fuzz on his face. He still practiced general medicine, and the people in the neighborhood still went to him, though he gave them foul-smelling poultices for their arthritis and prescribed nothing but laxatives for headache. "That old man should have his license revoked," Richard had said; but Katya and the others would have gone to him anyway. He had never married, and he lived alone in the first-floor apartment where he saw his patients. He stayed for tea and kissed Katya's hand as he left.

"He walks ten miles a day, that one," Katya said.

"We've always known that, Mama. He goes to the Battery and back, morning and night."

"Keeps him in health. Now your father, he never walked."

"He died of bone cancer, Mama. Walking wouldn't have helped."

"Your husband, now, he kept himself in shape. Such a shame."

"Oh, Mama." Marika put a hand on Katya's arm, then lifted it. "I can't stay in here. I've got to go out. I'll walk, too."

"Go! Go, my darling girl. Breathe the fresh air."

Presaging what would become a routine in days ahead, Marika walked away from the neighborhood where she had known Justin and with quick, short steps covered the miles of concrete that led uptown. The encrusted snow lay like brown skirts on the crowded window fronts, assaulted by the billowing exhaust of buses. Yet while the cold bit at her legs, she watched a group of snow-suited youngsters step off a bus and seemed to see the gang of Lethe children that swarmed over a hot courtyard in the fishing ghetto, brandishing sticks in pursuit of a hard black rubber ball, their shrieks merging with the cresting wave of a siren. The siren was headed down toward the water, toward the docks where they were hauling Florence's husband and the others from the black water into which the rifle shells had pitched them. Richard's face, hearing the news, went sharp as a knife, his hand clenching his sleek little tape recorder.

Heading through midtown in the low afternoon light, she passed rows of West Africans hawking elongated wooden icons and bracelets of elephant bone. From their accents, she could tell they came mostly from the French-speaking countries. They watched warily as deer for the police while they tried to barter away their goods in a tongue strange to them. Turning away from their faces, locked over their knees as they squatted by their shoddy merchandise, Marika found herself facing the pasty visages of New York's European descendants; and as she scrutinized them, one pair of blond women detached themselves, laughing, and turned into a health club. This time Marika saw herself, moving through the sauna heat that followed harmattan, when, during the days when bicycles instead of army trucks had roamed the streets of Revenir, she had spent such hot afternoons with Florence, first in the hospital and later in Florence's gabled bungalow. Florence had served sweet tea and millet cakes and taught Marika to make mash to ferment for beer; and her daughter had been there, too, withdrawn and gawky, peering from the curtained-off sleeping area, her hair braided and tied with bits of cloth.

Marika's unmindful steps led her into Central Park, gray in its January dormancy. Somewhere in the miles up from the apartment she had bought a roll and eaten half; the rest she broke up to feed the scrappy seagulls and pigeons by the lagoon. And again an image hit her—the chattering flock of flamingoes, a hundred or more, that had broken the surface of a stagnant lake in the Yumana uplands and flushed it to the color of the pale, inner flesh of an orchid, the surrounding hills like petals cupping the ferocious sunlight.

It was not, she would have said, that she mourned. Rather, an intense confusion, like a flock of gulls descending on a patch of the lagoon, had fallen on her from the moment the plane touched ground. It had trailed her, in fact, all the way from Yumana. As she headed south, her legs aching under her, she turned as at a footstep coming from behind; but there was only a bum leaning against a bench, kicking at the snow.

Nothing followed her but uncertainty. What would she do the next day, and the next? How would she begin to live? The Americans she had left behind in Yumana saw her course as predestined to move, like a career diplomat, from one bed of unrest to another. Claire had waved at her from the Lovells' porch as if she expected to see Marika at the next Washington function on the arm of the consul to Kuwait or of Pioneer's new foreign director. They saw no other path. They didn't know anything of Justin, of course—but then, did she?

How much easier it had been with Richard, who had harbored no interest in Justin. Shortly after they met at the United Nations club where Marika sang jazz, Richard had begun taking her home, to the address she gave him, the loft below Canal Street. He had claimed he worried for her safety. He would leave her at the warehouse entrance when he saw she had her key in the lock, and he would take a cab up to Central Park West. What Richard had wanted of Marika's past had been her engagement with history, the origin of her name, her childhood religion, her languages. Not her young loves or her singing; not the smell of oil-rendered flights of fancy that emanated from a painter's loft.

As dark fell she stood, shivering, by Carnegie Hall, trying along with dozens of other helpless, waving arms to hail a cab. She hadn't planned to walk so far. Unpracticed, she let the others grab the fleeting yellow cars, their lights like fireflies in the bluish haze. It had begun to snow. She backed away from the curb into the vestibule of the building, which was warm and dry and filled with young people going to and from performance classes. As she had done once.

Idly she scanned the directory. Among the studios and offices she found him, still on the eleventh floor—Claude Thrush, the round-bellied, asthmatic tenor with whom she had trained during those few years in New York with Richard. He had reworked her breathing, her *glissando*, her vibrato. He used to say singing jazz had ruined her. Himself, he sang only for his pupils and his dog, a St. Bernard who sat always panting in the corner of the studio.

She thought she should call Katya; but instead she went up to the eleventh floor and down the dark, musty corridor, with none of the eager students from the vestibule behind her but with a vague sense of being followed. She walked faster and arrived breathless at the glass-paneled door with the old sign, cracked and peeling. CLAUDE THRUSH, VOCAL AND OPERATIC INSTRUCTION.

"Well," he said when he saw her. "You're a real ambassador's wife now, not just one of those foreign service Ivy Leaguers hanging around New York waiting for something. You should be at parties. You shouldn't be here."

His voice, if it were possible, had grown even more pinched and wheezy. He sat behind his little desk, a schoolboy's desk, with scores piled on the file cabinet behind him and a music stand set up in the center of the bare-floored room. He combed his hair, Marika noticed, over the top of his bald head, from one ear to the other; if he let it fall back, it would reach on that side past his shoulder. The room smelled the same as it had when she used to come here, a young wife and a headlong performer, like some of the older ones, downstairs.

"What am I doing here, then?" she asked him calmly, the warmth of the room making her more tired. Too tired, at last, for stark remembrances of Yumana. Her face flushed as from drink. By "here" she meant not just the studio but her mother's apartment, the city, the United States. Maybe Claude Thrush had an answer.

"You've come for me to hear your voice, obviously. You barge in unannounced, you haven't done a note of warming up, it's like Alaska outside, and you want me to praise you and say you haven't changed in the slightest." He shrugged and took a stick of gum from the pack on top of his desk. Every time she had returned to New York with Richard, Marika had promised herself she would look up Claude Thrush, and then she had failed to. He would have ridiculed her. Never could she have told him—his head as perfectly round as a pumpkin, his smile a straight pencil-line of lips—about her music school in Revenir. Always he would have made her feel like dozens of others who brought him their unfinished lives.

But now she had come. Her first day alone in New York, where somewhere Justin waited for her. "I don't want you to hear my voice," she said. "It's thin. I haven't done an exercise in six years."

"Well, just look at you. You're slouching."

"My husband's dead," she said, as if he were the first to hear.

"Sorry to hear that. Cancer?"

"Bullets."

"Well, that's quicker, anyway. Bernie's dead, too."

"Who? Oh, the dog." Marika glanced toward the empty corner.

"Not that it's anything like losing a husband. But then, I wouldn't know that side of things." Still he seemed to smile, like a mannequin whose expression, once painted, never changed.

It refreshed her, this flat emotion, the dusty room with its sweet smell of chewed gum and lingering odor of dog. A scratched and yellow-ivoried spinet took up one corner. "You do still give lessons, though," she said.

"I still have to pay the rent."

"Maybe I'll stop in again. When I'm warmed up, I mean."

"What for? You still got that fire in your belly? Nah. You want to stand out in the church choir, maybe. Or you're just looking for an outlet. So you don't have to think about what you do without him. You don't like the parties. It's suddenly occurring to you, 'Hey, I used to be a singer!' "

"Maybe," said Marika, her smile reflecting his the way she used to mirror his facial contortions. "Or maybe none of those things. Why should it matter to you?"

"Why indeed?" Gentle, porcine Calude Thrush took the gum from his mouth and stuck it to an ashtray. "My job is to do some good and earn my keep. Hey, I was sorry to lose you. You had a good *bel canto* voice." He pulled out a desk calendar. "Come see me tomorrow. I've got noon open. We'll start with halftone scales."

"Wait. I didn't say—"

"So you don't have to. But it'd probably be the best thing for you. Don't you think?" He rose and patted her shoulder—patted her, it seemed, right out the door. The small lobby downstairs was still filled with bundled, breathless students, the street outside dark and calmer. A solitary West African stood playing an ocarina by the door to the vestibule, a medley of wood and reed instruments spread over the dirty, once-colorful blanket at his feet. Dressed in traditional robes, the bright woven *boluwo* cap on his head, he resembled the chief's tall, long-faced son who had danced for her and Richard in the north country. She dropped three quarters on his blanket, among the instruments. He kept his face down, rocking on his feet to keep warm as if in the early stage of a trance. Turning away, Marika lifted her arm, and this time a bright new taxi stopped for her within seconds. Luck was with her. But what was this sensation she had, running down the spattered sidewalk toward the car, as of a train of phosphorus fading behind her—as of being followed?

Justin was—had become—a living fact. Without trying, Marika found his name everywhere. In lists of paintings acquired by one museum or another, his fell at the top. Advertisements for SoHo galleries used his name; so did the ones on Fifty-seventh Street. The fourth Sunday after Marika's arrival in New York, the Sunday magazine section boasted a cover of Justin Kilroy, straddling a rickety wooden chair, his body and face turned away from the camera and contemplating a huge shimmering sweep on black canvas captioned *The Glass Mountain*.

"KILROY," the title read, "COMING OF AGE."

Slowly she opened the magazine, thumbing through lipstick ads and an article on covert war until she reached the inevitable spread—Justin before the camera, close up to one of his paintings, a whole plethora of objects seeming to spill out of the flat surface behind him. The cheeks that years ago had been taut were now rounded, the beard gone again, the nose as always an appealing loop in the center. His chest and shoulders massed under a stained red flannel shirt; he had exercised to gain strength, she remembered, not wanting ever to tire before an unfinished canvas. The writer used words like *visionary, meteoric, charged*. Reluctantly, Marika turned the pages to confront the facts of Justin's life, facts she had avoided for years. The text swam before her eyes—but the pictures chronicled a public and glamorous life, in the new loft he had bought in TriBeCa, in his house on Shelter Island, with his son Adam in the studio. A discreet mention of a certain Rose, now estranged.

On her walk uptown early that week, she brought the magazine with her, tucked into her bag, like a talisman. With remarkable rapidity the days had acquired a routine. She would leave her mother's apartment by ten and hike through the city to run trills for Claude. On the way back, she stopped at the Museum of Modern Art to spend time with Justin's paintings. For hours she wandered through the square, white, partitioned galleries where she knew Justin himself would never appear. Afternoons, she talked to apartment brokers or answered the letters and phone calls that still flowed in—accepting condolences, rejecting invitations to receptions and lunches.

This time she took a cab from Claude's studio to the Guggenheim. The exhibit touted in the magazine was titled "Postmoderns and Fantasy" and boasted at least a dozen Kilroys along its Charybdian wall. There was a new *Flounder*, a floating half-human creature in night-blue space; *Hansel and Gretel*, a thick pastiche of celluloid woods, with real breadcrumbs embedded in the paint; there was *The Glass Mountain* of the magazine cover, a transparent slope in which broken bottles, syringes, mattresses, parts of bodies were buried while a figure strained to climb the smooth surface above. A frenetic authority locked into every cryptic detail.

Looking at the new works, she remembered how he would go painstakingly through other artists' paintings with her, pointing out the significance of the brushstroke in this one's work, the recurrent turtle-images, symbols of birth and eternity, in that one's. She had nodded and asked questions, all the while transfixed by the muscles of his arms as he traced a theme through the air, by the stance of his legs as he stood squarely before a sculpture, as he moved around it before rendering judgment. Sometimes he had held her in front of him as if he were presenting her to the painting, setting up an exchange between her eye and its pigment, her hand and its wattled surface. Always the curators had come forth to pump his hand and ask when he would be ready for an exhibition, a question he evaded. Always he announced that he would be painting Marika for his next work. She had smiled and shaken her head.

He had painted her anyway, of course. In thick strokes of red and black, her head like a pin on the molten globe of her body; stretched out asleep, shiny and translucent as a glass bottle; in a tumbling, vulnerable abstract that he called *Rika's Voice*. But she would not sit still for him so that he might study and recreate the curve of her hip. "I'm not a model," she had said. "If you find me in your mind, paint that. I thought art had stopped copying from nature." The truth was that she had been unsure of him, afraid that he would put her onto a canvas and have no more use for her in real life.

In the picture window that looked over the Modern's

courtyard, Marika saw her own tall form, softened by layers of wool. The face, with its long delicate nose and eyes like a pair of dark smudges, skin nacreous as skim milk, filled the void framed by finely waved, overgrown hair, a diffuse cloud spun by the tinted glass. *I will die*, she thought, *if I can't have him back*.

Still she postponed him, journeying uptown rather than down, letting the street carry her away. As winter wore on she accepted a handful of invitations, to purposeless seminars with foreign service wives who hugged her and loaned her their sympathy. In the small Carnegie studio, Claude Thrush knotted and expanded his facial muscles and made her place her hand on her diaphragm as she breathed. At night, Katya took her along to meetings and dances at the Ukrainian Institute, where the same aunts and uncles that had sent condolences came for folk dancing and asked her to sing and play the *balalaika*. They blew their bulbous noses and kissed her on both cheeks; the director welcomed her to teach evening classes on the music of the Ukraine, "just for amusement," making it clear he knew she had no need of money.

She postponed also a visit north to bring Richard's ashes to his father. In their few talks, Morton Hooper seemed not to care about his son's remains with a fierceness that alarmed Marika. "Why the hell would you want to come to these mountains in the winter?" he said. "Can't even break ground for a burial. Let's settle our scores with the living first, Marika. Call me in May."

The time went by. In the February damp she caught a cold and allowed it to linger. She turned down a soirée at La Maison Française given by francophone Africans, a Washington's birthday weekend in Alexandria. She came almost to crave the close moldy rooms of her childhood, the smells of meat and onions seeping through the walls. Katya snatched the invitations out of the pale blue wastebin by Marika's bed.

"Look how you fester," she said, "when the world wants you to have a good time!"

"Mama, I don't know those people."

"Your husband's friends!"

"His associates. He didn't like them, either."

"So now you don't like people you don't even know yet? Some enjoyment you get from life, wandering the streets like a tramp to make yourself sick, singing like a schoolgirl for some little perverted man. You forget your position, you forget the life you should lead. Yah, and going to see those paintings, too, I know about them."

Then the news came that her shipment had arrived from Yumana, and Marika's spirit seemed to stretch itself like a waking animal and trot out to find sustenance. She woke in the morning with the old sour taste in her mouth, and the old desire knocking.

"I can't live here indefinitely," she told her mother.

"Of course not. A year or so."

"Another week or so. I'll keep the things in storage until I find a place. You can move, too, you know, Mama. The money's not a problem."

"Where would I move? All I need is here."

"Don't take me wrong."

"You're not well. You should rest a bit. You're grieving." Her mother knotted and rubbed her hands in her lap, as if she were washing them. "You should go talk to Dr. Dniprovsky."

"There is nothing, Mama, that Dr. Dniprovsky could give me to make me better."

That afternoon, filled with new energy, she surveyed sets of empty, clean-swept rooms with views of the park, of the river, of the reservoir. She told the realtors who she was, or had been, and they glowed. But as she looked down from these heights there came to her the panorama of Revenir spread before her each evening in Yumana, and she stepped away. "I can't stand views," she told one realtor, "of any kind."

So the realtor showed her quiet interior apartments that only made her long for the breadth and height of Justin's loft—not the one in the faded magazine picture but the old loft, the untouched space that had come down with the cheese factory years ago. She left the realtor and walked, following the broad curving asphalt paths of the park, mottled and banked with hardened snow, down to the museum. She stopped in at the dusty studio and listened to another of Claude's pupils, a broad, blond soprano, sing the opening aria from *Bohème* that had been Justin's favorite. She checked into the health club where she had watched the two women enter, and took a dry, silent sauna.

So it was she floated, like a mote of dust in the light, bathed in the warmth of Justin so tangibly near. Often she sensed she was being followed, but imagining it was he, she dared not turn. Even in her thoughts she kept from calling to him, knowing what would be his constant refrain: *Come to me now. Why do you wait? Now. Come to me.*

# Chapter 7

The wet snow turned to pelting rain, day upon day of it, until the whole island floated waterlogged scraps of newspaper and half-eaten bread on its spreading whitish-gray puddles. Marika flew through rain to Washington and stood under the protection of Charles Hallerin's umbrella, surrounded by foreign service officers with their matching wives, while a salute went up through the cold drizzle over Richard's memorial marker in Arlington cemetery. She flew back in a muddle of sleet and fog, Manhattan bobbing below like a cluster of upright spars. Next morning, sitting in the warm alcove of Katya's living room, she watched through liquid windows as the pigeons huddled and cooed under the courtyard eaves.

"Who killed him, do you think?" Katya called from the back room where she sat stitching odd little bits of cloth together. Her mother had always moved needles through cloth, Marika thought, as if the thread were Katya's mind working, hooking and pulling free, rhythm of the cerebellum. "Your husband, I mean."

"Oh, Mama," she answered, not turning her head. "I don't care."

"Blame everything, don't they, on the communists." Katya came to the door. "Maybe so, but we learned, you know, not to believe the simple story. They told us the *Führer* was killing only Jews."

"Mama, I saw them. They wore yellow armbands. They were guerrillas."

"Simple as that." The hard note in Katya's voice made Marika look up.

"I'm not asking questions, Mama," she said. "He's dead either way, isn't he?"

Who had killed Richard? As she emerged from the apartment into the rain making fat holes in the stubborn crust of brown snow, the act of someone clapping shut Richard's life seemed as remote to her as the steaming summer monsoon was from this gray metallic chill. More impossible still, the idea that she might be living with Richard now, rather than slipping from museums to vacant apartments to her mother's home, lifting at intervals the steady lid on her memory like the pressure valve in an aquarium. Justin was her only possibility, and she was afraid to go near him. Until she had solved the one mystery, the secret of who at this moment was loving Justin, no questions about Richard could command her attention.

Who was with Justin? There lay her urgency. Shaking off the drizzle as she entered the Whitney Museum, Marika noticed around her women who appeared, all of them, to be twenty-three, serious, and beautiful. Their hair was cut to fantastic shapes, hugging the head on one side only to break into polished spitcurls on the other. Their broad-shouldered jackets tapered to cinch their boyish hips, with knit leggings below, or sharply cut leather or velvet pants that stopped just short enough to catch the taut muscle of the lower calf. Marika shrugged off her coat and headed straight for the elevator. Justin had worshiped her broad, low-slung hips, her full chin, her large mouth, but these sleek women had not been among his available choices. Already he had divorced the wife Rose—Marika saw her as diminutive, sparrow-like, anxious to please—and was seen, if one believed articles, at conspicuously elite gatherings. But Marika straightened her shoulders and tossed her rain-frizzled hair as she stepped out into the sparse setting of the museum's traveling show, "Art as Social Conscience." When she had imagined herself with Justin, true, she had been as he last knew her; but she had not aged precipitously in the last few months. Men had wanted her over the years. She had no need to beg.

The Kilroy in the exhibit was drawn from Swift's Gulliver, the battle of the Lilliputians. The tiny figures rushing toward cataclysm smacked of Hieronymus Bosch and Bruegel, with their tails and claws, their heads between legs, their multiple eyes and orifices. But unlike the other artists' monsters, Justin's were transparent, like fish, nymph-like, lovely.

"There is always," Marika heard at her ear, "that essential lyricism in his work, don't you think?"

The young woman, one of those from the lobby, tanned after a week in the Caribbean, spoke to a spindly, worried man beside her. "*Lyric* is too weak," he said. "It's the fantastic minus the grotesque, if you ask me."

Marika moved away to let them get close and analyze Justin. Backing into one of the low, black-cushioned benches they condescended to place in these rooms, she tried to hum to herself the Poulenc air she would have to sing for Claude Thrush. Her upper range, he would tell her, had failed to grow in force; her vibrato was too loose. He would crack his pink gum and focus round, tired eyes upon her. Afterward, if the rain had subsided, she would again take up the hunt for an apartment. She might even return home to

Katya and allow her to argue who had killed Richard. Anything to stave off her obsession, to make plain the impossibility of looking Justin up, of facing him, widowed and out of season as she was. Yet here she sat, surrounded by his work.

"I remember," spoke a familiar voice behind her, "when you could see the guy's stuff whenever you wanted. Just wander into the place and look over eight, ten paintings. I'd frame 'em so people could pick 'em better when they come to visit, that's all. Now one's done and out the door to go hang somewhere, and you gotta hoof it over to these other places. Ain't it a pain?"

"Sure is," Marika said reflexively, then turned to see this companion who spoke to the air. He wore a familiar sheepskin hat on his round head, his jaws working a toothpick as he shifted on the bench and faced her. The thick forehead was now creased, the thin stubborn mouth starting to pucker; and the added pounds, gained one each year for fifteen years, had left him walrusy where he had been porpoiselike, Justin's roly-poly pal. "Milos," she said.

"Our own Marika." He removed the toothpick and grinned. "More gorgeous 'n ever."

"You didn't know I was in town, did you?"

"Thought you was off making voodoo with the Pygmies."

"I wasn't, I—my husband died. So I came back here."

"You surprised?" He tilted his head toward the painting.

"Not really. I followed his career, till recently."

"You married that older guy from the government, right?"

"He wasn't that old."

"Pissed the old Texan off. Jeez! I remember."

"I never thought he minded so much."

"Shows what you girls know. But what's he expect? You're gonna sing nightclubs and support him the rest of his life? How're you supposed to know God's gonna take a shine to him?"

"Oh, it wasn't that," said Marika, shaking her head. How could she tell Milos, after fifteen years, *He started to scare me?* "What about you? You still making the frames?"

"Sure! And I get other work, too, now *he's* made it big. I'm rolling in green stuff. Look at me, I got nothing better to do with my time than hang out at museums and look up girls' dresses."

"Funny, running into you like this."

"No, it's not. I been thinking I saw you other places, too. I come around to check out the frames, you know. I knowed it was you, even in those tweedy clothes you got on. And I thought, 'Well, looky there who's back.' "

"Does Justin know?"

"Well, he don't talk to me much about you. When you was first gone off to Africa, he says to me, 'Milos,' he says, 'you let me know if she dies over there. I want to hear it from you first. And then I'm gonna break every bone in that sonofabitch Hooper's body.' That's what he said, I'm just quoting."

"Someone else," said Marika, "got to Hooper first."

"Yeah, like you said. I'm sorry. But whether *he* knows you're in town or not—hey, you're asking the wrong guy."

"Well, you let him know you saw me, will you? And—and—" Her hands fingered her pocketbook, worrying the clasp. A hum started up—the humidification system, protecting the paintings. "Just tell him you found me here."

"Hey, I know that bit about offing the messenger," said Milos, holding up a stubby hand. "Why don't you see him yourself? I'll tell him you're coming, I can do that much. He's having a bunch of folks over to the place tomorrow night. Corner Franklin and Hudson Street. You oughta just show up there. Eight, nine o'clock. Be a reunion."

His eyes, impish under their heavy lids, glinted at her. "I'm not sure I'm free," said Marika.

*I like to cook for my friends.*

"Well, you better be, baby, because I am not telling the man you'll be there and then you not show."

Instead of answering, Marika stood up. Justin's Gulliver, still half-hidden by its admirers, was flanked on the walls by strident, declamatory paintings, the curator's notion of social conscience. "What do you think," she said slowly, "of his work now?"

"Stuff like that, there? Hey, the man's famous, it speaks for itself. Incredible. And he hasn't changed a bit, you're gonna see that, he's the same crazy guy."

"Well, the art has changed. A lot." The Lilliputian grotesques, the carefully constructed holocaust.

"So he didn't know exactly what he was doin' before. Hey, the man's tremendous. Are you accepting this invitation to his place or not?"

"I'll go," said Marika, nodding her head as she spoke. "I'll do it."

"Thataway! Us Slobovniks have gotta stick together, hey? My god, the old guy'll be surprised!"

"Oh, no," Marika answered. "Justin couldn't be surprised to see me."

Part of her, as she exited the museum into the rapid twilight, the sidewalks slicked black with rain, believed what she had said. Hadn't this sense she had had of being followed really been Justin, close at her heels? Three years ago, when Biswandi came to search the house for a nameless *dai* who was crouched in the basement between the wine cases and the gardening tools, hadn't Justin talked her into toughness until she stood fast by the door? Hadn't he whispered litanies of memory in her ear as she watched a lone truck roll out of the city at dawn, its cargo heavy with those whose destiny had broken the night's quiet? Hadn't he made love to her time and again, even as she aged, bringing her back with him to New York or coming to her in the fierce heat of Yumana?

Too vivid to be solely of her imagining, the encounters tracked her and Justin along their separate paths to their inevitable meeting. If the *dai* had not killed Richard, Justin would have found another way to bring her back. Never would he have let her go but to make himself dear to her.

*—But you used to hit me,* she told him.*—That year before I left, whenever anything went wrong, you descended on me. You bruised my eye once.*

*—You cried more when I broke your piano, my love.*

*—Then you spent all your money to buy me a new one. You couldn't afford paint for six months.*

*—I was a child.*

*—I want to give you a child.*

*—But I have a child.*

His name was Adam. The wife, Rose. And all those voguish, clever young women to hover around. The bleached white house in Southampton. This new Justin would never strike out, would never break all his canvas frames, would never drink himself oblivious and miss another's concert, would never—

*—Come on, Marika, you think I care about the old Justin and the new Justin? I care about your lower lip, how it pushes out when you get above high F, more than I do this whole* famoso *routine. God, why don't you come to me?*

It was the man in the magazine pictures speaking, those pictures that had jolted her ever so slightly before she admitted that he looked a little different—only a little—from what she had imagined. The eyes slightly less focused, more gray in the hair, the neck thicker. But he spoke the same as always, and his rough scent, with the lingering turpentine on his hands and dried paint flecking his shirt and shoes, remained. Hers.

High up in the Carnegie building, Claude Thrush's studio was lit, a small square of white by the southwest corner. She was late for her lesson, but not so late that she couldn't have sung for him. Behind the closed, rain-swept window he might have been playing the Poulenc on his spinet. Guilty, she turned to catch a cab downtown. Claude knew nothing—had never known anything—of Justin; but he would call her out for what she was or feared to be. He would hear the hope in her voice and dash it. As the cab sped away, she hummed the *Mi chiamano* from *Bohème*, the only aria Justin loved her to sing, otherwise preferring the jazz she did at clubs. Claude said jazz had ruined her. And Richard? Richard had liked it all equally and blandly. *Who killed him*, Katya wanted to know, as if the answer would make any difference now.

The rain let up. Marika got out at Fifth and Broadway, where a bag woman stood in a puddle at the corner, crying, "Disease! You're full of worms! Plague and disease!"

"No, old biddy," Marika said, "I just recovered."

She walked past the bookstores and antique wholesalers, past buildings masked by scaffolding that advertised co-ops, into the old neighborhood. From the brownstones, low and quiet beneath arching street lamps, came the sound of radios playing opera. Tomorrow she would look again for an apartment—but there was no rush, there was no telling what the future held. Breathless, she turned her key in the old lock.

"I worried sick for you!" Katya greeted her. "You're gone all day, and me with no idea where."

"I had to sort out the things I stored in the warehouse," Marika said, "and there was my voice lesson."

"Lessons! For what, I'd like to know."

"Because they distract me."

"Your supper's cold. I'll have to heat it."

"Please," said Marika, hanging up her wet coat, "don't. I haven't got much appetite. We'll save it for tomorrow."

"You'll catch pneumonia."

"Mama, I am forty years old!" Marika heard her voice rise and crack. "Women my age have stopped telling their own children to eat."

"Don't mention children, please. We're all sad enough." Her mother sat in front of the color television, her body facing the set but her head twisted toward Marika.

"Yes, we are. We are all sad. We have all been sad for a long while." Marika felt her lower lip tremble. As slowly as she could, she walked down the hallway to her room and shut the door. After a few minutes she heard the television switch off, then her mother's footsteps approaching.

"It's that artist, isn't it?" Katya said, her voice quavering on the other side of the door. "You aren't mourning your husband. You're mooning around after that artist again. Well, he's dead, Marika! Do you hear me? He might as well be dead! He's no better as a man than he was as a boy. Marika? Do you hear me? If you loved your poor husband, you'll stop this terrible dreaming. He is dead!"

Marika covered her head with the feather pillow and sobbed, her forehead pressed against the hard mattress, in utter silence. She sobbed because she hoped, and she had no reason to hope. It had been fifteen years. His voice had kept her from chaos; but no one can live forever with only a voice, it drives them crazy, like the bag woman. Tomorrow she would see him. Overnight, she would will herself into the image he had no doubt molded in his mind, of a woman light and warm, wise and playful, a spur to his work and a haven for his soul. She had only to stop crying and concentrate, in order to make it happen.

The streets of TriBeCa wore the dank, brackish smell of early spring, of concrete that pressed upon the earth's natural fecundity. Above, the precarious labyrinth of fire escapes clung like centipedes to the blackened buildings. Between their rungs the smoky blue of Manhattan's night sky filtered down. Marika had walked down from Katya's through the lamplit awakening of SoHo to this once-familiar territory of sleeping warehouses with the lit artists' lofts like white fire blazing on the upper storeys. Her steps fell with small, hollow clicks on the dry cobblestones. In Revenir the monsoon had begun. The Parambo Dam was spewing water from the engorged lake above, while the incessant rain slicked the street with thick layers of red mud.

But here there were isolated, drifting human conversations and the boom of trucks topping the ramp to the Holland Tunnel. With nothing in nature against which to measure oneself, one quickly became small and forgettable. Standing on the curb of Franklin Street across from Justin's new building, her back to a mailbox, Marika felt herself shrink until the large door facing her across the intersection seemed too heavy for her to open alone, the steps behind it too steep to climb. The bright light from the four loft windows above emanated out and up, leaving her below in a pocket of darkness. Turning into the street, a limousine paused between Marika and the door, and a blond couple in fur coats stepped out and sailed through the wide opening, a ripple of conversation spilling down the stairs in front of them, cut off as the door swung shut.

She had not left Justin, she reminded herself, standing

shivering in winter's leftover damp, for Richard. She had left, first, because of what Justin had done to her and, second, because her mother had convinced her she was a failure and trash to throw her life away keeping alive a tall violent Texan who called himself an artist. She still remembered how she had come home, one of the last nights, from singing at a gin mill in Hell's Kitchen and, as he stood mixing his paints, had parroted her mother at him: *I might as well be turning tricks, it's easier on the feet.*

No. Neither the things he did nor her mother's voice had been the main reason. She had left so that he would follow her and beg her to come back, so that he would see he needed her to become a great painter. Only he had not followed, and he had become a great painter anyway. It was time for her to admit she had lost the game, and to come back without his asking, to beg him to take her.

*And Richard?* he would still ask. And Africa? She would have to persuade him that she had not loved Richard, never, he had been acceptable but that was all, and she had certainly never loved Africa. She had drifted for a while, that was all. She had not borne Richard's children, had she? So how could she have loved him?

The rightness of her argument struck Marika like a bell and propelled her across the cobblestoned street to the door. Her heart beat as though, after the weeks of hesitance, she were coming to Justin *just in time;* as she pressed the button below the metal speaker her every breath attended the sound of his voice. Instead, the opening buzzer was pressed, without anyone's asking who she was or why she had come, and the harsh sound followed her up both flights to where the party was.

"Look, what the hell, I am going for a Guggenheim," a young man with a red Mohawk haircut was saying as

Marika entered the foyer. "Have you noticed the yoyos they chose this year?"

"So you want someone else to call you a yoyo in twelve months?" his partner answered. She was older and drank champagne, a wry smile set in her face. The room, Marika saw at a glance, was filled with artists and agents, a few she recognized from the old crowd, many with the same tinkle in their voices, the same innocently affected arch of the eyebrow. Some people glanced curiously in Marika's direction, and one wraithlike woman glared. Eager to seal herself within the circle before the open door beckoned her away, Marika shrugged off her coat and took a glass from the fastidious serving boy. That morning she had dug out a black silk jumpsuit bought two years ago in London; despite the deep cut of the front, it seemed to fold around her, demure as a frock. Justin's guests wore costumes, feathers and fringes and unexpected patches of bare flesh—they dressed as the Lethe might for a harvest dance, only in bulkier clothes and heavier shoes.

From the corner of her eye Marika spotted Justin, slamming his fist against his palm as he argued with an excited group. As if he were bright light, her eyes refused to take him in all at once but darted around the room, catching the hand motions and the vehement shake of his head in their sweep. A small voice told Marika that, had she not been looking, she would not have known it was he—the body was not so large as she remembered or the magazine hinted, the shoulders less broad, the face busier, less of a portrait. But all she needed was the glimpse. At once everything in the room reduced to a hum and a wash of color, backdrop for the event she had set in motion, the moment when he would walk out of her imagination into this room, when she for him would come alive, a plain and simple offering. Slowly, anticipation galloping and going nowhere in her breast, she sidled through the crowd toward the kitchen where Justin stood expostulating.

"What the hell do you mean, the geometry of the line is invigorating?" Justin was saying to one of his listeners, a lithe black man with jeans cupping his buttocks. "The geometry of the line is *meaningless*. You cut a painting in half and then you think people have to see the image as flat. Cavemen saw paintings as flat without any lines slashed through them. The difference is, we have supposedly lifted the spirit a fraction higher. Geometry, shit. Study it in grade school."

"But illusionism—" the tight-jeaned man protested.

"Is a word people who can't paint made up. Like Shakespeare was into story-telling. Like why don't we have films that show the frames so people don't get fooled into thinking there's movement on the screen."

"I know a guy doing that," a woman with a husky voice put in. She stood behind Justin, in sunglasses, smoking nervously. "Had a thing at the Forum."

"So people are crazy in every medium, what's it prove?"

Falling on Marika's ears, so lately attuned to argument on a different plane—tribes, insurrection, international debt—their talk had the ring of an old and familiar tradition, of stories told on the front stoop. She herself was out of practice. Drink in hand, she stood outside their charmed circle and gazed in at Justin. She would not enter, she already knew that. She would just finish the drink and go away; suffice it to have seen him.

Then Milos spotted her. From across the kitchen, where in shadow he leaned against a counter drinking Hungarian beer, he shouted, "Hey, boss! Look what blew in from the cold! Mine own discovery!"

And Justin turned. Like a lone horse breaking free of the herd, he turned his head and then his body, allowing his guests to argue on without him, around the focal point he had vacated. "Well, well, well," he said, his voice flat and taut as a strip of rubber, "if it's not Marika *Hooper*."

"Rybak," she corrected quickly. They had to get over Richard right away. "Rybak, to you."

He came one step, then another. His eyes on her, she saw he knew why she had come, what she had come out of. She had not been wrong in her blind and relentless, her uninvoked communication. He *had* been with her. Here was not the Justin of the magazine picture nor of her feeble imagination, but the Justin who had been always waiting, his large rough hands making his art, his eyes slightly protruding, intent on the space just in front of them. He and she had only to begin, now; the time ahead was theirs.

Then he stopped, the space between them a cave of air. "What," he asked, not taking his eyes off Marika, "is this woman doing here? I didn't invite her."

Milos rolled out of his dark spot, stepped right into the dangerous vacuum. "I brought her, pal," he said. "Found her loiterin' around your stuff in the museum and thought she oughta come see the genuine article."

"I have lots of groupies. I don't invite them all to my home."

"Hey, reunion of old friends. You know. Past is past. She come all the way from Africa, boss. Her husband got wasted."

"What a shame." The edges of his mouth flickered upward. "But he must have left a nice annuity."

"Justin, please." The words escaped Marika's throat like gas. Under his stare, her whole body dissolved. A twisting pain locked her stomach, her esophagus. The arm holding her drink had gone stiff, fixed forever with the glass cocked in her hand.

"Justin, *please,*" he mimicked. "Please be a robot and not a painter. Please show my mama your portfolio—stocks not sketches, thank you—and your salary stub, and then I'll up and marry you. Please finance my little singing career, Justin."

"It was you as much as me," she found voice to say. "You told me to go. You said you couldn't live with anyone, it made you drink."

"Ah, wasn't I noble." He lifted his bourbon and drained it. "Wasn't I, Milos? Wasn't I, folks?" Milos looked dour, but others, their curiosity damping their own conversations, let go to a nervous titter.

"I'll go," Marika said. "I shouldn't have come at all. Thank you anyway, Milos."

"Wait." Justin's arm was just long enough to whip through the air between them. He gripped Marika at the elbow and pulled her abruptly close. Later she would remember the smell of the bourbon, of his chest, of the flannel shirt he had worn since morning. "You think," he said so swift and soft under his breath that she was not sure of the words she heard, "I didn't have you on the brain every goddamn day? For years it went on. Every painting I'd do was like a bar loose on your cell. Then I get the whole thing pried open, and you don't come out. Ten years I've been making it! And he's gotta *die* before you'll even look me up."

"Justin, I—I have, too—" she started. Had devoted herself to him, committed cardinal sins, refused grief as if Richard's death were a test of devotion to Justin.

"Uh-uh. Too late. I stopped making it for you years back. I got a little son. And you can just leave us alone, Widow Hooper. You got your life, I got mine."

He let go her arm. A dozen pairs of eyes were fixed on her. She knew none of these people. Slowly, mustering dignity, she retrieved her coat. They parted like a wave as she headed for the door.

Suddenly Justin's voice boomed behind her. "Leaving, Mrs. Hooper? Without singing us a little ditty?"

Marika turned, her mother's pride welling inside her. "Mrs. Hooper," she said, "doesn't sing anymore."

"We'll take Miss Rybak, then! Come, come." With the lightness he had possessed as a young man, Justin swung himself over a long couch and swept his arm toward the baby grand that stood in the corner. Marika thought of the tinny upright he had bought for her, while they lived together, with high C missing and middle F reduced to a flat fuzz. The baby grand was sleek and polished, like a Doberman pinscher. She shook her head. "You had a drink," Justin reminded her. "Now you have to pay the bar bill."

Ten minutes before, her glimpses had bathed him in desperate affection. That they should meet, touch, speak to one another with the muscles of tongue and lips. Now his cocky, self-serving grin ignited an old, unrecognized strain of aggravation. She opened her purse and drew out a ten-dollar bill. "For the whiskey," she said, letting it drop to the floor.

"Pah!" Justin spat on the green bill, his saliva a quick, fine spray. He wiped his mouth. "We want a song, a song! You know this lady used to sing at the Met?" he asked the woman to his left. She shook her head, staring down at the money. "It was in the *chorus*, of course," he went on, "but *I* thought she was good. I *always* thought she was good, know what I mean. Shows how ignorant *I* was, huh? Let's have a song!" He turned back to Marika. His unshaven face had lost, in an instant, all its time-nurtured charm. The skin looked loose and oily; the eyes were a lizard's, watching. "Sing"—he clapped his hands—"a song! Sing"—another clap—"a song!" From guest to guest he went, showing them how to clap their hands. "Sing a song! Sing a song!" The rhythm pressed on Marika like a hot iron. She blinked and stared at Justin, hoping to find a stranger in him. What she found instead was her old response, the gut heaving and choking, the way it always had before when he tortured and taunted her—the way she had forgotten, had made herself forget. What had she done that he would hate her so? And the answer came: she had given him what he asked for. "Sing"—Justin and his excitable guests shouted and clapped—"a song!"

Out of frustration, out of shame and despising, she drew herself up and parted the crowd to reach the piano, the black carved monster that she suddenly hated as much as she had loved her old tinny upright. As she sat down on the neat round stool, they fell silent. She refused to look at Justin. Her hands touched the keys and she knew that, despising him now, all at once, she would sing better than he had ever heard her, better than she had since she had left for Africa. She would sing to knock him dead.

"*Mi chiamano Mimì,*" she began. "*Ma il mio nome è Lucia.*"

The *Bohème* orchestration flowed beneath her fingers. Her voice flew from her throat as her vision of Justin—unchanged today, as much a bastard as he was when she first had fooled herself—crumpled like a stack of cards.

*Things that talk of dreams and fancies*, she sang. Pauses fell like petals between the notes—unrushed, savored. But when she reached the first cadenza, the moment Puccini had written in for Rudolfo to cry yes, yes, he understood her, to prompt her voice to rise again in the *Mi chiamano*, she stopped short. The sound of the piano keys died away in the surrounding silence. She closed the lid and rose, her skin damp with perspiration.

"Now that's what I call a voice," the young man with the Mohawk said eagerly. He stood by the piano; his Adam's apple jumped up and down.

"Sorry I can't stay to entertain you." Wondering glumly what the young man would be like alone, she turned to find herself facing Justin. The stupidity of the grin planted on his face failed to stem the rush of blood to her cheeks; that he whom she had held in her mind stood bodily before her baffled her senses. "Well," she managed to say, "if you can still paint, I can still sing."

"I can't paint. I do it with mirrors."

Every second that she stayed wove a delicate thread to him. She could not, must not, want that seam sewn. "May I go now?" she asked, though she did not move.

He shrugged; detecting her abeyance, he was quick to seize the advantage. "You paid for your drink."

The others had turned away into little clusters, though one wandlike woman hovered behind Justin. With effort, Marika broke her gaze from his and headed for her coat. "Sorry to have barged in on your party."

"It was an interesting diversion."

"Not exactly what I'd planned."

She reached the door, her back to him, when he gave way. "Look, let's have a drink tomorrow," he began. Unseen, his voice fell familiar on her ear; at least *that* part of him she had not rose-painted past recognition. She stepped into the hallway and started down the steps. He followed. "Where are you staying?" he called, the question echoing as her heels hit the metal stairs.

Still she did not respond, tightening her lips as she made it through the wide door into the damp cool night. But she knew he didn't need her answer, he would find her at Katya's. *And how,* she asked herself, emotions leapfrogging for ascendancy in her mind, *have I won by his knowing?* She could not still want him, not now, not ever. Her Justin had been an illusion, easy to put aside.

Yet the real Justin, the arrogant and spiteful success who had just humiliated her, stuck in her mind, as though she had opened a door and could not close it. The world beyond the door was not new ground but familiar turf, and what she stopped herself just short of admitting was that she wanted despite all she knew to tread it again.

# *Chapter* 8

They had taken one long trip together, to Mount Desert Island, off the coast of Maine. Justin had wanted to study fjords, and Mount Desert contained the only fjords in America. As soon as they arrived on the island—in a car borrowed from Milos, a low-slung station wagon ten years old that ate a quart of oil each day—he drove out to the high cliffs overlooking Desert Strait.

"What makes it a fjord?" Marika had asked.

"The depth of the water, the U-shape of the bottom, the steep descending banks. All of which give evidence of glaciers. But what I'm after is the depth."

In early June, there were few tourists on the island. The park's campgrounds were closed until the next month. Rumbling into one of the commercial grounds by the bridge, Marika studied one site and Justin another until they picked a flat area behind a thick row of bushes by a rain-bloated stream. They spent the hours of waning light collecting wood for a fire, and Marika swept pine needles to make a soft bed nearby. They crawled into Justin's oversized sleeping bag and soon after were making love, struggling against the padded confines of the bag until Marika reached down and loosed the zipper. Moving over Justin, she watched the light of the fire sculpt his arms and chest while it played over the sway of her breasts, his hands too like the lick of flames that traced the breasts' outer curve. As he turned her over, the side of their bodies that had faced the cold melted in firelight, the other side cooling quickly as he spent himself in her.

"I like this outdoor life," Justin said. "Somehow, I don't remember it being so much fun when I went with my brother."

"Maybe your brother didn't know what I know."

"No one does," said Justin, rolling off and pulling the sleeping bag over them. He had just started his beard, then; the roughness of it lingered on Marika's face and chest.

It was on Mount Desert, the next day, that Justin persuaded her to move in with him. "My mother," Marika protested.

"What does your mother think you're doing when you show up to change clothes and rush off to voice lessons? Spending the night in the U.N. bar?"

"My father keeps getting sick. She needs an anchor."

"She needs a sail," said Justin. Marika had told him how Katya had gone along with naming her daughter after her husband's old love in the Ukraine—*Marika*, a woman unrelated to them all, who existed only in memory. The original Marika had died, but rather than fight with a ghost, Katya had never contested her right to a place in Katya's husband's affections, her right to his daughter's name. "Your mother's been becalmed from the start," Justin said. "Now she wants to be like he is, moored to the past."

"I'm only saying it'll be hard for her if I go."

"*When* you go. I won't let you live away from me much longer."

"Why? You've got your painting."

"It's my painting that needs you." For the first time since Marika had known him, Justin looked needy, his eyes cast down, his fingers picking nervously at the stick of charcoal he held poised over his sketch pad. They were sitting by a cliff, overlooking the fjord. "When you're not in the loft I stop working," he said quietly. "I pace around. I can't hold on to an image for more than a few seconds—I dip my brush and it's gone. When you're there, just running through trills, the sound ought to make me nuts, but I—I explode with ideas. There's no limit to what I can do."

Marika hugged her knees. She was twenty-two and had been prepared to wait long and patiently for the jewels of life. Yet here they were, sparkling like the June sun on the cobalt blue of the inlet far below. "Give me a little time," she said.

The air warmed quickly in the days they were there. A small beach on the north shore of the island, protected from the wind, became warm enough for swimming, and with no one there they stripped and went in. The salt water numbed their skin, tingling when they emerged. Marika wanted to stay, then, to read in the sun, while Justin went to hike the long bluff to the east and make sketches. "I'll be back in a few hours," he said, waving.

But he hadn't returned by dusk, when Marika threw on her thin sweater and went to the top of the cliff by the beach to look for him. A cold breeze edged into the cove; the lights of boats far out on the water flickered on. The station wagon sat at the top of the rise by the road, useless. Justin had the keys. To keep warm, Marika jogged in place. She started to follow the path along the bluff, but it diverged at an early point; taking it, she might miss him if he came back the other way. She called his name, her voice blending with the sharp cries of the gulls. As night pressed in, she stopped calling and sat huddled on a rock. No cars passed. She knew it was ten miles at least to a town, and the road to the campground curved far around the south shore.

This is Maine, she told herself, watching the moon creep over the top of the opposite cliff. There are no wild beasts here, no cannibals. She knew Justin would want her to wait, and soon she became very still, like the stones around her, except that they didn't shiver from the cold. In her mind she saw the fall from the bluff, the sharp rocks and numbing water below. As night drew on, Justin fell and fell against those rocks, his body breaking into wreckage.

When she heard footsteps on the road she dared not hope. Only when he called, "Hey, Rika Rika!" in his familiar sing-song did she look up to see him swaying above her on the road. She scrambled up the path, stones skidding behind her. Her arms wrapped around his neck.

"Ooh, you're cold," he said. His breath hung in the crisp air.

"I thought you were dead!"

"Poor little Rika. I left you all alone."

"You said a few hours. I didn't know where to go—" She realized he was leaning on her, his warm chest pressed against her face.

"Justin's been bad," he said. "Justin let the time go right on by."

"Where have you been?" she asked, stumbling with him back to the car. He slumped into the passenger seat.

"Here and there. Found some friends, over the next hill. Poor Rika."

"You've been drinking." She said it out of wonder, the overhead light of the car pointing up his protruberant eyes, shot with blood.

"Naw."

"Yes. You have. You left me on the beach and ran into some people and started drinking. Where's your sketch pad?"

"I lost it," he said, his big face sad as a small boy's. "I looked and looked, but it got dark. Can you take us home, Rika?"

"I can't believe you did this," she said, but with fingers numbed by cold she reached into his pants pocket and dug out the keys. She could think of nothing to say, and so in silence she started the engine and drove up the road until she found the signs that led them back to the camp. There, she started the fire and slipped into the sleeping bag. She did not try to rouse Justin, who had fallen asleep in the front seat of the car, his head against the window. Her shivers quieting, she stared at the fire until unconsciousness took over.

The next thing she knew was the light of early dawn and Justin starting a fresh fire with twigs and scraps of paper. "Hi," she said.

"Hi. You all right?"

"Yes. You?" He nodded. Raising herself on one elbow, she remembered everything. "But Justin," she began, "why on earth did you—"

"Ssh." He came around the fire and crouched beside her. "Don't ask me, Rika." He bent his head into her neck, his hand reaching down the back of her sweater to stroke her spine. "It happens. And even if I want you too much to let it happen again, it will. Can you stand me for it?" His hand moved up to the back of her neck, cradling her head as he looked down at her. Faint lines of pain crisscrossed his face.

"I don't know."

"You got to," he whispered, and let her go. Standing up, he walked briskly over to the car. "You stay there, now," he ordered Rika in a new voice, sounding like a Texan. "We are having breakfast in bed. Pancakes, bacon, hot coffee, and oranges. Move one inch, and you'll be shot."

She had lain there and watched him bustle. That day, as if at a signal, they left Mount Desert, Justin's sketches lost somewhere on the bluff. Soon after, he painted something that he called *Fjord*, but it bore no resemblance to the colors and shapes they had seen. The only painting that brought her back to the island was the portrait that had hung in her bedroom in Revenir, of the flounder hooked and washed in with the high tide, its scales green with algae, its black eyes staring promises and truths.

"You're drowning in the tub, or what?" Katya asked next morning as the melting strains of *Bohème* floated from Marika's lips through the bathroom door.

"I'm almost out."

"You'll be happy to know I've come to my senses." Katya was leaning against the wall in the hallway; Marika could hear her sipping at her mug of coffee. As for herself, she was leaning across the washbasin, trying to discount the feverish glow that had come into her eyes. She frowned, stretched the small lines in her lower lid, covered her face with her hands, then peeled them away as if removing a masque. The gleam of desire remained unwanted, uninvited.

"What does that mean?"

"I have realized you are an adult woman. Older than I was when I raised you. Needing no help of me."

"I wouldn't say that," Marika said. Wrapping herself in a robe, she emerged.

"I mean that if you choose to throw away your body

to scum it is not my affair. I can see the way you look. I don't try to stop the sun from coming up every morning, either."

Over the brim of her coffee cup, Katya's red-rimmed eyes stared moistly up at her tall daughter, then with her hand shaking she returned the cup to its china saucer and shuffled past Marika to the living room. The belt of her red robe had twisted across her back. Her pincurled hair, gray roots showing under the dark blond, bobbed against her neck.

"Oh, Mama, you're adorable," Marika said, pressing her hands together and smiling.

"What's adorable? All day and night I'm trying to see some good of it. Your poor husband shot down in his prime, and you going right back to where your trouble started. I never see you crying for him. You had no Mass. His ashes are going unburied, your own husband's, you don't know where his soul waits. But I pray and the Lord gives me strength, so I say you go with my blessing to ruin your life."

"I don't want Justin Kilroy, Mama."

"Don't tell me you don't want. Look at you."

"What about me?" Marika spread her arms and made a show of looking down at her swathed body—shaped still, she had thought in the bathroom, like a pear.

"You're a middle-aged widow looking like a sixteen-year-old who just got her first kiss. Pah! It's disgusting."

"Mama, I *went* to see Justin. And he's just a bitter, arrogant, conceited artist. I want nothing to do with him. I'm fired up about getting an apartment, that's all. I'm looking at a place today." With an edge creeping into her inexplicable high spirits, she followed Katya into the kitchen. Pouring coffee, Katya eyed her suspiciously.

"You going to take a place down there by *him*, or up where your husband's friends live?"

"I thought," Marika lied, "I'd take a second glance at a place up by the park. I have *no* desire to be near Justin."

"Those are good people, your husband's friends. They are trying to make sense of his death. You should talk to them."

"His name was Richard, Mother. You may call him that. I know he was my husband." The edge had taken over. Marika pushed past her mother to get milk.

"You should help them. Not moon around after the past."

"I told you. Justin has no interest for me. I don't help State Department people because they are *not* trying to make sense. They look for an excuse for what they do in Africa, and Richard's death is convenient."

"Not so."

"How do you know, Mama? You've never met this species."

"One of them called last night. I told him you were gone to late Mass. To my shame."

Marika poured the milk too quickly; it slopped onto the countertop. The past—that meant Richard, now, and Yumana, not Justin and New York—bore down on her and refused to be thrown off. "Which one was it? What more can I tell them?"

"He left no name. Sounded foreign to me, with all those manners. He wanted Mrs. Hooper, the ambassador's wife, if he could trouble her to come to the telephone. Said he was a close associate of her husband's."

"Richard's."

"He will kindly call back tomorrow."

"Tell him"—Marika took a draught of her coffee, which, for all its caffeine, calmed her—"when he calls, that I've gone."

"Gone where, I'd like to know?"

"Moved. I'll start moving today. I won't have a phone for a while. Just put him off for me, Mama, whoever he is."

She could just picture the man, someone like Charles Hallerin or Curtis Lovell, mouthing off about insidious plots, communist conspiracies, these appendages of a giant beast who had mistaken Richard for America and performed a symbolic execution. They wanted her cooperation, meaning not only that she should not ask questions—she hadn't—but that she should help them point the finger at the *dai*.

"You *are* going to that artist."

"No, Mama. He wouldn't have me if I camped naked on his doorstep. Right now"—her high spirits had evaporated. Justin's face, as she had caught a glimpse of it at the peak of her short, forced aria, the forehead beleaguered but the mouth soft, almost naïve, swam before her eyes—"I'm going uptown."

She took an apartment on Riverside Drive that a scurrying, paunchy broker had shown her twice before. "I know you'll love the place," he rasped at her as she signed the papers. "Super's a swell guy. Swell neighbors. Got yourself a couple real live ones in the building, know what I mean." He gave an exaggerated wink.

There were three rooms besides the kitchen, high-ceilinged and newly painted, one looking out on the tidal river. She had decided at the outset not to take a view of the park. What memories she had stored of Richard were of that overlook and of his foreshortened figure as he darted across between cars and headed on his daily loop along the bridle path. Once or twice she had worried that in the hazy dawn he would be killed by a car tearing down Central Park West; but that threat he had survived.

The movers worked swiftly. By the time Katya came

up the next day in late afternoon, the furniture that Marika had stored was in place, Richard's files and desk in the small room. "So, you're right at home," her mother said, nodding approval.

"Any calls for me today?"

"Nah, nah. Your phone's working now?"

"Sure. You can tell—" Marika hesitated. Only one person of any significance could be trying to reach her, and she wanted nothing of him. A dozen times his voice, his stubbled cheek, the odor of his flannel shirt as he had gripped her arm, had intruded on her. Forcing him out, she had concentrated on unpacking, on moving her sparse sticks of furniture from place to place. But her resistance was low. "You can tell whoever calls that I'm at the number on the dial, there."

"Never lonely with the telephone." Stoic, Katya copied out the number and moved to the window, where the sun had cast a line of orange that reflected straight up from the river to the sill. "I don't understand still why you're having to pay this good money for a different place. It's seven miles from our home. I watched the meter."

"Mama, we've talked about this. I need space. I'll be putting a piano in that corner, there. I'm going to make a lot of noise. I'll probably take a few students when I get settled."

"You won't be eating right. I know already."

"I lived for fifteen years in Africa and managed to put on ten pounds."

"You had natives to cook for you. You come on home for supper tonight. I got a roast for Sacza and Dr. Dniprovsky, he's back from Florida."

"I know he's back. You cooked for him last night." She had avoided that meal, too, the doctor mopping his plate with his bread.

"He's a lonely man, and too thin. He needs a good meal, like you do. You're in this place since last night already."

"Thanks, Mama, no. I've—I've got plans."

"With friends?"

"Sure, with friends. A little dinner on the town." Crossing to where her mother stood, Marika watched the sunset with her. "Now don't *you* be lonely," she said, touching Katya's shoulder.

"Oh, my darling girl! Don't talk crazy. Sacza will eat up your lamb and be looking for more. If there's one thing we learned coming to this country"—she glanced at Marika's strong frame—"it is how to eat."

When the evening had gone to pitch, Marika showered in her new pink-tiled stall and dressed in clean soft challis. For once the keen sense of being watched or followed had abated. Stepping out of her building, she hailed a cab and, without reflection, took it down to Little Italy, to a small *trattoria* on Mulberry Street. They had always come here, she and Justin, and as she walked in she was unsurprised to find the same waiter, with his pointed nose and chin and small round eyes; when she was seated in the back he listed for her the same specials he had ticked off a decade and a half ago: stuffed artichoke, tile fish, pasta angelica. His shiny black hair sported spots of gray, like a pigmatism, and he stood shorter than Marika remembered. For his part, he gave no sign of knowing her, but then he had never indicated recognition with more than a slight, sharp nod of the head. She ordered the stuffed artichoke and a glass of wine, then another glass, which he served without asking what she would have for the main course. He had served many women like her, over the years, women who could pass for thirty-five, who rented freshly painted apartments, women who read paperbacks while they drank or who tried to look the way the men who did this sort of thing looked—preoccupied with financial problems and shifts of executive power; impersonal, faraway concerns.

*—It started in Maine,* Justin said in her ear, *when I let you see the crack in my lining. From then on you thought you had me in your pocket. I wasn't the Texas romantic, I was a lousy drunk.*

*—You left me on the beach. I thought you'd died. I didn't care if you were an ax murderer, just don't go off and leave me alone in the cold dark. How could you do it?*

*—Had to. Part of loving you was killing you off. Want to know what I did that night?*

*—You told me. Met with a bunch of locals and finished a fifth.*

*—What if I bought the bottle myself? At the store? And went off to a lonely cliff to swig it down?*

*—Then you lied to me.*

*—With the moon pale and refusing forgiveness, stripping me of the big-shot painter pretense. And me yelling at it how Rika loved me, and it calling back that you didn't know me.*

*—That's why you treat me like a stray circus dog, now, with your friends?*

*—Those people don't matter.*

*—Neither do I, anymore. You wanted me to leave you, Justin. You never came after me!*

*—And I let you sit there on the beach. I am your wild card, Rika, you love for me to hurt you. It would kill your love to see me tamed. When I'm good and ready I'll lock you back inside my heart and cast your image in stone. You'll sit for me until I have those hips just right, and people won't understand my painting. They'll throw me out of the museum, where I never wanted to be.*

Marika shivered as a couple came through the glass door, followed by a draft. The last time she had come with Justin to this restaurant, she remembered now, they had wrestled over a commission he had turned down from a shipping magnate afflicted with yearning for the avant garde. Some people, Justin had said, he would not produce for. Marika had said he'd be producing for himself, just taking the magnate's money instead of hers. He had spat on the floor, by her shoe, and walked out, leaving her rooted to her seat with the red wine gone rancid in her mouth. When she had paid the bill and wandered back to the loft, he had been waiting with champagne and yellow roses.

Recalling the scene, she called a glimpse of herself as the glass door swung shut. On her drawn face, tired from the day of moving, was the look that lone men had as they finished their third silent drink and returned to the gregarious world. Maybe they weren't thinking of finances, or executive privileges, or of any of those things at all.

The doorman at her new building greeted her with a nod and an abstract wave of the hand, as if she were a passing ship, entering the musty hallway. As she stepped out of the elevator and fished in her pocketbook for keys, she heard the shrill ring of a telephone from her apartment. He had found her! He must have called at her mother's, and not recognizing the voice after these years, Katya had given him her number. She fumbled with the keychain; Justin never let a phone ring more than four times, and he might not call back for days. She did not stop to consider how she hated him. Freeing the door, she raced across the polished wood floor to the slender blue instrument the phone company had sent. The voice, not Justin's, was low and mellifluous, vaguely familiar. "Mrs. Hooper?" it said. "You remember me?"

"I—I'm not sure."

"Amet. The boy who brought the meat."

"Oh, no." She backed against the wall, her hope frozen. *This* was the voice that had impressed Katya. This was what had followed her to New York. "What do you want from me?"

"We are needing your help."

"You murdered my husband."

"Na, that's foul slander, Mrs. Hooper." The voice flowed, never losing its honey. "We *dai*, we honor Richard Hooper. Where our dead are consecrated in the hills, there is planted a stone for Hooper, too."

"I don't know why you did it. I don't care. I don't want to listen to your lies."

From the open door to the hallway she heard the elevator snap shut and whirr away to another floor. The voice on the phone erupted. "It was a setup! Why are white people stupid as cattle? The devil Biswandi butchered your man, lady, are you blind and deaf also? Who else would want him dead meat?"

The name of Biswandi stung Marika like a wasp. She took the receiver from her ear as if to drop it, then slowly brought it back. "I don't believe you."

Amet muttered a curse in Lethe; then, "You must be ignorant of everything. Your man, your husband, he was never speaking to you of the dam?"

"The Parambo Dam? He was up there, with Biswandi, the day before you—before he was killed."

And Biswandi's round face had looked in, over the broken glass, minutes after the greenhouse floor had tasted its first blood. "Richard knew all about the disease up there," Marika said, "about Pioneer taking the land and breaking its contract. That dam plagued him."

"Your man, he was passing us its plans," Amet continued in a steady voice—feeding her information now, his temper aside. "For to dynamite that dam. To make the Parambo run free, he was telling us where to go, what to wait for. But he is not clever enough, and they hear of it, so they kill him. Na, Biswandi kills him."

"But the man from Pioneer—what was his name—McGrath, he got hit, too. They had to be *dai*, to do that."

"Exactly as Biswandi would be having you thinking, Missis."

"But McGrath couldn't know what Richard was doing."

"McGrath, no. Pioneer, yes. They tell the soldiers to wound him, nothing serious."

"I don't believe Richard was helping you," Marika said, lowering herself to the polished wood floor, a fine layer of dust like silk over its surface. Biswandi could strike anything down in cold blood, but Richard—Richard moved his mouth, he posed no threat. "He was never a violent man," she told Amet. "He'd have told Ngebin to forget any plan like that. Destroy all that electric power, that could have lighted your villages? Not Richard. And the people living below! They'd be destroyed! No, it's impossible."

"And why," Amet asked softly, "would my people kill him?"

"To scare Biswandi! To scare the United States! Because he couldn't or wouldn't get you money and guns. I don't know. But it makes more sense, for the Richard I knew."

"Perhaps you did not know the same Richard as we. Allow me to show you some documents. Some evidence. I am coming all this way, Mrs. Hooper, you must spare me a moment, hey?"

Marika had taken off her shoes; her toes made tight

spirals in the dust. The Richard she knew was a shadow in the bare living room, watching her for a spark of interest. He had anticipated her hope for Justin's call; he had sent this man to pique her. "No," she said to Amet. "We have nothing to talk about but the past."

"Are you afraid to see me, then?"

"Yes." Her throat was dry; she shook off her coat as she cleared it. Amet had her phone number, he knew where she was staying. He could even know about Justin.

"You need time." He spoke like an older brother. "I will call you again. Is it so fearful, Mrs. Hooper, that we are bringing our past days with us?"

When the line went dead, Marika gently replaced the receiver in its cradle and lifted herself from the floor. From the west window, its surface chill with the night wind, she watched the red lights of a barge plowing its way up the Hudson with the flood tide. In just this way she had stood uncountable nights in Revenir, the ships' lights glowing like fireflies in the harbor below. But she was in New York, not Revenir. She had seen Justin. From outside there came no sudden bursts, like hail, of gunfire but only the arbitrary trumpeting of car horns, the whirr of rubber on pavement. So let Amet call. She would tell him next time that she did not care who had killed Richard and that his country could rot.

Standing in the center of the empty room, a room devoid of memories, Marika knew with her eyes closed exactly how far she stood from each doorframe, each wall and window. She was going to hold on to this, where she was and what she wanted. Light steps ran across the floor of the apartment above; a stereo played, the welcome music of strangers. Unclenching her fists, Marika went to take the phone from the hook. There would be no more calls that night.

# Chapter 9

Like a seed planted in rocky soil, the call to avenge Richard Hooper grew slowly and untended in Marika's mind. That Amet had planted it at all, after weeks of Katya's annoying prods and questions, owed something to the *trattoria*'s wine and something to the stark, judgmental blankness of the walls that bore down on Marika in her three rooms; to an unbalanced space of time, purged of Justin, into which the call could enter unremarked.

At first it was easy to bury deep the seed and forget it. At Marika's next lesson the unceremonious Claude made her a proposal. "There's a new group in the East Village," he said, "with some money to stage *Fidelio*. Their Leonora is a wreck—can't sustain a single *fermata*. So I told the fellow, why don't I bring Marika down?"

"You think I'm ready?"

"Not in the least. But they don't start rehearsals for a month. Gives us a little time to build up your strength. Give me three octaves now, slow as molasses. Follow my beat. Use your diaphragm."

Long dormant, Marika's upper range swelled and warmed with the extended passages. She left Claude's studio with the *Fidelio* score tucked under her arm like a small, bright portent.

A few days later, when the telephone rang in her apartment, the caller was Justin Kilroy.

"You have to treat me like a stranger," he said.

"That's easy. You behave like one."

"Only at a full moon. Other times I'm just—changed. I don't burn as hot as I used to, Rika."

"Could've fooled me."

"That was a fireworks show. Let's say my guests bored me, and leave it there."

She could not, she told herself, refuse to see him. That afternoon, after a long session with Claude, she journeyed downtown. Alone with him in the loft, she watched him move around his canvas as if he were a statue come to life, each step and gesture a miracle. "This is Uhuru," he explained. "African god. You should know him."

"He created the world of the Lethe," she said absently as she studied the sharp strokes of Justin's arm, "by coupling with a python."

"Got to finish this by April for the Pan-African Congress. Pain in the ass."

"If that's a face I'm making out in the center, you've got his single eye right."

"Yeah, well, I read up on it. African mythology books, reproductions of artifacts, that kind of thing."

"Did you think of me, doing that research?"

"No," he answered simply. "I never thought of you as being in Africa."

He was, indeed, cool. *Tamed*, Marika almost thought. He talked about business. His accountant hounded him with investment strategies, tax shelters, write-offs right down to his paintbrushes, his dealer wanted him to go into partnership on a warehouse space in Brooklyn, some reporter was after him about a book, there was alimony to pay. He showed Marika pictures of Rose—not at all what she had imagined, but rather a large woman with a cornflower look—and of Adam, at eight already looking muscular like his father. He seemed to have an endless supply of words to anesthetize the minutes and hours they were choosing to spend together. Marika almost wished she could get him drunk again. As a bastard, Justin had been recognizable. But as his words worked the afternoon into evening, she studied with growing alarm his modest chuckle and his nods of agreement, moving the conversation along while they faced each other in identical fan-back chairs. He asked nothing of her music, of Africa, of Richard. Still, to be within reach, within sound of him carried the infinite pleasure of expectation. After this first step there must come a second, and after it the breakthrough of a third.

He would not drink, not even at dinner, which they ate not at the Italian hideaway but at a large columned and chandeliered place on a stark street by the Hudson piers. The waiter who knew him here was a willowy, delicate, and aristocratic young man with a silver earring; he inclined his head and murmured, "Hello, Justin," as if they had shared some intimacy. Others came up, recognizing the painter, and Justin made a show of bashfulness, a quality Marika had never remarked in him. Then there were the faithful: "You remember Beverly, don't you, Marika, she ran that shabby little gallery on Varick Street—"

"It *wasn't* shabby, darling, only a bit camp. I spent all I had on good lighting. Marika, it's been ages."

"Too long," said Marika, wondering what connection this spare, dry-fleshed woman had to her past.

Though he drank nothing, Justin insisted on a bottle of Bordeaux for Marika. As her glass emptied and was refilled, the room gradually acquired a slight tilt, like a large sailing vessel. "D'you remember," she heard herself saying, high-pitched, to Justin, "the time we found that llama on Fifth Avenue?"

"No."

"Of *course* you do. It was after two in the morning, right? And we'd been up at Milos's brother's place in Yorkville—"

"He calls it the Upper East Side, now."

"What*ever*. And we'd spent our last dime on these chocolate *breasts* for him, because he was *always* saying he thought black women had sweet skin. Right?"

"Well, I remember Milos's brother—"

"So we didn't have any money and figured we'd walk home. But on the way there was this bag lady with a *llama*, of all the incredible things, and you asked her if she'd sell it? And she said anybody'd sell anything for the right price?"

She raised her eyebrows and blinked at him, waiting for the click of recognition. "Go on," he said, forking his salad.

"Well, as I said, we didn't have a cent, but you promised this woman that if she'd let you have her llama, you'd paint her portrait and it would hang in a museum! My, but you were cocky!"

"Hey, it'd be worth a million today."

"But just then the smelly old llama reached over and *bit* you, right on the shoulder. Don't you remember? And the bag woman said nobody whom Elsinore would bite could paint worth shit. Those were her words, not mine."

Marika giggled, the room expanding and contracting like a lung around her. She had been through the llama scene five thousand times in Yumana, where every saddlebagged camel made her remember that night with Justin. He shook his head and smiled indulgently. He had not replayed the incident since it happened, not once. "It seems so long ago," he said.

"Not from the way you acted the other night, it doesn't." Loose from the wine, Marika nudged him with her knee. She would *make* him behave like her Justin.

"I still have my tantrums, that's true. Anger's an easy catchall for emotional stress."

"Justin," Marika said, looking up from her plate to catch his eye squarely on, "that doesn't sound like y—"

With the acute distance vision that sometimes comes with alcohol, Marika saw past the haze that was Justin, past the globed candle on the table, the diners whispering close around them, to a lone figure seated behind the small empty stage where a band would set up later. Gaunt and black, spiderlike, his face obscured partly by an old-fashioned white fedora and partly by a black patch over his left eye, he was inhaling slow puffs of a long cigarette with one twitching side of his mouth, and he was watching her. A short cry cut off her sentence.

"You see a ghost?" Justin turned his head, but she had already dropped her gaze so that he might not follow it. The room was crowded; anything could have caught her eye.

"I thought I saw someone I recognized. From Africa. But it couldn't have been the same person. That ever happen to you, in a strange place?"

"New York's your home town, Rika!"

It wasn't Amet; she knew it wasn't. Amet was built like a young bull and would have made this club look like a china shop. That was just a black businessman over there, one of the owners probably, or one of the musicians, staring into space, locking arbitrarily onto her vicinity. All the moment showed was how that phone call had rattled her. She would have to get back to her apartment, to touch the urn that held Richard's ashes, to prove to herself that he really was dead and couldn't be sending these apparitions to plague her. She had been faithful in his lifetime, she owed him nothing.

"My biggest danger, believe it or not," Justin was saying, his attention undiverted, "is becoming a has-been by fifty. That's the big jump-off. Only a few make it. Lichtenstein, Moore, O'Keeffe. The ones who find their style and stick with it—so the imitators stay imitators while the real thing keeps getting churned out."

"I thought you wanted to fall off the ledge."

"What ledge?"

"Of fame. You wanted to stretch your work until you plunged back into obscurity. 'The grand excitement.' "

"Forget it. Lautrec painted whores long after he couldn't look at them anymore, he was syphilitic and sick of the bunch. But they made him great."

"And you've got apocalyptic myth."

"With an innovative use of the short, heavy brushstroke. I tell you, Rika, if I get a vision these days, I take it right down to Goodwill and let some other slob pick it up. Now's the time for strategy."

So cool, so self-possessed he looked, perched on his comfortable ledge. Marika glanced back to where the dark figure had been sitting, but it was gone. She felt a need for fresh air.

"Look, this has been good of you," she said as they exited the restaurant. "I'll just take a cab on up to my apartment."

"Won't allow it," he said with a trace of the other night's imperiousness. "You can't leave a man lonely on a spring night. Walk me home."

So they went on together, speaking variously of Justin's agent, Justin's house being built in the Carolinas, of Adam down in Virginia with his mother, of old friends of Justin's who had married or divorced or borne children or committed suicide. Marika followed along easily, granting Justin the small part of her attention that he seemed to require. The rest she focused outward, her eye quick to see if the black man had followed them; and inward, to her dormant desire, asking herself if it were possible that she did not love this man walking beside her, finally so near at hand. He was not so different from her imagining, her transplanted Texan—elegant and crude at once, his genius inspirited and satanic by turns. Rather, it was as if she had lost track of what it was that she loved, of what obsessed her in him; or as if she had chased down the passion too fiercely, only to find it tired and needy of respite when she captured it at last. Or was she callused from the lashing he had given her, ripe and full of hope, when she had invaded his party?

It was not an absurd thing to do, on the surface: to look up one's old lover and have dinner, to listen to his babble for a few hours. It need mean nothing. What chafed like a small wound was only the unseen presence of Amet, the scent of danger that in Africa had always sent her flying to Justin as to a haven. Now Justin walked beside her, and she had nowhere to fly.

"Come and see the lights from my window," Justin said when they reached the wide metal door. "I paid an extra twenty grand for them, I ought to be able to show them off."

"I don't know, it's a long way uptown—"

"What are you, an old lady? The Rika I knew was a night fox." He raised his eyebrows at her, flirting. With a sidelong glance at the empty street, no sign of a man shadowing them though black skin would be hard to detect, she followed him up the stairs.

Perhaps, she thought later, she stayed in part because she was afraid of being accosted on the way home. The odor of the loft, overhung with turpentine and gesso, wrapped her like a cloak. Then, too, what remained from fifteen years was her inability to say no to Justin. He took her as he would any date, as if intercourse were simply the way men and women conversed. Had she been blindfolded, she would not have recognized his lovemaking—nor, she supposed, would he have known hers, tepidly as she enacted it. "What did you mean, the other night," she asked as they lay naked on the bed, "when you said you made paintings like prying bars loose on my cell?"

"I was drunk." He kissed the top of her head.

"But you thought of me. It made you angry that I never came back."

"I did some great paintings by playing tapes of you singing, I'll admit that. The last great one I did, you're wailing away at Porgy in the background."

"Which was that?"

"*The Glass Mountain*. You saw it in the museum with Milos."

"Tell the story," Marika said, settling onto her back, looking out through the skylight at the city's pale night as she had in the early days when Justin spun out his tales.

"It's an easy one. This princess lives alone at the top of a glass hill, and everyone tries to scale it to reach her and get her father's consent to marry. This one prince actually makes it up the slope, and then wham! he's got about a dozen other trials before she's his. All he's supposed to do is get up the glass hill on his horse, but as soon as he's there the king hits him with the gamut. In the painting, I buried in the hill all that shit he's got to ride over to make it up the glass—bottles of booze, women, highways. Images of death, mice and snakes, flowers like vaginas. And

I saw this deformed beast of a man trying to ride a broken-down horse up the slope. I felt so sorry for the guy. Like, what did he think he'd find once he got up there? He'd just have to go after a gold dagger, empty a stream with a thimble, more shit."

"How long ago was that?"

"Was what?"

"*The Glass Mountain*."

"Four, five years. Five, I think. It was before we separated, Rose and me. I never finished it, in fact. Let the museum take it as is."

"Why'd you stop?"

"Who says I stopped? Look over there—" Propping himself on his elbow, he waved a muscled arm at the long wall of the loft, lined with stretched canvases. "Does that look like *stopped* to you?"

She had meant stopping painting *The Glass Mountain*; but instead she came out with, "Stopped thinking of me."

"It was the last painting you were right for. The last dream of glory, making it up the mountain. These others"—again a wave of the arm—"are just plain dreams. Like the kind you have when you sleep."

"Maybe if you'd finished this one," Marika said carefully, tucking her arm behind her head, "you'd have found whatever it was he found."

"The princess."

"You could call it that."

"But I've got the princess right here," Justin said easily. He turned and cupped himself against her hip. "I stayed put," he mumbled, "and the princess came to me."

Lying flat, Marika ran a finger down his spine, still the same knotty bumps scooping into the hollow of his lower back. "Did she?" she whispered. He smelled so close. She had his scent in her skin, in her lungs; she shut her eyes and breathed it in, like ether.

But in fact she lay awake long after Justin had drifted off, and she watched as his face rearranged itself into the round contours of satisfied unconsciousness. For her, there had been no satisfaction, but in the backwash of the wine and the brandy they had finished by the window, which did, indeed command a view of the city, the slow stirring of hope reasserted itself. There, unmasked, lay her Justin. No trail left by Richard Hooper would lead her away from him just yet. Still, as night faded from the room, she slipped down from the high bed, and dressed, and escaped into the cold nip of morning while he lay still dreaming, heavy and warm and alone.

Why she came back that night, and the next, she could not exactly have said, except that he asked her to—phoning late in the afternoon when she had drained her day of energy by painting the apartment or buying shelves and fixtures, as if she needed to settle in without delay before something snatched her out of it. Over the weekend, she canceled out on the dinner her mother held each year to mark their arrival in the United States and went instead with Justin to an opening at a packed gallery downtown. There, she flattened herself against the wall like a still life while Justin drank—for the second time since she'd seen him again—and slipped away for an hour with a childlike creature before returning to take Marika home with him. The next morning she allowed him to penetrate her without so much as the illusion of pleasure, as if she were doing atonement for all the times in Africa when she alone had enjoyed his body—without license, without even his physical presence, rendezvous with a spirit who had now come to exact his toll.

But soon after, at the end of the school term, Adam came up from the farm in Virginia where he lived with his mother, Rose. While Justin failed to call, Marika paced her apartment. Vainly she went over the libretto that Claude Thrush wanted her to memorize. The words swam before her eyes. What to her was the story of a woman diving into a prison to save her husband? Why should she thrust herself among a group of starry-eyed young warblers rehearsing in a dusty East Village annex? Claude himself acted morose and cut her lesson short, leaving her to head home at twilight, there to keep the television on as she wrote to decline foreign service invitations, her ear always pricked for the phone. Surely there was a woman whom Adam knew, who was playing the role of stepmother—a young divorced artist with children of her own. With this woman—Marika convinced herself as her feet criss-crossed the hard floor—her red-blooded Justin, quick with life, reappeared. And he was the one she wanted back.

To escape the luxurious cell of her apartment, where neither the real nor the imaginary Justin had entered, where her own voice, running up and down scales, bounced like a hard rubber ball off the high walls, she went to see Katya. With spring in full bloom, she took a full morning to walk down through the park, past the flowering trees and the fenced-off lime-green grass. She had not been back to her mother's in almost a month. They had met instead at the Ukrainian Institute, and Marika had told new lies—which Katya saw through—about her social life. Katya had stopped harping on Richard, speaking instead of Marika's last tour to Africa as "while you were away," as if there had been a long cruise or an extended stay in California. While you were away, Uncle Led died. While you were away, the church started a mission to the old country, we send them books and blankets. There was a tone of reproach to these reports, as if Marika had turned her back at just the wrong moment and so missed what her mother could hardly be expected to recapture for her. Katya's lower lip pushed outward as she sat embroidering her part of the Ukrainian Home Flag and cataloguing events, and the other women in the room, Sonia or Elise or Sacza, sighed and shook their heads.

Not only had Katya wiped Richard's name from her lips, but she had stopped dropping hints about the "important people" Marika was failing to see, and she seemed to have let Justin go free from her venom. Where, for years, her round eyes had beetled at Marika, lancing the tenderest secret, she watched her now as if from a distance, impersonally, as though her daughter had never and could never hold secrets from her. Instead of ticking off questions, she unearthed stories, usually in Ukrainian, challenging Marika to keep up with her. The time we rolled ourselves in rugs and got flung onto a ship for Sweden. Your father's rich uncle in America, who was going to take us in and treat us like kings but he was just getting let out of jail the day we came ashore. The old one lying by me on the deck, she died, Jesus help me I took her clothes, her arms like cold metal pipes.

As Marika walked downtown, the sweet scent of the flowering trees blew like baby's breath through the harsh air and lifted her spirits, sunk by the presence of a Justin who was not her Justin, the absence like a death of the one she had come to find. In the park, small children sprang up before her, fresh and plentiful as grass. She spotted a boy about four, his legs churning over the dandelions, running nowhere and from no one, on his face the stamp of unalloyed delight. There was a newborn, making gurgles in a blue carriage, rocked by a girl in cutoff jeans and a T-shirt who clucked and then giggled in response. A somber dark boy sitting crosslegged on a freshly painted bench next to an unshaven man absorbed in his pipe and newspaper. Others, scattered over the lawns and rocks. Marika counted them as if assuring herself that they were still there, the toddlers and the babies, washed and fed, their golden platters of hair and the perfect moons of their buttocks. The mothers were half her age—but so long as the babies still grew up to scramble on the beaten grass of the knolls, she stood a chance. They hadn't all been taken from her, the bountiful supply of children that had passed by her and Richard. At the edge of the park, she turned to look.

themselves in the trees. Marika took a step forward, as if to call them out. At the base of a spreading Japanese maple, next to the path, lay a slender curved form, half-hidden in the unmowed grass, the sun glancing off its caramelized surface. Her knuckles at her teeth, Marika's scream darted through her throat like a cold snake.

It was only a branch of the maple, its bark stripped and the bare wood polished by winter's ice. On hearing Marika shriek, one child appeared and ran, weeping, to its mother, who shook her head menacingly until Marika had backed out of the park, onto the crowded street.

# Chapter 10

Katya was rarely alone. The people with whom she had come over the ocean did not believe in the telephone, and they stopped in with their bits of business, their pieces of gossip, like so many squares of cloth they were leaving off for Katya to quilt together. Only when one of them had lingered would another join, and then they would stay standing until there was a third in the doorway—and so on until they sat and brought forth the vodka and the little shot glasses, and so they would settle in, Elise and Sacza, Dr. Dniprovsky, Aunt Zirka, the Pleskayas. The things they spoke of, simple essential things like life and death and the infinite permutations of illness, had the same litanic ring as the complaints and the gossip that had passed among Seki's friends and among the village people Marika had seen in Yumana. Even the rhythms of the Ukrainian bore a resemblance: the rise, the stop, the fall into worn adage. It was these voices that Marika had escaped when she first entered Justin's painterly world. The same voices, out of African mouths, had found her in Yumana with Richard—and again, now. Back in the old country, where we could get the cow's milk warm, the babies didn't die like here when the mother's milk goes. The gods will not smile on those who build this dam, the rains will dry up. The time we rolled ourselves in blankets. Seven seasons ago, when the chief's son killed a python. While you were away, the church started a mission.

The day Marika came over while Adam visited Justin, the others stayed no more than an hour, then drifted off to their stores, their shops, their tiny professions. When they had gone, Katya stood awhile before the picture of Marika's father that hung on the wall.

"Dr. Dniprovsky wants me to marry him," she said abruptly.

"You can't be serious!"

"And why not?"

"He's addled, Mama! Why, even Papa used to make fun of him."

"Your papa is dead."

"That doesn't change Dr. Dniprovsky. I can't believe you and Sacza still go to him, he can't even hear through a stethoscope anymore."

"But it does change Dr. Dniprovsky, your papa's death. I am a woman alone, my darling girl."

"There are worse things in life," Marika said, "than being alone."

"So maybe. But Dr. Dniprovsky is not one of them."

"So you'll *marry* him?"

Katya shrugged. "I must go on. Like your father, he went on, to me. I married the fisherman, the *rybak*—now I join with the river."

"The Dnieper. You always loved it." Marika began gathering up the glasses, the little plates of salt crackers they had eaten, the crumbs like sawdust making a ring on the table.

Katya sat down in the velvet armchair, not moving to

help, her hands folded in the shape of a church across her lap. "We never thought," she said, as if she were answering Marika, "making the trip over here, like a ragged herd of goats, we never thought we would give birth to anything beautiful." She studied the steeple formed by her index fingers. "But you were beautiful. I never told you such a thing, it would go to your head. But when you grew to a woman, and you used to put on the dress from the old country, you looked just like her."

"Like who, Mama?"

"Her. You know." The eyes flickered to the box in the glass-lined cabinet. "You never saw her picture?" Marika shook her head. "Take that out, then, we'll look."

Marika pulled out the small stationery box, and her mother sifted through it—yellowing photos of their first house in Brooklyn, water-stained cameos of Marika's grandparents, scraps of newsprint in Ukrainian. "Ah." She drew out a small gray leather folder, a pocket frame, and, opening it with cautious fingers, she handed it to Marika.

Inside was a faded portrait of a young woman, leaning against a fence, her full skirt caught by the breeze while one arm tried to hold it down. Her face, the hair drawn straight back, held an unspoken gravity through the deep, close-set eyes and finely cut cheekbones, but the wide mouth was open in a laugh executed for the cameraman. "Daddy's Marika," Marika said softly.

"Some—the ones who knew us well—they said it was because of the name, that you took on her features. Myself, I wanted sometimes so much that you would take after me! I saw him sitting with you the way he did, and you know, I almost hated you then, and you just a girl. And then—" She stopped abruptly, sinking back against the velvet, and took a long, slow breath.

"Then what, Mama?" Marika asked, still staring at the photo. How had she never seen it, this coincidence of the past?

"Then," Katya said slowly, "I was so grateful. For your beauty. That I learned—to love—*her*. She didn't belong just to him, anymore. Take it." She patted Marika's hand. "Take the picture, she's yours now."

Her eyes on the photograph, Marika saw not the young woman, but her father, tall and slender, eternally abstracted, puttering with his plants. He had spent hours talking orchids with Richard, the winter before he died. She and her mother had shared him like an acquaintance in the house, who ate and slept and spoke with them as if he were on an extended visit from the place where his true ties dwelt.

"And he never stopped loving her," Marika said.

"Of course not. Why should he? She was safely dead, she's not going to disappoint him." Marika puckered her lips, but her mother went on. "I could have killed that, you know."

"Killed what?"

"His love in the old country, that was meaning his youth. His freedom. But oh, so much changed after you left us for—" She stopped at Justin's name as at a wall. "When you left home," she went on. "It was like he knew me, then. He recognized *me*, your father did. Like I had been in some disguise before. Then we had all our struggle together to look back on. And you—you that we'd brought up like that, without thinking we could make anything new. He was thankful, then, he gave thanks. You don't know, you were away—" Katya's eyes misted over.

"But Mama, what," Marika began, timidly, as if she felt herself a dense child, "has this got to do with Dr. Dniprovsky?" A plate fell to the rug; she stooped to sweep the cracker crumbs into her palm.

"It has to do with me." Katya pointed her finger at her broad chest. "It was me, the one that your papa went on to. Was he expecting something, a miracle, maybe? No, but he got one. When we got you, for us a miracle. So I go on, yes, to Dr. Dniprovsky who can't see so good. And I'm not expecting nothing."

"He's really asked you? Dr. Dniprovsky?"

"He has."

Marika took the plates out, leaving her mother in the armchair. It was not Dr. Dniprovsky's eyesight, nor his persistently mistaken English, nor his lapses that upset her. Her mind flew from what Katya had said of her father, to the children in the park, to Justin as she had felt him in Yumana to the way he was now, slipping from her like a piece of music that slips past a real climax to a forced and unsatisfying coda. She had mastered languages, she had lived among artists and diplomats, she had circled the globe and conversed with those who ruled it. Even now she was ready to tackle Mozart's opera. How then could her mother, who had stayed within ten miles of Irving Place, who steeped herself in the pasts of a dozen friends from the Ukraine, make her feel as though she were treading water while Katya swam blithely ahead?

It had always been so. She could remember evenings, long before she met Justin, when she was just entering her teens and would finish her schoolwork in order to drift out from her desk to the living room—crowded, then as now, with musty furniture and bric-a-brac. Her mother would be bent over the kitchen table, making lists, getting up every ten minutes to answer the phone, to hold a brief impassioned conversation in the old language. Her father, meanwhile, would be sitting in the little alcove by the glassed-in shelves, his chin in the palm of his hand while his arm rested on the back of the chair, and he would gaze at the curtains barely fluttering out from the half-open window. Marika would pass by the brightly lit kitchen to slide silently into the armchair facing her distant father, and wordlessly she would assume his position, her eyes on the wavering edge of the hemmed cloth. Without venturing to ask what he was thinking, she had allowed herself to enter that blazing summer world where she knew for a fact he was living, and where for her, too, there lived a godlike phantasm, still unrevealed to her. Her father got up and left, eventually, to wash up for bed—but she stayed seated in the dark reflection of a world closed to Katya, the same world that her image of Justin would inhabit when she lived in Yumana, the world she had come back to New York to find.

While Katya, with her satisfaction in small miracles, was going to marry Dr. Dniprovsky, as if she like the young mothers in the park possessed some secret that Marika could not learn, the secret of going on.

"Mama," Marika said, coming back to the claustrophobic living room. "Mama, do you think I should leave the city?"

Nothing but Katya's eyes moved, examining her daughter without surprise. Justin's name pulsed from the walls.

"There came a time," Katya said when the eyes had made their scan, "when the days with your father stretched out, like so many blank leaves in a fat book. Then I thought, 'If I could only give him back his dead Marika, how happy he'd be!' All those evenings, instead of staring like he did at his paper, pretending to read, he'd be saying the things to her that he was saying in his head, already. I could hear him! And I looked at you, like I wanted to bring her back and give you to her. Oh, I was crazy! Do you know why I was crazy, to think like that?" Marika shook her head. "Because she would have failed him. She was not anything but his childhood, all dressed up in the fancy furs of his memory and not human no more. She would have gone and got wrinkled and burned the roast once or twice, and he would be always wanting to dress her up in the fancy furs, and she'd be hating him for it. No, no. He loved her best when he packed her up and put her away in that box"— she motioned toward the stack of old photographs— "and knew himself like a man without her."

Marika dropped her head. "I don't know why I . . . have to see him," she said.

"Tch! You are doing what you want."

"Are you doing what you want, marrying Dr. Dniprovsky?"

"I'm not so young, like you."

"I'm not so young either, Mama."

"Ach." Katya waved her hand. They were back at their old impasse. "If I were not such a selfish mama," she said, "I would send you back to Africa."

"Ha! I'd never go. You don't know how ugly it is, Mama."

"Don't I?" Katya pushed out her lower lip.

"How could you? You and Papa never made it there. He wouldn't take the plane."

For a few moments as the two women faced each other, the room filled up with men—Marika's stubborn father; Justin; Richard dead in Africa; even Dr. Dniprovsky, who would lie with Katya. Then like an alarm the phone rang, and Marika stepped past her mother to pick it up, prepared for the billing and cooing of Elise or Aunt Zirka, the first to hear "the news," what a good pair the new Dniprovskys would make and they had hoped for such a thing these many months.

But it was none of the aunts calling. "It is I, Amet," the voice said. "You see that I allowed you time."

"Time?" Marika repeated. Crooking the receiver in her shoulder, steadying one hand with the other, she brought the plates to the kitchen counter.

"That you will say, to be helping us or no."

"You're wrong to call me here." Marika cupped her hand by her mouth.

"There is no further time to wait. I am finished in my work in this country."

Marika crossed to the window that looked over the street, where two women straight below had stopped pushing strollers to stand in the shade. One of the strollers was blue, the other a dark red plaid. The babies were hidden. "Well, I'm not," she said, "finished in mine." She thought of the children in the park, of Justin's Adam. She would have her own Adam, she would make it work.

"Meet with me once." In his voice persisted the rhythms: *The day we rolled ourselves in rugs. Some seasons ago, when the chief's son.* "I swear no one of us will harm you."

She pictured Amet's finely chiseled face, the nostrils flaring as he held up his hand. "Don't swear," she said. "I believe you."

"Then say only where and when. I will show you what we are needing."

"I—I can't say. I was never involved with Richard's politics. I never saw what you were fighting for. I can't just take up a cause like that."

"Accept that I speak for Richard Hooper. He wants this of you!"

"I have another life. Richard's not alive." *Damn Richard.* The muscles in her stomach bunched as if to expel him. Richard, Richard and Yumana, every breath she took.

"Then, lady"—the voice paused, worn out with urgency—"why you don't put down the phone on me? Why you hang on? We cannot be waiting for you."

As he spoke, Marika realized she was still holding the folder with the photograph that Katya had given her, the photo of the woman her father had loved. *He loved her best when he packed her up and put her away in that box.* With her free hand she let it drop open. They were wrong, she thought. I look nothing like her.

She cupped her hand closer. "All right," she said. "Tomorrow at noon. There's a new park they're building, on the Hudson River, down by Harrison Street. Can you find that?"

"Anywhere, I'll come."

"I think we'd be—safe, there." Behind her, she heard her mother's muffled steps across the carpeted living room. "I have to go."

"We are thankful, Mrs. Hooper. *B'nago b'maradi.*" He gave the Lethe blessing and hung up.

Marika held the receiver, like a piece of food she was about to eat, until the dial tone reasserted itself and she heard her mother behind her in the kitchen. "So, who's that calling and hanging up?" Katya asked.

Marika turned to answer and found she had to swallow hard. Gone from her mouth was the bitter taste of disappointment; in its place, her tongue touched the dry roof of fear.

That night, she went to him without love or hope or memory; without jealousy, without cognizance of his stature as an artist or his slippage as a man. She went to him—

surprised, actually, that with Adam gone he was merely alone in his loft, doing quotidian things like answering mail and punching in expenses on his small computer, his unfinished paintings like silent companions—because he was alive and the only one who could make sure she did not think about Richard's death.

Whether Amet's calls had made her fix on Richard's killers, or whether her own unacknowledged investment in the truth had invoked the presence of Amet and his mystery, she could not say. She had understood the death in the greenhouse to be an erasure, an act of fate. But she would have had to admit, had she gone home alone from Katya's that night, that the cause behind that fateful moment had teased her ever since, like a door she could choose not to open only for so long.

Justin let her wander around the fringes of the loft while he finished his bits of business, then he made *bombacitos*, a stuffed chili concoction that he had always sworn originated in his part of Texas. Grinning like a boy, his white teeth flashing in his new growth of beard, he pulled out the old Parchesi game they used to play and set it up with the *bombacitos* on one side and a bottle of tequila on the other.

"There's an opening in Southampton tomorrow," he said, throwing the dice. "You come with me. I know a place we can stay, a dancer named Lucille. She just built this Spanish place on the shore."

"I don't know. I've got to meet someone in the morning."

"What is it, another one of these government guys? Let him wait till Monday. They make a living out of waiting."

"Not government. A friend of Richard's—he's got some things of Richard's to give me."

"So see him, then we go."

"I'll let you know tomorrow. Your move—you've got me blocked. There's Mama to think about, too."

Justin poured the tequila for both of them. If he regarded Marika's presence as a triumph for him, he failed to gloat. After they had finished half the bottle and all of the fiery chilies, and he had brought home his men while Marika's lay scattered on the board, they crawled into the loft and undressed one another. He kissed her until she came, without expecting to, suddenly and in floods, her hands laced into his mane of hair as she rocked him. Then, wanting no more, he fell asleep.

It should have been enough, more than enough. Adam's visit had knit his father's personality together, and a small hope breathed into the loft like the June winds. But Marika could not lie still. Knotting one of Justin's robes around her small waist, she went to sit and smoke on the low couch among his paintings. In the pale light that silted in from the glass roof, her dark eyes scanned the quick, expert roughs on canvas and saw among them one image after another of potent, inevitable death.

Think, Richard would tell her. Sort it out. Just so, he had rearranged the pieces of other killings—like that of Ngebin's sister—until they made a coherent picture. Marika had told him once that he had missed his calling as a detective. "A diplomat *is* a detective," he had said, "only he can never proclaim the butler did it, since the butler always follows the master's orders, and the diplomat is that master's ward. A diplomat is an accessory to the fact."

Noiselessly, Justin came, naked, to join her. Squatting beside her, he pulled a stray lock of hair back from her shoulder. "Posing for the moon?" he asked.

"No." She clasped her knees and smiled, her long nose as if sniffing the air.

"Whisper it to Uncle Justin, then." He tipped his head.

She pulled him down beside her and looked at his face and saw how much older he looked. Before, when they had lived together, he had never asked what she was thinking; she had lost the habit of telling. Now he was older, a man with a child, he wanted to know things. "I realize," she said, measuring her words, "that I don't have any idea who killed my husband."

"I thought you didn't care."

"Of course I care. It'd be unnatural not to care. Wouldn't you care if Rose—"

"Ssh." He placed his finger across her mouth. "We're not talking about Rose."

"But you would."

"You don't swallow the story you told me about the guerrillas?"

"Not entirely." Amet maybe, even Ngebin. But not Florence. Not when she had sent her only daughter up to the house. "I'm the only one who'll ever find out who did it. Everyone else wants *not* to know."

"So what's your stake, sister?"

"I feel like I haven't buried him. Like I can't go on with—with what I want to do, until I put the question to rest."

"And what might this thing be that you want to bury old Richard in order to do?"

"Oh, you know."

"Tell me."

His eyes glittered at her in the faint light that came from the bulb they had left burning by the kitchen. It was late at night, and still. The words that fell from her mouth had the unreality of jewels: "I want to marry you, and have your baby."

His grin remained fixed on his face, the same half-lidded grin he used to wear when they set off in a helicopter to take pictures from above the charred Apollo launch pad; only much later had she learned he was fearful of heights. "You don't mean that," he said, giving her a reprieve.

"Half of it, I don't."

"But the rest." He moved onto the wide couch and slipped his hand under her borrowed robe. "What great breasts," he said. "God, feel how they stand up. Let me see them." He untied the sash.

"Not even the other half," Marika protested, her words ordinary again, meaningful.

"You want a baby, there's just one way."

"Wrong time of month."

"Practice run."

"I've got Richard on the brain, Justin."

"There's more than one way to bury a ghost." He squeezed the side of her breast as he pressed her to his chest. In a little time he would be inside her. She felt herself swell for him.

"I won't be free of Richard," she went on, fighting desire, "until I find out who did it."

"I ever tell you the story of the frog and the lyre-bird?" His hand had discovered her swollen vulva and massaged it as he talked. She shook her head. "Well, there was this frog that the lyre-bird tricked—never mind how—into letting her take his food. So the frog's left hungry, and he drinks up all the water in the stream where the lyre-bird likes to bathe, and he thinks he'll hold the water inside him until she gives him back the morsel she's taken. All the other animals around, thirsty as they are, go to the frog and beg him to let the water go. Now, the frog isn't happy with his belly full of water, but he can't let the stream go free until he knows where that morsel of his is. Of course, the food's eaten already, but he won't believe that. So you know what the animals do?"

"No."

"They dance and carry on in front of him, and finally an eel—phallic symbol, notice that—gets up and does a little dance in the dry creekbed, and that does it. The frog bursts into laughter and the water pours out from his mouth. He's free, see?" Justin's hand flew up to Marika's waist and with quick soft pinches produced a spasm of laughter. "See? See?"

"Okay, all right, I'll forget about it!" Marika cried out to make him stop. As soon as the tickling ceased, she was about to say something more about Richard. But then, his story over, he was inside her, and she caught her breath.

# Chapter 11

*A diplomat is an accessory to the fact.* Richard had coined the definition long before they ever left New York for Yumana or heard the rattle of gunfire below the stronghold of their bedroom. Shutting the door on the last departing guest of an evening on Central Park West, he would give a great groan of relief and say, "Big Bird, I believe there are more accessories to the fact in the United Nations than angels on the head of a pin."

And once, sweeping ashes from the coffee table, her feet bare on the plush white carpet of the living room, sated with brandy and heady talk of the three worlds, Marika had asked him, "Aren't you afraid you'll get to be like them?"

"Why, do I show signs of it? Am I getting puffed up? Green around the gills?" He had grimaced at his reflection in the hall mirror.

"No. But there are other professions. You could teach, for instance."

"I fall asleep in class."

"You could go into politics here. We could travel for fun."

"Ah, Big Bird." Slouching down on the couch, he removed his glasses and squeezed shut his eyes. "I have this unalterable conviction that there is more than one way of thinking, in this world. But I won't find out unless I'm out there."

"You think there'll be fewer bureaucrats out there than back here?" She dropped the ashes into a tray and wiped her hands.

"I'm not naïve. I meant something besides bureaucracy."

"Beautiful women."

"I *did* meet a tribal princess once—"

"Well, if that's your aim," she interrupted, sliding onto his lap and hooking her knees over his long legs, "I'll just have to tag along and chaperone you."

He had laughed and fondled her, and they had sat like that for a long while, the lights from the street filtering through the blinds, the room rich with the smells of wine and ripened cheese. Finally, realizing he had dozed off, she lifted his hand from her breast and kissed it, and woke him, and led him to bed.

She had not expected ever to wake next to Justin only to find herself dwelling on Richard. Beside her, as he lay on his back, Justin's upper body rose and fell with the shallow, even breaths of late sleep. He had kicked the covers away, and there lay useless the strong but slight stalks of his legs. This was how men should be built: the trunk living up to its name, heavier toward the front, waistless; poised, when the man stood naked, on hips so narrow, almost delicate but for the weight they supported, so like the hips of the boy he had been, that they drew one's eyes and hands toward them, and then to the flexed buttocks in back and the tender scrotum tucked under the belly. Richard's build had differed utterly, slender from thigh to shoulder.

Spreading over his midriff, her hand would lie flat, nothing to hold. She made the gesture upward in the air, the arm finally wrapping the smooth torso.

He refused to vanish. Slanting across the high window, the yellow light asked if this was mourning come at last; and the still air answered that it was not. Mourning showed itself in cracks and crevices, and Marika's spirit remained seamless as an egg. Yet he had infiltrated—through Katya, through Amet, plucking the strings of Marika's fear. Fear of? The old addiction to Justin asserting itself, with the faded kick of a familiar drug. Fear of returning to a solitary and obsessed life—or, to change the tune, of embarking on a life alone and perilously free of obsession. She wasn't mourning. She was escaping the present.

Unlined, Justin's cheeks in sleep relaxed to a perfect convexity from temple to chin, the lashes of his closed eyes tangled like feathers. She thought of his question from the night: What was her stake?

Answerless, she left him, as before, sleeping. The sun rode high, the morning almost gone. By the time she reached Claude's studio, he had started a lesson with a young bass, a beautiful Scandinavian with a head half-shaved and two earrings in one ear. Claude scowled at Marika, and she pulled away from the door, only to lean against the outer wall, listening to the boy's sonorous voice. Fear lurked here, too, fear of falling for the music only to fail in it. If Richard had exiled her from success, he had exempted her from failure, too.

At midafternoon she found herself walking, as if descending a steep row of stairs, down Harrison Street to the new park near the Battery. Before her lay a sea of pale green, new grass planted in imported sod, the yearling trees ringed and held upright in a symmetric group, like ballerinas in a frieze. A low brick wall banded the Hudson. Crossing the industrial boulevard, Marika thought again of Richard, who had disliked this part of the city, or anywhere south of Central Park, because it contained no expanse of green on which to rest one's eyes. The new park, its first crop of grass the color of parrot feathers, rimmed by a waist-high fence, might have begun to satisfy his craving, as it swept down to the slate promenade edging the Hudson.

*It'll be fifty years,* she could hear him object, *before those trees take root and give any shade. I'll stick with Olmsted's creation.*

But Richard wasn't here to criticize the spindly, staked trees, just as he wasn't here to circle the Central Park reservoir with the morning jog that left him intolerably brisk and optimistic. Someone had cut him down at the peak of his time—and until now, she had not much cared who had done it, or why. Richard had been wrong, that was the main thing—he had thought they would leave him out of their rumble, and instead they had tossed him straight into it. Both sides—Biswandi's army and Ngebin's *dai*—had killed plenty before. And every killing was unforgivable. So what did she care which faction had chosen Richard Hooper for its target that night?

But now she was going to meet one of them, and in her slow steps fell the burden of Richard's knowledge—for he must have known, looking up as the glass crashed inward, who was pointing death at him. What had he said to Ngebin, the night before? Had he moved to compromise once too often? *I see them all, finally,* he had said. *If you think I don't, you're making the same mistake Biswandi's making.* His thin body, like a pale wand, moved by rote in the bathroom, his desire for her tucked away along with whatever deeper secrets he kept.

She stopped at the rim of the park. Those secrets had burned to cinders, along with Richard. She had confessed herself to Justin Kilroy, who desired her the same way he desired food, the same way he snored at night—with no intensity, but at the visible surface. *He* hadn't sent her down here. She could turn back right now and catch him as he gessoed a freshly stretched canvas, the turpentine pinching their nostrils.

But the disembalmed questions whined like mosquitos in her ear. If not Ngebin, then had Biswandi fulfilled his allegory—the scorpion stinging the bridegroom? Like Amet, she counted herself among Biswandi's enemies and so wanted to believe that he had wronged her. No one in the State Department had pointed a finger in Biswandi's direction, but no one there knew of the fable or of the microphone planted in the kitchen. If they were to learn, they would say the *dai* had planted it, and logically they could be right.

She took a bench. Gulls keened around her, lamenting everything the city gave them. Justin might think she had gone to her mother's; Katya believed her to be arranging her living room in anticipation of parties that Marika failed to envision; Claude thought that, shamed, she had taken her music home. No one had any true idea where she was. Her heart squeezed within her chest like a force pump, pushing the blood too quickly through her veins. *You listen too much to your Slavic heart*, she chided herself, as if wrestling with Richard's analytic mind.

"Why do you smile?"

Marika looked up. Before her, silhouetted by the early sun, stood a thin brown man in a rumpled, oversized cotton suit, his head recently shaved and just beginning to show stubble. A large black patch covered his eye, from which a scar cut into his drawn cheek. His right shoulder was hitched over a wooden crutch, which Marika followed down to the point just below the knee where his pants leg was pinned back. "You can't be—" she began.

"Amet. The boy who brought the meat."

"Who did this to you?"

"What, these things?" He pointed at the patch and sawed-off leg. She recognized the voice now. "The same one who got your man. Always the same. May I?" He motioned to the bench beside her.

"Yes, of course."

Amet lowered himself carefully and leaned his crutches against the iron benchrail. He smelled of Ivory soap and unwashed cotton. Like the man in the restaurant, he pulled his mouth to one side, the cheek muscle jerking with a slight tic. "We were showing, you know, pictures we had got, of army boys lining up the hill people against a wall and shooting them dead. And stories we had, too, from the metal plant, like these men who are losing an arm, a leg, and they go back home with nothing but bauxite dust in their pockets, na, and their lungs, too. So anyway, the boys find me and pluck out my eye to teach me what to see, and they shoot up my leg, full of holes, so I know where to go walking."

"They didn't try to kill you?"

"No, no. They are letting a few of us live, you see, in the hoping we might lead them to the bigger ones."

"To Ngebin."

"Yah, him." He nodded sharply, the name a thing one did not speak aloud. A light breeze, tinged with salt, blew in from the harbor. At the other end of the park, a young woman was walking next to a little girl who jumped rope as she skipped along. As they drew near, they would notice the white woman and the shabby black cripple sitting together on the bench, and the mother would draw her little girl aside, sure that they were trading drugs, that Marika was getting her fix. *I am like them*, Marika wanted to say, but turning to Amet she knew she was not. In everything about him, now that she had recovered from the initial shock of the eye and leg, she saw Yumana—that mahogany skin, distinctively Lethe among all the hues she had passed on Sixth Avenue, the turning up and down of the palms as he spoke, the mention of *dai* with all the mythology of the dauntless individual god behind it. She had thought to slip Africa from her like a cloak, only to find patches of it clinging to her skin. Amet was either her enemy or her ally, no stranger; and Biswandi, five thousand miles away, was still nemesis to both of them.

He stared at her, reading her thoughts. "You should state your business," Marika said.

"It is so simple." The palms went up, then down. "We cannot begin reform while the dam is there, and we cannot bring down the dam without knowledge from inside. It has long been discussed. Your husband—he began the work. Now we turn to you."

"I don't see why I should help you, even if I could." Marika watched the mother and daughter settle into a round sandbox at the center of the lawn. "Pioneer Aluminum and the Mayume government are two separate entities, whatever you people might imagine. And just because white colonials oppressed your people doesn't mean they left no good behind them. Someday you'll want hydroelectric power—you'll want to bring light to the villages. Destroy what you have, and something worse'll take its place. Why don't you just stage a coup and give yourselves a decent government?"

Amet had taken out a short brown pack of African cigarettes and was thoughtfully tapping one against the heel of his thumb before lighting it. "My people," he said, "are dying at a rate of one hundred a day from disease and death squad." He spoke slowly and crisply, with hardly a trace of dialect. "Work in the smelter and the mines weakens our bodies, and in the rot of this great unnatural lake"—he paused, his lips curling—"we breed these small and greedy parasites. You know them." She nodded. "The dark green snail, no bigger than my thumb, that burrows into the huts where we sleep and sucks at our children's blood, giving them in return the fever that eats out their guts and makes them mad with hunger and dysentery. The tiny buzzing mosquito that the British boast they had wiped away, who spreads among us malaria like it was this confetti I see here in the parades. The tse-tse that puts us to dead sleep. Oh, yes, and the water itself, that we need like always to drink of and wash with—we Lethe have always been clean people, fanatical—it robs us of our sight and gives us stinging, infested orifices that make for unquenchable thirst. Doctors we have, but they get no clean water to heal with."

"But what do you—"

He stopped her, his lower lip stuck out in another Lethe gesture. "Farther upriver, just south from the plains country, there is a waterfall. It plunges with enough force to light the villages as far as the coast. We are a small country, you see. And only twenty kilometers from this waterfall is the greatest deposit of bauxite in Yumana."

"But Pioneer wouldn't build a plant there?"

"And lose the bauxite they can get so cheap from the tiny countries from the south, which are themselves poorer than we but that they have the short monsoon? Hey? Should they give our land itself cause to prosper?"

"Okay." Almost mechanically, Marika reached for his brown cigarette pack and drew out one of the short, tightly packed sticks. She had smoked these before, with Florence, late at night, when they had drunk palm wine together and uttered wives' common grievances. The taste was rich and harsh, like a nut with the skin on. She lit one and drew in the smoke. "Why don't you—why doesn't Ngebin—take over the country and order Pioneer out? Isn't that the first step, to gain some kind of rule? Why do you resort to grand, violent gestures—stealing documents and blowing up dams?"

"One dam. Only one." He smiled, with a glint in his one eye, secure in his resolve.

"And besides, what do you know about me?" She turned to face him squarely, the cigarette hanging like a splint from her hand. "You don't just go out and hire somebody's widow as a spy. Why do you think you've got a chance with me?"

"Oh, we know mostly everything."

"Like what?"

"We know you are grieving little at your husband's death."

"You don't know that."

He scratched his stubbled scalp and went on. "We know you have the one mother, here in New York, and that is all your family. We know you are staying away from U.S. government parties—like this one, here." He pulled a square envelope from his breast pocket and handed it to her; inside was an invitation to a reception that the Council on World Affairs was to give for Curtis Lovell when he arrived in Washington next week.

"Where did you get this?"

"From your *boîte postale.*" He grinned.

"You got into my mailbox? You are thorough. So you know where I live."

"And who you are seeing."

"What do you make of my—attachments here?"

He shrugged. "You leave him behind you."

"This is absurd." Marika ground her cigarette with her foot and rose. "If you really knew anything about me you wouldn't have wasted your time coming over here. Your cause is none of my business. There's no reason it should be. My husband rarely shared his political activity with me. We were—practically estranged. I lead a private life here. It has nothing to do with Africa or its—its troubles. I don't know what to tell you to do, but stop this—don't keep on with me!"

She walked away toward the river but not so fast that Amet couldn't pull himself up on his crutches and follow her. When he caught up they walked side by side, saying nothing for several minutes. On the river, a tugboat was bringing in a British luxury liner, its human cargo leaning over the rails, waving and waving at the city.

"He knew he would die," said Amet finally.

"No, he didn't."

"I saw him, the last night with our leader. He had almost all the plans with him by them. He said—"

"You couldn't have seen him!" Marika broke in. "Richard didn't even know who you were, the next day. I asked him. I used your name."

"Oh, he's not knowing me. We're all together there, in the leader's compound, you see, but only the two of them talking. We others watch; we *listen.*" He lifted his pink-palmed hand, thumb pressed against forefinger for emphasis. "And this Richard Hooper, he says he thinks they're on to him. Says this McGrath has come to play watchdog. And he's been hearing little clicks on his phone wire, too, and people who stop talking when he enters a room. He says McGrath will not find anything, and that will only make Biswandi more angry. And the government wants more money from the dam, too, so they have to scare the

American giant just a little bit, you see. He says—na, I remember, that night, this low table and the rest of us on the dirt, while they sit across from each other—he says he can feel the web tighten. So the leader says, Leave them some clues, let them find us, instead. But Richard Hooper says no. He thinks he can maybe keep them guessing until our work is done, and then he can persuade the Americans not to strangle us. 'A peaceful transition,' he calls it. But the leader is just looking at him, like that, until Richard Hooper stops talking big and says, Yes, the odds are not good. I remember he is snapping his finger against the edge of the table—so."

"Yes, I know," said Marika, watching as Amet executed the familiar motion, clicking his fingernail against the wood of his crutch. "He had a nervous habit."

She stopped and leaned against the wall. Learning, months later, what Richard had said that night made her head swim with Richard's voice and face forming words she had never heard. She could see him, his lean form folded onto a short stool in the low hut, candlelight pointing up his pale whiteness against the barklike skin of the rest.

"They have altered the layout," Amet was saying, "and changed the schedules, for security. Little of the information we possess is of use to us now."

"And you want me to come back to Yumana and get more." Marika spoke through her own confusion, staring out at the luxury liner still climbing the Hudson, trying to rule out this version of Richard that Amet was bringing to her, trying to hold on to Richard as a spineless, compromising American diplomat, who drank coffee with too much sugar and called his wife by pet names. But Amet's version refused to disappear.

"This McGrath, he has no wife," Amet began, touching Marika's sleeve nervously, "and he has been seen after the curfew with one or two of the whores near the market, so it is known he has an appetite."

"Well, why don't you get the whores—"

"He is too clever for that. He brings an armed man with him, in fact, to avoid kidnapping. But to an American lady, a beautiful widow, he may be more susceptible. You need do no more than charm him," he added quickly. "Anything more is dangerous and unlikely to gain results."

"This thinking comes straight from Ngebin, I take it."

"Yah, in fact."

"Ngebin met me only once, years ago. How does he know I have such charm?"

Amet looked away from her, toward the river, so she could see only the black patch over his missing eye. "*He* spoke of you," he said.

"Who? Richard?"

"He said that you saw straight through everything. We had asked what you would do, you see, if you discovered all these plans. And Richard Hooper said you had one allegiance only, to the truth. It was said in the manner of a warning."

"Richard, Richard." Marika shook her head. Suddenly she remembered how, in their first years, he would come home from the embassy angry and puzzled. He would pace the living room, at the edge where it sank, brushing his thin hair back from his forehead, exclaiming, "I don't get it! I am supposed to be working for the State Department, not Pioneer Aluminum! They act like I'm their *man*. And in return I get to act like Otomo is *my* man. Well, I don't *want* Otomo as my man."

And yes, she had even seen through it all and explained it to him. It was not long after that time that he began to cultivate his orchids—his escape, she had thought, from the compromising role he played and the anger it engendered. *How young you were,* she thought, looking out at the Hudson and seeing the man she had married. Younger than she was now, and angrier from the start than she had guessed, if Amet spoke the truth.

Amet waited, his slight form hanging on his crutch, like a coat on a peg, for her answer. His lips, still sculpted smooth as marble, pressed tightly together, as if holding in the numbers that Ngebin used to flood Richard with—number of limbs, like his, blown or sawed off, number of infants born with snail fever in the upper valley, dead at a few months, number of boys conscripted from the villages into Biswandi's army, where they could not tend the cocoa and plantain fields. Amet held the numbers back and attended her.

"I have to sort things out," Marika said.

"Yes, of course."

"I may be pregnant."

A pause. "I did not know that."

Glad to have stopped him short, in his omniscience, with a simple lie, she went on. "I won't know for another couple of weeks, at best—" Panic closed her throat. Two weeks was no time at all. What could two weeks tell her about Justin that she did not already know?

"I return to Yumana tomorrow," Amet said. He knew she was lying, was stalling him. "I must be hearing from you in fifteen days, if you are helping us. After that time, we are going in ourselves. There will be much more fighting, more violence. But in the end the stool is ours."

He smiled grimly. Marika recognized the old saying, symbolized in the golden stool the old chiefs had cherished, with its figures of men massing together on the sides: "In life, one is always sitting on another."

"You will send a wire to this address," said Amet,

handing her a folded slip of paper. "You will say you are enjoying your trip but have sprained your ankle. You will sign it 'Bandele.' Then you will write your friends and tell them you are coming to visit—you are lonely and miss their company. You make flight arrangements yourself. Use your own name, let people meet you at the airport. We will contact you in Revenir, not before."

"And if I decide not to do this?" said Marika.

"Send us nothing. Say nothing to anyone."

Amet cleared his throat and spat cleanly over the wall into the river below.

All at once, where there had been days stretching infinitely forward, nothing remained. Marika hurried past the old factories and new loft buildings, the warm June wind whipping at her dress. She might have been standing in the park talking to Amet for days or years. The wind that had started up could have whisked away Justin's loft and Justin with it, back to Rose and Adam on a Virginia farm. Katya could have married Dr. Dniprovsky; she could have grown ancient and died. Marika would be left alone in this island city with no hope of replanting her roots here, her chance for a child torn away by the wind.

Amet expected her to return to Yumana. Where the people moved like cattle through the streets, the sweat coursing off their backs and legs. Where the setting sun caught the stained ivories of their eyes in a look of stricken panic as they hiked their sacks around the hood of her Renault crawling upward to the red hills, she, like the swarm of them, meeting dusk as if it were her ancestor summoning from the grave. Where Biswandi's car scattered children before him like dogs skittering from its path. Where the fecal odor of the open latrine in the quarter that spread from market to river permeated the mangoes and cassava even after Seki had scrubbed them with soap and left them to dry in the clear air of the hilltop. Where that stench blended also with what lingered unmistakably in the still early-morning air behind a pair of olive drab trucks leaving the city: the trail of human vomit and meat.

A truck swung around the corner where Marika had wandered from the sidewalk to the cobblestones. "Ya wanna watch it, lady?"

"Yaw, yaw!" Marika shouted back. The driver's face that mugged at her from the open window was pasty as milk, a cigar stuck like a wooden peg to pry the lips apart. He hailed from Queens or maybe Staten Island, and the only things that scared him were communists and old age.

She could say no. Amet had convinced her of nothing. That *he* was not behind Richard's death she could believe; but the *dai* were scattered and secretive.

So Richard had had a cause—a grand scheme. He had woven it around his orchids like a gauzy, sticky web, and now she had stumbled into the greenhouse. As she hurried back through the streets, Amet's recital, *I can feel the web tightening*, jangled in the loud honking of horns and clank of metal grates. Without pause she had been running toward Richard, who had spun and been caught in his own mesh.

But she was running to Justin, and she could say no. Over the grate, through the iron door and up the slanting stairs to the loft, Marika's feet clattered louder than the street sounds. "No," she whispered at each step, "no, no, no, no," each *no* like an inkblot over mahogany hands that pawed at her, that shook their grimy fists at her, that nudged her with the blunt muzzles of guns shattering greenhouse glass, their unseen faces taunting her.

"Justin!" she shouted. "Justin, talk to me!"

He opened the door, surprised, his face half shaved and his arms spread wide to take her in. He did not talk to her but let her beat her head against his chest. "Poor Rika," he said, "you ought to have yourself a baby." Then he pressed her face to him until his skin was all she felt, all she smelled and saw, and his heartbeat was all she heard.

# Chapter 12

Justin went alone to Southampton. On Monday, Marika flew to Washington. By Thursday she had gone through Mr. Jacobson, Mr. Schuyler, Mr. Kline, and finally Charles Hallerin, as if they were all gates that led from one dry, flat pasture to the next. Familiar, all of them, with the tragedy of Richard Hooper's death, they frowned and nodded briskly with the certainty that an investigation was proceeding. *Where* it was proceeding, well. . . . They examined their fingernails and coughed up something like a laugh. Culpability in a country like Yumana was the needle in a fat haystack, they said. Mr. Schuyler, Mr. Jacobson, and Mr. Kline had identically shaped heads of dark brown hair, and wore suits tailored to a sharp V, while Charles Hallerin, whose pale tan jacket resembled a packing box, seemed to suffer under the dome of his bald head as under a metal helmet.

On her second journey to see Hallerin, her third day in Washington, Marika was waylaid in the broad gray corridor outside Schuyler's office in the State Building, by a stranger whom she recognized, after a blank staring minute, as Curtis Lovell.

"You ought to know better!" he bellowed. "We Africans can smell each other a mile away. And it don't wash off!"

His round face gleamed as he pumped her hand. He wouldn't forgive her for standing him up at his reception—he thought she'd come to town just for the party—but he'd take her for coffee anyway. Hallerin wasn't going to see her for an hour at least, he was tied up in there with some amnesty proselyte.

"The day doesn't go by," he said, sliding into the booth, "that Claire doesn't mention your name. 'If only Marika were here!' she keeps saying."

"If I were only there, then what?"

"Why then, the damned natives'd behave themselves, and the rain would stop, and we could get up a regular set of bridge! No, seriously, she misses you. And we all feel awful without Richard. But you look swell! Considering."

Freshly shaved, Curtis appeared young and decent, like the first flank that had met Marika in the outer offices of the State Department; as enthusiastic as emissaries to a thumbnail democracy, they had bobbed their heads and listened to her, knowing all the while that beyond their inner doors lay hours of stalled and wasted time.

"What *are* you doing in town, since you didn't come to see me?" Curtis asked now. His voice carried over the narrow booths of the coffee shop, and the counter waitress sneaked a sidelong glance at them.

"I'm finding out who killed Richard."

"Who *what*? Those Marxist baboons did it, you know that already."

"Did they?"

"Look, I know this has been a terrible loss for you. But just because there's no arrest, no trial, no single person to point the finger at—"

"There was an arrest. They let them go."

"Because *you* wouldn't identify them," Curtis answered too quickly, leveling his finger at her. He had been forewarned, Marika realized; he hadn't really been surprised at all to find her in Washington.

"But I'd never seen those men."

"Don't you understand?" He pushed aside his coffee cup as if it impeded her understanding. "You can't ask which one of *them* did it. In a lineup they'd all look alike. They act with one mind. They kill with one hand. You can't get individual revenge, Marika. You've got to think, 'It was a disease that got Richard.' Then we stick together and stamp out the disease."

"A bullet," Marika answered, "got Richard. All I'm asking is who paid for the bullet."

"Karl Marx."

"That's what Mr. Schuyler tells me."

"Then believe him! God, no one could be angrier about what happened over there than I am, but face it—"

*—Lovell knew it was coming.* As if he stood just behind her, Marika heard Richard's voice in her ear, and she gave a barely perceptible start. Listening for more, she caught only Curtis's loud drone. What had he known was coming? The *dai*, the gunshots? Curtis and Richard had attended college together. They formed the perfect complement, the diplomat and the businessman. But as if at a signal, Marika knew not to ask Curtis about Biswandi, or to object further to Curtis's explanations.

"—so England let them go too early, is all. You don't turn children loose before they've learned what's right and what's wrong. They'd kill each other over a game of marbles. You ever read that book *Lord of the Flies*?"

"Of course you're right," Marika said tonelessly, in her ear still the echo, *Lovell knew it was coming.*

"It's understandable. You're bereaved, cast adrift back here—God, the States are just a foreign country after all these years, aren't they?"

"I'm adjusting," Marika said. Her words rolled like smooth pebbles across the table. "But of course I miss everyone over there. It's like being away from a family."

"Exactly how we see it! Say, why don't you fly over for a visit? The situation's stable at the moment—not that you can predict! But we'd love to have you in the guest room. You and Claire can cheer each other up. Revenir's not much more of a jungle than Manhattan, eh?"

He was beaming again. Accomplishing the small favor that Schuyler had asked of him—to distract Marika from asking messy questions about Richard, to put her mind onto the bright and homey future—he saw his morning neatly sewn up.

*Score one*, Marika thought, looking over her chipped cup at Curtis's bland, useful face, *for Amet*. She held her breath, half expecting Richard's voice to drop inside her head in response, but there was only the rattle of steel spoons in the waitress station over her shoulder. She had, unexpectedly, an invitation to Yumana, planted and soon ripe for the plucking. And why would she have planted it, if not to pluck it later? "Washington, too," she said.

"Washington too what?"

"Is a jungle. Hallerin's not going to tell me anything, is he?"

"He may not have anything to tell! Look, I'm going to give you the same advice I gave old man Hooper."

"Richard's father?"

"Last time I was stateside he called the department. Asked a lot of nonsensical questions to which we haven't got a clue of an answer."

"What kind of questions?"

"Christ! He wanted to know it all—why we hadn't had security at your house, whether there'd been threats, what kind of covert activity we had going on over there, the whole shebang. Let's get the check." He waved at the waitress.

"And you told him—?"

"I told him what I'll tell you: Let it go. Believe me," Curtis went on, though Marika had already checked her protest, "I'm giving you the advice Richard would give if he could. When can I tell Claire you're coming to—hey, watch it!" he broke off as the waitress, trying to tear off their tab with one hand, lost the balance of her tray and a water glass tumbled onto the table.

"I'm sorry!" the girl cried, ridding herself of the tray and scrambling to wipe up. "Oh dear, your hand!"

Quickly she dabbed at Curtis's hand, which had caught a shard of the broken glass and was bleeding from the palm. "It's nothing," he said. "Just a sliver. Here, it's out already."

Marika stared at the place where the glass had gone in while the frantic waitress found a bottle of peroxide and a bandage. *You turn round*, Florence had said, her rough hand tracing in Marika's hand the V that Curtis now held out for the waitress, *right here, at the broken glass again*.

"Hey," Curtis said, "don't get upset! It's just a scratch."

"Sorry." Marika pulled her gaze away from the omen. "You were asking me something?"

"Oh yeah. When can I tell Claire you're coming to visit?"

"Oh, soon." Maintaining control, Marika watched her fingers reach out and graze Curtis's swathed palm. The blood was only a sign, not a directive. She smiled generously at Curtis as they left the booth. "As soon as I'm able," she said.

"Good! And we'll try to keep the natives peaceful while

you're there, eh?" He patted her shoulder with his bandaged hand. "So you can stay till the flies drive you off."

At her hotel Marika learned Justin Kilroy had called.

"I'm leaving here tomorrow," she told him when she phoned back, "but I'm not coming back to New York just yet. There's someone I've got to see."

She heard music in the background, laughter, tinkling words. Justin's loft was filled, again, with people. "I thought you wanted to marry me," Justin shouted, "and have mah *bay-bee.*" His drawl was harsh with marijuana.

"We'll talk as soon as I'm back in the city."

"Last time he had to die. Does he hafta come back to life now?" The party seemed to roar in the background. Marika winced and shut her eyes.

"I thought you understood. I just need to know."

"Yeah, well, I got women here who don't want to know a damn thing, and their comp'ny's plenty fine!"

"Don't yell at me."

"They wanta do a feature on me! On the boob tube! The educational boob tube! Ain't that legit enough for you, Mrs. Hooper?"

He was gone again, like the first night; the dark side of Justin's moon.

"You're drunk. And boring."

"Yeah, well, y'know what I'm gonna do when they get me on that camera? I'm gonna spread out my arms and I'm gonna shout, 'I love you, Marika Rybak, you fucking bitch!' And all the girls in Artland'll cry 'cause they just lost out on the richest goddamn heterosexual painter in America! That do it for you? That what you came back from the jungle for?"

"No. No, Justin, no," Marika repeated faintly as she set down the receiver. She sat down on the dark brocaded bedspread. For the first time she realized that Justin had never changed. While she had thought she was preserving him in her mind, she had been slowly changing him, day by day and year by year, until she had wholly replaced the man with the fantasy. While the man himself loved her unto bitterness and anger but finally left her cold. Had Richard never lived, she still would not have borne Justin's child.

Dry-eyed, she phoned Claude Thrush and left a message on the static of his answering machine to say that she could not sing *Fidelio,* that voice lessons would have to wait awhile. He would nod wryly as he heard it, thinking that he had had her number all along, that she lacked even the courage to tell him face to face.

Next she reached her mother. Below her motel window, a shoal of limousines swam through the traffic, as she told Katya she would be traveling to upstate New York to bring Richard's ashes to his father. "So *now* you do your duty," Katya complained. "When your mother needs you back here to help with the engagement feast."

"I'm—I'm pressed for time, Mama. I'll be back in a week."

"Someone's after you."

"No, Mama. I'm just settling some things."

"It's that artist. He's making you crazy. He's hurt you?"

"If anyone's done hurting, it's me."

"So we'll wait for you, with the feast, my darling girl. We old people, we can wait."

"Thank you, Mama."

"We'll say a prayer, here, for the burying. The whole neighborhood will say one. Hey?"

So she journeyed from the close heat of the capital, up the narrow, converging tracks of the railway to Port Henry, New

York, to bring Morton Hooper his son's ashes and to search the Adirondacks for clues to an African death.

As the train climbed into the hills, it traveled backward in the season; the dogwood and cherry blossoms that had already dropped from the trees in the city reappeared, dotting the landscape like confetti. Marika leaned against the window in the dining car and let the clack of the wheels turn her, too, back in time, let it return her to the infrequent trips made up here with Richard, past the gilded, dying leaves or over white-cloaked, slumbering winter mountains, her luggage burdened with carefully selected gifts for Morton, offerings he delighted in scorning.

"What in hell am I going to do with a carved African bowl—out of mahogany, yet?" he'd ask.

"Well, you could use it for salad—"

"Have you ever known me to eat *salad*, Marika?"

"Or you could just hang it on the wall. Your walls are bare, Morton."

"That's just fine. They're not ashamed."

Richard had sat on the sidelines, not saying much. It was after Marika had gone to bed in the narrow, vaulted room upstairs that he stayed up to talk for long hours with his father. She had heard their voices, low and unintelligible, floating up the broad stairs. To interrupt them would have produced the same shocked, shamed silence as walking in on lovers. Not that there was any love evident between Richard and his father: they faced one another like trees, one gnarled and the other still smooth-barked, but alike in their steady growth, their affection for distance.

To Morton, Marika knew, she held the place, not much revered, of Richard's woman. The first time they had made the trip up here, the widowed doctor had looked her over as he might a local girl who through foolishness had contracted an infection. "I can't tell," Richard had answered the first time she had asked him what his father thought of her, but years later, when she had ventured to ask again, huddling under blankets in the cold guest room upstairs, he had smiled laconically and said, "He finds you passable. Which in another tongue would translate as terrific."

"I don't believe you."

"You will."

She never had. And yet, over the years, during the required four days spent in Port Henry on each trip back to the States, she had come to realize that the pairing-off worked out so that Richard stood on one side and she and Morton stood on the other, where they could clearly see him and bend their heads in a collusion of opinion on him.

Once only, four years ago, had Morton come to Yumana. His first morning there, Marika had found him standing straddle-legged in the door of Richard's greenhouse and scowling. "Flowers" was all he had said.

She had nodded.

"Can't you find a way to help him out of this?"

They were refreshing, these sparse conversations, because they reminded Marika that someone cared to talk straight about Richard—because each exchange conveyed a clear nugget of understanding. "Underneath the complaints," she had said then, "he thinks we thrive here. In any case, he turned to the orchids first."

Morton had never looked more the New England aristocrat than he did that day, his skinny legs dropping out of newly pressed khaki shorts, his jaw jutting below dark glasses that unfairly obscured the stamp of his keen eyes. Behind him, the blood lilies shone unnaturally, tropically bright in the African daylight. Marika had been relieved to send him back on the plane to his native habitat; yet in his short time there he had dipped into the country and gathered up his son's predicament like a clean scoop of wet sand.

Now Marika pressed her nose against the window of the train and watched the beribboned trees fly by, with the desideration she should have felt going to see the experts, the Schuylers and Hallerins, in Washington. Of course they had told her nothing, refusing even to pick up on her hints that Richard had been friendly with the *dai* and so was unlikely to have been killed by them.

*—Had you gone hoping for something more?*

There it was again, that voice sounding just like Richard, clipped and dry, dropping into her head. She held her breath, her nose cold against the pane of glass, and listened.

*—You wanted them to stop you from going back to Africa. Big Bird, that's not their job.*

"Enough," she said aloud, and held her hands to her ears to shut him out. It was going to see his father that did it. Echoes of the past.

Morton drove her from the train station up the chiseled road that led through the hills to the ramshackle Victorian he had bought when Richard's mother died, just after the war. Here he had practiced his medicine—the sign still hung from the wraparound porch, MORTON HOOPER, M.D., GENERAL AND INTERNAL MEDICINE. ("Playing the village saint," Richard had always said, turning Marika's attention to what he himself was doing in the outreaches of Yumana.)

"You've put on weight," Morton said as he followed her up the path. The paint was flaking from the posts that held up the sagging porch, and Marika tripped on the frayed edge of carpet in the dark front hall.

"You've lost it," she retorted.

"Have I? I do look in the icebox now and then for something to eat, but usually there's nothing there. So I stay lean."

He took her suitcase up the broad-planked stairs, lifting his long legs high, as Richard had, though his upper body had contracted with age. When they were settled back in the airy living room, a bottle of whiskey on the table between them, he asked her to bring out the urn. She had left it in the hallway, in the dark leather satchel in which it had sat now for seven months: Richard's ashes packed like a maternity bag, prepared for the inevitable trip.

"It's so damn *small*," he said when she had set the clay pot next to the bottle. He stared at it with his hand over his chin and mouth, pondering the size.

"I should have brought it up to you right away," said Marika.

"Why? To bury him? Ashes don't need a ceremony, Madam. They're the final thing."

That night they left the urn there, like evidence, and after a small supper finished the whiskey, lifting the bottle and replacing it by the side of the dun-colored pot. The windows were open, the screens in, and in the warm night, closer than the ululating crickets, they heard the whine of mosquitoes hitting the wire mesh.

"So you're back in the ozone factory, the big city," Morton said.

"My mother's there."

"Friends?" He lifted the half-full bottle experimentally, testing its weight.

"Some." Her face flushed as she thought of Justin.

"Haven't been there since I visited the two of you in seventy-five. You staying at the old place? By the reservoir, there?"

"No, I—" Marika bit her lip. As she had done when she was barely a woman, she forced herself to expunge Justin and enter Richard's world, a world more strange to her now that she had lived in it than it had been those many years before. The sheer curtains of that remote apartment, blowing in the night wind that came across Central Park. "We gave that place up awhile back. I'm renting farther west, overlooking the river."

"Your mother's well?"

"Marrying again."

"Bravo." He raised his left eyebrow, exactly as Richard would have done. Had Richard been allowed to grow old, in fact, he would have come to match his father in every detail: the ungainly limbs, the circlet of gray hair around his narrow head, the large freckled hands that grasped the neck of the whiskey bottle. He too would have been working late into the night, like a country doctor. Abruptly, Morton pointed at the urn. "Did he want it like that?"

"No." Marika poured more whiskey and sipped it. The smooth burn ran down the sides of her throat. "He wanted to donate himself for research. In his will he had a place for his eyes, his organs—everything. But there's no research facility within five hundred miles of Revenir."

"Funny." Morton leaned forward and tapped the urn, gently, with one finger.

"What's funny?"

"He had time to change the document."

"But—"

"He knew. Come, girl, you're aware of that."

"Richard didn't—" Marika chose her words carefully, remembering Amet saying confidently, *He knew he would die*. "He didn't share his worst fears with me. Perhaps I wasn't listening."

"P'raps." Morton rose and stepped across to the screen door that looked out over the valley. His free hand folded like an army general's across his back. "I spent a few nickels talking to those robots at the State Department," he said. "I even thought for a while of going on one of these wild-goose chases you read about, poking my nose around there, flying over to the scene of the crime, coming up with just a scrap of evidence to indict the bunch of 'em."

"You mean the *dai*," Marika said tentatively.

"I mean"—Morton's voice, like Richard's, could wither like a dry wind—"the snakes who paid my son's salary and shed his blood, that's who I mean."

"You don't think *we*—"

"I don't think 'we.' I think 'they.' I *know* 'they.' Those white-palmed murderers eating goose liver down in Washington killed Richard as sure as those are his ashes, there." His voice never rose. He stood silent by the window, his back to her, feeling her unspoken challenges, her pressing need for proof. "The last time you two were here," he said at last, "he told me what he was up to. With the dam and the land rights, the people in those hills I saw from your window, over there. He says to me he's gone all the way and they're on to him. I press him a little, and he says he's been stealing plans and passing them over. I thought he should resign his post, be a missionary if he has to, help people on the up-and-up. He told me it was too late for that, and anyway he couldn't see you in it. But he says to me, 'It'll be a race to see who finishes me off, Pioneer or the intelligence agency.' I asked him if he'd let me know, just send me a hint, however he could, when he thought it might happen."

It was one of the longest speeches Marika had ever heard from Morton. In the thick stillness that followed, she traced the ribbing of corduroy on the arm of her chair, the chair in which she had always left Richard at night to stay up and exchange truths with his father. "I just found out about the plans," she said, "recently. But I think—when it happened—it came as a surprise to him. He looked—startled."

"You stay here." Morton pushed himself up from the

couch and walked quickly over to the rolltop desk that dominated one corner of the room. "This arrived," he said, rummaging through a stack of papers he pulled out from a pigeonhole, "the very day I received your cable. It had been opened and resealed. As he knew it would be."

The stationery he waved at her was the familiar light gray, engraved stock that Richard had used all his years as ambassador. "Dear Dad," she read. "When I last saw you, you asked how my new orchids were coming along. The black *africuus*, I'm happy to report, is beginning to flourish, despite the inclement conditions here, but my *Rebellis Hippocraticus* is in a dangerous state. The disease that threatens the plant is hard to detect. It strikes from within and without warning; I'm afraid this one will fall prey even before its flower is quite gone. Still, for an orchid lover, its time has served some purpose."

The crickets' song rose, drowning out the mosquitoes. "Not even a tough code to crack," Marika said. "The *R* and the *H*."

"The doctor's rebel."

"He never warned me." She thought out loud, under her breath, but Richard's father heard and leaned forward to grip her arm.

"I told him," he said, his voice rasping with the whiskey, "*I* could see you in it. But he wouldn't take the chance."

"Why didn't you contact me about this?"

"I was waiting." He raised his glass and winked at her, his neck creasing as he nodded his head. "I knew you'd come asking, sooner or later."

In the pitch black of a moonless night, the walls of the bedroom converged, damp and close as a tomb. Marika threw open the windows, but in the stifling air the night sounds only hemmed in her own silence. Restless, she turned from the windows to the door and back again. She had not wanted to come asking. To encounter Morton, who was Richard's only family, the only one who knew Richard as himself, the only one who could hold Marika accountable. She felt herself a criminal who had made an almost clean getaway, only to stumble at the sound of a familiar song, the sight of an old friend. Morton would not have wrung his hands, like Katya, over her being with Justin Kilroy; he would have smiled over it. He would have smiled and gone to weep and rage over his Richard, with a wild grief that Marika would never see.

And in his grief or its aftermath, he had fingered another killer for his son, and that killer had white skin. Now that she had paused in her getaway, the three killers of Richard surrounded her—the *dai*; Biswandi; America. She had walked into their circle, and now they trapped her, ordering her to choose. Richard's letter, finally, pointed nowhere. It only hinted that he had premonitions about one of the three in the triangle. He had left his death like a magnet, drawing her into the trap.

Utterly silent now, with the crickets' song fled, the night pulsed like a giant heart. Where was Justin to take her out of this? Always before, when her stomach buckled at the crowd's cheer rising up from the white wall where *dai* were shot, when the facile conversation of Americans chittered against her ears, she had reached for Justin as for a door that let her out of a cave into the light, that closed Yumana off like a bad dream. Now she had walked back into the cave, and where was he?

She knew, and knowing, she could not summon him. Justin lay in his own bad dream, his nightmare of success, his paintings drowning in an ocean of acceptance. He would spend a morning with his accountant, an afternoon at an exhibition opening, an evening at a sleek loft party; and the next day he would go on a bender. He had been right, she could not love him tamed. She had preferred even the worst of the old days, when he hurled obscenities and threw his canvases across the room. She saw him heaving them, one by one, into the hallway to go out with the garbage. His face she could not see, nor summon his voice—only the arms swinging the heavy frames with their thick mottled surfaces, one by one, slinging them onto the pile. Like a silent pendulum, the movement of his arms, in their work of destruction, pushed her toward sleep.

Finally, she must have fallen unconscious, because she awoke to the blunt impact of a nearby thud. Her eyes flew open, but she lay utterly still while she unraveled the half-heard and barely familiar sound. It did not come again; instead she heard the noise of water running and gingerly raised herself on one elbow to see.

What she had heard first, she realized as she looked down the long bedroom to the adjoining bath, was the drop of Richard's briefcase as he returned home in Revenir. He had always let it go without bending down, so that it fell with a thump on the hard wooden floor. Without asking herself why the sound should have awakened her here, in Port Henry—for certainly she was awake—as it had for years in Yumana, she fixed her stare on the lit bathroom, where she had flicked off the wall lamp hours before; the amber light that emanated now from that small space was filled with steam, as if from a scalding bath. Slowly, as her eyes adjusted, she saw him, Richard, leaning back in the tub under the sulphurish glow, soaking away his fatigue.

Marika did not feign sleep, as she had the other time, the night before he was killed. She held herself attentive as a tuning fork to the sights and sounds of his evening ritual, the lifting out of the bath, his pink flesh, the muted scrub of the toothbrush. How clear it was now: the heavy secret that he harbored, betrayal and untried hope. He would not let her in on that secret, but even as he stood, naked, his back to her, he ravened for her quick warmth.

Motionless, not daring to breathe, Marika awaited her visitor. Outside, an owl hooted low; below Marika's window, the old well sucked and rumbled. There could be no doubt where she was.

As before, Richard wrapped the towel around his waist and moved from the bathroom to the bed. He did not shut the light, which glowed behind his silhouette, and he did not head for the left side of the bed, which Marika still out of habit left empty. Instead he shuffled slowly to a point where he stood above her, looking down at her upturned face. Her heart pounded in her throat. As if that other night had been yesterday, she anticipated his warm, urgent hand gliding along her hip, the desire waking in her. But he did not touch her. He bent his knees and lowered himself to where he knelt almost at eye level, and the amber light from the other room seemed to brighten, bringing his face into its glow. For the first time she saw his eyes, blue and burning, drilling into hers as if they would seize on a vein of gold deep below the surface. At the same time, in those bright pools she saw grief and pain drawing her beyond everything she had yet known.

"No," she whispered, her voice like smoke.

Almost imperceptibly, he nodded his head. Yes. She would go back.

Bursting away from that stare, Marika scrambled for the light. Her hand twitched over the cord of the bedside lamp until it found—precious!—the switch. Light flooded the room, and Richard vanished.

She sat up, back against the headboard. Disparate objects in the room faced her with their ordinary opacity, their lack of remark. In the white electric light, she could move freely; she would encounter no visions.

Swinging her legs from the bed, she wrapped her robe around her and headed downstairs, lighting the areas before her as she went. In the warm oak kitchen, she fixed a cup of stale instant coffee and lit an even staler cigarette from a pack she found in the drawer of utensils. With these she moved to the living room and settled on the deep couch before the coffee table and the small urn that held Richard's ashes. It, too, looked doggedly plain, devoid of mischief. She was tempted to remove the lid but held back. Flicking the end of her cigarette into a white tray, she studied the tobacco's cremated texture, gray, fine and dry.

Yet she did not doubt for an instant that he had visited her and that she had seen her own decision in his eyes. Her body still hummed with the expectation of that last night. If she had only turned to him, if she hadn't thought, *Let him take it all the way, then*. But he would have been killed anyway. Next time, when he came to her, maybe he would give her a chance. To touch his smooth skin, feel his breath over her face. And she knew, too, where to find him: where the grief and pain lived, in the place he had called home.

—*That's my woman*. She felt his voice drop into her head once again, and this time she let it settle there, like a shell drifting to its place on the ocean floor, pulsing in the silence of the space around her. Uncapping the whiskey bottle, she poured a jigger into her black coffee and swallowed it down, then stretched out on the couch, just to lie there awhile, near the dust of Richard, before heading back to sleep.

"He liked this hill, as a boy," said Morton by way of eulogy. "He used to come out here with a little telescope he'd got for his birthday. Looked out over the fields by day and up to the stars by night. I asked him once if he didn't get tired of it, straining his neck like that over the same view, and he said things were always changing. This is the highest point, here, on the property. You can see fifty miles on a good day."

He pointed, turning his face from her to hide the water in his eyes. It was the next morning, and in the heavy mist hanging over the Adirondacks, they could see a mile at most. Marika and Morton had taken turns digging a shallow hole, and together they had set the pot inside. Then Morton had spaded it over with the moist earth and hammered in the stone that the State Department had sent. It was engraved with Richard's name and dates, a waving flag, and the words, "Died in noble service to his Country above and beyond the Call of Duty."

"They've got one just like it in his spot at Arlington," Marika said. "I went to the service in the winter." The person she had been then, sleepwalking toward Justin Kilroy, had stood stiffly on the small stage under a hastily erected tent while Charles Hallerin made his speech about freedom and martyrdom, and the soaked air muffled the fire of a dozen guns. Walking back under Hallerin's umbrella, she had smiled at black-suited strangers who—it had seemed odd to her then—perceived her as in mourning. Now, standing across the grassless patch from Morton, the morning mist cool on her cheeks, she began, distantly, to mourn, but for a Richard who had died as if before he was born, before he ever spoke to her as he had these past days or looked at her as he had last night. Still a stranger to grief, what filled her instead was a nascent rage, moving toward its time.

"I was always so proud to be a doctor," Morton said, swinging his trowel at the bushes as they started down the hill. He talked unnaturally, embarrassed by his short spate of tears. "I thought I had it over the others simply because I could stave death off from my wife and son. And what a trick, it got both of 'em."

Back at the house, bustling in the bare kitchen, Morton looked suddenly older, as if the trip up and down the small knoll in back of the house had cost him five years. His shoulders sagged; his slacks hung loosely on his legs. "Someday soon you'll have to stop working," Marika said to him with accustomed bluntness. "What'll you do then? With this big house, and all?"

"Guess I'll die in it, like a stubborn old mountaineer," he said, his thin lips parted in a grim smile. "What'll you do? Now, I mean."

"I'll find out, if I can," she said, "who killed Richard."

He had been hoping to hear such words more than she had expected to utter them. Had Richard come to him, too, in the night, kneeling by his bed, whispering as they used to? Morton put away the dish he had been drying and went over to Marika. Stooped as he was, he stood a head higher than she. His hands, damp from the dishwater, strayed over her face like a blind person's while she stood mute. The pools of his eyes filled again as he spoke. "I never thought you loved my son."

"I didn't love him well."

"How then"—his hands still straying over her cheeks, memorizing their bone structure—"can you be angry enough? What can you wield for him?"

"Everything I never gave him, before."

"If only that were enough"—the old man spoke fiercely as he cupped her head—"to bring him back."

Locked against his shoulder, Marika could see through the window up the hill to the clearing where they had left Richard's ashes. Like a *dybbuk,* Morton's anger had fled him and entered her. Her cool blood had caught fire, and in this moment of peace she wanted restlessly to be moving. To take care of business, to strike out, to find Amet, to kill Biswandi.

If he were the one.

Whether it brought Richard back, or not.

# Chapter 13

"He calls here for you again, and again and again," said Katya, waving at the phone from her overburdened stove.

"I know, I was here," put in Sacza. "Your mother tells him, but he won't believe Mrs. Hooper is out of town. No answer at your place, so he thinks you've come down here. What's he suppose, we've got you tied up in a closet? The other day I see him on the corner outside my place. I go out to the stoop, yes? And he calls over to me, 'Where you got her stashed?' Like that. People turn and stare. But I don't say a thing, I don't tell him what's your address, I just go back in my shop. His eyes, I'm telling you Marika, they burned holes in my back."

"I'll go see him," Marika said, turning over the mail that had come for her at Katya's. One letter bore an African postmark. "He shouldn't be bothering Mama."

"I'll say he shouldn't!" Sacza came over and put her long-nailed hand on Marika's shoulder. "He's got young girls now, you know that," she hissed into her ear. "Your Uncle Yuri saw a photo of him with two of them in yesterday's *Post*. He showed all of us. For your own good, a woman of your reputation—"

"Leave her alone, Sacza!" Katya called out from the kitchen. "It's Marika's matter, yes?"

"A little friendly advice—"

"Thank you, Aunt Sacza." Marika drew herself up and smiled down on her mother's friend. Sacza had always meddled. "I'm back at my place now, so people can call me there."

She withdrew with the mail to the room Katya had kept fresh for her. Six months ago its familiarity had rankled. Now she drew strength from the patterned walls and dark wood. Coming down the Hudson on the train, she had looked out her window and seen faces emerge from the watery expanse of the river. First Justin, his features large and liquid; then Richard's face, like a fine etching on the surface; Biswandi's pugged visage as he leaned gingerly over a jagged edge of glass; and finally Amet, his hobbled form as she had left it by the park bench, rising now from the water. She would lean back in her seat and shut her eyes, but soon they would open again, drawn by what the river held.

Quietly, sitting on the edge of the bed, she opened the thin airmail envelope, as if the sound of paper tearing would give her away. She expected a letter from Amet, but the note inside came from Claire Lovell, writing on the night she had spoken long-distance to Curtis and had learned that Marika might "stop over" for a visit. Claire was tickled. She wanted Marika to bring her some Bloomingdale's pantyhose and a supply of malt diet wafers—Curtis never knew the right size or kind. She had a very *presidential* secret to tell Marika, but she would keep her in suspense until she arrived. Claire signed off, "*B'nago* to you (guess who I learned that from!)"

Of course Amet would not write. Still, Marika sensed,

as she had since she left him standing like a statue in the freshly made park, that the sands of the clock he had handed her were funneling away. She had to act on the rage that Morton had bequeathed her. She had to move.

Hearing Sacza leave the apartment, she opened her door. Out in the kitchen, her mother was humming a rondele from the Ukraine, mixing the heavy fruitcake she would soak for the feast celebrating her engagement to Dr. Dniprovsky. For a small moment Marika regretted that she could not stay for Katya's wedding.

"You take strange trips," Katya broke off to say when she saw Marika. "To Washington, to other places. Why?"

"To see Richard's father, upstate. You wanted me to go, Mama, it's not a strange place."

"Strange men call you and then stop calling you. Men who knew your dead husband, that you say you did not love."

"Did not—" Marika caught herself, her throat tightening. "There have been some inquiries, Mama, that's all. Some things to clear up."

"And your famous artist friend, he can't clear nothing up for you?"

"Stop before you start, Mama!" Marika warned. She would not let Katya rake over the coals of her hope. Justin's only fault, his disjointed soul regardless, lay in being human. The rest lay with her. She had loved a different man, that was all, and too selfishly to trade him in for the man who lived and breathed.

"You're not giving him money?"

"Mama, he's got millions. And I won't be seeing him again."

"So it's just a little trouble your poor husband left you, is that it?"

*Richard*, Marika stopped herself from reminding Katya. She said, "That's about it."

"Makes a difference when you put him in the ground, hey?"

The morning mist on the knoll, rising like Morton Hooper's rage into the bright sun of day. The sharp cut of soil. Richard had lingered, along with the rest of night, in the chill shadows around the open patch.

With studied insouciance, Marika took a handful of raisins and did not reply.

"Remember"—Katya leaned forward to taste the batter from the wooden spoon and then pointed the spoon at her daughter—"remember that this one is gone from you. Nothing you do is bringing him back. Yes?"

"Of course yes, Mama."

Marika turned to leave the kitchen, but Katya, wiping her hands on her apron, followed her out and, taking Marika's hands in her own, led her to a couch. "Your papa," she began earnestly, "was not so good to his Marika, either, when she was alive."

"No?"

"So many times, in the night, he woke up crying. He was so sorry he hadn't wanted marriage with her, he never knew, it was his parents' fault, so on and so forth. Then worse—" Katya wiped her face, flushed from the heat of the stove—"worse are the nights he wakes laughing. He thinks she is there, you know, and when he looks around and sees the old room, and me, ah, then. . ."

"Then what, Mama?" *Then*, Marika thought, when Richard had walked through the room toward her, in his father's house. She pressed her mother's hand.

"Then she died again, for him. Again and again, she had to die."

“And you think,” Marika said, forcing a smile, “that something like that is happening to me. With Rich— my husband.”

“I see you turning,” her mother replied, studying the hands she held like a palm reader, “and still it’s backward you’re facing, each time you turn, my darling girl.”

It was an infection she had caught. This burning desire to know, and the fire that bred it. Like an apostle, over the next few days, Marika assumed the cloak of Richard’s logical mode of thought and went after all he had learned about the Parambo Dam.

His files were stashed against the white walls of the second bedroom in her still-cluttered halfway house of an apartment. In them she buried herself, beginning with the initial prospectus submitted by Pioneer Aluminum in the early seventies, when Richard was first sent to Yumana. Seeking funds from the federal government and the World Bank, Pioneer’s plan showed how the new hydroelectric power plant would generate electricity for high-country villages and so raise the standard of living for the Lethe and other tribes. A further proposal drew up charts that gave the amounts Yumana was spending on imported oil and the reductions that would be accomplished by the dam. Finally, a long article movingly drew a picture of the bauxite resources that were going to waste while young men from the villages idled their way into the black market, into stealing, into poverty.

The Parambo Dam, Marika read, would relocate fifty thousand people to better the lives of millions; the ten-mile lake it would create meant billions of dollars’ worth of power for Africa, as well as jobs for the indigenous people of Yumana. The architects’ clean, faded blue-line renderings showed a high narrow trapezoid with a peaceful lake above and a rushing stream below, flanked by the arching canopy of the rainforest.

Next, Marika sifted through the reports and clippings Richard had saved: the early medical testimony of the probability—high—of waterborne diseases increasing above the new dam; Pioneer's pledges to Otomo to use Yumanan bauxite; data showing the expense of transporting the raw material over the high Yumana plateau; newspaper reports of heavy layoffs during an early series of malfunctions at the plant. Richard had underlined a policy study that proposed a series of small-scale hydro projects and public health programs in place of the big dam, and attached to the study was a ledger sheet on which he had recorded, year by year, the incidence of dam-related deaths. Over the decade since construction, Marika saw, snail fever among children had gone from ten to ninety-five percent, and malaria had tripled; sleeping sickness, which had been virtually wiped out twenty years before, now infected almost half the population. Croplands, gone saline from irrigation, had been replaced with beef and cotton for export, and the farming people had hired on for the government or for Pioneer, which bought the ruined land for a token sum. The lake had grown from ten to forty miles in diameter, flooding the homes of a half-million Lethe.

Interspersed through the disordered stack of information were copies of letters from Pioneer Aluminum to Presidents Otomo and then Mayume, explaining that the importation of bauxite was only a temporary measure, that they planned to build a pipeline to Yumana's native reserves in the near future, and that at the same time they would set up power lines to the villages. In the corner of each photocopy Richard had written an amount: forty thousand dollars on the first letter, a hundred thousand on the fifth, two million on the last. These were the amounts that had flowed into the Yumana government's coffers while the mines to the north tried to bargain away their bauxite ore on the glutted world market.

*We were a fishing people,* Marika remembered Seki saying, *and my uncle was being chief. A little girl, I saw these dances he made for the trout running. So fine, the scales on his back! He's not going, he says, when the flat water comes. Na, we carry him up the hill, away, so he never sees the Parambo.*

*Is he still a chief?*

*No, Missis. No more chiefs! All the golden stools been drowned. My brothers, they are living*—here Seki's eyes had dropped, picking a lie off the ground, the brothers were all *dai—south, in the next country, they find work in the mines there.*

In a separate folder, on white onionskin, remained Richard's cumulative cry of protest, in copies of crisp letters dictated to Suzanne and addressed to colleagues at the State Department and at Pioneer Aluminum, letters attempting the fraternal, clubbish style of Ivy League teammates trying for the same goal line, just dickering over strategy. Still, he put it to them: the numbers he got from Ngebin, the tented hospitals he had seen for himself, the greasing of palms. The dam, Richard wrote, was only fuel for a flame already building. Just because the regime had held for ten years without a coup was no reason to assume its stability; there was a level of repression and authorized murder going on here that no population had ever tolerated for long without kicking. Richard wasn't beating his breast for the common people, he wrote, he just didn't want us to back a losing team.

And then he submitted his list: medical aid for the back country, a dismantling of the Parambo Dam, a new plant in the north near the Yumana mines. Better millions lost now, he said, than billions later. He wished everyone's wives the best and hoped he and Marika would see them on his next trip stateside. On the bottom of one letter, sent to Richard's predecessor, who was by then safely ensconced in the United Nations, was scrawled the reply: "Hooper: Why hasn't Biswandi staged a coup? The military's what you want to watch for, not the people. What holds him back? Regards." The other letters had gone unanswered, or perhaps it was their answers that Marika had seen Richard crumple with one hand and drop carelessly in the wastebasket at home in Revenir.

From the bottom of the file she drew out the tapes on which he had recorded reports of each new visit to the hills above the Parambo, descriptions of each new disease that he came to link with the dam. His familiar, modulated voice talked only to himself, spelling out the horror as it unfolded itself to him. She had seen him switch the machine off when she entered his office; and there, at the end of the last cassette, she heard him as if she had been listening at the door:

*I just learned the identity of the girl. Ngebin's sister. Tried to convince Ngebin, this is a tease of the worse sort. If he strikes back now, we lose the dam and the whole nine yards. He asked me what if it was Marika.* There came a pause of static, then a click. *If this Pioneer character proves the messenger I suspect him to be, I'm getting Marika out.*

He clicked off. He had been alive when he spoke, as immortal as anyone else. And all this time, while he complained freely to her about the pompous asses at Pioneer, about the medical disasters above the dam, about Biswandi's bloodthirst and Ngebin's impatience and above all his own political impotence, he had been telling her nothing, nothing. Because she wouldn't hear. "Like brick, my head!"

she accused herself aloud, thumping her forehead in Katya's way with the heel of her palm. And her stomach weak as a kitten's, she didn't want the knowledge, she had pushed it away. —*You might as well have married Claire Lovell,* she said to Richard.

—*She didn't have your hips.*

No. That was something Justin would have said. She didn't know, yet, why Richard had married her.

Justin. He was there, at the streetcorner by Katya's apartment, waiting. "I've been telling you I saw him, didn't I?" said Sacza, coming up behind Marika where she stood parting the curtains on the living room window. "Every day he's there. He goes and comes back, you know, like a policeman."

"I'll talk to him," Marika said.

"A tongue in anger," said Dr. Dniprovsky, wagging his finger at her from where he sat opposite Katya on the sofa, "is a snake biting its own tail. So my papa told me."

Justin had started his beard again, and in the two weeks since she had seen him it had grown to a woolly muff over the lower half of his face. In the morning light, his eyes in their deep sockets burned low, like candles that have been going the night through. The day was warm; she approached him in her light clothes, defenseless.

"Yo," he said.

"Hi. I hear you've been checking out the neighborhood."

"I'm a painter. I have to know everything about my subject."

"I'm not your subject, Justin."

"Not yet," he said, leaning against the streetlamp, his strong arms crossed over his chest. "But you will be."

He took her by the elbow, and as always, however reluctantly, she went with him. His hand on her skin felt rough and warm, like sand, and for an instant she remembered their long walk, years ago, on Jones Beach. *I could take you right here*, he had said, but she had not let him.

"I don't get drunk very often," he said now, his voice the same as then, unaged.

"Is it just booze that does it?"

"Naw. It's a special recipe—a little coke, a couple downers, and then the hooch. Gets me high off hating the world."

"You were going to tell the world you loved me, as I recall."

"Yeah, well." He squinted up at the sun, the creases running out from his eyes like the grain in wood. He would be still handsome at seventy. "The lousiest things seem funny, in that state. It's under control, though. Not like I was before. Marrying Rose kept me tethered for a long while."

"I never asked why that ended."

"She left."

"Why?"

"Same reason as you."

"What's that?"

He stopped, his hand drifting affectionately to the nape of her neck. "She's a survivor," he said. "Like you. And I'm a destroyer. I'll confuse and abuse a woman till she cracks."

"You really think you've got all that power? Poor Justin."

"Yeah, I do," he said, his sea-blue eyes on her, seeing through her like an artist, perceiving her surface and her depth. "Ain't that the worst of it?"

They stood at the edge of Union Square, the tree above them in new leaf, its sap barely scenting the city air. "You know I'm going away," she said.

"I figured, one way or another, you were," he said. "Quitting the show?"

"The singing, you mean. I wasn't in the show, yet."

"Oh, you've always been in the show," he said, his eyes pinning her through the spotty shade below the trees. "It travels with you."

"And you?"

"I talked to Rose last weekend. She's coming up here with Adam. This place downtown's hanging some of her work."

A dying envy threaded its last needle through Marika's heart. "I'll miss you terribly," she said, her eyes diverting from his to a thin stream of water that ran along the gutter beside them and into a drain at the corner.

He laughed, low and nervous. "Those are the exact words you used fifteen years ago. You survived. You came back." He brushed her cheek.

"I had you to talk to. In my mind. When I felt the need to, I—I touched you."

"So? I'm still here. Making worse and more expensive paintings, with no one to sing to me."

"Oh, you're still here, in New York. But here"—she put her fingertips to her forehead—"you've disappeared."

"Don't say that, Marika." He pulled her hand away and stepped closer, his body heat igniting hers. "I've been either painting or standing on that corner for two weeks with you in my head. I don't even know where you live. No one would tell me. And all I wanted was to ask for a tiny space—in there."

He cupped her head in his large hand, his wrist to her cheek. "It used to be," he went on, "when I thought I was dead—as an artist, I mean—I'd think of you remembering me. Or maybe I'd get this snatch of time we had together, and it'd wake me up again. That's all I'm asking of you!"

She bent her head away. "I can't anymore, Justin. There's too much else. You were—you're a great painter. Not what you're giving the museums now, but what you're going to paint. As soon as you jump off that ledge. When you're a 'has-been.' "

Quickly she raised both his hands and kissed them as if they had been hurt, the broad knuckles against her lips. For years the remembrance of those hands had warmed and steadied her blood. "I have to go," she said.

"Wait. You can't just *go*—you can't!" The edge of his voice cut the air. He took her by the shoulders. "You have to promise me you'll come back sometime. When I need you! Who've you got to go to, anyway?"

She shook herself loose. "You'd weigh me down," she said, soft but cruel.

"You can't shake me, Marika," he said, planting himself in her path. His lips curled, making a joke, regaining control. "I'll haunt you!"

"You won't."

"Oh, Rika, Rika," he said in sing-song. Before she could protest, his bearish arms stretched out and wrapped her up. He had got his control now; generosity was his trademark. "You let me haunt," he begged, pulling her close. The scent of flannel against his chest struck her again, like a cadence. "I'm no evil ghost."

He released her, and she turned to cross the street. "You'll have to come back, though!" he called to her over the rush of cars, "to sit for me! Till I get those hips right!"

As the traffic stopped at the light, Marika's sandals clicked loudly over the pavement, the still air like a cone of pressure surrounding her. If she turned around now, Africa would cease to exist, and the life she had invented would triumph finally over the one she had lived. But the traffic closed between her and Justin. A warm gust of air brushed her bare legs as she walked forward, and his voice behind her melted into the general din.

That night at the apartment, they held the engagement feast. "I am become a stuffed goose," Dr. Dniprovsky said, running hands up and down his small ribcage, when they had all finished and sat back in their chairs.

"You are become maybe half a man," said Uncle Yuri, his arms wide to his sides. "I think maybe you don't get rid of the hookworm you bring with you from the old country. Hey, Katya? You going to pour food down this hollow pipe, here?"

"Better down a pipe than into a pot!" Katya answered with a glance at Yuri's belly.

"I remember, on our farm," Dr. Dniprovsky began, his beadlike eyes glancing at each one of them to be sure he had his audience, "my father had parasites, they said. Everything he eats is running right through him. He's a skinny one, like me, you know, so my mother is wild—he'll die of starvation, she says. But you know what they do? They keep from him food and water for a few days. Crazy, you think? Then they hold a side of fresh ham to his rump. Yes! They all came running out, the squigglers, hungry by then. Little shiny things."

Marika sat among them, drinking sweet white wine. They soaked her up, Katya and the aunts and uncles, like sponges. When they had cleared away the table, Katya put on records and they danced, circling slowly around the small room. Marika found herself with Dr. Dniprovsky; he held her by both shoulders and squinted mischievously at her. "So you're going to make your mama set the wedding day, I hope?"

"I couldn't make her if I tried. You should know that."

"I'm wanting a summer day. My Andrea and I, we were married in the summer. In a little church in Plyetsk. You know Plyetsk?"

"No."

"Well, it's gone now, anyway. Like a little jewel, it was. And Andrea's sister standing next to her, like two flowers. You must stand with your mama."

"I don't know if I can make the wedding, Dr. Dniprovsky."

"Why you don't call me Uncle Reuben, like you do the others?"

"Habit," said Marika, smiling at him. He smelled of tobacco and paprika, as her father had, but with a sourness, whereas her father's odor had exuded rich and sweet.

"We marry when you're back here, your mama and I," Dr. Dniprovsky said, leading her around the edge of the couch. "We're old people, we don't have to be rushing, hey?"

"No, no," Marika answered quickly. "Don't wait for me. You tell Mama I said not to wait. I've got to go on a trip. I don't know how long."

The music stopped. They stood in the corner by the glass case, away from the others. Dr. Dniprovsky leaned against the windowsill, his eyes like a ferret's, protruding, the brows short white tufts. "Your mama," he said, "worries about you. She thinks you should rest."

"I've been resting. I've rested too long."

"She talks to me about you, you know. She says to me you were not"—he examined the case, as if finding her in it—"a *warm* child." Glancing around the room, he seemed to locate the spot where Katya had spoken. The eyes went rapidly back and forth. "She says you went hot to cold. It was to her frightening. We all think, hah, she's a little dramatic, yes? But now I feel this chill off you, like a frozen lake. Underneath"—he put his gnarled hand to his chest—"I feel a fire."

Marika laughed nervously. "Not enough to burn anyone, I hope."

"Ach. Who can say? It must melt the ice."

Marika leaned into the open window. From below, beyond the ordinary street noise, came the syncopated clopping of leather drums—the African street sellers, their bangles and scarves put away, peddling their music in the hot July of New York. "I didn't want you to marry Mama," she said. "I didn't think you were a match for her. But I'm glad now."

"You are going back? To all that trouble?"

Marika nodded, content not to explain. "I'll tell Mama tomorrow." She turned back and saw her mother on the other side of the room, lifting the arm of the phonograph, the heavy black disk poised in her hand.

"You return when?"

"When my work is done." She smiled wryly. "I've never said that before, you know? I've never had work that had to be done."

"We all of us have work that has to be done," Reuben Dniprovsky answered. "It makes war on us, and we surrender to it, without love and without hope." His brown ferret eyes glistened. As the music started over again, soft and scratchy, he took Marika's arm and led her like a novitiate back to the dance.

# Chapter 14

The leather drums of that evening pulsed in Marika's temples as she stepped off the plane into the driving rain of the late summer monsoon. Flight attendants waving huge umbrellas scurried back and forth to escort each passenger over the muddy field to the shelter of the terminal.

"Well, look at you-oo!" Claire cried out, stretching her arms forth to give Marika an angular hug. In the dark throng of the Revenir airport, Claire's skin with its tropical tan bore an almost jaundiced cast. Curtis stood next to her, paler and beaming.

"Didn't I tell you she'd be white as a sheet?" he said of Marika. "Got to hit her with some African rays, eh? Heh-heh!"

"Nonsense, she looks fabulous," Claire retorted. "Tans are *passé* this year, isn't that right, Marika darling?"

"Right," Marika answered. Dizzy from the flight, she thought only how Claire had never called her "darling" before. "I was expecting Suzanne."

"Well, the embassy kids," Curtis said, steering them past the babbling crowd—Lethe, Sacatra, Nebo, Marika saw them suddenly distinct one from another, she had forgotten the physical traits—"are all caught up in this student thing now. So we thought we'd better fetch you ourselves. This your only bag?"

"I've got the overnight case. What student thing?"

"It's absurd," said Claire. "General Biswandi arrested some American students—"

"So-called," Curtis put in.

"—who were somehow involved with the underground here."

"What underground?" Marika asked casually. They had reached the Lovells' Peugeot, and she stepped ahead of Claire to take the back seat.

"I don't know, dear. Running guns, I think. You'd think they'd have enough guns from the Soviets. Anyway—these were all blacks, of course, they were studying political science—they appealed to the embassy for amnesty, and now it's a pretty kettle of fish."

"Where are the students?"

"In jail, where they belong!" Curtis said, glancing in the rearview mirror as he started the car. "Next thing you know, they'll claim they were starved and tortured and given cockroaches for bedfellows. Biswandi's got his hands full, I'm telling you."

"President Mayume," said Claire, turning to wink at Marika, "has got *his* hands full, too."

The rain slapped the car in sheets, and the red clay of the road spattered the windows. Curtis was shouting that they had finally paved the roads around the southern hills, wait till she saw.

—*In the monsoon season*—Marika could hear Richard's voice on the tape—*you get infestations of hookworm overnight. When the river ran smoothly, the high waters and fast current bore the parasites away in monsoon. Now they stay. They breed. They live in children's guts.*

"You have to fill us in, Marika," Claire was saying, "on your funny little mother in New York. I'll never forget those liver and rice sausages she used to send you back with."

"Now Claire. Marika needs family."

"She's remarrying," said Marika.

"You see?" said Claire, as if the announcement proved something. "Marika is expatriate, like us. We're her family. This is like a homecoming."

"I'm not so sure," Curtis put in, "that Marika wants to think of this place as her home! Things are not exactly Mom-and-apple-pie peaceful around here, Marika."

"I had not expected them to be." Marika smiled gently, rubbing the side window with the back of her hand to clear off the moisture. She and Richard had invariably returned in monsoon, steam rising around them on the road in the intermittent spells when the rain lifted and left them like travelers arriving in a dream, the fog settling onto insubstantial ground. Richard had preferred the harmattan, because the heat dissipated at sunset, yielding a night of dry breezes—*good sleeping weather*—but to Marika it was the fecundity of monsoon, the clay-rich riffles running like blood down the streaked hills, that broke her open like a seed meant to grow large and wild in the rich heat. When they had returned to the house on the hill, she used to peel off her traveling clothes and stand out on the patio to let the rain drench her skin, her sweat mingling with the water that pelted her shoulders and breasts.

"One thing I will tell you," Curtis began as the three of them settled into wide, canvas-backed chairs in the Lovells' living room, "I underestimated this McGrath. I thought he was just some loser that Pioneer was shipping out of the States, but he has got the makings of a world-class businessman. Tough, you know. Decisive. Doesn't take shit from the Afros. He's laid off a bunch of 'em, tightened things up at the dam. And he keeps cozy with Mayume, keeps the president's palm slick, if you know what I mean."

"And he is," Claire added, pulling wine from the refrigerator, "such a *lonely* man."

"His wife isn't here with him?" Marika asked innocently.

"Darling, he hasn't *got* a wife. He made a play for little Suzanne, bless his heart, but she fended him off. He'll be driven to the natives if we don't help out."

The spacious homes that ringed the southern hills above Revenir contained an infinite variety of European leisure-class architecture. The U.S. ambassador's house imitated an Alpine villa; the Lovells' was an English country home, crossbeams, gables, and narrow churchlike windows looking down on the city. Marika undressed in the guest room, a small alcove off the head of the banistered stairway, complete with a cushioned window seat and a carafe of sherry on the nightstand; and in the white-tiled guest bath she took a long shower, her hot skin steaming under the cool water.

Her blood seemed to flow and dance in the moist heat. In spite of fatigue, she surged with health as with strong drink, as if Revenir were not a gun-pocked city but the fountain of youth, as if Yumana *were* her homeland. She took a rough sponge and scrubbed away her imported dirt.

*Ah, Richard,* she thought, *you in your bath, rosy and unprotected. You hated showers and you wouldn't tell me why.*

How he had wanted her, that last night. And she withholding, challenging him as if he had no higher concerns than marital power-play. And he, murmuring, *We've got all the time . . .*

In the midst of her surge of strength, hot tears mingled with the cold fresh water. Marika stepped out, her flesh tingling, but she couldn't stop the flow. "He can't be gone. He can't," she whispered aloud, holding the damp towel over her face. Suddenly, Richard's eyes, his mouth, his teeth, his long arms with their sinewy muscles, the slender pillar of his waist gripped between her thighs, his whispered *I'm coming* like a secret, the thin silk of his hair, drove through her at once like a shock of electricity, and her knees went weak. It was not she, staggering toward the guest bed, the towel draped weakly across her breasts, who had held him on the greenhouse floor that day; his ashes had not gone into a clayish hole at the top of the rise by his father's house; he had not died while she sifted through his filed secrets in New York: he was dying now, now, while she folded up like a fan, the life was leaving him before she had touched it, before she had comprehended anything.

The smell of his sweat through the soft shirt cotton. His fingers, stained from the loam he packed around his orchids, the thin green line that stayed under the quick of the nail. His voice like worn leather when he let go to fatigue. His laugh, no more than a chuckle, so rare that she had known him six months before she heard it. Her gut constricted as if a snake were strangling her at the waist. She folded down farther, head between knees. Richard Richard Richard.

"Marika! Marika!" Claire burst into the room. "My god, darling, I've been banging and shouting myself hoarse, and you in here screaming like a squaw! What is it, what's wrong?"

"Go away." Marika made no effort to push the words out, but they looped back, roaring, at her; they pushed Claire back from the bed.

"Well, what have I done to *her*?" she heard Claire say,

and she knew Curtis was in the room too, staring at her crumpled on the bed. She gulped for breath.

His pale eyes. His chin long like a blunt instrument, he used to massage her neck with it. The white heat of his anger—it burned her now as it died with him, the ashes of his rage left inside her. She twisted as if possessed on the bed. Claire shooed Curtis away and sat down on the edge.

"Let it out, honey," she said, and it was not Claire speaking but the oracle finding its mouth. "It's high time."

Marika howled. She crawled up the bed to the headboard as if escaping this death, Richard's death, that had come so unwarranted upon her. The blood that had been singing through her veins curdled and went foul. It forced her to live while he burned to cinders within her. This death was not possible and still it was, it was, it had been for these seven months and had lain in wait for her while she came full circle and back to Yumana.

Marika's stomach heaved, and she spat sherry into the small gilt wastebasket by the side of the bed. Then, with the sour taste filling her mouth, the roar in her head quieted finally and she looked, dazed, at Claire, as if she had never seen her before. Claire pulled Marika's damp head down onto her lap and covered Marika with a soft cotton blanket, because in the hot airless room she was shaking with chills. Every few minutes, as the two women remained there, the demon of Richard's death would take hold of Marika again, but each time as she began to thrash with it, Claire held her down until it had passed. It would come back; but for the time being Marika gave way to a black puzzled exhaustion.

"Don't you think it's time we woke her up?"

She heard the voice of Suzanne. Her eyes fluttering

open, Marika saw them gathered by her open doorway: Suzanne, Lisbeth, Tom, and Claire like a nurse guarding the portal. "In a while," Claire said.

"What brought it on?" Tom asked, glancing toward Marika. "You didn't mention his name or anything?"

"I tell you, darling, it's the place," Claire answered coolly. "Brings it all back for her, we should have expected it. You know how she loved him. Their happiest times were here."

"I didn't notice that," Lisbeth said, her low alto voice cutting under the others.

Outside, the rain had momentarily stopped, and a gray morning light filtered into the room. The heat was like a fist. Marika felt the utter lassitude of her limbs, the hollow pit of her stomach. Then she remembered the howling catharsis of her grief, and in the same instant thought, *Richard*, and was plunged back into a chamber of despair, small and dark as a tomb. He was dead and cold dust, and nothing to replace him. But now, propped up by the wall of sleep, she knew where her grief had brought her, and why for him she needed her strength.

She stirred, and they descended on her.

"Darling!"

"You look so well rested!"

"Tell us how the flight was."

"Can you eat?"

"Can you walk?"

"Should we let you sleep?"

"I'm fine," said Marika. "Please, I'm fine."

Claire had dressed her in a nightgown and tucked the sheet around her. Newborn from grief, she sat up and smiled gently at the Americans looking at her. From this moment, her work began. "What a night," she said. "I'm so sorry, Claire."

"Don't you dare apologize! Hungry?"

"Starving."

"Good. It's a good sign," Claire said. Marika laughed. "What's so funny?"

"You sound like my mother."

"Well, that's exactly what I'm going to be. Now let's shoo these children out of here and talk."

"No!" Marika almost cried out. The night past had been her first and last collusion with Claire. "I mean, I think I should eat something, mostly. I'll dress and come downstairs. All right?"

They all nodded and smiled, approving of her, of Richard's widow, back in the bosom of the family. When they had gone, Claire shutting the door behind them, Marika stood up from the bed and almost collapsed to the floor—her knees would not support her. She grasped the nightstand.

*—Richard, tell me what you want me to do.*

*—Hey, Big Bird. You've never scared easy.*

*—I've never had to take action.*

*—The first time I drove into the bush, Marika, I pulled over at the first sign of an army headlight and just sat there, shaking. My hand wouldn't move to turn the ignition back on. You get over it.*

He was smiling wryly at her. She picked herself up and dressed. Downstairs, the others would be waiting for her. They would take her to McGrath, and McGrath to the layout of the dam. Somehow she would find Amet, and Florence, and Ngebin, the ones who counted. Her work was cut out for her; but it was Richard who had cut it out, dead as he was, and dust.

Claire and Curtis led her to McGrath that night. In the A-frame theater built by Pioneer Aluminum on the flats next to what was left of the Parambo River below its fall from the dam, the concert series at Revenir University was opening its first season, underwritten by Pioneer. Mayume's dream of an orchestra had come true.

From the causeway, they drove past slipshod houses, built for the Lethe when they first descended on the city from their flooded farms, to the grassy campus of the university. The amber lights of the hall glowed through the steady rain as they approached, three hours before curfew. Inside, folding chairs were set up on the concrete floor, facing the small stage, and behind it a triangular window looked over the river, swollen with monsoon.

Fewer than a hundred had come to listen. Marika took short, fragile steps as she entered behind Claire and spotted first Mayume in the front row in an armchair, then the few professors she and Richard had known, dressed in their carefully tailored suits, their hair cropped close. Six months earlier, she would have faced them all with equanimity, amusement, even pride at this little orchestra she had nurtured. Now she loved Richard and had lost him, and that loss left her as naked as a bush woman who in a fit of amnesia might have stumbled into this cultured gathering.

Biswandi was not there. But of course not. He had his squads to maneuver before dark fell.

"Come *on*, Marika," Claire hissed, reaching back and taking her arm. "You're white as a sheet, they'll think we poisoned you. Yoo-hoo! Bud!" she called out. "Look who we dragged in from the rain!"

"Well, I'll be buggered," said McGrath, rising from his chair. His face was rounder and ruddier than Marika remembered, the neck fleshy above the open collar of his short-sleeved khaki shirt. He hitched his pants up before he took her hand and pumped it, smiling from one side of his mouth like a cigar smoker. Hot and sticky with some kind of lotion, his hand grappled hers. "Thought we'd sent you back to the Waldorf Astoria," he said, stressing the *r*'s.

"I thought it was time I visited," Marika answered, her voice as thin as skimmed milk, "all my good friends."

"Well, that's exactly right, isn't it?" McGrath said. He stretched the left side of his mouth farther. "Isn't that right. Sit, now. Sit!" He patted the folding chair next to his, and Marika sat. In front of them, the performers had begun to set up onstage. Almost all Marika's former pupils, they held and warmed up their instruments with a dexterity that astonished her. Most were Sacatra, young men and women she had known as adolescents, their names a blur of French and English nomenclature, their faces like strangers in a dream, the features familiar but interchangeable. Those with parents in the government had gone to Paris or London until the university was built, and then they had returned. Their tall, pockmarked white conductor, Marika knew, had arrived last year to carry through Mayume's dream, but she had spoken to him twice at most. Her job had been with children, not with the president's grand plan.

The players seemed not to notice their meager audience. In their somber black, so far removed from the bright *dashiki* and *kanga* that marked most formal occasions, they went about their preparations like actors in a play. "This is a goodwill gesture," McGrath said, leaning toward Marika and lowering his voice as far as he was able. He motioned toward President Mayume.

"How so?"

"Well, you might have heard about those *assholes*—do you mind strong language?"

"Not a bit." Smile *charmingly*, Marika told herself, and did.

"Good, I like a woman who can cuss. Those young do-gooder pricks who are now sitting in the box at the harbor were enrolled at this institution, here. They were supported by American dollars in a country supported by those same dollars, which they wanted to blow up, and now old Mayume's saying he doesn't blame the dollar-providers. Which is not to say he had any choice, but it does make it easier."

"You mean to turn the students over."

"Egg-zactly. One of them was supposed to play at this affair, here. They got that nigger boy on the left to take his place."

Marika looked up to see which was the nigger. Poised at the end of the row of violins, his short feet barely touching the ground, sat Constantin Mayume, the president's sad, gifted son. His skin was a scant shade lighter than the small tuxedo into which his limbs were thrust like sausages. The program listed Bach's Fifth Brandenburg, with Constantin on the violin. Smiling, Marika lifted her hand, and the boy gave a short, dignified nod of recognition. Remembering what he had said about going away to school, she made a wish that the time would come soon, that he might rise out of his homeland as he would from this ragtag orchestra.

They finally joined to an A. "Time for my nap," McGrath said, folding his arms across his barrel chest.

"You're not fond of music, Bud?" Marika forced herself to use his name.

"I believe I recall telling you," he answered, his eyes shut, "that I was not an appreciator of the arts in any form. Now your painter friend—what's his name, Killjoy?—might get inspiration from this stuff. Me, I get hemmorhoids."

The first half of the program was the overture to *Carmen*, played at halting tempo, violins sawing away with what appeared desperation and castanets a half-beat late. Marika stole side glances at the others in their company; they all wore bright, patient smiles, and Suzanne nodded slightly in time with the music, like a teacher.

Had Richard been there, his face would have settled into an earnest study, but his mind would have flown miles from the concert hall, above the dam with the *dai*. Marika tried to follow him, to the back hills where the monsoon now was swelling the huge lake, the noxious water hyacinth forming gases that rose from the clotted surface and spread over the waterlogged land; where Ngebin and his cadres hid among the local population whose daily industry had gone from fishing to cattle farming for the beef they could not afford to eat but would sell to the Revenir export market. Richard's mind would have been swirling among multiple causes and effects, all of them traceable to the dam and thus to Pioneer, finally to the United States and to him as its representative. He would have glanced up to see Mayume seated in front of him and would have added that to the churning mix: the expediency of a frightened and frightening government, the awful need that had created Mayume and Biswandi both.

But Marika knew only the bare facts of these things and could follow only as far as the image of Richard himself. As the ragged orchestra launched into the second theme, she pictured herself seated across from him in the wicker chairs in the lesson room, overlooking the harbor at a time when the city stayed lit at night. Many nights in the first few years they had lingered there, and now, as if he had remained in the wicker chair, balancing his brandy on his knee, she traveled back to frame questions for him, questions he would never answer. *—Did you think I would ever catch on to your tricks?* No, that was too mocking.*—I think,* she began again, *underneath you must have known I would love you like this. Because otherwise why would you have married me? And did you think of me as you bumped up* *those roads to meet Ngebin? Or did you leave me behind like that, like a wife, while you went on to your higher calling, your passion for these people?*

The orchestra paused and retuned. *—Because, Richard*, she finished, framing her warning carefully, *I am not one of your saints. I can't carry it through unless you're there.*

"Hsst!" she heard at her side. It was McGrath, his mouth cupped to her ear. "You can't fool me. This stuff bores the shit out of you, too."

"They just need practice," she whispered back.

"Yeah, like a dog needs practice to become a cat. How long you figure till intermission?"

"I'd say ten minutes."

"Let's you and I stroll on out of here while they're all milling around. Hm? Dredge up the past."

*You and I,* Marika could have said, *have no past;* but instead she nodded noncommittally and motioned him to hush while the overture struggled to its close. The privileged audience, no different from colonials proud of having "raised up" the natives, clapped with a strained heartiness as the piece ended, the last notes a surprisingly lyric flourish from the harpist, a non-Sacatra whom Marika recognized suddenly as the daughter of Florence 'wa Mthongo. The girl looked taller and stiff in her starched black dress and refused to smile as the pimply conductor made her stand alone.

"Excuse me a moment," Marika said to McGrath, and slipped down the aisle to the stage as the audience rose and mingled, scraping the metal legs of their chairs on the rough concrete. "I don't know your name," she began, touching the girl's wide sleeve.

Florence's daughter turned. "Olanda," she replied without expression, but then she recognized Marika. "Why, Missis!" she cried out.

"No time to talk, Olanda. Are you in touch with your mother?"

"Why yes, of course."

"You must tell her that I'm here. She must pass the news to Amet. You know Amet?"

"I am not so sure." Olanda bent her head away, mistrustful.

"I—I sent a telegram to him. I have to know if he received it." Olanda only looked at her. "I told him how I was enjoying my trip. I said I'd sprained my ankle."

"Bandele."

"Yes!" Marika clapped her hands despite herself. She almost detected a smile across the girl's lovely impassive face. "Well, you just pass the message to Florence, then," she said, a little calmer. "Tell her—I don't know what to tell her. They must find me. I can't venture out."

"I am understanding you, Missis," Olanda said, her flat expression restored. "*B'nago b'maradi.*"

"I'm counting on you, Olanda."

"*B'nago.*"

The girl was right to send her away; no other visitors were talking to the players. They had all moved away toward the open porch at the far end of the hall.

"How *perfect* to hear a live concert, don't you think?" Claire was saying as Marika joined them.

" 's all right," Lisbeth countered, shaking back her black halo of hair as she lit a cigarette, "but I wish they'd let them play their own music."

"What do you mean, 'their own'?" Tom asked.

"Tribal music. You know. Drums, native instruments. They're not eighteenth-century Europeans, this isn't natural for them."

"Well, let's just throw all the old stuff out, then, why don't we, and start from scratch with sticks?"

McGrath, standing back from the others, raised his eyebrows significantly at Marika. "Let us vamoose," he said in a low voice.

"Why, are you two playing hooky?" said Claire.

"Bud and I," Marika answered, keeping her voice even, deliberately using his name, "thought we'd take a stroll. I'll be back before the concert's over."

"Better be," said Curtis. "Curfew."

"Oh, you old dog," Claire countered. "Bud can always get an escort. We'll see you whenever, then, darling!" She winked as the lights overhead flickered and the sparse audience drifted back into the hall.

Turning to McGrath, Marika felt Richard's silent presence, lending strength to her limbs and voice. "Rain's stopped."

"Got to take a break, doesn't it? They tell me this goes on for another month. Shit, I'll have snails crawling into my socks by then."

"Must keep you busy up at the dam."

"Sluices are going day and night. It's a wonderful thing, this power. You know. Just plain old elemental power." The others had gone in. McGrath looked away from the city, toward the steamy hills from which they heard the constant crash of falling water. "I stand there behind the Afro working the pressure gauges, and I watch that little red light glow, so fierce you can hardly stand it. Two million kilowatts an hour. We get that just from plugging up a river."

"You get a lot else, too." It slipped out, and McGrath looked at her skeptically. They had walked over the stone pathway to the marsh built up around the depleted yet swollen river, where the loamy smell of thallus filled the air. Circling over their heads, invisible, fruit bats tinkled like bells.

"I've been told that's how Hooper used to think," McGrath said.

"What do you mean?" Realizing her error, Marika remembered Amet's claim: *That one knew.*

"Well, your husband, rest his soul, had some—different ideas—about what we're doing in this country."

"Richard took his work very seriously. But we didn't talk much about it. I never could follow politics, could you? Always such a mess. I just serve the hors d'oeuvres and make small talk and hope they resolve their differences without throwing daggers." Her speech accelerating, she put on what she hoped was a flirtatious smile and felt the muscles of her neck jump underneath. From the second McGrath had mentioned Richard, she had forced down a breath-stopping wave of anguish with its unutterable cry: *He is gone.* She let her foot sink into the ground, like an anchor.

But he seemed pleased, his spongy face soaking up all her attempt at charm. "I seem to recall those hors d'oeuvres," he said, edging closer. "Haven't had eggplant so good since I set foot on this continent. Not bringing up bad memories, am I?"

"No, no. That is, I've—I've gained some distance." Her knees were jelly; she had to walk. Moving around him, she started slowly back up toward the A-shaped hall. From inside came the strains of the Brandenburg, Constantin Mayume's violin quivering above the rest.

"Because I have done a great deal of thinking since that night. A great deal. They say it's being close to death that does it to you."

"Does what, Bud?" It was better now, her legs moving. She had a mission; she wanted to hear her pupil.

"Makes you value a couple things. You know, I lay in that crummy little hospital here and I thought, 'Why him and not me?' Here he was, such a great guy, and he had you crying over him and all. And I don't mind telling you, I was in trouble when I came over here before. My job was about on the line, my ex was after me for alimony, and I couldn't even buy toothpaste with my credit card."

*So*, Marika finished for him, *you became Richard's Judas*. Her pace quickened, then slowed; she relinquished Constantin. Hatred calmed her. She could have slipped the shining, razor-thin tip of a knife through McGrath's khaki shirt and the soft, barely resistant flesh underneath and watched the blood come without so much as a gasp. "It was just luck," she said.

"Well, it changed my life. This country here, I never heard of it before, and I tell you I plan to put it on the map. Afros or no Afros"—he glanced sharply at her, suspecting her sympathies—"the next Eiffel Tower, the next Empire State will come out of here. We're going to work that dam like Babe the Ox till she quits on us. Only she won't quit. And what's more—can you keep a secret, Marika?" It was the first time he had used her name; he pronounced it like *America* without the A. She nodded. "We have got diamonds tucked away in the far north hills. There's a guy who's done some tests there. He showed me, and I believe him. Just have to convince management, and we are sparkling."

"Where in the north? They've had rumors before."

"Not at this spot, they haven't. Right by the mouth of the river, that little valley up there where they do nothing now but grow yams. We'd have to do a little dynamiting, but underneath I swear there's a treasure chest. But I want to move quietly. Buy up the land, get a license from the government, make sure we've got an American passport for the proceeds, if you understand me. Shit, I'm boring you. You don't even know where I mean."

"Oh, yes, I've been in that valley." The trip she had taken with Richard—the open tent with mosquito netting by the purling river. In the cool morning, eating the bean mash they called *futu* with her hands, clear water washing it down. The trees thick with birds—she jumped when they squawked, and the village people laughed.

"With him?"

"With Richard, of course. He was my husband."

"Awful for you, huh?"

He shook his head and tentatively grazed her bare shoulder with the short fingers of his hand. "I'd rather not talk about it," she said, her voice slightly hoarse. The skin of her shoulder crawled away. How dare he speak. How dare he touch.

"I'd like to do what I can to help. As a friend. A special friend. We were blood brothers, you might say. No, don't look like that, you're right. Army buddies is what I mean, we went through it together and I happened to be the one who came out. I'd like to think he'd want me to take care of you." He leered. Some unintelligible, grateful response must have come out of Marika's mouth, for he went on.

"Know what Hooper said to me that day? He said some people just blossomed here, and you were one of those people. I think you oughta stick around awhile, maybe we can get you to bloom again."

Behind them, the polite riffle of applause rose and fell. Constantin's debut. "Maybe I will, Bud," she said, wanting in spite of what she knew to believe him. "Maybe I'll really boom."

*Boom.* She had meant to say bloom, but she had formed the word in her mind and it had changed. Bloom, boom—not a flower, but the crash of the Parambo Dam.

# Chapter 15

"I'm telling you," Claire said three days later, "I have come to know Bud McGrath, and he doesn't fool around. He is very interested in you, and I don't see why you'd want to pass up the opportunity."

"Because I didn't come to Yumana to find a husband, Claire, that's why."

"I know, darling, you're still abject about Richard, and I don't blame you. Everyone knew how happy you two were together." Claire's eyes glinted, as if the other night had joined her and Marika in a secret joke. At his name, Marika's heart plummeted into her stomach, and she held her breath. "But you have to find consolation somewhere."

"Well, he's a nice man," Marika answered, expelling her breath with a sigh, "and I appreciate his attention."

"We do—*crave* attention, don't we?" Claire leaned across the bar in the Lovells' den and blinked her large eyes at Marika. She wanted to spill her secret about Mayume, Marika could tell.

*What does that woman do all day?* Richard had asked one night when they had finally shut the door on the Lovells.

*I don't know. What do I do all day?*

*You teach music. You talk to unwed mothers at the hospital. You stand on the bridge and sing. You get frustrated at having nothing to do. That woman*—he had motioned toward the door as if tipping his hat to Claire—*is incapable of teaching, talk, song, or frustration.*

—*You hush,* Marika said to him, now. —*She was there for me, the other night.*

"What's up, Claire?" she said aloud, tasting the margarita Claire had made. The heat of the monsoon had reached its worst, at the point where the rains began to abate but the air still hung as heavy as overripe fruit, waiting for the harmattan, almost a month away.

"Oh, nothing!"

"Come on. Curtis isn't acting like an infatuated sophomore, but you are."

"Am I?" Claire came around the bar and climbed onto the stool next to Marika. "Does it show? Can you tell?"

"*I* can, but I'm sure Curtis just thinks you've found a new hobby."

"Well, I have."

"What's his name?"

"Amoz," Claire whispered with awe. "Amoz Mayume. The *president.*"

"No!" Marika let her mouth hang open and her eyes go wide in feigned disbelief. "You can't mean it! How did you—"

Claire sat back on the stool and sipped at her drink, pleased with the effect she had created. "It happened at one of those ghastly dedications," she began, and went on to outline her careful campaign for Yumana's president's bed. "Amoz," she said, tracing a circle in the light dust of the smooth wooden bartop, "is a much more *sensitive* man than the people around him think. He was never a military type;

he trained at Sandhurst because he saw it was the only way to help his people. He's intimidated by whites."

"Really."

"Well, who can blame him? We come in here and work technical *marvels* in his country, and he's got to take the blame for all the savagery going on around us. He's very sweet, really." Claire ducked her head, and for a moment, with her thin hair gracing the nape of her long neck and her eyes half-lidded, she looked almost shy. "He's my first black man."

"You shouldn't be telling me this, Claire."

"But I want to. I can't talk to anybody else here. His skin was warmer than Curtis's, you know. I had thought it would be. And he didn't—fuss around, the way our men do. You know, 'Did you like that, how does this feel?' He just shut the door and told me to undress, and then—he took me."

She finished the rest of her drink in one swallow, and with it her beauty fled and left her looking pale and wretched. "I don't know what to tell you," Marika said finally. This wasn't the truth she had come to Yumana to learn. Her cheeks flushed with embarrassment, not for Claire's story but for the desperate telling of it.

"You wouldn't tell Curtis, would you?"

"Christ, no."

"It's been going on for almost a month now. We don't make dates or anything like that. We'll just be at one function or another, and suddenly he'll find a way to slip away and get me to follow him. There's always a room waiting somewhere, and even if it doesn't lock, no one ever comes in. I think his guards know. Anyway, it never takes long. He strips me and—and—"

"Fucks you."

"Yes. That's what he does." Claire tipped the dry glass

to her mouth. "You can't call it making love. He's violent, sometimes, actually. But I find it terribly exciting. Those quickies, you know?" She put down the glass and began to laugh, giggling at first and then louder, and not knowing what else to do, Marika laughed with her until she saw that Claire was crying, her arm shaking as she tried to pour herself another drink.

"Oh, honey," Marika said, and folded the sharp-boned Claire in her arms.

"I—can't just—give him up. Not yet. He doesn't even *talk* to me, but he—he—he makes me feel like a woman. He does! Like one of those naked women you see in the bush, that our men are always drooling over. I wanted it to be—like that."

"Maybe it is," Marika said, gently patting and rubbing her back. "Maybe it is."

"No, it's not." Claire sniffed and, regaining her dignity, pushed Marika away. "Because I'm a rich American wife with a fat white husband. What would he want with me?"

"What does Yumana want with us?" Marika answered. But Claire, pouring herself a refill, had tuned her out.

The day before, Marika had seen Florence. Behind the plaster-mended corrugated metal labyrinth of shacks in the Lethe quarter behind the market, under the wide lean-to where one woman guarded her five precarious washer-dryers and the rest lined up to do the week's wash, with the rain like a gray sheet over the side of the lean-to, they had met and embraced. Olanda had sent the message to Marika by way of the Lovells' old gardener, his face wrinkling like a prune as he handed her the white paper, and Marika had used the easy, though risky, lie of having lunch with Lisbeth.

Florence was in hiding. Sitting heavily in the webbed

plastic deck chair in the far corner of the lean-to, away from the gush and rumble of the washers, she told Marika they had revoked her license to sell yams in the market. A short time after that, she had begun noticing one of Biswandi's small jeeps parked across the road from her flat, waiting for Biswandi to give the signal to take her out. And so, late at night and risking the curfew, she had packed what she needed and slipped across town, running like a rat from doorway to shadowed doorway, while Olanda went to live with Kikuyu cousins and enrolled at the university under a new name.

"Na, and they know I'm here now," Florence explained. "Olanda is maybe lost to them, she is light-skinned and blends in at the school. But me, so long as I'm not coming out, they figure it so, that I set an example for the people. That I have lost my freedom to sell—na, to *live*, because I am connected with the *dai*."

"Did Amet get my telegram?"

Florence smiled slyly, her cheeks round as plums. "He's saying he doesn't know you'll help. I'm putting it to him, na, she'll be fine, she's needing a little time. It's just now you're finding out this thing or two about your man, isn't that so, now?"

Marika looked at her straight. "You never told me what Richard was ready to do. For you, for your people."

"Is she a baby, then, that her mammy shows her what the signs mean? Na, Missis, you knew what you wanted."

"Why'd you tell Amet I'd do this, then?"

"Because, so it is, Missis" —Florence leaned close, her eyes puffy and bloodshot from little sleep—"that the world calls us"—she motioned to the wall of rain as if it were a voice heralding—"past what it is we want. You will meet Ngebin now. He is a man who wants no violence, is not wanting to speak of violence, is like a deaf-mute when they come to him with their guns and their bloody talk. But yet he will be doing violence, this one. It is outside himself. He must bring himself to it."

"But I'll never understand why he doesn't stage a revolt. Surely he'd get the support of the people. He might not even have to draw blood to do it. It's happened in other African countries. Why does he need me?"

"In other countries, too," Florence said, giving a light sigh, "there is the coup and there is then the army ruling. Na, the *dai* are not the army. And once he"—she jerked her head in the direction of the southern hills, toward Ngebin— "is sitting in the palace, why then you don't think your businessmen of your country are coming to him with talk of money and deals? Or if he will not open the door to them, there are assassins quick to work for the white man and take him down. It is not the head we must topple, Missis. Like the insect, our government can grow new heads. It is the arms, the legs, the muscle. So we are needing you."

"I guess the muscle," Marika said, brushing from her skirt the lint that blew out of the dryers, "is the dam."

"That is part, yes. So then," Florence sat forward, her voice taking on the edge of strategy-making, "you can get us these plans, you think?"

"I think, yes. He"—she could not bring herself to say "McGrath"—"is attracted to me. He wants to take me on a tour. I imagine I can show interest in the architecture or something and get him to lend me documents."

"Do not expect it to be easy. Do not push his resistance, eh? We can take what we need from you in pieces and assemble them far from Revenir. You are understanding me?"

"I'm understanding you, Florence." Marika felt herself suddenly white in the midst of the dark-skinned, Lethe-chattering women carrying bundles and folding clothes around her. It was rare, to feel white in Yumana—one blended in, the struggle was black against black. But Florence wanted to make use of her, wanted her to accomplish a mission that only a white woman could accomplish. Florence had no time to speak of Richard—he had been killed, as her own man had been killed—or to hear how Richard's neglected spirit had risen like a phoenix and come to dwell in Marika's heart. Florence was on one side of the wall, Marika serviceably on the other.

*Politics*, Marika found herself thinking, *means living with walls*. Or maybe it had been Richard's thought, lying in wait for her. She seemed to live with his thoughts.

"We must all move very quickly," Florence was saying. "This month ends the monsoon. By harmattan, we must know the plans, we must begin alerting the people who live now in the river's path. This is the short harmattan, the summer. We must be moving before it ends and we lose control of the Parambo in the rains. Na, more. Mayume is taking a trip, so we hear, in the late summer months."

"Where?"

"Some are saying Hong Kong, others Pretoria." Florence spat. "He has investments, his palm wiping itself off far from Yumana. But we must be knowing when he goes, we must have advance notice. We are not wanting—na, *Ngebin* is not wanting—to destroy him. This is another bit for you to dig up, so. The time and destination."

"Haven't you got spies in the palace? Why do you need me?"

"This man, this Mayume," Florence said, shaking her finger, "he is scared already for his life. He comes out, yes, he goes to concerts, but he speaks only with a small circle, the rest being rumors. But such is not the material thing.

If we are to destroy him, *he*"—again the short jerk of the head toward the hills—"must bring himself to it. The main thing is being this dam, now. It is, how do you call it, that small nugget of metal holding the wheel—"

"The linchpin," Marika said.

Florence winked and nodded. "Na, the linchpin. We pull it, you know, and the wheel that is Yumana, she rolls. You will be here, Missis. You will see."

So it was that Marika had left her, smiling through the steam, while Marika's own purposes seemed to swirl like the miniature eddies that ran along the mud-slogged streets.

*—Tell me how it was, Richard. The days we spent by the source of the river.*

*—Shall I tell you the thing I remember most? It was the sheen on your legs as you rolled your shorts up to your hips, as high as the other women tucked their* kanga, *and you went in with them after trout. The water eddied around your thighs, and I could see the fish gliding by, like silver arrowheads. I thought how your thigh must feel to them, naked and smooth in the water. I sat like a lug with the other men on the bank, drinking palm wine, and we were all watching the women's legs, though none of us talked about it. It wasn't the nakedness of them, you know—no one was exactly modest with their clothes. It was the water, licking at those smooth stalks.*

*—I remember that water. So cold it numbed us.*

*—You kept looking back at me. Like a girl, seeking approval! I told the men I was sitting with that I called you Big Bird, and they all laughed. They loved it. One said you were a flamingo, another a swan, another a white crane that had magic powers.*

*—I never knew. I couldn't guess what you were laughing at.* He had thrown his head back and finally fallen

backward, the others with him, all of them drunk on palm wine. The women with Marika had pointed and called Richard "the spidery one," not the white one, there was not then the wall that Marika had felt the other day with Florence.

*—But there was a wall between us two. Something in being happy with you frightened me.*

*—Whereas I never took hold of you. You came out of the river that day, and I touched my hand to your chilled calf, but I wanted to sink my face into the cool of your thigh, and I did not. It was not the others that stopped me, nor the palm wine. It was myself already bluffing you. Getting you ready for my orchid days. By the time they came, you were already lost to me.*

Bud McGrath lost little time. Coached by Claire and perhaps by the girls at the embassy as well, he was quick to follow the reasoning that Marika had spelled out before she left Yumana: Once a foreign service wife, always a foreign service wife. Like doctors', generals', politicians' wives. Whether the foreign service was government or industry made little difference. Marika's mourning period was clearly due to end, but her vocation must go on. And he, McGrath, was up to the challenge.

"People your age don't just hop into bed, do they?" Lisbeth asked when they did have lunch, several days after Marika had seen Florence.

"As opposed to people your age?"

"You might say." She shrugged, her face small and piquant under the growing globe of black hair. "I think the curiosity level drops. It's happening to me already. I used to wonder who'd make the first move, what the man would do if I wanted to hold off. Now it's like, you touch me here, I touch you there, and *pow*."

"You meet many men here?"

"They pass through." Lisbeth smiled artfully. "And they're generally on the look. Like Bud McGrath."

"With whom, if that's what you're attempting to find out, I have not jumped into bed."

"I'm not prying," Lisbeth protested. "But admit, you are attracted to him."

Oh, the temptation to speak truth. It called like a siren. But Marika held herself in, curled her lips upward, looked shy. "I'm just beginning to look at men again," she said, adding after a pause, "and he is kind."

Her words would travel from mouth to mouth as an overland package passes through trafficking hands, back to McGrath. They would give him confidence. Already he had told her his history, over a row of drinks at the bar in the embassy building, where he knew a dozen or more Americans would see them together. "Would you believe me if I told you," he had asked, signaling the Nebo waiter for another round, "that up to the age of twenty-five I never set foot outside Denver, Colorado?"

"If you told me, I guess I'd have to believe you."

"Well, it's not exactly true. My dad used to take us deer hunting up in the mountains. But for the most part—for the *most* part, I was content to keep the other places of the world where they belonged, in those pastel blobs on the atlas, and let my territory be Denver."

"What changed your mind?"

"My first wife. And getting fired from my job. Oh, you don't have to wonder what for," he said, winking at her. "I got caught with my hand in the till. Insurance, you know. Everybody does it; some get caught. They didn't press any charges, but my name was pure mud, and my wife had some cousin with a steel company in Detroit that was hiring what they called management trainees. I tried that awhile. Trained monkeys was what they were. So when she left me I thought at first I'd head on back to Denver, but just then Pioneer came recruiting, looking for inspectors for their foreign plants. They talked exotic places, Samoa, crap like that, you didn't have to know languages, and I signed on. Felt like an army recruit."

"The pay's better," Marika said pleasantly, letting herself sink, like waterlogged timber, to the level where McGrath lived.

"Also the companionship." He raised his glass in a toast. "And hell, since then I've been everywhere—Turkey, Brazil, you name it. Never thought I'd end up in a nigger hotbed like this, though. Do you realize"—he leaned close, and she could smell the bourbon on his breath—"that before Pioneer took an interest in this country, they had had a new government every two years since independence?"

"And only one of those governments was elected. And that was probably fixed."

"Well, hell, I'd hate to see what these people'd do if you let them *vote* for their leaders! All they understand is a big stick! Really, Marika, you should see them, up at the plant. Now, I've been to a lot of weird countries, but the way they just herd in, like cattle, and wait till some strapping black foreman burbles at 'em and makes them kick ass!"

"That's typical colonized behavior," she said, unable to resist countering him even as she saw her opening to get into the Parambo Dam. "Whichever way you move, the boss man's got you under his thumb. So why move at all?"

"But they're not *colonized* anymore, damn it! It's each *other* they're warring against now. You let them vote, they'll probably pick their great-uncle ancestor, every one of 'em."

She saw her chance slipping by. "They seem to get a lot accomplished at the plant, even if they are lazy."

"That they do."

"Richard said it was a magnificent feat of engineering up there, too." Sighing, she looked away, only half-feigning nostalgia. "He kept promising to get the fellow who was here before you to give me a tour, but it never came off."

"You think"—he put down his drink and, moving forward in his small seat, brushed his knee against hers—"you think if you went up there now it'd bring back—"

"Memories? How could it? We never got to see the plant together, I just told you."

"Do me a favor then, Marika." He still pronounced it like *America*. "Let me take you around." The knee came to rest and did not move.

"Sure, if you don't mind—"

"Nothing would give me greater pleasure. In fact, nothing *has* given me pleasure since I got to this shithole. I won't take you into the bowels of the place, they stink like a zoo. We'll just make a pass around the dam and take a glance at the shiny stuff."

"Oh, but I want to see everything, Bud," said Marika, opening her mouth slightly as she smiled.

The next day she thanked the gods of the Lethe for a steady downpour that made a ready excuse, and the day after she had the date with Lisbeth. When the third day dawned cloudy and dripping humidity but with no rain, she made herself ready for McGrath to call and invite her to tour the dam. But then a message came from Amet by way of Florence, who again sent word through the Lovells' gardener: Ngebin was ready to see her.

"I've just got widow's blues," she told Claire when McGrath called. "Why don't you go up, instead? You'd enjoy it."

"Don't be absurd. He wants you up there. In any case, Curtis has got me meeting this truly awful couple for lunch and showing them the harbor. Cocoa people, British, I hate them."

Marika thought of cocoa people and could see only the dusky stream of returning Yumanans she had joined at Kennedy airport. "Well, you go on into town and try to have a good time. I'm giving Bud a raincheck."

"That's a laugh. Today's the only reprieve from rain we've *had*."

"And I might take a walk later."

"That is not apt to cheer you up, darling, given the state of things you'll pass on your walk. And you could run into trouble; there are a lot more trouble spots in the city since you left."

"I thought I'd wander down to the market. I like the bustle."

"The market is exactly one of those spots. Don't go near it. Amoz tells me"—she could not resist the creasing of a dimple—"they're cracking down on some of the market women. You know, those old blacks sows who hoard their tins. And *he* says they've had violence. I don't know, it's not in the papers, *naturellement*, and I just send the girl."

"I'll poke around the garden, then. Don't worry about me, Claire. I need some time alone."

"All right. Just don't mope."

"I won't."

"Promise me."

"I promise." Marika bent her head, like an ingenue, half expecting Claire to pat it. Instead, Claire swept out of the room, leaving Marika to gather a few of Richard's papers and slip into the kitchen. There she handed the gardener a return note to run back to Florence.

By noon, following the course taken by her messenger, Marika had arrived at the labyrinthine compound where Florence lived in hiding. As soon as she rounded the corner of the entranceway, as if by a signal, a small van appeared to her left while Florence exited a doorway from her right and motioned her quickly to follow.

Marika had dressed in faded khakis, sandals, dark glasses; few of her acquaintances would have recognized her taking the circuitous route she had chosen down to the quarter. Still, as she followed Florence to the back of the van, there appeared a further disguise, a small mound of white cloth and a twisted rope to tie a headdress, as well as a jar of dark cocoa butter.

"You shall be Nebo," Florence explained, pulling Marika close to her as the van jerked and started down the road that led to the western hills. "You hold your head so"—she tipped Marika's chin downward as she began wrapping the white robe over Marika's now-bare shoulders—"and you drop your eyes as you speak. You don't speak much."

"Are we going to be stopped?"

"Man never knows," called one of the two in front. Marika glanced up at his profile, round and smooth—not unlike the face of Paul Ophalete, the young man she had met on the plane flying away from Yumana. "We got American money handy. The dog watching the road, he likes the taste of it, hey?"

They all laughed. Florence was streaking the butter over Marika's upper cheekbones and eyelids, turning them a light walnut shade. The rest of her body was sheathed in white cotton, the turban tied low on her forehead and masking her auburn hair.

"What about you?" Marika asked as they wheeled around the circle by the market. "Won't they recognize you, if they stop us?"

"I am a sack of yams," said Florence. "You sit on me. One can hide, no more. They know when the cargo, it is heavier than it ought be."

"How far are we going?"

"Not so far. Two hours," said the other sitting in front, a short, musclebound bushman, his face wrinkled like a dry fig.

"I wish you could've given me more warning," Marika reproached Florence. "There are only so many places I can logically go off to. They'll send someone out to find me by cocktail hour."

"It is not always possible to know," said Florence, showing no sympathy. "Who will there be, na, sending someone?"

"The Lovells. And McGrath, probably."

"McGrath. He has taken you through the plant?"

"Well, no," Marika admitted, slipping off her shorts under the tent of white cotton. Florence handed her a small pocket mirror, and she studied her face. Under her darkened lids, her eyes shone bright hazel. She did not look Nebo, but she no longer looked white, either. She rubbed the last of the cocoa butter over her hands and neck. "I would have gone with him today, but your message came—"

"You are here now almost one week," said Florence. "We must move more quickly."

"Look, I have to get oriented, make sure my old friends accept me—"

"These are not your friends. They were not your man's friends, hey?"

"How do you know?"

"Who turns him over to Biswandi?"

"I don't know!" Marika pushed herself back to a seated position, straightening her turban, as the jeep recovered from a pothole that had thrown her against the canvas side. Suddenly angry, she glared at Florence.

"The man we send you after, that is who. We give you your vengeance, Missis. But you must be exacting it."

"Maybe McGrath did set Richard up. Obviously I've believed you, otherwise I wouldn't be here. But you *people*"—her eyes swept around, taking in Florence and both men in front—"are not giving me anything. You need me so you can win out in a—a—tribal conflict, that has nothing to do with what I want. Richard thought you were right. Richard gave his life for Ngebin. So I"—the jeep bounced over a large rock, and one of the men in front shouted something, cutting her off. "I am helping you for now," she went on. "And if I'm not so good at it, well, you'll just have to make do."

"Get her under!" the guerrilla in front was shouting. "Quick! Quick! Trucks ahead!"

Florence threw Marika a look of pity and accusation that penetrated to her marrow. Then she bent down and quickly scuttled herself in the huge sack of yams. "Sit! Sit!" the muscled passenger whispered to Marika. She moved herself over in the back and sat gingerly on the sack, her legs under the flowing robes straddling the mound that she knew to be Florence. Marika's cheeks had flushed with irritation, and as they approached the roadblock she pushed her mouth outward in a pout. Her heart hammered. They were approaching the enemy, *her* enemy so long as she sat in the dark van, she who had known no enemies in her life. For years, in tamer circumstances, whenever her mind clenched, whenever she needed a magic carpet to waft her away from what was brutal and sordid in this country, she had opened herself to Justin and he had borne her away. Now, as the van slowed and finally came to a stop, while she felt the warmth of Florence's skin travel through the sacking to her swathed white thighs, she tried to turn to Richard to perform the same trick. Shutting her eyes, she concentrated on his voice, on his hands tending orchids, on his sure, quiet presence. But she could not escape the steamy, blasting heat that suffocated them as the van stood halted or the staccato voices of the soldiers searching the vehicle ahead of them. "You're dead, damn you," she barely whispered to Richard as she hugged herself in her Nebo disguise, trying not to stain the pure white with the thick cocoa butter covering her hands.

They seemed to remain like that for an eternity, though in fact it was a matter of minutes before the tall Sacatra soldiers approached the van and asked the driver in English what he was carrying and for what destination. "Yams," the driver replied, "to be sold in market, but they are not letting this woman"—he jerked his head back towards Marika—"pawn her stuff. They say it's rotten. My cousin and me, we are for tapping a little palm wine, hey?" He winked at the soldiers. "But the *vendeuse*, it's her truck. So we load up, we drive. Is free trip, man!" The last was spoken low, as if he didn't want Marika to hear, and she saw him slip the first soldier a five-dollar bill.

The Sacatra turned to Marika. "Your name!" he shouted in Nebo.

"Ousmane," Marika answered, her voice thin. Ousmane was the path that led from the rainforest to the high plain of Mecca, and dozens of Nebo women bore its name.

"Can't sell your fruit, hey?"

"They're good yams," she replied, her eyes downcast, the Nebo words twisting her tongue. "I'm no market woman, I come down to sell and then I leave. I'll sell these in the village, you'll see. Pah! In the city they eat dirt, they forget the one God."

"And where is your husband, Nebo woman?" the other soldier asked, leaning through the side door into the van. Marika fisted her hands to hide the poorly stained palms. Nebo women, she knew, rarely did business without their husbands near at hand, following their version of Muslim law.

"He is dead," she said, meeting his eyes, willing hers to darken to the sable brown of Nebo irises.

"Let me see one of these rotten yams you cannot sell."

"Not rotten," she said, reaching under the sacking. Her hand touched Florence's, and in it was a large rough yam. "You see?" She held it out to the soldier, who took it.

"Not such a bad yam, na," he said in English, turning it over. "Thank you, Nebo woman!" He held the root up as a sort of flag, and without waiting to be told they could go, the driver started the engine and followed the line of cars around the roadblock.

"Hey, you are speaking Nebo goo-ood!" the passenger in front said when they were clear. Grinning wide, he turned to Marika.

"I'd have done better with a little warning," she answered, smiling despite herself from sheer relief.

"A little warning," said Florence, struggling out from the sack of yams, "is a precious thing. And the *dai*, they can afford nothing precious. I had remembered," she went on as she dusted herself off and squatted across from Marika, "how you are babbling with your languages in the hospital. So proud, you were. I thought, na, you would not forget your Nebo."

"Not entirely."

"So, you are wanting maybe to go back? To join your people? We will not be giving you anything, it is true."

"No," said Marika, pulling off the hot turban and fixing her eyes on the road. Now, the crisis past, Richard's spirit flooded her—the sense of him driving this road alone at night, his headlights licking at the tall grasses by the side. "I think I'll last awhile longer."

Florence nodded, shutting her eyes; she looked very tired. The men in front talked to each other in Lethe, but Marika tuned them out. They bumped and heaved over the roads, the two hours like a badly scarred dream, until they reached the end of the labyrinth: the camp of Ngebin, the leader of the *dai* and Richard's friend.

# Chapter 16

The one time that Marika had seen him, eight years ago, Ngebin had been living in exile in London and had worn the undernourished, dependent look of many African expatriates with whom Richard sometimes rendezvoused on his way to or from the States. They had met in a small pub near Victoria Station, and as the night wore on they had ordered plates of meat pies, pasties, fish cakes. Eating and drinking, Ngebin had regained his animation. He had debated with Richard until almost midnight, stopping now and then to break into a guffaw at Mayume's latest presumption or at Biswandi's idiocy as reported by Richard. In the corner seat, sipping her stout and nibbling a sausage roll, Marika had succumbed to the drowsy heat of the pub and had let the men's talk flow around her and enclose her in the safe, reassuring skeins of discussion. At that time, Ngebin had seemed to her less a revolutionary than a professor, down on his luck but sure to write a great book one day when he overcame his *Weltschmerz.* He had been about forty, then, and looked older, his short mat of hair receding from his narrow forehead and the features of his face set in tense, intractable lines.

The man who came to greet her in the light rain that ran off the broad canopy of rainforest under which the van came to rest seemed larger, stronger and younger, in spite of the time elapsed. "Welcome to the palace of *dai*," Ngebin said with a distinctly British accent as he helped Marika down from the back of the van. "I hope the journey was not too hard for you?"

He held Marika by the elbows, as one holds a child to see how much it has grown, and his eyes traveled over her face, still oily from the cocoa butter that she had tried to wipe off. His hands gripped her arms with a tensile firmness, and her legs steadied on the muddy ground.

"Not hard," she heard herself saying. "Shorter than one would think, considering."

"Oh, they could find me, if they wanted. There are many roads, and the right ones are triggered with landmines, but still they could root us out. That wouldn't look pretty in the foreign press, though, would it? They would rather draw us out and butcher us in self-defense." He smiled down at her, his teeth crooked and discolored, the only imbalance in his face. "Come," he said, leading her by the elbow, "we may have tea in my compound, where it is dry." His voice had the lilt and inflection of Cambridge, where according to Richard he had lived and studied for most of his ten years in exile. Like the others who gathered as they approached the round hut of the compound, he was shirtless, dressed in a pair of fatigue pants and rubber moccasins, but he held himself upright and supple, his dignity unimpaired. The others fluttered around him like dark attendant birds, and Marika recalled Richard saying, one night when he had returned from meeting Ngebin, years ago, "That man is never alone. He sleeps surrounded."

Squatting across from her on a low wooden stool, he

gravely passed her a plate with a large kola nut. Marika split the nut, a sign of respect and peace, and handed back the side nearest her heart. Then Ngebin rose.

"We shall talk in a moment about your task here," he said, pouring tea from a copper kettle that hung over a small fire in the center of the hut. "I know you haven't very much time. But first I must tell you. Richard Hooper was my closest ally, my greatest friend. And I daresay, in some rather complicated way, I was his. I mourned his death greatly."

"I received your card," Marika said. "Thank you."

"But you had your doubts, did you not?"

"I did. I still do."

"We knew you would. Richard knew, too. When he saw his protection slipping away, he said to me, 'They will pin it on the *dai*, and they will try to convince Marika of that. But,' he said, 'they will fail on both counts.' "

"Did he talk to you, ever, about me?"

"On occasion." Ngebin brought the tea over and sat down opposite her at the rude wooden table. Carrying the mugs seemed inappropriate for him, beneath his aura of dignity, but the others who had followed them into the room stood dumbly by the doors. "He expressed guilt."

"Guilt for what?"

"For bringing you here, far from the life of the mind that intrigued you. You were married, once, to an artist—"

"No," Marika interrupted. "Not married."

"No? In any case, Richard saw you were living in the past. He regretted taking you from your artist. He said he had robbed you. You had no interest in the people here, and you were incapable of frittering your time away with the silly wives of businessmen. Yet he would not give you up, he told me, and he would not give up Yumana's *dai*."

"He sounds like a man with a mistress," said Marika, thinking of Richard's orchids, his passion.

"Ah, but do you think"—Ngebin took a sip of his tea, his black eyes challenging her as he peeked over the rim—"that one is likely to find the man's wife helping to save his mistress's life? No, Marika Hooper, I think he was a man who did not fathom the full range of his wife's interests. *I* knew you would come to us. I knew you could live not in the past but for the future, as we do. And I know that Richard is watching us now, consorting together, and he is laughing at himself for his own blindness."

"I did—" Marika started to say "live in the past," but a small voice inside her kept her from confessing it. Ngebin wanted her to talk on, wanted to soften her. What she had heard and seen on the road kept her on her guard, even against an engaging freedom fighter. "I did wonder whose idea it was to bring me here."

"Not mine. Amet's."

At that moment a tall figure hobbled out of the shadows, and Marika recognized the young man who had sought her out in New York. Though he was too old to be her son, she felt a wave of protection toward him. He looked even thinner than when he had last taken leave of her, and his khaki pants hung, frayed, from his stump of a leg. And yet, for the first time since he had played his joke on Biswandi by dropping the concealed microphone into a pot of boiling water, he was smiling, and his youth won out over his scars. "I am so pleased," he said.

"Did you think I would come?" she asked him.

"No. The others, they hoped, but I thought not. I am glad to be wrong." Releasing one crutch, he clasped her hand, and all the words of resentment and denial that she had flung at Florence faded away.

"Now," Ngebin said, putting aside his mug of bitter tea, "we must make plans. You understand what we need from you, and why?"

"I think so."

"Let me explain a little ways farther. You know we seek freedom for our people and we seek the destruction of the Parambo Dam, all at once. There is a reason, you see—this took the longest time for Richard to understand—why the people in the city do not rise up on their own against Mayume and the death squads. The reason is that they actually fear the dam will be taken from them."

"Why should they fear that? It causes disease, it devastates the forest—"

"And it provides jobs. For the people of Revenir, and especially for the Lethe who forget quickly that they came out of a better life, it is the job that is sacred. If you bring down Mayume, the rumor goes, you frighten the United States with your uprising, and they take their dam and their jobs elsewhere. That your job pays you a starvation wage, that the fumes of the smelter fill your lungs with aluminum dust, none of this do you recognize. You are addicted to the Parambo Dam, morning to night. You are a job junkie, and you cannot free yourself."

"So if the *dai* destroy the dam, the people will hate them."

"Not so. If we destroy the dam, we destroy the reason for Mayume's government, and it falls of its own accord. Then, too, most Yumana people are not in Revenir. They gain nothing from the dam, but they have been too poor, too scattered to fight it. When the dam goes, they are at one with the people of the city, Lethe and Nebo and Sacatra alike."

"And the jobs? Your so-called junkies with families to support? What do they do?" Marika spoke not with rancor but with curiosity. Richard had talked this way with Ngebin, and Ngebin had given him answers.

"There is no lack of jobs," Ngebin said, shaking his

oblong head as if he, too, were reliving the evenings spent explaining to Ambassador Hooper. "Everywhere that has been neglected is replete with opportunity. The cocoa plantations, ceded to us by the British, threatened now by the siltation of the lake. The bauxite smelter in the north that Pioneer chooses to ignore. All we need do is improve the road to the harbor, and we have a rich mineral to export, in any season. And then we have a waterfall, far in the back country—"

"I know. Amet told me about it."

"Well, there you see. Our villages do need hydroelectric power, only we must create it at a better place, where it will not kill the herds, the people, the wild life."

"But all this"—Marika spoke slowly, testing the weight of her argument—"needs funding to get started. Especially if you cut off the flow of dollars from Pioneer. Where do you find it, Ngebin? How do you make that leap?"

"We shall find it. Where we can."

"You mean, if the United States can't accept what you've done, you'll go to the Soviets."

"To a foreign power, Yumana is an investment. Whoever will invest with us on our terms is welcome." Ngebin spoke patiently and rationally.

"You might as well hang me for a traitor, then," Marika said.

He shrugged, his eyes fixed on her all the while. "So they perceived your husband to be. One chooses one's loyalties." He paused, his body erect as a statue. "Are you still willing?"

Marika bit her lip. Acutely, as with Florence days earlier, she felt her separation from them. Only now Florence was waiting outside, and she was a stray woman among men as well as being white amid black. "If I don't help you," she said finally, "I don't know what else to do with myself."

"Good then." His manner turned abruptly businesslike. "You have four days to get the plans we need. Here are their file numbers." He pushed a sheet of paper, listing computer codes, toward her. "The most essential ones are starred. We need to know the entrances from the top of the dam itself, and we need the control room. There is also a mechanism for overflow, channeling the water into a large holding tank. We must be able to operate it. The valley will be evacuated, but without control, after eight years of dry riverbed, we risk flooding the plain."

"I understand."

"You have no—reservations about what you are doing?"

"I've said I'll help. I'm not going to back out."

"I mean with the man."

"McGrath?" Marika felt the blood rise up her neck. "He repulses me."

"But you will act—as you must?"

Marika met his dark eyes. "I thought you loved Richard."

"He was my best friend," Ngebin repeated. "But he is dead. And he does not sit in judgment on you."

"I'll get the plans in four days. That's all."

"I am grateful. Later, we may talk of the next step. You have, I think, a personal connection with the president?"

So he knew about Claire's liaison with Mayume. Marika nodded.

"When the time comes, we must know he is out of the country. Believe me, this is for his safety. We do not want violence. There is no call for it, no lust for it."

"But it may call to you," Marika answered, parroting Florence's words.

"It has called to me many times," Ngebin said, a whisper of a smile on his lips. "But I have learned to abjure the siren."

By the time Marika reached the Lovells', it was almost dark and was raining heavily. The amber lights of the house shone like fireflies and cast a trail on the slick asphalt. Wiping the last vestige of cocoa butter from her lower face and neck, she pushed open the front door of the house, and they fell on her.

"Darling! We have been *terrified*," said Claire, squeezing Marika's shoulders.

"About to send out a posse," Curtis added. "Don't get me wrong, I like an excuse to bring people together, but—"

Marika glanced around the front hall, where Lisbeth and Jeremy stood openmouthed and Bud McGrath, fidgeting, was edging up to her. Leaning against the wall was Biswandi, his visor as always shading his heavy face, a cigarette hanging from his mouth. He said nothing but watched her intensely.

Riding back in the jeep and ascending the hill to the house, Marika had thought of a half-dozen stories, but facing the group, she abandoned them all for flat, unapologetic innocence. "My goodness, you all look alarmed," she said, giving a slight giggle. "Why, I can't have been gone more than a few hours! Is it after six?"

"Almost seven," said Jeremy, "and the curfew's at eight."

Untying her scarf, she shook loose her hair. "Well, I'm flattered that you're all here," she went on, "but if I'd known I'd cause such a disturbance, I'd have left an itinerary." She paused while McGrath stepped between Claire and Curtis and took her hand, forcing her to speak directly to him rather than to the others. "I just went for a walk," she said.

"*Nobody* just 'goes for a walk' around here, darling," Claire put in. "You know that. Why, we thought you'd been raped and pillaged by now."

"By whom?" Marika asked, managing to shift her gaze from McGrath to Biswandi.

"By the rebels, of course. First you tell me you're going to the market where no sane person sets foot, then you disappear for over six hours! So I called Curtis at the office, and he brought the whole gang over. We were just on our second round."

"And you look," said McGrath, still holding the fingers of her hand in his palm, "like you could use a drink."

"That I could, Bud." Marika turned full-face to him: she would plunge in, beginning now. "Why don't you fix me whatever you're having?"

"Pleasure," he said, squeezing and releasing the hand.

"So where did you go?" Lisbeth asked as they moved to the living room. Leaning close to Marika, she added, "You look a *mess*."

"Do I?" Marika put a hand to her hair. "Let me just freshen myself up," she said to Claire, "and I'll try to entertain you all, since you've been waiting for me."

In the cold light of the bathroom, she examined herself. A film of road dust had clung to the layer of oil on her skin, and her shirt was stained with perspiration. Quickly she soaped her face and arms and combed the snarls from her fine hair, gone limp under the scarf in the damp heat. Rummaging through Claire's makeup, she discovered foundation, rouge, eye pencil. She would make herself back into an American widow. Carefully she smoothed on the creams and powdered them over. Yet still, when she was done, she looked at her own eyes in the uncompromising mirror and saw there the fear of the roadblock, the bone-weariness of swampy road, the determination with which Ngebin had injected her. What she could not hide from herself she was sure to give away to those who waited, curious and suspicious, in the other room.

—*How did you carry it off?* she asked Richard.

—*I thought of myself as a silly little boy playing spy games. And silly boys never manage to look like spies.*

—*But in games the guns are plastic. They shoot streams of water.*

—*You think, in Yumana, that your fear will give you away? No, Big Bird. If you betray yourself it will be out of American guilt.*

Guilt. She had told Ngebin she was a traitor, but seeing her compatriots in the living room, she had felt no remorse. She sprayed her neck with Claire's spicy perfume and went back out to the others. There was a place for her next to McGrath, who had poured her a Scotch. Like a fond bulldog, he looked softly down on her. "Well, this *is* a relief," Claire said. "Though we are going to have to rein you in from now on, Marika. Mr. Biswandi was just telling us how they have to enforce that awful curfew."

"For your own protection," Biswandi put in, his eyes once again focusing on Marika, leaching out any clues. "We cannot be controlling who comes and goes at night. In the morning, there are goods stolen, there are human people dead, and in the city they say it is my soldiers, but you know that is a foolish idea. They are dressing as us, they wear the uniform, and they attack without regard."

"Who *is* 'they'?" Claire asked loudly.

"He means the *dai*," Lisbeth answered. "The Lethe fighters. Who else?"

"The communists," Biswandi corrected her.

"Same thing."

"Well!" Claire clapped her hands to close the discussion of politics. "Since we're all here and we're all hungry, I took the precaution of heating up a rice casserole. Anyone interested?"

"The curfew," said Jeremy.

"Nonsense. Mr. Biswandi will drive you home. Won't you?"

Biswandi inclined his head. "I cannot stay long," he said. "I have my duties."

"He has his death squads," Lisbeth whispered to Marika.

On her other side, McGrath was also bending to whisper. "You still want to see that dam?" he asked.

"You know I'd love to!" Forced animation made her voice jump. McGrath looked at her with desire.

"Tomorrow," he said, his warm breath on her face.

One by one the members of the small party admonished Marika for her outing, but except for Biswandi none seemed to doubt her sketchy alibi. Lisbeth, however, hovered nearby. When Jeremy mentioned the letters the embassy had received asking for the release of the American students, Lisbeth grunted. "It hasn't been proved they did a thing," she said.

"The hell it hasn't," said Curtis. "General Biswandi's men found napalm in their trunks."

"And guns," Biswandi said. As the eyes of his audience rolled in their heads, he added, "The explosives came from Cuba."

Lisbeth grunted again. As the conversation tapered off and Claire, delighted at the chance to play impromptu hostess, brought out the casserole, she drew Marika to one corner of the room and said in a low voice, "You cannot have come all this way just to flirt with Bud McGrath."

Marika laughed nervously. "That wasn't my intention when I started out, I'll admit."

"Look, I knew what Richard was up to. None of these other jokers did, but Suzanne kept his files, and I saw what she didn't want to see. Now honey, you can't tell me you weren't in on that."

"In on what?" Marika faced her levelly.

"Why, who do you think killed him?"

"Please, Lisbeth. I don't like to think about that."

They were standing close together by the screened porch that looked over the city. Away from the others, Marika began to relax; the fatigue of the day seeped through her muscles and slowed her mind. She needed someone to lean on, and here was Lisbeth, whom she had always liked, whom Richard had trusted. With Lisbeth she needn't feel the isolation she had known with Florence or Ngebin. She remembered how Lisbeth's remarks, for years, had carried the same subtle irony as Richard's, even when it came to the propaganda she was hired to create. Lisbeth was an ally.

"I came all this way—" she began; but then she caught sight of Biswandi, on the other side of the Lovells' couch, watching her steadily while he talked to Claire. Maybe Richard had had allies, she realized, but she could not afford them. "To see my friends again," she concluded.

"And do you think he"—Lisbeth jerked her head backward toward Biswandi—"is your friend?"

"No," Marika answered truthfully, then added, "but I hope you are, and Suzanne is, and the Lovells. Why, you must be! Look at how you all worried about my little walk. I feel grateful."

"Yeah, just look," said Lisbeth, following Marika's glance around the room. "Just look at us safe and sound while this country blows itself up."

She moved quickly away across the room. Marika opened her mouth, then shut it and made no attempt to call her back.

Next day the clouds broke, the first whisper of the coming harmattan. Marika met McGrath at Pioneer's Revenir office, in a tall building adjacent to the embassy, and he called for his car to take them up to the dam. Waiting for the black Mercedes to pull around to the front of the building, Marika realized that this was the first time she had been alone with Bud McGrath since the night of the concert. She had had a few days to hone her acting skills, but at the same time their flirtation had grown and would soon hover on the brink of seduction. She swallowed hard.

"Don't you be scared at this fellow's driving," McGrath said as they climbed in. "He knows these roads like the back of his black hand. He just likes to go fast. Don't you, Cyprian?"

"Yes, man," said the driver.

"So you just sit back, now," said McGrath, hooking his short arm over Marika's shoulder as the Mercedes roared out of the city and started the long twisting climb up the mountain.

Marika said nothing, looking out the window at the clearing sky, thinking of Richard's last trip up this road with McGrath, thinking of her own driver, yesterday, the taut faces of the two guerrillas in front. Suddenly her vision was blocked. McGrath's square face descended over hers, and without a sound he pressed his lips over her mouth, forcing it open. As her body twisted, a wave of nausea came over her. She forced herself not to resist but to respond, if possible, though as his hand pressed against her breast, shoving her back on the seat, there was almost no way for her to move in either resistance or response. His fat tongue filled her mouth, moving lazily around its corners while his weight bore on her with an insistent ferocity. Open-eyed, Marika caught a glimpse of the driver; Cyprian took no notice of them, humming as he swung the car around potholes and sharp curves in the road.

Finally McGrath let her go. She gulped for air. The force of the car as it whipped past another turn would have flung her at him, but she gripped the seat beneath her. "Such a sweet piece of flesh you are," McGrath said, leering at her now, his face red and glowing with sweat. He loosened his tie, unbuttoned the top of his shirt, and came over her again.

At the taste of his saliva she gagged and backed away on the seat. "No," she gasped, short of breath.

"Come on, honey, don't get coy, give Buddy that sweet mouth, now." He pulled her back by the shoulder and crushed her against him. Still she avoided his mouth. His hands groped under her blouse and squeezed both her breasts until she cried out.

"Bud, please—"

"You want it, too, I know you do." His lips found hers, and she forebore, but nausea hit her again and she pushed him away. "That was a nice one, wasn't it, Big Bird?" he asked.

Before she knew what she had done, she had struck him twice. He fell back against the corner of the seat. "Don't!" she cried, her voice hoarse. "Don't you ever call me that! You killed him!"

"Aw, honey, honey, I'm sorry. It just came out. I got so carried away. Hey, don't cry now, Buddy didn't mean to bring back memories. Come on." Clumsily, he helped straighten her blouse. He seemed not to have heard her last words, and she let go her breath in relief. "You're so young and precious. I forget you're a widow."

—*You have to act*, Richard's voice was ordering Marika. —*You've got him now. Hold him steady.*

She found her voice again, shaky but normal. "I—I overreacted," she said, smiling sheepishly. "Just that—name—"

"I understand, don't mention a word of it. Shush, now." He touched her lips with his index finger, then turned to face front. They were approaching the dam. After minutes of awkward silence, he said, squeezing her arm, "So long as I know you want it, babe. I can wait."

"Thank you," said Marika, not knowing what else to say. Her inner mind raced ahead. —*Oh God, Richard. They didn't tell me it would be like this. And there's worse to come.*

—*Just pull yourself back from it, Marika. Remember who you belong to.*

—*Rescue me, Richard. Take me away.*

But they had reached the dam. From its mile-wide bridge, the water fell in deafening cascades over the cement wall to the riverbed thousands of feet below. Cold spray struck their faces as they left the car. "Stupendous sight, huh?" McGrath called over the thunder of the dam.

"Magnificent!"

"It's quieter in here." He ushered her through the wide glass doors, and as they snapped shut the sound of the dam was cut to a low rumble. "You've met Alice," he said, gesturing toward the petite receptionist, "and Stan, my assistant, and Peter Abeche."

"Yes, yes," said Marika, nodding at the two whites and the one African. Peter seemed almost to smirk at her.

"You are a sight for sore eyes," he said, stepping across

the lobby to take her light hand in his dark one. Shaking it steadied her, and she remembered she had always liked Abeche. What was he doing on this side of the conflict? From where came his derision?

"First we descend," said McGrath, pressing an elevator button, "to the sanctum sanctorum. After that, we'll go outside and look at the fun stuff."

As soon as the elevator door slid shut Marika stiffened. But McGrath, though he leaned against the steel wall and grinned at her, did not make a move. The door opened onto a low-ceilinged white corridor, and as they walked through it Marika felt the floor shaking beneath.

"That's not the dam," said McGrath. "It's the machinery that runs it. You get used to it after a while. Get your sea legs."

"Are we underground?"

"Tucked under the waterfall, you might say. We run things from here. Farther down the hill's the smelter, where the boys work. You know how they say, 'They put them down below'? Well, that's where we've got 'em."

"I don't understand."

"The *Titanic*! They let the no-touchables sink first. Here we got a dam instead of an iceberg, but the smelter's what'll get hit."

"I've never heard of a dam this size bursting."

"Oh, it's not gonna happen! Just an expression. Here's where we pull the switches."

He led her into a wide, hexagonal room where a half-dozen white men were monitoring computer printouts and large tracking machines that measured pressure, kilowatts, amperes. A number of red and yellow lights blinked steadily. Glancing quickly around the room, Marika tried to memorize the layout, the position of each machine, while McGrath breezed through, greeting their operators.

"Impressive, isn't it?" he asked, hitching up his pants.

"What's that door?" Marika pointed toward a gray steel portal, heavily bolted, on the opposite side of the room.

"That goes right out to the dam, that does. You get an awful drenching if you open it—I know, I tried. When I was up here with your husband, in fact. They didn't want to put any windows in the place—security, you know. But they figured you'd have to have a way to take a direct look if all these little lights here started going haywire. So you've got a door that sounds the alarm if you open it, and outside you've got a little bitty terrace you can stand on for a few seconds before you get dizzy from the height. Nothing but cliffrock around it. You know, what with the crazy political climate they got here—not to mention the plain old weather, hah hah!—they figured they'd better make the place impregnable. After all, you've got American dollars at stake!"

"That you do," Marika agreed, thinking of the children Richard had seen at the hospital above the dam, of the devastated cropland around the edges of the swollen lake. These things had not touched her when she lived close to them. They had been Richard's quarrel—like the orchids, his world apart. To her, they had borne no connection to the gunshots that disturbed their sleep or to the shallow graves she had seen dug just outside Revenir. Now, after splitting kola nut with Ngebin, she felt the violation of the dam like a parasite in her belly, as if the land and the families torn up were her land and her family. Had Richard, walking these rumbling corridors, felt that same violation twisting him inside? Was this what had drawn her back to Yumana—these humming machines, this fortified gate on the river?

"Seen enough?" McGrath was asking, bending close to her ear.

"Yes!"

"Let's vamoose to my office, then. Can't hear yourself fart in here!" He nicked her with his elbow and guffawed.

Leading her out of the control room, he turned left down the corridor, passed the elevator bank, and followed another fork to a locked door, which opened onto a short hallway with a second elevator.

"This," he said, unlocking the button that read UP, "is what the great architects at Pioneer Aluminum figured would keep little me from getting assassinated."

"Well, it seems to have worked, thus far." She attempted a coy smile.

"Didn't exactly protect me in your greenhouse, though, did it?"

"Didn't it?" Marika asked softly.

"Beg pardon?"

"Nothing. I think it's wise to protect yourself in—in any foreign situation."

"You mean any *African* situation. You don't see the director of our Australian office with this many keys! And don't start in on how we treat the aborigines different than the Afros. I know that sweet little brain of yours has got some notions."

Marika said nothing. As McGrath unlocked his carpeted office, her eyes darted around as they had in the control room, but this time she focused on files, on binders that might hold plans or documents.

"Quieter up here, isn't it?" McGrath said behind her.

"Yes."

"I like to get away from the boys now and then. You just sit here now." Coming up behind her, he led her by the shoulders to a broad couch by his wood-paneled wall and pressed her to sit. "You are nervous as a chicken."

"I've just never been in such a labyrinth."

"Wait'll you see the smelter! But we'll take a little break before we head down there. No, no, don't look scared, I'm not gonna paw you. We'll just have a little drink and talk. Bourbon okay?"

"Fine," said Marika. With relief and apprehension, she watched him go out of the room, wiggling his fingers at her to signify that he would be just a minute. As soon as the door shut, she sprang from the couch and headed for the low, flat file she had spotted behind his bare desk.

"Distribution," she read on the drawers. "Kilowatt printouts. Production estimates. Damn!" She turned to a set of hanging files. "Renderings," she read aloud. Flipping the narrow sheaf toward her, she saw the words PARAMBO DAM, REVISED 1986 at the top. Just below was the red stamp FINAL.

"Got to be it," she muttered, and pulled the file out. The stiff cardboard was almost three feet wide, impossible for her to hide. Quickly she glanced toward the closed door; her ears felt like radar, attuned to the slightest sound of McGrath's approach. Then she opened the file, fumbled for the metal clasp at one end, slipped the sheaf of architect's papers out, and dropped the empty folder, with a smooth whish, back in its place.

Just as she folded the papers in half, she heard the clink of glass—McGrath, holding both drinks in one hand in order to get to the door. Swiftly she crossed to the couch and sat on the papers, spreading her skirt. He entered.

"Do hope I didn't keep you waiting too long."

"Not at all. I was admiring your heads." She motioned toward the stuffed tigers baring their teeth from the other wall.

"Oh, those! Wish they were mine! Goddamn bleeding hearts won't let you nab 'em anymore. Mayume says he wouldn't care, but he doesn't want the headache. Fellow before me got those." He handed her a large tumbler of bourbon and sat at the other end of the couch. "To us," he said, holding his glass aloft. "You'll drink to our—new friendship, won't you?"

"Sure I will, Bud." Marika moved slightly to face him, keeping the papers tucked under her seat.

"You do like me. I can tell. I just never knew you were such a shy woman."

"Well, I'd been with Richard so long—"

"Such a tragedy." He shook his head. "Ever screw around on him?"

"Of course not!"

"Good, good. I like a faithful woman." He patted her knee. "Now don't go getting jumpy. We're just going to sit here and talk a little while. You tell me about yourself. Lots of little secret things, hey?"

Marika talked to him without keeping track of what they were saying. Aware only of his movements and expressions, she adjusted her own to keep an amorous distance. She sipped her bourbon as quickly as she could without losing her head, and she watched as he kept pace with her. Take a drink, then answer or ask a question, then take a drink. She kept the pattern up until he laughed at something she had recounted and, finally rising, relieved her of her glass. He would have to leave the room now, she thought, to get refills.

But he said, "I can see you'd like another. Hey, so would I! Let's just take a quick peek down at the smelter and come back for the afternoon, whaddaya say? I have to check on that Afro foreman, otherwise they'll think I don't do my job. Heh heh!"

Marika looked longingly at the empty glass. If only he would leave without her. But there was no time for wishing. "I think a quick peek, and then I'll have to get on home," she said. "Claire'll be expecting me. I'll just powder my nose while you put those away."

"Why, we've got a restroom, the others don't use it or anything—" He waved vaguely toward the closed door.

"No, no, I'll just give my hair a quick comb. Go on, now, don't watch. I'll be done in a sec." She opened her oversized purse and pulled out a compact before he could make another objection.

"Hell, I'll use the can myself, then," he said, and lumbered off. He left the door open, but she needed little time. She slid the renderings out, folded them again thickly, and stuffed them into her purse. He couldn't ask what made her purse bulge. He wouldn't dare. She rose and walked smoothly through the door into the softly lit hallway. After a minute, McGrath emerged from the bathroom at the end.

"So you like my digs, do you?" he asked, coming close to her.

"They're very impressive."

"We'll take you up top the dam before you go. Let you feel that *power*." Reaching for the small of her back, he drew her sharply to him. "Give Buddy a kiss now, and we'll promise to show you. Gimme that mouth."

She didn't have to touch him now, she had the drawings safe in her bag. But as McGrath's lips sought hers, relief and gratitude ran through her veins, and she embraced him almost with desire, almost as if he were Richard and had reached down to lift her up, to grant her a life that could leap ahead and not be caught any longer in the backwash of time.

And as they released, McGrath grinned, delighted with his prize.

# Chapter 17

In spite of what had taken hold of her that first night, in spite of grief burning her like the prairie wind that leaves a fine dust for new growth, in the scant week since she had arrived in Yumana, Marika had failed to detach herself completely from the small, circular, and separate worlds of Justin and Katya back in New York. She had received one brief postcard, mailed by her mother the day she left; on it, the picture of the studded Byzantine cross that hung in the dark, dusty Orthodox church off Irving Place backed a message that read simply, "Today is the saddest of all my days since your papa's death. Come back soon to your mama." Sitting on the Lovells' humid porch, Marika saw again her mother spinning through their living room, her round form like a top, her forehead gleaming in the light of the wall lamp as she danced with Reuben Dniprovsky. It became easy to forget that Katya too had tackled a strange land with a new tongue and hidden threats. Pressing her hand to her forehead, Marika was sentient of the warm, rough palm her mother had laid there, winter after winter, checking for fever; of the safety in that hand.

She had not heard from Justin, and she would not. She had spoken the truth when she last saw him. She would miss him terribly. Not in the flesh: pierced with pleasure, those moments had vanished as soon as they passed, like the taste of a certain food for which one can hunger without knowing why. She would miss instead the Justin of her dreams, who would never come back to her and whose burning eyes and mad schemes would never meld with the ghost of Richard, quick and warm as gold, who had come to inhabit her soul. That is, she would miss Justin later, when she had done what she came to Yumana to do and when her life had settled into some hitherto untraversed path. Until then, out of habit she found herself checking her impressions against what Justin would have thought, only to discover that she had no idea what Justin would think—they had been separated so many years, and he had changed so much. Still, a few hours later, she would catch herself doing it again.

What she had come to Yumana to do grew hazier rather than clearer as she drove with McGrath down the mountain and returned to her false life of paying a fortnight's visit on the Lovells. Not Amet's persuasion but some other urgency had impelled her to help the *dai*. She had told Richard's father that she would track down whoever had killed his son, but it seemed as she played out her role that she was instead tracking down Richard. And just as she would draw close to finding him, his spirit eluded her, like a child growing old before her eyes, his essence vanishing at the moment she realized it was there. She could not run fast enough, her mind racing down the corridors of memory, to catch him.

These thoughts had been coming on her in the afternoon heat, or late at night, when the others let her escape to her small room at the top of the stairs. She would sit, knees up, on the quilted window seat and chase Richard's elusive spirit until he and she stalemated at their present liaison, in which he gave her no comfort but rather the sharp erotic charge of risky collusion. Where Justin had roped her back to safety, Richard impelled her toward danger. His was the hand that reached her through a barred window, his the voice lipping her ear as they lay hidden together in the dark, his the cool teal eyes that faced Biswandi down and told lies with the innocence of a farm boy.

Except that Richard had taken his risks without her, and lost. When he could have bestowed his dark plans on her, he had caressed the petals of his orchids and she had unburdened herself to Justin. Now, late at night, she would finally let him go, not, like Justin, back to the dusty cradle of memory, but into the hollow shell that had bodied forth this impossible rudiment of their unlived lives together. She would lie flat on her back and hang onto scraps of him—his deep, even sleep sinking into the bed, the vein in his temple that throbbed with fatigue, the way he took hold of her breasts and turned them slightly, like soft handles that opened her up.

The night after she took McGrath's file, Marika had no time to wallow in a dream of Richard. The Lovells and their dinner guests—tonight, Mayume and his Paris-educated wife—had pulled out a board game that Curtis had picked up in London called "Espionage" and labeled *Adult*. They had passed the evening together stealing state secrets and waylaying one another in several "hotel suites" sprinkled over the board. "This *is* naughty," Claire kept saying. On being assigned to the Middle East, Amoz Mayume let drop that the game was foretelling life. Marika's ears pricked up.

"You're taking a trip?" she asked.

"Ah-ha, state secret! You have to draw the right card to ask that question."

"No, I meant—"

"He's being silly," Claire put in. "President Mayume is taking a little trip to dance the *hora*."

"Israel!" said Curtis. "Now that's nice, I like our country's buddies to be buddies."

Mayume's wife glared at Claire, but Marika was still unscathed. "Leaving soon?" she asked.

"Not so soon. August, maybe. Jerusalem and Paris," Mayume added, smiling at the froncophile wife, who still glowered. "A short trip. Still uncertain."

Tucking the news away, Marika maneuvered herself into being first to lose the game, to *suffer an untimely death*, according to the rules. The party let her go, and she escaped to her quarters. Pulling out the architect's drawings and the list Ngebin had given her, she retreated to the bathroom, where she could lock the door.

The drawings were done on a blued, parchmentlike paper, the fine lines and numbered call-outs in dark blue ink. Running down the right side of each rendering was a long legend identifying the parts and describing the vantage point of the design. Finally, at the lower corner, Marika spotted a row of numbers. Turning to Ngebin's list, she uttered a short cry as she identified the first rendering—the roof and back view of the smelter, where McGrath had taken her for a brief glimpse before leaving the dam. He had been right—the stench of the chemical refiners, mingled with men's sweat, had been overpowering. Though the foreman, a short, furrowed Nebo named Jimmy, who called McGrath "Boss," stopped every few minutes to bark something unintelligible into his portable microphone, the stupefying pace of the workers, hard-hatted and shirtless, had never altered.

The second drawing was of the interior of the main building, with its long, low corridors and hexagonal control room. Some changes had been penciled in. The next was a minute rendering of the dam's sluices and was also identified on Ngebin's list. Marika had eight drawings in all, but the list contained ten starred computer codes. The two that read UNDERGD MN BLDG TO DAM and SPLLOVR MCHNSM were missing.

Marika rocked back on her heels, suspended by a curious elation, not at what she had accomplished but at there being more to do, another hurdle to dare. It had not been so difficult to get this far. She even had the bit about Mayume's trip. Rolling up the drawings, she tucked them behind a bookcase. Downstairs, she could hear Mayume leaving, the spy game over with, and then Claire and Curtis arguing in low tones.

*—You enjoyed that, today, didn't you?* Richard asked her as she crawled into bed.

He was sitting across the baobab table from her, his face haggard from overwork, his hair matted like straw, sticking out from his head. She put her fingers to his and, at the touch, felt herself grow moist. *—I thought I did all right.*

*—You didn't have to give your body to him. That's the main thing.*

*—I won't have to. The job's almost done.*

*—Just watch yourself, Big Bird. Don't get too cocky.*

One by one, he pinched her fingertips between his thumb and forefinger, starting with the pinky and moving slowly to caress the thumb, as she fell off to sleep.

When Marika got to Florence's hidden bungalow with the drawings, Amet was waiting there, hunched over the table with Florence and Olanda, drinking palm wine. "Have some," he said cheerfully, pouring Marika a glass. "The leader man, he's not allowing it in the camp, so we must fly our kites in town, hey?"

The wine was sweet, without the sour fermented aftertaste of cheaper brews. Marika laid her findings out on the table.

"He may have more in his office," she said, "but I'll never get in there without being with him. It'd be hard to show a general curiosity about the structure of the place—it wouldn't fit in with his image of me."

"Good," Florence said. "You keep this image."

"Anyway, if you ask," Olanda added, "he'll go to look for these, no? Then we see trouble coming."

"She doesn't go asking," said Amet. "She finds another way in. Not so direct. You, na, meet the man there and so go out together. Or you think you leave something behind in this office. But these two missing, they are a big thing. We are needing the underground tunnel to trigger the dam itself. And the spillover sluices to relieve the pressure, or we flood the valley sure. You must get them."

"What if I can't?"

"I hear a breath of wind," began Amet, and the others laughed. He wasn't going to hear the word *can't*.

"Listen, Missis, now serious," Florence said, leaning her heavy bulk on the table. "They going to come take me out soon. Many signs. At the university, too, we got demonstrations. Olanda, she is keeping quiet, but they going to sniff around and find her. You know those boys from U.S.? They dead."

"They can't be!" Marika cried. "They're being deported to Washington. Curtis Lovell was talking about them last night. Mayume was there."

"He's talking about corpses. They dead two days now. Biswandi is not thinking yet of any good way for them to officially die, is all. We got pictures of the graves, now, I give to you for safekeeping. You stitch them into your suitcase, you hide them till we say to show."

Olanda brought out the pictures, and Marika looked at them: black and white snapshots, taken from behind a thick growth of swampgrass somewhere near the shore. There were several shots of four men unloading two bodies from a truck, then laying them in shallow ditches and spading the earth back with small shovels. Evidently the pictures had been taken in the rain—the diggers' faces were hidden by hoods, and the downpour hazed the quality of the photographs so they looked old and smeared. But the photographer must have come out of hiding and dug out the graves after the truck drove off, because there were a half-dozen views of the corpses, the earth caking their naked bodies but their features clear. Two shots took in the arms and legs, with their hands and feet chopped off in the traditional way of execution, so the dead one cannot walk or hold things in the next world. Their tongues, too, had no doubt been cut out.

"Who took these?"

"I," said Amet.

"Okay," Marika said, swallowed hard. "I'll keep them." She saw Amet hobbling over the marshy ground, kneeling to scrape away the fresh mud. Like the corpses, he had been maimed: in their eyeless black heads he looked at his own fate.

"Good!" Florence stood up. "Amet, you must go, is not safe for you here."

"Oh, one thing," Marika remembered as Amet pulled himself up by his crutch. "Tell Ngebin I may know when Mayume is leaving the country."

"This is for sure?"

She told him what she had heard after dinner, the president's mention of Israel and Paris. Though in her mind she saw Mayume's wife glowering at his mistress, she did not mention Claire.

Amet nodded his head vigorously, up and down, then let it hang as if in shame. "Marika Hooper," he said. "Not so long ago I flung my speeches at you, like poison darts. I was a little angry boy. I had no hope for you. Forgive me."

"I'm not so noble," Marika replied. "I'm doing this for my own selfish reasons."

He shook his head—these, too, were words he would not hear. His long hand covered hers from palm to wrist. "*B'nago b'maradi*," he said.

Olanda, Florence, and Marika gathered at the small window that looked out onto the enclosed courtyard, as Amet made his way around kidney-shaped puddles and sticks of broken furniture. "He is worse than Ngebin," Florence said.

"What do you mean?"

"The heat of his fire burns too hot. And still he throws more wood on, and everything they do to him only is fanning the flames higher. He will consume himself."

"He is needing a woman, is all," Olanda said.

"You?" asked Marika, turning to her.

"Maybe, when we have won the war." She spoke matter-of-factly, watching the tall lopsided form as it hesitated in the intersection of the courtyard and the path to debate the safest way out. "He is still beautiful to me, as he was before. But he will not believe me, when I say it."

Suddenly Amet's head snapped back, as if he had seen something in the sky. An instant later, the sound of the shot followed, then the next and the next. His crutch dropped to the ground. Bullets flying from both ends of the courtyard threw his body into a contorted dance and held it upright while his arms flew out from his sides as if to welcome his assassins. At last he folded and fell to the wet ground, but again the shots ratted out, and he jerked, first in pain and then without feeling, grotesque twitches on the ground. The bullets rained onto his body.

"Can't they stop it!" Marika cried in horror. She sprang for the door. Before she reached it, moving without thinking, she perceived a shadow standing between her and the wire screen, as if blocking her from the sight of Amet's death. Richard, it was Richard in her way, trying to protect her, as if *this* were not what he had intended. With a sweep of her arm she pushed him aside; but as she gained the door a strong hand, flesh and blood now, grabbed her waist and pulled her back.

"What you want," Florence hissed in her ear, "to sacrifice you'self?"

"But he—but he—"

"They coming to take us out now. Move quick."

Marika struggled against Florence to press her nose to the window once again. From there she saw the familiar form of James Aholo Biswandi himself, stepping out from the shadows in the finally silent courtyard. Alone, he approached Amet, sprawled on his back, both of his legs now useless, twisted underneath. Like a soccer player, Biswandi reached one foot back and gave the body a hard, sidelong kick. His laughter filled the space between the bungalows. Then he turned to face Florence's house, and Marika drew back from the window.

"Come *now*," Florence whispered. She had a brown duffel on her back; Olanda had gathered a stack of papers, the renderings among them, and a few blankets. Opening a waist-high door that Marika had thought led to a cupboard, Florence disappeared through it, and Olanda pushed Marika to follow. Shutting the door behind her, Olanda switched on a flashlight to illuminate the tunnel, and Marika saw her cheeks drenched with tears.

"Go," was all she said. "They won't take long."

Marika ducked her head and followed Florence down a crumbling set of clay steps and through a narrow, dank tunnel. Florence moved like a crab, her knees splayed and her hips low. Trickles of water ran down the floor of the tunnel. None of the women spoke, but they moved as quickly as they were able through the narrow, airless space. Marika kept hearing the percussion of bullets scoring Amet's body, the gunfire that refused to cease long after its work had been accomplished. Olanda wept silently, moving close behind Marika, her flashlight steady in the utter dark.

Gradually Marika became aware of a broadening in the tunnel, of firmer ground underneath. Florence, in front of her, straightened up, and they could make out a light that ran along the floor. Panting, they reached the end, another small door, and Florence motioned them both to check their breathing. She began to peer through the chink at the side of the doorway, but at that moment they heard behind them a distant scraping and the echo of voices.

"We have no choice, Mother," Olanda said. Florence nodded and, throwing her shoulders back, turned the knob on the door. They stepped out, blinking, into what was left of the market.

# Chapter 18

Where once the marketplace had throbbed with trade, there now huddled hungry families from the hills where Biswandi had sent his soldiers to rout out *dai*. They tried vainly to keep dry under the rusting tables, piled high a year ago with tinned goods, and their vacant eyes followed the three women as they emerged, breathless, and moved quickly into the narrow, protected space between a corrugated metal wall and a crumbling stucco hutch. The smell of human feces rankled in the air.

"Return quickly to your white people," Florence ordered Marika. "Do nothing surprising, nothing not ordinary."

"What about the plans?"

"We take these drawings to a safe place. We must have the other two, the two"—Florence hesitated, glancing at her daughter; Olanda stood stonefaced—"the two that Amet was asking you after. You must be moving without hurry, but quickly. You are understanding me?"

"But where will you be?"

"We shall be sending to you. Soon." Florence raised her head and peered over the top of the metal fence. Few police ventured into the market; they roamed its perimeter, more to question the refugees who had resolved to leave it than to prevent anyone from entering. No uniforms were in sight. The pounding of *futu* and the cries of hungry infants, answering each other across the broad square, were the only sounds. "Amet," Florence said, "is not the first, na, nor the last. You had twelve thousand dead, *n'est-ce pas*, Missis Hooper?"

Marika shook her head, not understanding Florence. Almost unwillingly, her hand had stolen to the back of Olanda's neck and rested there, in apparently useless comfort. Olanda did not move or speak.

"For you, for your revolution," Florence went on, smiling faintly. "Now is our turn. But we have no time. You are American lady. Holding your head high. Anyone ask what you be doing down here, you be acting a little bit tipsy, hey?"

Florence pulled her daughter back from Marika's hand and gave Marika a small shove with her free arm. As Marika backed slowly away, Florence continued to make the same shooting motions she had made months before, when the market teemed and one of Biswandi's men had sidled over to eye her yams. Finally Marika was out of the confined area and in the foul-smelling open. Following orders, she turned and lifted her head and walked stiffly and without haste until she had safely passed the scattered line of police and was once again in the streets of Revenir.

Claire had locked herself in her room. "For hours now she is shutting herself up," the cleaning woman, a coal-black Hausa from the interior, told Marika. "My hand is on the telephone so, to call the boss. But each time I say, na, I'm to do it, the lady's screaming like a jackal."

Reeling still from what she had witnessed, Amet's body

like a flag flapping in the wind of the bullets that whistled across the court, Marika shrugged impatiently at the closed white-painted door. Instead, she took her own refuge in the Lovells' back garden, tamer and more landscaped than the sprawl she had kept going on the next hill, but bulging nonetheless with the monsoon-nurtured vines and bushes of tropical Yumana. The gardener had gone home, but no matter—she had no messages to send to Florence, or Amet. As the sun cut through the diminishing rain, the green of the broad-leaved plants thickened to an intense opacity against which she shaded her eyes.

She walked slowly around the perimeter of the garden, watching her feet as she set them down on Claire's graveled path, as if each step were a small marvel. Again and as always, the choice lay before her. She could make her excuses to the Lovells and take the next plane out of the country; or she could dare McGrath's office once again and try to come out with the final clues for destroying a dam that no one had heard of, a dam that, conceived in a mixture of hope and corruption, had ended in misery and death and could bring more misery still if Ngebin were wrong and she helped him to achieve his end. As her steps fell, she wondered where Florence had gone, if she was safe. Olanda. Amet.

The thick vines of the mahogany trees that shaded the garden reached as low as Marika's shoulder. She recalled Justin's tale of the lyre-bird and the frog, the frog letting loose the water of the river as he broke finally into laughter. There stood the Parambo Dam, its metal struts like the striped underside of a monstrous frog's mouth, clapped shut. From deep within her rose the urge to tease the frog's mouth open, to let the water roar forth as if being birthed, to run to the sea and never circle back. "Oh, Justin," she said aloud as if admonishing him for putting the idea into her head. Or Katya, saying as if Marika herself were a dammed-up lake, *I see you turning, and still it's backward you're facing, my darling girl.* "Oh, Mama," she said, remembering, and then as if to complete the trilogy, "Oh, Richard." But instead of seeing Richard, she saw Amet, sleek-skinned and muscular as he had been the first day he came up to the house, and then as he folded like a half-empty sack into which Biswandi could pump his muffled bullets.

Passing by Claire's bedroom window, Marika heard her give a low, prolonged groan. At first she turned back to circle the garden again, ignoring Claire's obvious bid for attention. But the sound continued and made her stop. The shades on the room were pulled, the curtains drawn, though the midafternoon sun had just managed to slant through the heavy clouds. Marika drew close to the window and, listening, heard a guttural plaint, stripped of Claire's usual affectation. She knocked on the window, and the sound stopped, but there was no movement from within the room. Marika went quickly indoors and around to Claire's locked door.

She knocked. "Claire? Let me in, it's just Marika." She put her ear to the door but heard nothing. "Stop moping now. Can't you talk to me?"

The groan came again, somewhat louder. Marika rapped and coaxed. The Hausa woman appeared at the end of the hallway but shook her head and went away. "Come *on*, Claire," Marika said at last. The day's tragedy had made her sharp and intolerant. "If you don't talk to me, what are you going to do when Curtis gets home? Hide in a closet?"

After a long minute, the door opened. Claire stood in a bathrobe, large dark glasses covering her face, her hair matted across her forehead. "Get in here quick," she whispered, and, shutting the door after Marika, returned to lie on the wide bed she shared with Curtis, her knees bent up to her chin, fetal position.

"Claire! What on earth has happened to you?" Marika said. As her eyes grew accustomed to the half-light filtering through the drawn shades, she made out the purplish bags below Claire's dark glasses, the fresh bruise on her neck.

"I guess"—Claire's voice cracked at the first word—"he got—a little too rough on me. That's all."

"Who? Mayume?"

"The president. Himself."

"Let me see what he did to you. I'm turning on the light. Don't argue," Marika added as Claire reached out a hand to stop her.

In the harsh overhead light, the bruises flushed like plums. "Let's see," Marika said, sitting on the corner of the bed to pull off Claire's sunglasses. One eye was swollen shut, the other shot with blood. "Is there more?"

Claire, nodded, mute, and, rolling onto her back, pulled her robe off her shoulders and let it drop to her waist. Flecks of red covered her chest and round breasts, the blood clotted into beaded strings of red where he had broken the skin. "Good God," Marika said, "what'd he do? Crack a whip over you?"

"He—just used—his hands."

"Well, he beat you up good."

"No. No," Claire protested weakly, bending her head like an obedient rag doll as Marika turned it to shed light on the worst eye bruise. "He just got—carried away. I should have told him. To stop."

"You mean you *let* him do this? You didn't even try to get help?"

"He says—the b-black women like it. He said I wouldn't cry out if I was a bush woman. Oh!"

She drew her breath in sharply as Marika coaxed her to sit up on the bed. Glancing at the white sheets, Marika saw the deep red stain below where Claire had been lying.

"Christ. You're hemmorhaging," she said, not wanting to guess the cause.

"He did that—last. I never. He cut. It happened so fast!" Claire slumped back onto the bed and gave a long low wail.

"Where did he cut."

"There. Y-you know. The way they do."

"What'd he use?"

"A little knife. It was so sharp, I didn't feel it at first."

"But now," Marika said, holding Claire's ankle. The bloody smell permeated the sheets. Female circumcision, the rite of passage among the inland tribes. *Clitorectomy*, Richard had always named it with the medical term, as if it were tonsils or an appendix. Outlawed, the practice continued unabated. But not like this.

Claire cried in gasps, hyperventilating. "Hush," Marika said. "It's done now. Hush." She slipped Claire's robe all the way off and rose to get a washcloth to clean the place where Claire had been abruptly initiated. "Some lover. This could be infected already."

"He said he was making me—a real *woman*. Like they do in the bush. Then he—"

"What! He didn't cut you more!"

"He—tore into me. Himself. Oh, Christ on high." Claire's face dissolved.

"I'm going to get a doctor."

"Oh, no. No!" Claire reached up and pulled on Marika's collar. "You can't trust anyone! He—he said he'd kill me! Curtis can't know, you understand? I've got to just—stay here, till this all goes away!"

"Don't be absurd! You'll take weeks to heal, and that's if nothing's wrong where we can't see. You can't just hide in this room day in and day out and expect no one to ask questions."

"I'll make something up. Tell Curtis I've got migraines. *Ai!*"

"Sorry." Marika pulled the washcloth away, rank with blood. "Blood everywhere," she said, half aloud, then bit her lip to stem the thought of Amet. "You've never had migraines."

"Then I won't tell him anything. Let him think I've gone nuts. I'll keep the door locked and the windows drawn, and you—you'll bring me food."

"What if I leave before you're well, Claire? What if you get an infection? You'll need a doctor."

"I will, won't I," said Claire, in a suddenly absent tone, her long neck arched back as her unbruised eye gazed at the ceiling.

"Well, I couldn't say for sure—" Marika began, when Claire abruptly sat up, causing a fresh spill of blood between her legs, and grabbed Marika's arm with her bruised hand. "You've got to get me out of here, that's it," she said in a low, tight voice.

"What do you mean, out? Out of the country?"

"Back home. Before Curtis sees me and tells Amoz he's seen me. Before Amoz sends his men around for me."

"To do what?"

"You know what they did to Richard."

Her words were like a threat. Thinking, *She knew, then, too,* Marika shrugged loose her arm and said slowly, "You think you matter so much, Claire?"

"Did *he*?"

Marika didn't answer; her gaze fell on Claire's swollen face, on the lesions scarring her naked chest. "They hate us all, Marika," Claire went on, her breasts swaying as she shook her head. "They only kill each other because they can't get to us. I swear to you—" Her voice dropped; she leaned forward, squinting into Marika's face. "I think if Mayume could kill me with his bare hands," she whispered, "he'd *come*."

Marika shut her eyes. Tired, she knew instinctively that more, much more, lay ahead. As if she had not arrived in Yumana until that afternoon, when she had watched Amet go down, cracking the surface. "Curtis?" she asked.

"I'll divorce him. I don't care. We've been nowhere since he brought me to this garbage heap."

"Okay. Okay. I'll book you on a flight. I'll get people to take you to the airport."

"No! He'll know about the flight! He won't let me out of the country!"

"Claire, I can't exactly rent you a camel—"

"You can go to Bud McGrath. You can get me on the company plane. He knows I can pay for it. He can send the car, it'll be over before anyone knows. If *I* call him, he'll go straight to Curtis. He adores you. He'll do anything you ask, just—"

"Just to sleep with me."

"You want *him*, don't you?

"Oh, Claire, Claire." Marika brushed Claire's hair back from the battered face. "I think you should go to Curtis."

"No."

"All right then." Marika pulled away and spread her hands over her knees, as if checking her fingernail polish. "Asking Bud McGrath is out of the question. I may know a place where you can stay for a while. But it won't be easy getting you there."

"I don't care. Where is it?"

"I don't know."

"Oh, that's *great.*" Claire fell back against the pillow and picked up a melting icepack from the bed table. Blood surely had soaked through to the mattress; she would be leaving clues behind.

"What I mean is, I wouldn't be able to find it by myself. It's a camp in the back hills. I'm pretty sure they've got a doctor there, and no one would give you away to Curtis."

"Let's go. Who knows the way?"

"A boy named Amet," Marika said. "But—"

"But what?"

"He is dead. And Florence won't come back. There have to be others in the city still who'll talk to me."

"Marika, I'm in pain, and you're not making any sense!"

"How long until Curtis gets home?"

"He's drinking with a candidate for the embassy. Till curfew at least."

"That's three hours away. Do you need anything? Can you just stay locked up in here till I get back?"

"I stocked up with ice and gin." Claire waved a hand toward the bathroom and tried to smile. "Keeps down the risk of infection."

"Try to sleep. Maybe you should wash yourself. For God's sake, don't open the door to anyone but me. Gather up a bundle of clothes—a *small* bundle. If you change your mind and decide to tell Curtis, then wait for me to return before you make a move. I'm risking other people. You understand me, Claire?"

"I got you." Claire made a weak thumbs-up gesture. She did not move as Marika left the room, flicking the latch shut behind her.

—*You said Ngebin swore a bond with you,* Marika said to Richard as she swung Claire's car back down into the city.

*—Yes, for each other. For our wives and children. We swore to sacrifice for the other, and to revenge.*

*—But not for Claire Lovell.*

*—Ngebin never brought me one of his people to hide. I could have saved them, maybe, but he let them take their chances. I repay him by handing him a battered debutante on the eve of a strike for the Parambo?*

*—He hasn't revenged your death yet, has he?*

*—Not yet.*

*—So he can keep Claire a few days, as vengeance.*

*—Big Bird, you're stubborn. This won't work. Leave her to Curtis.*

*—If she had come to you,* Marika asked, pinning him with her eyes,*—would you have left her to Curtis? Wouldn't you be looking for the* dai *right now, just as I am? Wouldn't you stretch your chance?*

She could hear him sigh. *—I might. But I would be wrong in it. And Ngebin would tell me so.*

*—So let him tell me.*

She left the car on a side street bordering the compound of bungalows, among a scattered line of abandoned cars inches deep in the hardening mud. The light wind, presaging the harmattan, made dust of the reddish top layer and swirled it against the concrete walls and metal fences. Marika wore dark glasses as much for protection as disguise while she found her way back through the doorways that had led her to Florence.

The washing machines were silent, and although curfew lay hours away, no women pounded *futu* in the late afternoon courtyard. Marika saw some movement behind a darkened doorway. "I'm looking for Florence 'wa Mthongo!" she called, knocking on the screen door. Inside, three women and a man with what looked like a baby drifted from the corners of the room and sat around a low table, talking in Lethe, as if they had not heard her.

She tried their language. "I was with Florence when Amet was killed. In the courtyard today. I must find her."

The man spat into the corner. The others buzzed softly, like heat-drugged flies, ignoring her. "I have to reach Ngebin," she went on. "I'm helping him. I am Richard Hooper's wife. It's urgent."

At the name "Hooper" the man's face shifted slightly in her direction. One woman lit a cigarette. Marika shook the screen door: locked. "Okay, you're scared," she said in English. "I'll find someone else!"

At each door, each waxpaper window, she called and pounded but only as if to numb the people inside. Everywhere the openings were locked, by twisted wire if nothing else, and the louder she called the slower these dark interior figures went about their small tasks. Frustration boiled into rage: they would abandon her, would blot out her existence. She ran from house to house, bruising the heel of her hand on the wooden doorframes. Finally she broke the handle to a tilted hut from within which a lone old man watched her obliquely. Flinging the handle behind her into the courtyard, she stood, arms akimbo. "I came ten thousand miles," she shouted at the inanimate man, "to help you people! Now I need help! Someone is hurt, she needs a place to go! What am I supposed to do, save your fucking country all by myself?"

The man stood like a statue at the waist-high icebox in the corner of the room. Then he bent down and pulled out a can of beer. Marika kicked herself back from his door and strode across the courtyard.

"You people deserve what you get!" she threw at them

as she crossed the place where Amet had gone down. Pools of his dried blood had turned brown in the sun. As her feet sidestepped them, the fine dust unsettled by his fall gathered on her shoes. "I hope the Parambo Lake *rots* all your villages. You don't give a *shit* about someone from outside. You're—you're not even Christians!"

It was a stupid thing that her mother might have said. Not a sound came from the wire-and-wattle houses. Sick with loathing, Marika passed through the narrow gate to the street. She would have to leave Claire to Curtis. And even in her hysteria Claire was right: Mayume would find a way to kill her rather than risk an incident. Mayume might even kill her first, before she got to Curtis. Marika's steps clattered toward Claire's car.

As she ran across the empty street, a brown jeep careened around the corner, almost grazing her. Jumping back, she remembered with a pang the delivery truck, far away and long ago in Manhattan, whose familiar danger had reassured her.

"Ho, la!" she heard as she started away. She turned. The face that grinned at her from the wheel of the jeep belonged to the bushman who had ridden with them up to Ngebin's camp. "Where are your yams, market woman?" he asked in Nebo.

"Oh, God." Marika backed up and walked toward him as if in a dream. "Everyone's gone," she said.

"What do you mean?"

"Don't you know about Amet?"

"Na, I'm just coming to the city now. The roads, they so free. I'm not understanding. Where be 'wa Mthongo?"

"You mean Florence," Marika said. Suddenly decisive, she went to the other side of the jeep and climbed in. "You've got to go where I tell you. I'll explain on the way."

"You with the leader," the bushman said, starting the jeep up. "I got no quarrel with you." He jerked into reverse, and they backed out of the quarter.

Timing at the Lovells' was lucky: the Hausa cleaning woman had left, and no one had yet arrived to prepare the evening meal. The house was utterly silent, and coming to Claire's room, Marika knocked loudly, afraid that she too, somehow, had gone. But Claire stumbled to the door, dressed still in her robe, her face white. She looked small, like a sick child, and Marika shoved her into the hands of the bushman while she went to gather a few of Claire's belongings and to throw the coverlet over the bed, to delay the inevitable panic that would set in when Curtis saw the stains. Docile, Claire allowed herself to be led to the jeep and bedded down in the back, and so they set out, almost an hour before curfew.

The driver had been right; there were no roadblocks or soldiers on the road. "They are raiding the quarter now, you know that," he said. "They got no time for what's outside. Once they clean up down there, they'll be coming after us."

The jolts of the potholed road seemed to fray the edges of Marika's nerves so that they finally fell away into exhaustion. She underwent a sleep filled with escapes overtaken—Florence, Claire, Amet, herself all crawling away from forces like tidal waves breaking over their heads. She awoke to the bushman's mournful, atonal singing, and when he saw she was awake he said, "We almost there now. See how your friend is doing."

Marika reached back and put a hand to Claire's forehead. It was fiery hot. "He circumcised her," she said. "Why?"

He shrugged. "This is a very sick man, this one in the palace," he said. "We in the bush, we cut our women when they babies. Then we put away the knife. The man is being afraid, he is like a caged beast. He is striking out. For him, the sacred rites are being like a weapon. Your friend, na, gets too near to him, she gets the knife like a lion's claw."

They entered the camp, lit only by the small fire from the main hut, the smoke rising like a white snake from its chimney. Before they drew close, the bushman reached under his seat and pulled out a rhino horn, which he blew from the open jeep. The long low note undulated over the camp. A man appeared from nowhere with a lantern. Speaking fast in Lethe, the driver explained his sudden return, and they drove on to Ngebin's compound. Marika's heart pounded. She had broken the rules, had gone against Richard's voice, bringing Claire here. Ngebin could hold her in contempt. But what should she care how this Ngebin saw her?

He emerged from the low door to his house, wearing only a pair of beltless fatigue pants, his anvil-shaped head recently shaved, beset by broken concentration, coming forward to meet the source of disturbance. "Mrs. Hooper," he said—the formal name like a military designation, discipline in crisis—"how did you make your way here?"

He did not ask why she had come, possibly leading Biswandi to their camp, the American women forming the perfect excuse for a raid. She told him about Claire, and about how she had gone to look for Florence and found herself ignored until she stumbled onto the jeep.

He smiled, looking tired. "Of course the people in the quarter turned their backs on you. What better ruse could Biswandi have concocted than to send *you* down there? But Mrs. Lovell needs a doctor."

"I think so. She's still bleeding."

Ngebin turned to one of the guerrillas who constantly attended him, and spoke rapidly in Lethe. "We can give her antibiotics," he told Marika. "Our facilities are poor, some of our people suffer greatly."

"Do you know about—" She could not speak the name.

"Amet, yes. Word came shortly after your driver left here, or I would not have let the jeep go."

"And Florence? Olanda?"

"They are here. They brought the news. We've given Olanda something to help her sleep. Come, you look as though you could use a nip of something yourself." He led the way back through the small door, Marika and then the attendants following.

"I'm afraid I've brought you only trouble," Marika said as he handed her a clay mug filled with warm bourbon.

"Nonsense. What else could you have done?"

"Her husband will already have started looking for her. With me gone, too, the trail points right here."

"It is only another reason for us to move fast. They will not come up this way by night—they know we have eyes for them in the dark. All of Biswandi's army would not stand a chance." He sat across from her. Between them on the low table, the architect's renderings of the dam were spread out and notated in bold red pencil. Florence had delivered them. "So in the morning we prepare ourselves. We set ourselves to move on the dam. This is where you come in."

"Amet said he needed the missing drawings."

"We're helpless without them. Can you get them in the morning?"

He put the question casually, as if he were asking her to stop by the stationer's. Marika put her hand to her forehead and giggled, feeling the bourbon. "Get them," she repeated, "in the *morning?* Why don't you just ask me to make myself invisible and fly to the Parambo on a magic carpet?"

"You are learning that the work is not so easy, hey? Now you'll learn that it is just possible. But you have not eaten."

He waved one of his men over and asked for rice, plantains, and olives. When the food came, Marika ate hungrily, suddenly aware of her empty stomach, of her legs cramped from the jeep; of her filthy hands, which she washed in the bowl that the man provided.

Ngebin drew short red lines on the edges of the renderings as he thought aloud, making Marika's plans for her while she ate. "We shall drop you near to McGrath's house in the morning," he said. "You'll stumble to the door, unwashed and unkempt, and you will tell him an awful story. You'll tell him, with some panic, about yourself and Mrs. Lovell being kidnapped and molested. I suspect that our missing plans are in his house—they were not with the others in the file, is that right?"

"Yes. But I didn't have time to scour the office, they could have been somewhere else."

"Doubtful. These plans were made consecutively; the ones missing were within the sequence. Our man at the plant tells us that McGrath often takes papers home."

"You have a man? At the Parambo?"

"Sure. Abeche. You know him."

"Peter Abeche. *That* makes sense. But why couldn't he—?"

"He has been always under suspicion. And no one but McGrath has the keys to his office. Abeche could only tell us what was on the surface, in the outer lobby. McGrath is certainly stupid, but those who run Pioneer Aluminum are not. Abeche could never catch them off guard, as you can."

"So I go to his house," said Marika, wiping her mouth with the back of her hand. "And he sends up an outcry. How can I get the plans to you from there?"

"Your nerves are shaken, you need to be alone. We send someone behind you to cut the telephone wire. McGrath must leave the house to alert the police to what has happened. He leaves you recovering, and you let our men in. Within ten minutes you should find those plans and be gone."

"What if Bud won't leave the house?"

The dark eyes shone mischievously at her. "You will be very distraught," he said. "Pathetic, even. And demanding justice. But how should I know what a beautiful woman does to get her way with a man?"

"Mata Hari again." Marika dropped the last olive pit onto her plate and leaned back in the low wooden chair. The food had lent her stability, but the alcohol in her veins still made her giddy and unnaturally relaxed. "You're very good to take in Claire," she said.

"Richard Hooper did many good things for us."

"Richard, yes." She tilted her head back and stared at the smoky ceiling. "I have done grieving for him," she said without thinking. "He was a good man and is buried. I won't find him again." She lowered her eyes to Ngebin. He sat contemplating her, his chiseled face younger than his years, alive with cunning and hope.

"You need to sleep," he said softly. The firelight reflected off the dark muscles of his chest.

"Is there a place where I can clean up?"

"One of the women can show you."

"And I'd like to see Claire."

He nodded and rose. At a signal one of the men, a young Lethe no more than fifteen years old, came forward and led Marika out of the compound, across the clearing to the infirmary hut, a long, low building fronting the jungle growth.

Inside, the central fire lit up the rows of cots and floor pallets that held the sick and wounded *dai*. A short, bunch-muscled bushwoman, ghostlike in a plain white *kanga*, was moving softly from bed to bed. When she saw Marika she pointed at the end of one row, and in the half-light they stepped around cots and over bedrolls to reach Claire. The stench in the room was a mixture of rot and antiseptic, but the close walls and smoky fire mercifully kept the bugs out. Claire was sleeping, a white bandage taped over her bruised eye, her loins swaddled under a light robe.

"Her fever is going down," said the bushwoman, coming over to Claire's cot.

"Are you the doctor?"

"Nurse." Her accent was more British than Yumanan. "He's been to look at her already. He sleeps, I wake. One of us always here, that way."

"Does he think she'll be all right?"

The nurse shrugged. "The flesh will heal. She is losing something more than flesh, of course. But I have known worse."

The young Lethe soldier led Marika out of the infirmary to the single women's quarters, where a metal tub had already been filled with hot water and topped with sweet papaya oil. There was no sign of Florence or Olanda. The women showed Marika her hut, then left her alone to bathe and wrap herself in a clean cloth.

Floating in the outdoor tub, water to her neck, the studded night sky above, Marika let the day with all its pain swim past her and disappear in the steamy, oily surface.

Half-animal, she knew the fullness of her belly, the lassitude of her limbs; and the slow itch of desire, brought on perhaps by the shock of Amet's death but for whatever reason aching for release.

Her hand sank through the water, to the depths of her vulva, and remained there as she rested her head on the sharp metal edge of the tub. Far off, in one of the last huts, a woman was singing a baby to sleep. She tried to focus on Richard, but drew a blank; and she could hardly move her lips to pronounce Justin's name. For now she was animal, cut adrift from memory and imagination, and craving the salty sting of a man's skin.

"You're just tired," she whispered aloud to herself as she stepped lazily from the tub and padded across the soft earth to her hut, where a broad blue cloth had been laid out for her to wrap herself in. But fatigue seemed only to rouse this newborn restlessness. She could not bring herself to want sleep.

Noiselessly, swaddled in the clean cloth, she passed by the quiet huts of the women and then the families, and finally the young men whose huts surrounded Ngebin's. Guards saw her but, recognizing her, did not stir from their posts. At the low door to Ngebin's quarters, she paused—aware, as of a breath of wind, of the wildness in her face, her uncombed hair, her trespassing. Had someone been watching the door, she would have turned back, but no one stood at guard and her steps went forward.

*He sleeps surrounded*, she remembered Richard's saying as she ducked her head through the door; but in fact he did not. Alone in his hut, the leader sat propped on his cot, writing in a small black notebook. For the first time that day his face betrayed that he had just lost one who was to him like a son. Two seasons before, he had shaved his head for his sister, and for her he had burned half of Revenir.

The fire had died down, leaving a red glow on all the walls. Ngebin was naked, slim hips harnessing powerful legs, the vulnerable scrotum between.

"I—I couldn't sleep," Marika began as he heard her step and looked up. Unembarrassed by his nakedness, he showed no surprise.

"Please," he said, "come in. Throw a coal on the fire."

She lifted a large chunk of coal with the wooden ladle and reset it on the embers. By the time she straightened, she had made ready with several excuses to escape; but as she turned she saw he had sat up, against the clay wall, the book laid to one side. The suggestion of a smile played over his lips, but there was no hint of scorn. His arms lay at his sides, the large palms turned up like vessels. She took a step toward him, then another. Like disobedient children, her eyes roamed over his body.

"The blue cloth becomes you," he said. His voice was patient and not completely sure of itself.

"Should I have stayed away?"

"Comfort should not be so difficult a thing. We should find it where we can."

One palm lifted, beckoning. He too needed release from sharp sorrow. Marika drew close, to where she could feel the heat coming off him, and glancing down, she saw that he had grown hard. She touched her hand to his cheek and gave a small cry at the electricity of contact. Bending, she pressed her mouth first to his chest, then his shoulders and neck, before she finally reached his broad lips, like velvet crushing as they molded to hers. With a deft touch of his hand he loosed her robe and she sank down to lose herself in him, in this stranger, this Ngebin. She caressed him with her tongue and teeth, his hard cock and tender scrotum a simple need she could attend to. Gravely he gave her pleasure, making the act complete with every corner and fold of flesh, until her breath came fast between her teeth and his lips found hers again in the vise of passion, his body deep within hers pounding and pounding, and the shared sweat covering them both. With a great sob she leapt into him, shuddering still as he filled her and drove far within her his comfort; as she translated her grief-spawned joy into rivers of tenderness, her hands tracing down his wide back, finally resting on his buttocks, finding one still, complete moment within the fractures of their time.

# Chapter 19

Morning made itself known like a cool, pink finger running down the length of one's spine, prompting not arousal but a slow stretch of the body, as if it reached for the dwindling night. The finger was the dry air of the harmattan, already skimming the top of the brown mud so that the clay dried to the dull sheen of caramel pie. Within a few days the wind would be whipping the ochre dust up the baked streets, leaving children screaming, blinded in its wake; it would silence the birds at night with its never-ending moan. But at this moment, after three months of steaming rain, the harmattan touched Yumana like a wand.

Languidly, Marika turned in her pallet, recalling in patches like torn magazine pictures her stealthy return to her compound in the night's dark hour, the burning fires in the huts as she passed them, the jeering laugh of the macaw. "I want to stay in bed," she mumbled aloud.

"Na, na, Missis," said a familiar voice. "You are having work to do in the day. Look how the sun!"

The sun indeed slanted through her open doorway, silhouetting Florence 'wa Mthongo as she stood blocking the light, tapping her foot on the hardened mud floor. Marika pushed herself up. "I heard you were here."

"I been already to see Mrs. Lovell. She's making a fuss for you, think we been eating you for breakfast!"

"How's she doing?"

Florence turned her palms up then down. "I have seen worse."

"I should go talk to her, explain all this."

"You are not having any time for chat." Florence held Marika's shoulder firmly as she rose from the cot, and steered her around to where her clothes, washed and dried but unpressed, hung on a metal folding chair.

"Who did that?"

"The girls, here."

Marika was reminded. "How is Olanda?"

"Olanda has shaved her head."

"It's so awful."

"He was being a dumb boy. Left his truck in the street, right outside. Then the men seeing you come in, they make for a demonstration."

"Biswandi knew *I* was there, too? Why didn't he pick me up, then?"

"He is knowing you and I be old friends. He's not going to go after ambassador's widow for her visiting, na, a friend. He is needing more from you than that. But he sent you a little warning."

Marika had unwrapped the blue sheet and stepped into her cotton skirt. "It's my fault that Amet is dead."

"It is the boy's fault and his alone. But hey, you are looking rested, Missis."

Marika's eyes flicked over to Florence's, as if she could read her reflection there. If Florence knew, the whole camp might know. And Florence knew.

"Good you rest up," Florence went on. "This is to be a hard day."

"Oh, Christ, McGrath. I almost forgot about him."

"We make you look bad on the way down the hills. I be coming along. Na, don't look worried, he is believing you already, this McGrath."

"You shouldn't have washed my clothes, if I'm supposed to have escaped the *dai.*"

"But you must be smelling sweet, isn't that so?" From the glint in Forcncc's cye Marika could not tell if she meant for McGrath or for Ngebin. They crossed the main courtyard, awash in the hazy morning sun of the early harmattan. In a week, at this hour, the ground would be already scorched and the women would pound *futu* in the thatched shade. At the end of the line of huts, Marika could make out Ngebin's tall, erect figure, waiting for them. She touched Florence's arm.

"I really should stop in on Claire first," she said. "She'll think she's been kidnapped."

But Florence was adamant. "You have work to be doing. You see her when you get back. She is no stupid woman—she is knowing her luck to be here, not in her big husbanded house, hey?"

So they continued, the two women, down the broad path that led inevitably to Ngebin, his head newly shaved and oiled for Amet's sake, a fresh shirt on his usually bare chest. He looked younger and, stripped of his mat of hair, markedly vulnerable. Marika tried to fathom how she could have lain tangled with him, and failed; but as they drew near, his scent caught and held her like a magnet. The blood rose to her neck.

"This is a frightening thing," he greeted her, "I am asking you to accomplish."

"You don't need to tell me that." She swallowed hard.

"If the documents are nowhere, you must turn around without waiting and head back here. We shall find a way through to the dam without them."

"I could just stay in Revenir and give away false clues."

"No. You would be examined. They would find your bruises to be chalk. They would find no evidence—of forced entry." His mouth as he looked down on her bore the vestige of a smile. "We can concoct another plan, Marika."

Ngebin's speaking her name was like a rope coming untied from her waist. Marika took a deep breath, and with it came a surge of energy. He had not forced politeness, he had not called her Mrs. Hooper, that name linked to Richard. He had not pretended. "I guess there's no time to waste," she said.

"Not a moment. *B'nago.*" In an unexpected, almost paternal gesture, he bent and, his hands to her temples, touched his lips to her forehead; then did the same to Florence. To the two men going with them, he nodded sternly. As they roared off in the jeep, the trees closed quickly as curtains, shielding the camp.

The first day of the harmattan always represented the one time that Africa seemed not the heart of the earth but only another of its living organs, the wind-swayed canopy of forest a bridge between the humming earth and the soundless sky. Monkeys skittered across the road as the jeep bucked over puddles; a mongoose lay harmless across a wide acacia branch; parrots shot through the dark leaves. And yet for all the tropical fauna, the crisp air might have been that of the central Ukraine, the summer morning when Katya had headed down from the hills to meet Marika's father and the rest at the Odessa docks. At this thought, Marika felt a tug of loneliness, the first since she had left Manhattan to return here. She was going to meet no one of her own kind, embarking on no risky voyage toward the future. What lay below for her was something Katya in her desperate flight had never known: vengeance.

She sat still as Florence took out a greasy bag full of ointments and rubbed the colors with her wide, rough thumb onto Marika's left cheekbone, a place on her neck, her upper arm. "They must be resembling fresh injuries," she said. "Pink and a little orange, not black, not blue."

"What if he touches one of them?"

"You wincc. You must bc thinking where they are. Now your shirt." Grabbing Marika's lapel, she tore it with one quick motion away from the body, the newly washed fabric ripping softly. In the back she did the same. The shirttails flapped their ragged edges in the breeze that riffled through the jeep.

Ever since she had begun relying on Justin's voice, memory for Marika had resembled a set of rooms waiting to be visited. She might leave a person behind in one chamber and be gone a long while, but when she entered that space again they would be there, as always, awaiting her. That images of Richard had not filled her mind for days meant only that she had not visited that one secret room.

*—Richard, are you still with me?*

No answer came. Florence bounced against her in the jeep.

*—Richard, damnit, I am avenging you. You have to communicate with me.* Still no answer, but as if caring little about the silence of her audience, her speech ran on. *—It gets to the point, doesn't it, when it doesn't matter whether one's side is right or wrong. One goes on what's touched them personally—for Florence and me, our husbands' deaths, for Amet his father—and one never steps back to judge the whole picture. Maybe* you *stepped back—but*

*you are the exception. And you know, no matter how involved you are, even if you do feel it in your gut as well as your head, you aren't bodily there as much as the rest of us. You say, "I do this because it's right," while we say, "I do this because they killed the one I love." The* dai *can make more use of me than they could of you.*

*—Still, the fight'll kill us both.*

So he was there, still. *—But eventually you'll be called a martyr. I'll be an accident, a piece of foolishness.*

She turned her thoughts out of the corridors of memory. She did not want to believe her use was to die, here in Yumana.

The sun had crested over the hills when they stopped the jeep in a thick patch above the lush neighborhood that contained McGrath's Pioneer-owned house. Eight o'clock at least, but McGrath slept late. The driver stayed with the jeep, a rhino horn resting on his legs, to warn them if he were discovered. The rest wove their way through the brush until they emerged near the small group of villas. "You go out to the road, right now," Florence whispered to Marika, "and you start right away to be running. We others, we vanish for you. You do not look back. You run, you scream. We shall be just outside of this house, na, to watch when he is going out. You must not have to call to us."

"All right," said Marika, but she did not move.

"Oh, my chicken," said Florence, and wrapped her with her heavy arms, her soft midriff like an ocean against Marika's ribs. "Go now." She laid her hand on Marika's purposefully mussed hair, then shoved her hard in the direction of the houses.

Like a top sent spinning, Marika ran down the new blacktop of the suburban road. Not until she was within earshot of McGrath's house and out of range of the others did she feel her throat open and give forth a cry. "Aiee! Ai! Help! Bud, Bud come quick! Ai-yee!"

He was at his door as she reached the drive, but only stood there, freshly shaven, as she stumbled across the lawn to the concrete steps. She was genuinely out of breath. "I—I—"

"What's wrong, Marika? What's happened to you?" Pronouncing her name right for the first time, his voice carried a cold edge. Had Florence gone too far? Did she look like a witch instead of a victim? But it was too late to stop.

"They—took me. And Claire. They've still got Claire." She sank onto the steps, her disheveled head resting on a dust-streaked arm. "Oh, Buddy. What they did."

She could not look at him. To this point, she had lied smoothly but never so outlandishly. "Come inside," he said. "Out of the open. Grab hold of my arm now."

If she had been worried about McGrath's excess of gallantry weakening her resolve, one look at his limply extended forearm reassured her. She should have known. He wasn't interested in damaged goods.

"I came here first," she said. "They left me somewhere, back—back there." She pointed toward the east, the scrubby high ground above the city.

"Claire was with you?"

"When they took us from her house. But they blindfolded us. They threw me out of the jeep alone."

"Scratch yourself?" Sarcasm, in his voice.

"N-no. It was soft ground. A few bruises, I guess. Curtis must be wild about Claire missing."

"Ahh, they'll find her. Drink?"

"Scotch, please. Buddy, I think I should get to a doctor."

"Sure, we'll call one pronto. You—uh—want to clean yourself up?" He motioned toward the bathroom. He did not steer her in that direction, did not touch her in any way. His capacious living room was decorated all in white, with tiger skins draped over the sofas and on the hardwood floors. She felt herself a beast. As she headed down the hallway to the washroom, she noticed how hollow her steps sounded. No housekeeper, no cook, and yet she knew he had these people in daily. She leaned a few minutes against the locked door of the washroom, afraid to look at herself. She combed her hair with her hands.

When she emerged, McGrath was spread halfway across one sofa, a drink in his hand. He motioned to a bottle and tumbler on the heavy glass coffee table. Now she could look at his eyes. They were small, plugged like bolts into his face. She detected no concern in them, but she had only this one card to play.

"I'm so shaken," she said, trying to prompt him. "I don't even know how many there were! They came while Curtis was away yesterday. They kept us all night, in this—in this—" She stopped to pour the liquor, spilling a string of drops that beaded on the table. Out of the corner of her eye she caught sight of a low credenza in the corner of the room, by the French doors that led to McGrath's garden. "This *hut*. We couldn't speak, they gagged us both. Then they just kept coming in after us. They—took turns. It was monstrous."

She gave an effective shiver. She could not be sure, but the size of the papers on top of the credenza looked the same as those she had folded six times to stuff into her purse at the Parambo Dam. The plans. It would be the first place to look, once she got him out of the house.

"Monstrous," he repeated, his beady eyes on her. Maybe she had been wrong, maybe he was not repulsed.

"Yes! Oh, God, Buddy," she said, taking a large swallow of Scotch, "I feel faint. Can't you get a doctor or something quick?"

"You want me to call up the hospital on the phone?"

"Yes! Why not?"

"Because the line's done been cut, that's why not."

He knew already about the phone.

Had he tried to call while she was in the bathroom? Her face registered shock. "No! Then they're nearby, somewhere. They know I've come to you. But you've got the car here, don't you? You can still get help."

"Oh, I don't think I'll need any help."

"For me, I meant."

"Oh, I should think you'd corraled just about all the help you'd want." Lifting his heavy bulk from the sofa, he took a step toward her, and without reflection she retreated.

"I don't know what you mean," she stuttered, "Buddy. I've been—I've—"

"You've nothing, lady." He took another step, and as though he had caught her by the arm, she stood still. "Come on, little Russki," he said softly. "You've got your Afro bucks lined up outside, now, haven't you? Ready to jump on Buddy from the bushes. Eh? Make me a new mouth in my neck?"

Her voice sounded dry as paper. "I don't know what you mean."

"We found Claire's car down by their digs. Sloppy work, Marika."

"They must've stolen it. They—took Claire's purse. With the keys."

"You think those"—he jerked his thumb behind him—"are the plans, don't you? You think I'm just that stupid, to leave them out for you like a calling card."

"Buddy, I've been hurt—"

"Not yet, you ain't." He did grab her arm then, his grip like a thick vise. "Now you tell me where they got Claire Lovell. You feed her to them? Yeah?"

He knew. Pain shot from her elbow to her neck. "You don't understand about Claire."

"I understand when I been blueballed for some baggy-lipped gangsters. Hey, baby? You put out for them?" He flung his drink behind him; it crashed against the credenza holding what Marika had hoped were the Parambo plans. With his free hand he took hold of the lapel of her torn shirt. "What were you gonna give me for those plans? A little tit, maybe?" Tight-lipped, she shook her head. He yanked, and the buttons of the shirt flew off. Without warning, he slapped her breast. "Maybe you'd get the knife out just when I shot into you, huh? All that hot seed, and then the blood, too. They teach you to like that?" He slapped again, harder, and she heard a small cry from her own throat. With the hand clamped on her elbow, he threw her to the floor. "Well, your nigger friends—the ones outside—they're getting it now. How about that!"

"I'm telling you, Claire and I—"

"We'll get Claire back. You didn't kill her. We'll get back what you stole from my office. 'Cause you'll tell us where to look."

"How—did you—find out?" she gasped, her arm across her stinging breasts.

Standing over her, he guffawed. "You think we got no moles, too? Hey, it took a few days, I admit. You had *me* on a string! Seems you were top secret. Took an Afro to clue us."

The name came like a flash. "Peter Abeche."

"Bingo."

That sardonic grin. No wonder Abeche hadn't taken the plans himself from McGrath's office. And he was the one who had chased, that long-past night, after the yellow-banded men who had gunned down Richard. "When did you know?" she whispered.

"Yesterday. When you led us to a nice prize."

"Amet."

He grinned. "They got names, your jungle bunnies?" Taking her drink from the table, he downed it.

Marika recovered her voice, full and loud. "You killed my husband."

"Man was a fool." His foot, large and heavy in a black leather shoe, lifted and set down on her waist. Slowly, methodically, McGrath unbuttoned his shirt. Marika twisted on the hard floor, and the foot pressed down.

"Murderer!" she accused him.

The foot flicked up, caught her on the chin, then pinned her again by the belly. "Watch your mouth."

"You've got"—she felt the blood run down from her mouth into her throat—"nothing on me. Hurt me, you hurt yourself."

"Hell, I'm no jury! I'm just taking what's been promised me."

"Nothing."

"You little fucking bitch." He reached down and, with a loud rip, tore her shirt. "You commie whore. You want to blast my gut open, huh? Make you all wet to think about it?"

"You got Richard in cold blood!"

"Yeah, the lily-white ambassador. He liked jungle bunnies, too, didn't he? He tell you their juice was sweeter 'n yours?"

"Richard never—"

"Ah-ha, but he did! Liked to flatten them out like little brown pancakes and spread his syrup. Whether they would or no. Like me and you. Not so much fun, is it, white on white?"

His foot had moved upward, the hard heel grinding on one nipple, then the other. Her muscles tensed like springs. "You don't know anything about Richard."

"I know you're a Russki cunt! And I am going to pop you before they string you up."

Unbuckling his pants, he lifted his foot, and Marika scrambled away. As she reached her knees, his fist landed to the side of her head, and she fell against the glass coffee table. "Pig!" she shouted. "Help! Pig!"

"Shut your shit-eating mouth." The back of his hand had broken her lip. Her head rang with the blow from the table. He stood over her, his white belly hanging over his erect penis, breathing heavily. "Off the panties."

Her mouth opened to cry out again, then stopped. Like the low wail of wind through a canyon, the voice of the rhino horn blew through McGrath's curtained windows. They had found the jeep. Suddenly Marika saw the whole truth of the trap, that outside there was no one to help her anymore. If McGrath knew, then there had to be others, waiting for Florence and the rest. "Don't do this to me," she begged.

"Off the panties!" The leather toe of his shoe jammed underneath and pulled them away, with a soft, sad sound. Then the same instrument drove, bruising, between her legs. She cried out. "Shut up, bitch!" he ordered, landing heavily astride her. With a last effort, she gathered the blood and saliva in her mouth and spat it at him. A palm cracked across her face, then the back of the hand from the other direction, then the palm again.

"Now you be quiet," he said, his voice softer, breathing hard, the sweat glowing on his face. "And you spread your legs good and wide. And I am going to rip you apart for what you tried to do to me. And you are gonna be quiet as death. You nod, now."

The place where his foot had struck had curled in on itself like a dying flower, dry and brittle. Within her head there remained no room for thought, as though each blow had knocked out another ray of reason. Through bruised eyes she saw him red above her, his head enormous, his breath a gas over her pinned and naked body. She tried to nod. When he broke her open, like the hollow stem breaking, her cry drove deep into her head and locked away there, in a sealed chamber, where even she could not hear its noisome, tortuous plaint.

# Chapter 20

The place where they put her smelled of rat feces. From the loose spot in the corner where the dirt silted in came the tang of sea salt, and she knew they had put her by the harbor. It would be the place she had viewed from above while visiting Richard's office, the same place McGrath had mentioned, where they had kept the American students before cutting off their hands and feet and laying them in shallow graves. A persistent trickle of lime ran, like a mucus trail from an unwiped nose, down the stone wall into the clay, still damp from monsoon.

For a long time the dark was thick, like a cool soup. Marika lay as if molded into the plastic mat they had spread on the floor for her, her legs and arms too heavy to lift or simply better where they lay, risking only the chafe of the plastic and the slow ache of gravity. Like anything in a shell, she was self-sufficient, relying on her blood warmth, her reserves of fatty tissue, her body's moisture. Then gradually the darkness sharpened and grew angular, so that first she realized her eyes were open, not shut, and next she strained them to see something through the dense opacity of air.

To attempt seeing, she first had to turn her head, then in a sudden and jarring move to raise herself on one arm and look across a horizontal plane. Propped on her shoulder, she realized for the first time since becoming conscious that she was wearing clothes, the same that she had allowed Florence to tear, the front of the shirt tied at the waist to hold it together. After staring at the space for several minutes, she began to see the smallest possible pinhole of light, a yellow sliver almost like a speck in her eye, gradually allowing her retina to widen and absorb its evanescent glow and to make out dimly the corners of the room, the pit at the far end, the run of lime water.

For what seemed a long while, that was enough—the recovery of sight, and the smells she could sort out and label in her mind. Gradually her hand moved off the mat onto the ground, her fingers digging absentmindedly into it, freeing the scent of fresh clay. She had not been unconscious when they brought her here, only slowed with a drug they had injected at McGrath's, to keep her from fighting and waking the residential neighborhood full of foreign businessmen. But then, she had wanted no sensation of her surroundings, only the blank oblivion into which the drug eventually pushed her. Now a set of basic urges came back, one by one like children, and the next one found her hiking her knees up to crouch on the barely visible ground. It was at that point that she felt the dull wound below her abdomen, and with its ravaged tissues her whole flesh became china, splintered into pieces and propped together with paste. One hand moved to her thigh, and bit by bit she touched herself, finding in the near-impermeable dark that she was there in every piece, every joint and distention. But the pain grew as she woke and pulled herself to her feet and in all consciousness brought herself to where she had been thrown.

Gradually she stood, her legs stiff and fragile as matchsticks. Neither McGrath nor the ones who had come into the house when he was finished with her had hurt her badly; no bones broken, only a spattering of warm glowing circles—the molecules making heat as they rushed to mend broken veins—that she knew were bruises, the fuchsia and orange kind that Florence had faked in the jeep, driving down. Reaching up her arms to test the ceiling of her cell, she touched with her elbows still bent. She walked, counting paces, from one end of the box to the other, and figured it as ten by about six feet, narrower from the door to the stone wall that faced outside. Then she sank to the plastic mat again and listened. From behind one wall, she heard a soft scratching—a rat, perhaps smelling her, digging under to her cell. After a long stretch of time she heard a clang of metal, far above her. Otherwise, silence reigned, pounding in her ear. She shivered, a strange thing to do in a tropical country.

"Oh, my darling girl," she said aloud. "You got yourself into a pretty pickle."

Clay and stone absorbed her words as soon as she voiced them. Laying a hand on her belly, she realized she was very hungry—she must have been here at least twelve hours. Perhaps they would allow her to starve here and die.

She knew Claire and Curtis had always been wrong about their nationality making a difference in the way they might be treated; one had only to think of nuns in El Salvador, botanists in Chile, political science students, just before her, in Yumana. Her mother would raise a query, maybe Morton would join in—maybe even Justin, with one of his temporary causes. There would be a column in the newspaper and a file in the State Department and a few questions asked of Mayume. There the matter would rest until Katya and Morton had both died and Justin had drunk or painted her into oblivion. A sweet, righteous wave of sadness swept over her as she imagined them all, asking for her and growing old, but the sharp odor of feces drew her back to reality. She shook her head.

She wondered where Florence was. Claire. Ngebin, the last man she had touched. No, not the last. She shivered again as McGrath loomed before her, cold as a slug and relentless, twisting her around and pinning her from behind, the rough carpet scraping her breasts as he wrenched her thighs apart. Curling into herself on the cold mat, she let out the same low moan that she had heard, a short time and a world away, from Claire. She wondered where Curtis was, if Claire had been found and had told him the truth, if he had turned on her, if he had been silenced. If Claire had been found and had lied. If Claire had not been found, and Ngebin were still safe, and Curtis Lovell knew nothing. What McGrath had said about Richard, flattening out African women—maybe she had understood nothing from the start, because they all played a game she had lost before entering the arena.

Time stretched, elastic and infinite. Marika stared bluntly at the low ceiling, indistinguishable swirls before her eyes. When she first heard a metal clank, closer than the one before, and steps following, she lay numb. It was only a guard or someone with heavy boots treading the hallway outside, who passed without pausing by her metal door. The longer she lay still, the more sounds she could distinguish—the wind of the harmattan blowing through the chinks above and around her cell, air whipping through ducts. From perhaps a mile away, the low flutey whistle of an oil tanker as the tugs pulled it into Revenir harbor. More movement, scraping and a sparse kind of chitter, from the walls.

After a timeless space, the steps came again, doubled,

and with them the jangle of keys at her door. Marika pushed herself up on her hands, her heart racing. She had nowhere to go and nothing to fight them with.

The light that hit her eyes blinded her; she covered her head the moment that the heavy metal door swung open, and tried in vain to squint at the two men who stood in its frame, laughing at her. "Hooper's wife," one said, too loud it seemed, in English as though she did not speak the tongue. The other stood behind him, peering over his shoulder. But to Marika they were both no more than dark silhouettes in the glare of the light; they said nothing else but kept laughing in a good-humored way as they set an object on the floor and left her in the relief of darkness.

She knew already to crawl, before the rats sniffed it out, to the wooden bowl they had left behind. Her eyes absorbed the darkness again; she could see nothing, but felt the bowl and the metal spoon, and smelled and touched the loose paste within before she lifted a mouthful gingerly to her tongue, feeling as much for the telltale filaments of insects as for the taste of the stuff. Nothing more than cold *futu,* it seemed clean and even fresh, and she shoveled it in before anyone came to take it away.

The one who came, uncountable hours later, was not so merry as the pair before. She heard him approach her door and this time shielded her eyes before he got it open. Between her fingers, her pupils adjusting quickly, she saw he was a large, older Sacatra, his loose features set in a scowl. She wanted to ask for water, but the words stuck in her throat. Picking up the empty bowl, he glanced over at the pit where she had painfully relieved herself, sniffed, and walked out, the door slamming loudly behind him and reverberating for Marika down to the last decibel of refracted sound.

Her mouth and throat dried out slowly, like fruit in the sun, the membranes going delicate and then hard with drought. She kept her mouth and eyes shut and dwelled on the thought of water. Her mind did not wander outside the dark space in which she was confined—one day, two, three, counted out by the arrival and removal of the bowl of *futu*. To recall the events that brought her here was worse than useless; the idea of planning ahead carried no meaning. She sucked the moisture from the *futu* and demanded water, loudly and more and more hoarsely, each time the men opened her door. Once the first one she had seen, who had called her Hooper's wife, took a pair of threatening steps toward her. She would not move but pulled her hands from her face and squinted at him: "I need water."

Then on the fourth day it arrived, warm but clean, in a tall plastic cup that sloshed on the floor as the one who cleared away the *futu* bowl set it down. She drank thirstily and too fast and had to lie on the mat determinedly holding down the *futu* and the water that her perverse body wanted out of surprise to retch up. Next time the water came, one or two days later—already the passage of time had slid into a category of no importance—she took it carefully, in sips, allowing the precious liquid to roll around her desiccated gums before it slid down her throat, devoid of song or speech, to the pit of her stomach.

There were things she could not help: that her body grew dirt like scales, that her scalp itched with what had to be lice, that her urine smelled of *futu*, that after only a few days her gums bled because the paste was all they encountered, that her eyes, like a mole's, tried vainly to blink each time the door was opened and the cruel rush of light was allowed in. That she had ceased so quickly to think about anything but these animal needs was a thing she condemned and tried to prevent in herself. She went over the libretto to *Fidelio;* she remembered Ukrainian songs that her mother had sung to her as a child; she dredged up images of the harbor outside as it had looked from the ambassador's house on the hill. At one point as she waited for the food to come, it struck her that she was alone, in her head—that no Justin or Richard was there with her, as if her suddenly reduced circumstance cut the life force for them. In a melancholy way she wished they would visit her, as one might a friend in the hospital. But they stayed home.

It did not fail to occur to her that Biswandi might have designed her death this way—scurvy from the diet, dehydration despite the occasional teasing cup of water. The time for her period came and went, her body unwilling to shed even a drop of moist blood. But after some indefinite stretch of days—at night, because the pinhole of light at which she stared sometimes for hours was not present—two men she had not seen before threw the door wide open and came in for her. Though she did not protest, they took one arm each and hauled her out into the blinding electric light as they might a thrashing monkey. They carried her, her soles dragging against the floor, down the hallway and around a corner, past closed metal doors identical to her own, the metal unpainted, gun color. When they had passed through an open doorway into a large, white-tiled room, they set her down, and her legs, though she had been walking lengths of the cell daily for hours, almost crumpled beneath her, so helpless did the light render her.

"Take off your clothes," said one of them, tall and muddy-skinned. Pistols wagged on his belt.

Marika consolidated strength in her legs, stood straight, and stared at him. Would they assault her, stinking and molelike as she was? Then her eyes, adjusting, open now, flicked around the tiled room. Other men had taken her mother's sisters, along with the Jews, to a place like this in Germany, and the innocent metal spigots in the ceiling had sprayed the sisters with death. Of course, they couldn't want her flesh; it was her life they would take. Her arms hung at her sides.

"Is not time to be wasting," said the other, a true Sacatra, short-necked and trim, his skin the color of bricks. He walked straight over to Marika and began untying her shirt, not roughly but with authority, as a strict parent would undress a child. When he had loosed the second knot, Marika pushed him away and finished the job herself, staring ahead as she slipped out of her dirt-stiff torn skirt and waited for them to do whatever they had been ordered. The mud-colored one reached forward, grabbed the clothes, and tossed them out of the room.

Marika thought for a moment, softly, of Richard, how he had liked to see her naked. Then the men stepped back, one turned a switch, and the showers came on.

It was nothing but cold water. The first drops nonetheless rained on her like knives, the pain clearing her senses. She saw the distance between herself and the two disinterested soldiers; the height of the room; the three walls with no way of escape. She remembered Florence, whom she had forgotten for days, and Ngebin with his pure cause. *They* had been trained for places like this. They would know how to focus and survive. Her body shivered under the hail of water, and lifting her head, she opened her mouth to catch some. Then, even as the men watched, she ran her long-nailed fingers through her tangled hair, combing out the lice that had spawned at the roots, the cold water washing them down. Her head drenched, she bent to perform the same operation on her pubic hair. The water trickling between her shaking legs caught the odor and spirited it away. Shameless, she raised herself up and gulped in the water again, its taste fresher than what they had so rarely brought her in the cell, the spray clear and without scent. The chill went through to her bones. Then abruptly, the switch flicked off, and she stood naked and dripping before the two men in uniform.

For the first time since the day when she had tried to blister them with pleas for water, she opened her mouth to speak. The sound that came out she did not recognize as her own. It might have been another voice, like Justin's, like Richard's, invented and not quite true. "What," the voice asked, "happens now?"

But the voice wasn't invented. The men heard her. "Now you go to the general," the tall muddy one said. From a small sack he had slung under his arm, unnoticed until now, he drew out a length of red cloth. Dumbly, Marika recognized the red dress she had worn on the plane. They had been to the Lovells', they had brought it to her from there. Next he pulled forth a thin brown towel that he threw to her. She clasped it to her chest, suddenly aware of her nudity, shivering in the clammy air.

"She has to hurry," the shorter one said in the bastardized French that the Sacatras used. "He waits already."

"Soon enough," said the other as she turned away from them to wipe the cold water from her body. On her legs the growth of hair, still stubbled but beginning to curl, accounted for the time since she had left to take Claire up to Ngebin's camp—three weeks, or more. Her belly looked bloated, most likely the *futu* and the sudden intake of water from the shower. In the utter dark she had not seen her own outlines, and she had used her hands only to stroke herself, as if her body were a pet cat. Now she encountered it, in its ghostly whiteness, shaming her. The tall one looked on. When she drew up from drying her legs, she wrapped the towel around her breasts and faced him. "Hand me my dress," she said, her voice unpracticed but her own. Leering, he stepped forward and gave it to her.

Barefoot, her hair rudely combed—the Sacatra had handed her a three-pronged implement, oily from long residence in his pants pocket—she walked between them through long corridors and up flights of stairs that seemed endless. Her legs took the steps one at a time; the walking in her cell helped not at all with lifting one foot then the other over the high concrete. Like any animal seeing its own kind, she could not hate the soldiers, who waited impatiently, their hands on her upper arms, for her to scale the stairs. "I'm sorry," she said.

"No time to waste," said the short one again.

Her dress, she thought, looked strange on her, but then everything that met her eyes looked strange, brighter than she had left it, the corners and angles of things sharper and more threatening. At last they reached the top of the last flight and turned off the corridor into a long, narrow room, with a guard dozing by a closed door at the other end.

"We are bringing her," said the tall one.

"Name," said the guard, sitting up and leaning into a long pad on his lap.

"Hooper."

"Shit. Get her in there."

The guard stood and unlocked the door. The two bringing Marika pushed her, gently she thought, and she found herself facing Biswandi.

She gritted her teeth to make her legs, gone to jelly from the stairs, hold her steady. "So, Mrs. Ambassador," the general said, his white teeth smiling in the folds of his cheeks, "sit down."

Next to Biswandi, behind a long table, sat two others, like him bedecked over their olive drab uniforms with pins and medals and ribbons—hungrily her eyes picked out the bright colors. One of the soldiers who had brought her nudged the backs of her knees with a chair and she sat.

"So," continued Biswandi amiably, "you are finding terrorism to your liking?"

"I don't understand you." She had not been trained for this—the questions, the playing dumb, the long silences and repetitions—any more than for the privations she had endured. They would get what they wanted from her.

"Ah, but Mrs. Ambassador, that is not where the problem lies. The problem lies in myself, not understanding *you*."

She sat silent. She did not have to speak. She was out of the habit anyway.

"What I am meaning is, that you had done nothing wrong but marrying yourself to a terrorist. A rather stupid terrorist. And you did not know."

"I knew," she said reflexively.

"No, Mrs. Ambassador, you did not know. You do not know even now."

All the words, the light in the room, the fresh clothes were beginning to wake her up. She shook her damp hair back from her face and leveled her round eyes at him. "I want a lawyer," she said distinctly. "And regular water. And some vegetables or fruit in the diet."

"Pomegranates," Biswandi said to one sitting beside him, and they all roared with laughter.

"I demand to know what the charges are against me."

"No!" The laughter stopped. "You are not teaching us our scales, music teacher. You do not demand of us anything."

She bit her lip but did not lower her eyes. The room was warm, drying the damp of the shower from her skin and drawing out perspiration.

"Your husband—" began the one next to Biswandi.

"You killed my husband."

"You see?" said Biswandi. "She does not know, she is ignorant. We are here to be helping you," he turned to tell Marika.

"Then I want a lawyer."

"We wish to educate you."

"A lawyer and fresh fruit in the diet."

"We wish you to meet your husband's murderer."

"You have no right to withhold water."

"Bring her out," the other next to Biswandi said to the guard. He walked quickly to a side door, opened it, spoke to someone on the other side. Marika held back her curiosity. Richard, Richard, where was he, to tell her what to do? Her mouth had gone dry again, the water from the shower inadequate for her sweating body. No counsel from Richard reached her.

The woman they brought in walked freely between two guards, her small head thrown back. Awkward in heels and a tailored dress, she looked straight ahead, not at Marika but at Biswandi.

"Seki," Marika said.

Seki did not answer or glance her way. Wobbling on the fragile heels, she came to a standstill where the soldiers stopped, perpendicular to Marika.

"We bring you," said Biswandi, even his voice glowing, "a victim of colonialism. Disguised, to fit the custom, as a free agent."

"Seki," Marika said to her, "we never hurt you. Why would you help these people? *You* didn't kill Richard."

"It is not for you to speak!" one of the other two barked. Bareheaded, he looked young, a boy acting tough.

Biswandi went on, "No one can blame her for what she did. The white man taking what he please, it's an old story. Many before, they have worn the clothes of the revolutionary, to get what it is they want."

"Cut it, Biswandi," said Marika, her voice harsh as a man's. "What are you telling me?" She felt herself losing the game, and she thought of water.

"Let *her* be telling you." Biswandi nodded toward the motionless Seki. "Go on," he pressed her. "Tell why it is you strike out at the American ambassador. You know who this is, here. You recognize her."

For a moment, Marika wondered if Seki did. She herself was ignorant of the bruises on her face; those on her arms and legs had gone to a mustard yellow, the broken places crusted with dirt. It was still such a miracle to her to see the bright things around her that she had not stopped to think how she, with her pasty face and small, blinking eyes, her hair streaked with oil, must look to these others. Her own dress fit her badly, as if it belonged to another body.

"Yes," Seki said. "I am knowing the lady." Her face was turned still to Biswandi, away from Marika.

"Tell her what you have done."

"I have not done anything!" Her small brown hands gathered into fists.

"You killed her husband—did you not?"

"No! I—"

"Richard Hooper, the American ambassador. You stood outside his greenhouse and shot at him until he was dead."

"Don't make me say it again!"

"Why not? You have confessed the crime. Say it once more for Mrs. Hooper. It is making no difference in what we do to you. Tell her: It was you who killed her husband."

"No!" Seki's hands had twisted, now, into a single knot before her chest.

"We know that you shot him till he was dead! But tell us why, na, tell the lady why you would be killing her husband!"

"—not my fault!" Marika heard burst from Seki's throat. The girl managed a quick sidelong glance in her direction, like a fleeing animal checking its tracks.

"Not your fault? Not your fault?" Biswandi was gripping the girl's words in a stranglehold. Marika could not breathe. "What would the American do to you that you would go to kill him? Hey? Hey?"

She wanted them to send Seki away—this was a ploy they were using, a weapon against her, and nothing to do with why she had come to Africa, to avenge Richard. Seki's legs shook on their high heels.

"Don't make me say these things," she said to Biswandi in Lethe, half-whispered, but he answered loud and in English.

"What things will you say? What things make you kill him? Do we have to make you say?"

A soldier stepped forward and gripped Seki's arm, but she screamed with the same ferocity as if he had twisted it to breaking. "Aii! I'll say! He—lay me down, he jump on me, he make me, he make me—!" She tried to pull away from the soldier.

"Make you what?" Biswandi pressed. "Make you do chores, make you do other things?"

"Other things! Terrible things!"

"He beat you?"

"No! He—" She waved her free arm in the air.

"He assaulted you." The girl nodded. "He flattened you out."

"He is making me do it many, many times," Seki burst forth, as if relieved that Biswandi had said the words. "He is making me, when I am just there alone, cleaning, to lie on my stomach and he does these things to me, in the one place and the other place. It hurts me and I scream, and he cover my mouth. And he makes me, with my mouth, to take him in. He is saying that he'll see me sent back to the hills if I am not doing this with him. So then"—glancing sidelong at Marika, Seki got rid of her story, fast and breathy—"then I get with child, you know, his child, and I know by my own smell that it is a man child. But he—"

"Richard Hooper," the young one by Biswandi put in, almost like a lawyer, checking the guilty party.

"Yes, I am in his house. I am keeping everything clean, the garden too—"

"A man child, you say you were carrying." Biswandi could not let her be distracted.

"And he says to me, Get rid of it. But my people, we cannot kill a man child, it is every way bad luck. Girl child, we can do this. I say no, it is a boy, but he tells me I don't go and he'll tell his wife, and she will kill me for sure. I must tell her instead it is just my child, nothing to do with him. So I tell her so."

*We never knew the father.* Marika's heart stopped her throat as she listened to Seki. Was this the wormlike truth she had come so far to hear?

"And you did this?"

Seki nodded. "I go to this place that they both are knowing of, and the people open me up, and hurt me, and they take out this child. I ask them to tell me, it is a boy or girl, and they are not knowing. But I know, by the smell. Then my sister in the hills, she is giving birth but the baby is dead. The day I hear this, I know the curse is on us, because I am killing this man child. So I go to—I go—"

"You got a gun and killed Richard Hooper," Biswandi finished for her.

"No!" cried Marika.

They looked at her, mildly amused, the young lawyer outraged.

"Richard couldn't *have* a child," Marika said tightly. "We tried and failed for years! Even if he had—*touched*—this woman, he would not have made her pregnant. Your whole stack of cards"—she looked up at Biswandi—"falls apart."

The smile remained fixed; Seki even seemed to join them, the corner of her small, pouting mouth twisting upward as if she was proud of what she could tell Marika, here in the protection of a low-ceilinged cellblock room that passed for a court.

"Go on!" said Biswandi. He had recovered his severity. "You say Richard Hooper raped you and made you pregnant. This one says no."

"He told me"—Seki looked down at her waist now, as if a child rode there and passed her the story—"his wife, na, she was barren. He says he's not wanting her anymore because she be dried up inside like an old fig. But then—but then, ai, when I'm giving him a child, he's making me to tear it out!"

"I won't believe this!" Marika erupted.

"You will not *speak*," the other one next to Biswandi, an angular red-haired Sacatra, warned her. One of the soldiers standing behind her chair took hold of her upper arm, jerked it, and let it go.

"You were saying," Biswandi continued with the disquieted Seki, "you went somewhere for a gun."

"To the men of the *dai*," Seki answered. "They need the money, they will sell anything."

"They are knowing you want to kill Richard Hooper?"

"No! He is helping them, he spies for them. I know

this. But it is easy to buy. I am Lethe. I chant their little song, and they sell to me. They are giving me also one of their armbands, so, like a little honor."

"So you go up to the house, and you see the ambassador in the greenhouse, and you shoot."

"I shoot," Seki repeated, crossing her arms defiantly over her ribs, "and I get him. I end this curse."

"So you see, Mrs. Ambassador." Biswandi turned his attention to Marika. His face had the happy puglike look of a dog who has jumped for a biscuit. "Your husband the terrorist dies in a crime of passion. Flattening out the help, hey?"

*Like little brown pancakes*, McGrath had said.

"It's not true!" The blood bursting in her head, Marika went for Seki, but both soldiers shoved her back and held her in the chair, their hands like iron clamps. She surged forward again and they knocked her back. Her breath came short. "He never touched you!" she shouted at Seki. "They're making you say these things! *They* killed him, the people in this room, they butchered him!"

Seki turned to her, calm and proud now with her story told. "He has a brown mole," she said quietly, "on the inside of his left thigh. The size of shilling coin. When he is at his peak, he is whispering, so: 'I am coming.' You see, na, that I know."

"No! It's a lie! Richard couldn't father a child! There were two *men* outside the window of the greenhouse!"

"No two men," Seki answered quickly. "Just me."

"You wore the armband of the *dai*, not so?" said Biswandi.

"I am not caring. I don't want to die for ending this curse. Let them die for it, they are evil, they hurt the Lethe." Her answers came fast, like a speech memorized, without inflection.

"A crime of passion," Biswandi began again, "which to spare the Americans embarrassment we are placing with the *dai* who kill so many. We save the good name of Richard Hooper."

"You—knew this—all along?" Marika asked.

"Before you are leaving the country, we know. But why shame the widow? Then you must be coming back and planting bombs like your husband, we must stop you. Not so? Then maybe you will talk to us a little, tell us about your new friends."

Glaring at Seki, Marika wanted to choke the truth out of her. Yet in their house, the girl had never lied. And she had told the details now of Richard's body, the words he used. *I'm coming.* "I have no friends," she hissed at Biswandi.

"The ones who sold this piece of filth the murder weapon? Not your friends? Tell us where they hide, now, where they keep their little toys."

"You already know," Marika answered.

"Do we? Then no harm in telling again. You came to Africa for vengeance, did you not, Mrs. Ambassador?" Marika was silent. "Here is your target. You want her head?"

"No!" Seki cried. "You promised no!"

"Shut her up," Biswandi said, not glancing the girl's way. The two at Seki's sides pulled her backward. "So, you want to sit with a glass of wine and talk?" he asked Marika genially.

"Talk about what," she answered in a monotone.

"Look, Mrs. Ambassador, we of course mean you no harm. You violate the laws of our tiny nation, you place yourself on the side of violence, but we are understanding your motives. So now I find for you the one who has done the deed. We can be doing one of two things. First"—he took the tip of one pudgy finger and pointed it at her—"we can send a very exciting little press release out, to this effect, that you have disappeared and this *woman* has been found to be accountable for Richard Hooper's murder. We have nice details for all the journalists, and we are parading the girl out to tell her story. But she is going free, and you are swallowed up, let us say, by the *dai.* Or"—the middle finger joined the index—"we say it is the *dai,* still, who went for Richard Hooper. We have many downstairs to serve this purpose. You saw some, did you not, before you left our country for New York?"

Marika stared at him, unable to incline her head. Amet had stood at the end of that lineup.

"So we bring them out, now, and you appear also, just as you are. We'll take pictures, hey? And you say, just so, it is the *dai* took you away and starved you and beat you down. This gets into all the papers, na, the TVs. Your government is sending us money and guns to put down these communists. And you may be there to see the girl shot."

"I don't believe," Marika said, barely moving her lips, "Seki did it."

"No? You want more proof? More little words, times and places? We have more proof, if you want."

"No! I don't want proof. I want—to think." She shut her eyes and saw in their darkness Seki, in her stiletto heels, her face ashen underneath the purplish rouge.

"Go then! Go think! Take all the time—ha ha!—all the time of your life, Mrs. Ambassador! When you are hungry for the girl's blood, then you'll have more to say to me. We all know more than we think, hey? Hee hee! Go on now, have a good cry, hey?" His body rocked with laughter. The others joined in. Her throat dry, her head filled with a boiling rage, Marika was dragged backward from the room, into the long low corridor again.

# Chapter 21

They did not take her back to her cell, her dark safe cubbyhole of ink-black air. Down different corridors, filled with human sounds, they took her past grilled doors. She was just able to catch a glimpse of the men, then the women crouched on the floors or plastered to the walls, before the guards pushed her along. Shaded overhead lamps turned the halls an eerie, uniform amber. Abruptly, they reached one of the last doors, and with a quick turn of a heavy key in the bolt, the two men opened the door and thrust Marika in.

The heavy clang of the metal closing behind her made the dozen women in the room wince in unison, as though they had all been slapped at once. Then they stared at her, their white sunken eyes in the pitch of their faces catching the refracted light that came through the grille. They might have been tigers contemplating a meal thrown to them. But before any could speak, a figure rose from where it was sitting in the corner, and hobbled slowly toward Marika.

"Missis Hooper, you are alive." The cracked voice came from a mouth that Marika could see was almost swollen shut. Florence's whole head, in fact, as she came into the ray of light, looked like a bowling ball, so swelled was it with bruises. She walked, bent far forward, as if she might pitch onto the ground at any moment; and as Marika stepped forward to catch her elbow, the heavy woman's weight almost brought them both down.

"My God," Marika said when they were seated, leaning against the concrete wall by the barred door, "what have they put you through?"

"I am thinking maybe my hip is broken." Florence leaned far back against the wall, her left leg thrust straight out. "And they are hoping, na, to make me stupid, knocking the head. We Kikuyu think in the stomach, so I am all right this time."

"How long have you been here?"

"Since you, Missis, since that morning."

"How long is that?"

"Thirty-nine days. The harmattan be soon over."

"So long!" Marika drew in her breath. "I lost track. More than I thought."

"Your skin, so yellow. They feed you what?"

"Bean paste. And no water."

"I keep thinking, they should not be killing you. I hear what they are planning for you. But then we get no word, and it is always: no word, no living person."

"I've been living like that. Like a dead person." Marika looked up and around her, still amazed at the voices, colors, movements. All the women were barefoot. She thought again of Seki in her high heels. "It might be better, dead."

"Shame, Missis." It came out *Mitthith*, and looking closely, Marika saw that Florence's teeth, once flashing white in her mouth, were half gone. "They are wanting to get you to think so."

"Of course they are." Marika dropped her eyes to the pallor of her limbs, stretched before her for the first time in more than six weeks; ran her tongue over her own teeth, hanging barely to rotting gums. Her breath stank. Now that she knew it had been almost six weeks, she was surprised that she felt no worse. She felt, in fact, some buoyancy of life within—until she thought of Seki's tale, and the bubble collapsed. She edged slightly away from Florence. "Did you sell Seki the gun?" she asked bluntly.

Florence eyed her from swollen sockets. "She was buying no gun," she said.

"So you know she killed Richard."

"I know what they going to be telling you."

"That he—what he did to her—"

"He did nothing." Florence shook her head sternly.

"How do you know?" said Marika shrilly, losing control. "How do you know what she said to me? How do I know you aren't covering up for what your people did after all? How do I know"—her mind racing, snatching at every strand of the web—"you aren't in on it, her telling me my husband's a philandering brute who got himself shot? Leaves you and Ngebin in the clear, doesn't it?" In shouting Ngebin's name, she cut herself short. She had tucked him away since they brought her here; he had become a presence in her mind with no name, no voice.

The other women in the room gathered above them, chattering in Lethe. "Hush up," one said angrily to Marika in English. "They will be punishing us, when they hear you."

"This Seki is," Florence said in a whisper when they had drifted back from the corner, "a stupid, frightened girl. They are making use of her to break you—with no torture weapon, na, it's easy. Then you will be testifying against *dai*. They can use you everywhere, pretty innocent American lady speaks out. More U.S. money, guns, armies. Nothing better for them. They kill us all."

"What if she's telling the truth?"

"You think your man would be doing those things to the girl?"

"I don't know! She—knew what he was like. In body. Things I hadn't even recalled."

"You are forgetting they be listening to you, in your home, years on years."

"It was true she conceived a child. I *helped* her get rid of it. I didn't know!"

"That child not your man's."

"I suppose you're going to tell me whose it was, then?"

"When you tell me how many men there are in the city!" Florence snapped at her, then after a silence said, "But you are so eager to believe them. You could never be having children, you and your husband. I remember."

"Maybe it was just me to blame. Maybe he hated me for it. Maybe he cheated on the *dai* the way he did on me, and you killed him!"

"So they try to make me say." Florence ran a pink palm over her crippled hip. "But if I'm not lying for them after they do these things to me, why am I going to be lying to you here? Hey?"

"Maybe because you want things I don't understand." From where she sat, Marika looked up at the women crouched or standing around her. Gaunt, their skin devoid of lustre, they picked their teeth and scratched their thighs with primates' obsession. There was no room in the cell for hate, for suspicion; crowded together, each was an isolate particle. She would not, she thought with regret, be able to walk the length of the room as she had before; her companions blocked her way. Thought that ventured beyond these walls held no use for them or her.

There was a small closet at the end of the narrow room in which the women could relieve themselves or be alone, and often, as the time wasted away, one would shout at another inside, to get her to come out and give this one a chance. The food came that first day, or night—it was even harder to tell time than it had been in Marika's unlit cell—in large buckets, yams and a sort of mashed guava; Marika leapt at it, hungry for the tang of fruit. Passing the buckets, each woman had a utensil. Silently Florence pulled a plastic spoon from the folds of her stained blouse and handed it to Marika. The women talked together in flat, slow Lethe, and while Marika could have understood them, she failed to make the effort.

"Who are they?" she asked Florence in a whisper, unable to maintain the chill of silence.

"All kinds. Mostly are in here for stealing or breaking curfew. One over there—you see the tall one, scar on the face?—is *dai*. When the river flood, they forcing her and her mother and brothers from this little cassava farm. One of the brothers was going to work at the dam, but a mechanism is faulty, and he falls, and he dies. Not so bad a history for a Lethe boy, but it was taking no more than that for this Fandella. She turns to the *dai*."

"What's she in here for?"

"This time, only leafletting. They will keep her here a year, maybe more. Once before, she had four years for spitting at police. She is not so foolish, now."

Marika knew, falling asleep that night on the concrete floor next to Florence, her blood humming with the hours of light, of voices, of movement, that she would be in the rectangular room with the other women for a long while. She recalled as from another lifetime the handful of Americans she had met who had been jailed, for marijuana or political incitement or being in the wrong place, who had begun by assuming the mistake would be cleared up, that they would be on their way to St. Louis or Tacoma in a day or two. They had learned through boomeranging emotions the elasticity of time. It stretched before her devoid of desire or psychic dread, like air before a flying balloon with the ballast of hope cast overboard. She had only to watch, listen, test the balance.

The next day passed in a fog. The one who brought food in the morning bent to Florence and whispered a few sentences as he left, but Marika did not hear and did not ask. The others—Marika counted eleven prisoners, all Lethe or mixed-tribe, all but Florence younger than she—shuffled in their shadowy way and waited for their portion. While they ate, Marika buried her head in her knees, like another woman at the far end of the room who spoke to no one, and tried to reconstruct the past—the days, the weeks before the awful night of the reception, eight months back.

Richard had pushed and pushed, she remembered, for a return trip to the Parambo, determined to make it before Pioneer sent another man in. Twice it had been all arranged, and then Biswandi had called to say the jeep wasn't running, or the driver had taken sick. Richard had ranted and complained and stormed out to the greenhouse to defuse his anger in caring for the orchids. Seki had been there every day, diffident and only a little lazy, arriving minutes after Richard left for the office, staying until midafternoon. It had been a month since Seki's operation, and the pale edge of vulnerability it had given her had already toughened up. The *dai* had mounted an offensive to the west—not far, Marika realized now, from where Ngebin was to have his camp—and from her lesson room Marika could see the long line of drab army trucks snaking around the ledge in the exposed side of the mountain. So close to the city, no snipers would touch them, but a stretch later on, about one out of ten would be picked off the unprotected highway. These and others would limp back at night, to the single hospital in the city, its wings clogged with men in makeshift cots.

Used to helping in the maternity ward, Marika had put in extra hours and had persuaded the squeamish Claire to come down as well. But the wounded and dying were all either mercenaries or Biswandi's men—the *dai* had no entrance to the hospital—and her spirit rebelled at healing one side that it might crush the other. So she had retreated, leaving Claire, who began just at that time to talk of her itch to one day seduce a man with coal-black skin. Outside the hospital, Marika saw the dozen students who still came for music lessons—the Nebo boy with his impossible flute, Constantin Mayume like a precious nut locked in a hard shell ready to crack, others scattered through the week. And she drove to the airport and dwelled on Justin, no more than a museful diversion by then, a screen between her and the portents of those weeks.

The month before, when Seki was having her operation, Richard had seemed in high spirits. He had told Marika—and the hidden microphone—that Ngebin was just outside the country's borders, that he wanted to negotiate through the United States before heading in. There had been cables back and forth across the Atlantic in an increasing volley until the answer came: No. The American ambassador was not to engage in diplomacy with rebel forces. Then Richard's mood collapsed like a balloon and he began pushing to see the high country again. He had several late-night encounters, foxing the curfew despite Biswandi's monitor. But he took no notice, Marika thought, of Seki or her pain. Or had Marika herself taken no notice of him, the nuances of his needs? They had made love hungrily, in the small hours of the morning, when she could not see his face.

He had always treated Seki like an unexpected guest, someone Marika had invited and he didn't want to offend or overburden, even though it had been he who brought her home from the embassy one blistering hot day. They never exchanged more than a few words. Before Richard and Marika came to Africa, he had had many women friends, colleagues' wives who hung on him at the dreary parties they all attended in Washington. He found them silly and kind. Before he and Marika gave up on conceiving, he confessed that he lay awake nights imagining the sound of a child's breathing and praying to a Being he had never believed in to give them at least one chance.

None of what Seki had said could be true. Or else Richard's capacity to deceive had been as great as Marika's. Which it well may have been. She had known nothing, after all, of the tapes he had made, nothing of a plot to destroy the Parambo Dam, nothing of what prompted his ingratiation with Pioneer officials; nor, for a time at least, had his government known. He had not begun, surely, by lying, but he had made the transition with incredible ease, only his moods darkening along the course. How easy it was, too, Marika reflected as she thought of her own deceit among the Lovells. And she had hidden Justin from Richard, so why should he not have found a small cache for Seki? And Seki's child, who never came to term.

His would be the invisible hand, she had once thought, reaching through a barred window. But in this concrete block there were no windows for ghosts to enter; there were only the walls and the metal door, the dulled women shut up inside. No room for belief, though Florence carried it within her like a vital organ, feeding and cleansing her.

The third day, Florence was unable to move. "I am feeling a fever, in my hip," she said.

"You talk to the guard. Can't he get a doctor for you?"

"He is already watched. I am hearing from him about the others."

"The ones with us, in the jeep? What happened to them?"

"One shot. The other is every day with being questioned. This week he tell them supply routes, or he is shot also. Me, they are waiting a little bit more on. I ask for a doctor, and they going to want a thing or two in exchange."

There was no place, within the four close walls, for trust or mistrust. Marika brought the food, when it came, over to Florence, and helped her sit up to eat. The tall woman with the scar on her face spoke quickly to Florence at intervals but kept a distance from Marika. The bruises on Florence's face had flushed to a deep purple. As she sat up, she gripped Marika's arm with a hot, dry hand.

It was perhaps a week before the two guards who had put Marika in the cell returned. She glanced back at Florence as they pulled her out into the wide, lit hallway, but all she saw was a pair of feverish black eyes threading after her.

Stronger with the light, the food and water, she walked solidly between them as they climbed the stairs, higher than she had gone before, and echoed their way through a maze of clear, light corridors, until they reached a locked door. Inside was a chair, next to it a table with her small overnight bag; inside the bag, her clothes and a hairbrush.

"In one hour," the taller guard said, "we come back."

Suddenly they had shut the door and left her on the other side, in a square, low-ceilinged room. In the corner was a shower stall; they obviously meant for her to wash away the accumulated dirt and to dress in clean clothes, her own clothes, taken from the Lovells' guestroom or brought to her by Curtis. Under duress or willingly, having been against her from the start?

Slowly she walked over to the suitcase, opened it, and felt first the plush lining into which she had once planned to sew the photos that Amet had taken of the murdered American students. She had left them behind, fleeing Florence's bungalow, those images so grim to her then, familiar now.

One by one she picked up the garments packed for her: a pair of pressed khaki pants, a cotton blouse, a sundress of African cloth. These were hers and belonged to a life she might hope to reclaim. At the bottom of the case was the black jumpsuit she had worn to Justin's party. How long she had held him like an emerald in her heart, only to happen on a handful of reluctant embraces, like a gift anticipated too far in advance and sure to disappoint. In the days when she had worn these clothes, she had been, in fact, like a child who expects gifts in exchange for waiting, who makes life out in such simple terms. Perhaps she had loved Justin; perhaps he had even been worth loving. Katya in her limited wisdom had loathed the sight of him. It mattered no longer. In the half-dark of the cell below, Marika had lost what he looked like. The past had become a day to be kept track of only to be crossed off, and whatever wheels these players—she, too—had set in motion were whirling away in the distance. Close by was this square room, this chair to sit in, the mirror on the wall.

With the greatest caution, as if it concealed a weapon, Marika approached the mirror. Bleached white, her face gazed back at her like a negative photograph of the dark people whose eyes had reflected her image when she looked at them in the cell. The skin color made a startling contrast to the deep brown she had come to see as essentially human, whereas the hair had darkened from dirt and lack of light and lay matted on her head. Her own eyes, sunken deeper than she had remembered, expressionless, asked her hollowly why it was she had chosen to conjure this picture from the mirror. Only the thin line of her nose and the high, close cheekbones gave the face away as hers. And yet she was pleased at what she found staring at her from the small frame they had left hanging on the cracked wall by the shower. A new and strange beauty had emerged, hard and cold as winter light.

She looked behind the curtain into the makeshift shower, a towel hanging on the wall, and then back again at the clothes they had retrieved for her. Biswandi wished her to wash off her odor again and put on pressed slacks; therefore she would maintain her oil and dusty reek and her unbelted red dress, as a shield against him. She sat on the chair and waited.

When they unlocked the door, laughing between themselves, they entered to find her there as they had left her. "Hey, na, this a *pig*hole," said the brick-colored guard. "We got no more time."

"I'm ready," Marika said.

"Phegh!" The tall one spat into the corner. "You being ready for worms. Take off and get in the shower, there. We watching now. Go on!"

"You brought me here," Marika said, her lips tight. "You take me wherever we're going next."

"Where you can go!" The first who had spoken stepped angrily to where he stood over her. "You do it?" he asked.

"No."

The flat of his hand cracked across her cheek. Blood rushed into her mouth; she had bitten the inner skin. "Now, bitch!" he said, but the tall one caught his forearm as he raised it again.

"Not a good idea," he said.

"Hey, na, the man going to be there. We got to make her to look okay."

"Is not blood going to do that." The guard picked Marika's hairbrush out of the suitcase. His hand like a hawk descending and clenching the back of her neck, he began roughly to pull the filthy hair back from her face. Tears started to her eyes as the brush yanked out knots. "Get the cloth, you, over there," he said to the other. "Get her face, na, with it."

The short guard marched to the washstand, wet the cloth with cold water, and scrubbed Marika's face as if he were cleaning a pot. When she beat at his arms, he caught both her hands in his pudgy mitt and held them there as in a vise. When his scrubbing hand strayed near her mouth, she bit, but his knuckle caught her teeth before she could draw blood, and then he was finished, and the one working on her hair as well. The cold water had pinched her skin to an old, gaunt texture. When the one brushing her hair was done, he reached for an atomizer of perfume in the case and sprayed it over her like insecticide. She coughed, eyes stinging, at the vapor; even the guard worrying her face reared back and spat into a corner. "Phegh!"

"Is enough," the tall one said. "We are not being in this army to make like a beauty parlor, hey?"

Reeking of perfume, her hair tangled and rank under the fluffy haze left by the brush, she marched between them back through the empty halls until they reached the same room she had been in before. This time the guards walked quickly through the open door; they were late. As they entered the room they let go Marika's arms, and she found herself again facing Biswandi, but to his right was a slight middle-aged Sacatra in a business suit, and to his left stood Curtis Lovell.

"God in heaven, Marika!" he exclaimed, stepping around the long table. "Thank God we found you!"

"Found me?" Marika said, standing stiffly as he tried to embrace her. She thought she detected a look of disgust on his face as he caught her rancid scent.

"We thought you'd been kidnapped! Christ, we were just waiting for the ransom note that never came. Then Biswandi here told us what you'd been through and where you were."

"He—told you."

"Everything. The brainwashing, the way they were going to use you for the plans, where they took you and Claire, the whole deck of cards."

"Claire?" Marika stood still, her hands at her sides. Curtis's white face loomed at her like a dream.

"Well, *she* told me about the place they took you, but she didn't know more."

"You've got Claire?"

"Rescued her, thank God. She's fine."

"Where is she?"

"At the house."

"I don't believe you."

"Come on, Marika, Marika." Approaching her again, Curtis took her shoulders in his large hands as if he would shake her awake. "It's over now, the whole nightmare. Biswandi's got papers for you to sign, we'll get them back for everything they did."

"How long do you think I've been in here?" Ignoring the papers in front of the Sacatra, Marika narrowed her eyes at Curtis until he sniffed and took a step back.

"Biswandi told me: overnight. Tragic. At least you're not with *them* anymore."

"Over a month. Without charges against me."

"Marika." Curtis took her hand and, pressing it, looked straight into her eyes. "I *know*."

Returning his gaze, she saw that he did. He was playing his role to the hilt, despite not only her but his own wife, disappeared for weeks now, Marika imagined, with no trace. The distance of his eyes chilled her. She felt her jaw drop like a snapped coil.

"These papers," Biswandi put in, "are testifying only against *dai*. How they make you steal documents, how they are holding you in their outlaw camp."

"How," the Sacatra added in a high voice—she surmised he had drawn up the papers—"they are torturing you, with telling you how they killed Richard Hooper."

Curtis guided Marika to the table, holding on to her elbow, as if by touching her he could persuade her to do what they wanted. "With these," Biswandi said, pushing the white rectangles across the surface, "we make our country safe again for U.S. visitors. We stamp out this communism. We are making a democracy, everything fair."

"What they want," Curtis said, bending his head to get Marika to look at him, "is to crush the *dai* once and for all. They *need* American help. When you're better—we'll get you out of here today, find a doctor, give you a good long rest—you'll be able to tell the truth to the press and the people in Washington. Our government'll have to jump in here feet first for once. Richard—rest his soul—will get his revenge, Marika."

"And if I don't sign?" Marika addressed not Curtis or Biswandi but the Sacatra, a lawyer, the one who had written the lies for her to attest to.

"Terrible things," he answered calmly, "are being said. Terrible untrue things about your husband."

"Seki."

"The scorpion, you may remember," said Biswandi, "transformed itself."

Marika blinked, remembering the fable about the man killed before his wedding. Biswandi could point the finger wherever he wanted; if he wanted Richard to have died of a sordid affair, the thing was done. Seki would testify and then disappear. She looked down at the papers, which Curtis eagerly spread out for her. With a shock she realized that she had not seen a printed word in weeks, maybe months. She could not concentrate on the text; the letters ran together.

"No way," she said directly to Biswandi. "You can shove your publicity campaign. Get your blood money from some other panicky government."

"She's upset," Curtis said to Biswandi, whose dark skin had flushed red. "Let's give her a little recovery time."

"She sign," said Biswandi. "And she is sticking to it, what she says in here." He thumbed the papers. "Or she stays like the others below."

"Got here last night, did I, Curtis?" Marika's voice rose, mocking.

"Look, Claire's been so worried about you—"

"You haven't seen Claire. For all you know she's dead."

"No, you're confused, she's at the house—"

"You thought they broke me already, didn't you? Well, me alone, maybe, but to sign a lie for Richard—forget it, mister."

"Marika, I can't just leave you here!"

"Then call Charles Hallerin. Get me out."

"They've got serious charges against you!"

"I haven't heard them."

"This is a fight against communism, Marika." His voice grew harder; he shuffled the papers in front of him like a man preparing to leave the floor. "Your family fled Eastern Europe. You know the dangers. And you know one can't always choose one's methods."

"Do your methods include gunning down American diplomats?"

"My dear"—he tucked the papers together—"I knew about Richard's—indiscretions. It wasn't so uncommon. He did love you, but—well, the girl's got an authentic story. And believe me, she'll be punished for her crime only if she *doesn't* tell it."

"Let her tell it and go free. Richard's dead either way. And what I've done had nothing"—she bit her lip—"nothing to do with him."

"Take her," Biswandi said to the guards. As she glanced over her shoulder, Curtis was waving his hands, as at an airplane being propelled out of the room.

"We'll get you out, Marika! Soon!"

"You and Claire?" she taunted him.

"Claire is—Claire—Claire'll come with me next time!"

His face, tense and agitated, moved her. "Claire's safe!" she called back to him, but the metal door had already swung shut on her words.

The concrete floor of the corridor rippled below her like a gray ocean. Waves heaved in her stomach. Having eaten nothing since morning, she still failed to balance the bloated baggage cradled in her hips, her arms and legs heavy with water. As she swayed on the steps, the two guards watched her with interest, then the taller one caught her elbow and prodded her along. If they were going back to the pitch-dark box in which she had survived her first weeks in this place, she thought certainly she would die there. Nausea spread upward from her gut to her head, where it rested in a heavy ache at the nape of her neck. Finally they reached the metal door, and she was ushered back in to the same glazed-eyed group of women she had lived with all these days and nights. Her sisters.

She stood stock still for a while when the guards had slammed shut the door behind them, as if she were hanging on to her balance and her tiny square of ground. At this her third incarceration, she felt for the first time the madness of the urge to freedom. To beat the door and cry to them that she would, she would sign, and emerge into the all-forgiving sunlight under the benevolent protection of Curtis Lovell's arm. Only buckling nausea stilled the violent dash for life, for space and air. As the echo of the metal door died into silence, the floor slid away from her. She found herself half-sitting, half-lying, supported by one arm with the other at her mouth, and freedom fled into the realm of abstraction.

As the others stared, then turned back to their listlessness, Florence pulled herself across the floor, her broken hip dragging, toward Marika. She had not stood, Marika realized, for almost a week.

"They are hurting you, is it not so," Florence said as Marika sank down beside her.

"No, no. Only with words. I feel suddenly sick, is all. It's been coming on like this."

"How long?"

"Some days. In the morning, mostly. But you, Florence, you can't even stand! You've got fever. If you won't ask for a doctor, I'll—"

"How long," Florence interrupted her, "is it now since you are having your monthly?"

When the women in the cell menstruated, they tore off lengths of their skirts and tied them around their hips. The strips had gathered in a heap by the square wooden seat in the privy. The scent of blood permeated the air.

"I've lost track. The food here is so debilitating, I—"

"You are not so skinny from it." Florence touched her upper arm, as if seeing that limb for the first time. Pale as butter, the skin had an unfamiliar puffiness.

"I feel full. But it's not food, it's more like a gas filling me."

Florence's rough black hand traveled down from Marika's arm over the hips of the loose red dress, to her belly, and rested there. Sucking in her breath, Marika resisted the urge to pull away. "You are with child, Missis," Florence said.

"That's not possible," Marika said quickly—knowing, as the words fell out, that it was.

"You had your monthly?"

"It's a few weeks late," Marika confessed. She remembered how the time had come and gone, in the solitary black cell, she had thought little enough of it then. She remembered thinking her belly bloated from water. "Oh God, a baby in this place. It can't be."

"Not to be worrying." Florence patted her hand; Marika felt a palm hot with fever. "This man I speak to, I'm sending him to get herbs. We clean you out."

"Wait," Marika said. "I have to think about—about this thing."

"You're not to be *wanting* this child, na, of the man McGrath?"

"I don't know. I mean if it's his."

"The guards are laying hands on you?"

"No! No, but there was—there could be another." Marika's look barred Florence from asking. The image of Ngebin, smooth and hard in the shadow of his kerosene lamp, his skin scented with palm oil and coal smoke, leapt between them.

Moments passed, motionless. Suddenly a new and different truth, like a bright stranger entering the room, laid its hand upon Marika. "Wait," she said, thrilling to the touch, "a *minute.*"

"We here are rich with time," said Florence.

"If I *am* pregnant," Marika said, "then I am fertile."

"It would seem so." Florence drew herself up against the wall and winced in pain as she adjusted her hip.

"Meaning that if Richard could father a child of Seki's, he could have fathered a child of mine. But he could not."

"Richard Hooper is not lying with this woman," insisted Florence, shaking her head in disgust.

"The *point* is, he's not forcing her to an abortion. She's got no reason to come after him."

"Of course she's not killing him!" Florence's palms went up and down twice. "Those are the men of Biswandi, the butchers outside your house! We tell you and tell you, and then you go to listen to tales told by young girls frightened for their life!"

"I needed proof," Marika said. She moved her own hand across her belly, tender to the touch. "Maybe I'm finding it in myself."

All around her, the room reeked of human females closed up together for a long while. Malnutrition and neglect exhibited themselves on the dun-colored bodies, the matted heads of hair, the torn clothes. Nothing dictated that they should not die like this, together, and together rot into the crevices of the concrete floor. One young woman in the opposite corner leaned on another, scratching softly at her shoulder and murmuring what might have been obscenities or secret passwords; her companion's lips parted in a sickly smile and gave utterance to soundless laughter. Another, who just a few days before had thrown a spoonful of gray rice into the guard's face and received a quick slap across the breasts, was cleaning an older woman's head of lice. To bring a new life into such a space—for who was to say that the days would not open and shut here endlessly like a swinging door, never allowing her to pass through?—would be madness. By the time a baby came she would be mad herself, along with the others, all of them scratching unintelligible signs in the dust like the tiny Nebo next to Florence.

—*Forgive me, Richard,* she prayed.—*For all I know, I'm got with child by a man who saw to your death.*

—*For all you know, you're got by one who loved me as a brother. Anyway, half the world is conceived in violence.*

—*We never spoke of names. It seemed bad luck, back then. But if it's a boy, he'll be called Richard.*

—*That's what your father did, Big Bird.*

—*No. It's not at all what my father did. My father could not go on. I'm going on, Richard. Past you, past everything. This is good-bye.* She waited, but he did not answer. —*Good-bye,* she repeated,—*to all that.*

After the dinner pail had been brought in and its contents consumed, she took a rag from the bucket of water the man had left and squeezed it. Then she bent to Florence, whose eyes had shut tight with pain, and pressed the moist cool cloth to her forehead. "Ungh," Florence mumbled as Marika lifted the cloth and pressed it down again over her burning temples, her still-swollen, purplish cheeks, her cracked lips.

"You just be telling me," Florence said, "if you are wanting the herbs."

Marika moved the damp cloth to the back of Florence's fleshy neck and held it there. The nausea was a flower opening inside her. "Not yet," she said. "We're not over the dam, just yet."

# Chapter 22

It was during the time the women had silently agreed to treat as night that the first explosion hit. It caught Marika in the midst of a dream in which Katya, not she, had given birth to a baby, safe in the apartment in New York, the aunts and uncles standing around it praising its tiny hands, its perfect nose, while she, ragged and rank with the smells of Africa, tried to push between them just to get a look. It was just as she had gotten past Sacza and could almost see the cradle that the ground seemed to give way under her, and she woke.

"Aiee!" a woman was already howling from the corner, then in Lethe, "It's an earthquake! They'll let us die in here! We'll suffocate! Aiee!"

"They've begun," Florence said weakly, lifting her head from the pile of clothes on which she slept.

"Who's begun?" asked another, coming to stand over her. "Begun what? Begun the war? Is it the war now?"

As Marika sat up she felt the wave of nausea come on, faster and more sweeping than of late, and while the ground shook under them she picked her way among the women and went to retch in the foul-smelling privy. She backed out into the main room as the second explosion hit, closer to them, and a thin sprinkle of plaster began running down one whole wall.

"It's the harbor, I think," she said, standing and listening to the reverberation.

"Mines," Florence called hoarsely from the corner. "The Pioneer Aluminum ships, they are coming in to pick up the main load from work finished in harmattan."

"Mines!" cried another, older woman. She stepped over to Florence and shouted in Lethe, too fast for Marika to understand.

"What's she saying?" Marika asked.

"She calls us terrorists and murderers. She is accusing me of the engineering of this mine, she says I am here in this place, na, on purpose. I tell her I am only obeying my own *dai*."

*Dai*, the inner voice. "What's Ngebin up to?"

"It is only for a distraction. They are but very few, in the harbor. The rest be upriver."

"At the dam."

Florence nodded, solemnly and without energy. The leg with the injured hip jutted out stiffly, like a puppet's limb.

"Have they got—" A third explosion interrupted; the plaster erupted into a steady fall, the dust lifting into the air. The women turned first, open-mouthed, to the windowless wall fronting the harbor, then to the prostrate Florence. Muttering began, some scowling at Florence; the one with the scar, Fandella, edged to that side of the room, flanking Florence and Marika. "Have they got the plans?" Marika finished.

"They got enough. They—they going to—" Florence turned her palms up and down; her head rolled. For the last several days, since the day she had declared Marika to be pregnant, she had been slipping. She scarcely ate, and she slept more than she was awake. Her skin gave off heat like a furnace. The guard who gave her news had also been bringing pain pills, but when Marika asked if he couldn't get medical help, he only smiled sheepishly and ignored her. Now she sat on the ground and brought Florence's large head onto her lap.

"Get us some water," she said to Fandella. The woman moved quickly past the mutterers and came back with the plastic scoop from the bucket brought in each morning. "Drink," Marika urged Florence, lifting her head. "You're all dried out. Drown the fever."

Florence opened her mouth for a short gulp, then shook her head and let it sink down again. "He is coming for to take us out," she said, her voice no more than a croak. A series of explosions sounded from a distance, shaking the floor, and the women around them gave a collective gasp. "But I'm not under the sun's eye so long after he comes."

"All you need is a doctor," Marika said. The morning sickness had passed; next to Florence she felt strong, abounding in health. The metal door rattled; the guard, not the one who spoke at intervals to Florence, but another, bringing the flat bread that served as breakfast.

"Hold her," Marika said to the scarred woman, and rose to meet the fat guard. He lumbered in and glowered at the dozen women, as if *they* had broken his sleep with shelling ships in the harbor. Dropping the basket on the floor, he was backing out when Marika pulled at his sleeve.

"Look at her," she said, pointing to Florence. "She's going to die if you don't help her. The prison's got to have a doctor. I don't care what she's charged with, you can't let her rot!"

"Oh, we gotta doctor," the guard said slowly. "We can be sending him pronto, too. You want him?" he asked Florence.

She shook her head. "No" came in a croak.

"It doesn't *matter* whether she wants him or not!" said Marika. "She'll die of fever and starvation if she doesn't have medical attention! You think the world won't hear about it, don't you? Well, they will!"

"Don't!" cried Fandella, holding Florence. "Send him away, we are needing nothing!"

"Sure, now." The fat guard fell to giggling. He winked at Marika. "We get a fine doctor in here. Have a little talk first, na. Hey, 'wa Mthongo?" he said to Florence as he unbolted the door behind him. "You ready?"

"—spit on you!" Florence managed to get out, and followed it with a stream of saliva. Then her head fell back, and the guard clanged shut the heavy door. Echoes of his laughter sounded through the echo of metal.

"Idiot," the *dai* woman said to Marika. "They'll kill her." She put the scoop of water back to Florence's lips.

"They can't interrogate an unconscious woman."

"They are finding ways."

"Only a few hours now," Florence put in, her eyes shut and her mouth scarcely moving. "If we be listening hard, maybe we hear the water, as she is running free. Lie still and listen."

The booms from the direction of the harbor had died away. For a long while, the women sat in their half-dark, gnawing at bread. The stream of plaster would not stop. For once, no one whispered or scratched at the floor. In the silence Marika heard the pounding of her blood in her ears and thought, *It's another's blood, too,* not thinking Ngebin or McGrath but only *another,* because it was impossible to think beyond. At moments in the days past when she had felt her stomach buckle, she had had the sudden sensation that the thing within her must be the seed of McGrath's violence and hate, and she had been ready to turn to Florence for the herbs that would rid her of it. But in the next instant she saw Ngebin and felt his hard-driving comfort, and she was convinced that he had planted that comfort within her. At this image her stomach seemed to rest, and the life in her became her *dai,* her infinitesimal god.

The silence grew unbearable and was bound to come unlocked. The women shuffled again; some moaned. At the time when it seemed the guard should come back with food, no one appeared. The yellow light of the hall silted into the room like an afterthought. Some women, snapping like twigs with hunger and fear, shouted epithets—first out into the unresponsive hallway and then at Florence, who lay unconscious with her head in the scarred woman's lap, her breathing labored. The hours washed by. About the time that a second meal should have come to them, they heard in the distance another explosion, like a roll of thunder far off in the mountains. But they could not hear thunder, underground by the harbor where they sat, any more than they could hear any of the manmade sounds—traffic, airplanes, ship whistles—that surrounded them. The sound was followed in a wave by another, long explosion, just as far off but louder, which seemed to ricochet down through the streets of the city and the halls of the prison until it came to rest in their tiny cell.

"*C'est la Parambo,*" said Fandella, holding Florence.

"You mean the dam," Marika said in French. Fandella nodded. "You really think they got it?"

"I have no doubt. It comes from the right direction, and the Parambo is the only place they would target now."

“Any chance,” Marika said, looking uneasily and vainly through the thin slats of the grilled door, “the water will head here?”

“I know only the plan as it was coming down to us in the city. I know only that there are sluices, channels for the water to take. Also that the shanty people are going to be told when it is coming to flood the banks. We had food stored up for them, rooms all ready. I know only that there were to be many little bombs going off, one at each time.”

“But eventually—”

“The whole river is running free, yes.” The woman’s eyes shone. Marika looked down at Florence, whose eyes lay closed in a face that resembled a wax dummy.

“I wish,” she said, “she had heard the sound.”

“ ’wa Mthongo will see it soon enough. If they find us.”

So Ngebin had done in the dam without her. Marika settled down on the floor and tried to picture the immense walls of the bridge tumbling before the force of dynamite and liberated water, or the cool executive office and corridors that McGrath had shown her, blasted into smoking rubble—but everything she conjured up assumed the proportions of a model built to scale, something Ngebin and Richard might have tinkered over, nothing so massive as the concrete blockade by the endless artificial lake that had so determined Richard’s fate and now prefigured hers.

“Will we hear the water?” she asked, but no one answered her.

They seemed all to be listening, Fandella and the other women—who may have known nothing of Ngebin’s plot but knew certainly what the dam was, knew who had put it and kept it there and what it had done to their people. When whatever they listened for made no further sound—the water running, if it *was* running, as in dreams, silent and deep—their awe gave place to new fear, new hunger, new rancor. They switched their anger onto Marika.

"Rich spy bitch," one broke the silence. "You coming in and out of here like a queen. You gone to be telling us when they bring the food, na, hey?"

"She got her bellyful," said another, "upstairs. Them, your friends, they be coming to blow us up? Or now you the other's whore, since they be giving you a bush baby?"

"You tell us why we not hearing anything. This be the soft spot before the lightning is hitting."

"Look at her, white cunt. She not caring if she dies, na, she going to take us with her!"

"Hey, say you, we take her first away. She's not needing this red rag, ya!"

"We make her to be yelling, na, then the man comes who has been laying her flat!"

"Ya!"

Marika sat on her haunches a little ways in front of Florence and the scarred Fandella while the black forms crowded above her, blocking the light from the grilled door. Her arms found their way across her belly, protecting it. "I don't know about the food," she said, her voice sounding refined and feeble. "I'm just like you, I don't hear about anything."

"She a white communist sow," said one from the back, "with spots!"

"*Voyons ces boutons!*" came from the loudest one, one of those who shuffled during the day like a restless elephant in its cage. She took a step toward Marika.

Looking for help, Marika saw Florence unconscious and Fandella watching out of half-lidded eyes. Probably she thought Marika was getting what she deserved, coming to their country and failing completely.

"I didn't ask to be here," Marika said in French to the

woman breathing over her—though she could have been talking to any of them—"any more than you. What I did, I did for my dead husband."

It stopped them for a minute. They had had husbands, most of them, and a woman in Yumana gave up all for her man. But then from the back came, "That his seed you be carrying, hey?"

"Let's see, now! Let's see how white and fat she be! She is needing to cry out for some milk, na, for this baby to come!"

A hand reached down and tore Marika's dress; the buttons that held it together at the front flew off. Scrambling to her feet, she backed against the wall, one hand over her exposed breasts and the other protecting her belly. Everything from the morning she had gone to McGrath's house came rushing back in that soft sound of cloth shredding, and reduced her. "Please don't," she whimpered, tears of panic rushing from her eyes over her face. "Don't hurt me, I can't do you any good. They brought me back down here because I wouldn't go along with them. I don't know about the mines. I don't know about the dam anymore. Please don't hurt me."

"Listen to the sow crying!"

"You be making us to starve here, hey?"

"Get her clothes!"

Hands darted at her. She backed away from Florence, against the wall. "Oh, Mama," she sobbed aloud. "Oh, Richard." They forced her around, pinned back her arms, pulled off what was left of the dirty red dress. Long fingernails slashed across her shoulder blade; she felt the hot release of blood.

"Strip her!"

"Throw her into the dung, yah!"

"We going to die for this bitch, hey?"

More women, more arms and hands than there had been before, they flipped her down onto her back and she kicked. Her legs churned at them in the dark as they came onto her, and her feet made contact with knees, hips, soft flesh. They screamed, hot with rage, "Aiee! Bitch! Sow! Kill her! In the shithole! Yah!"

Even as she kicked, they were dragging her over to the closet, rank with excrement and menstrual debris. She shrieked until her voice rode over theirs.

Suddenly another, distant sound joined the cacophony. It was not an explosion this time, nor the rush of a new river, but a human melee that grew louder, pressing in on the walls themselves. "Hey, hey!" one woman said. "Ssh!"

But the rest tasted blood and could not stop, and Marika churned her legs like a piston. Her heel clipped the fat woman, the first who had gone for her, on the chin; she punched the hips of another as if they were ears she could box. Fighting each other in their fury to get at her, they blocked the light from the doorway. Claws and fists lunged at Marika from the darkness; she was fighting the dark, the roar of voices outside no more than a curtain containing the struggle.

Then came the familiar turn of the key, the clank of the bar being lifted. The door swung open, and the women prisoners left off their beating as suddenly as they had begun it, to rush into the arms of the crowd filling the corridor. Instead, as light flooded the room, they were met by yellow-banded soldiers with guns pointing them back into the cell.

"Hey!" said the large woman who had led the attack on Marika. "You not going to be setting us free, na, or what?"

"Political prisoners here!" called another.

"Some of you, yes," answered a deep voice familiar to Marika from the other side of the doorway. "For now, you stand back. There are three women only who must come with us."

The guns that pointed into the cell silenced the rest as a young man read off the names: Fandella, Florence 'wa Mthongo, Marika Hooper. Marika backed into the corner, her arms folded over her bare chest. Her dress lay in tatters at the other end of the room.

"She is ill," said Fandella, nodding down at Florence when their names had been read. "She is needing at once a doctor."

"Florence?" said the same familiar voice, and Marika saw Ngebin, for it was he, step out of the lighted corridor into the shadowy corner where Florence lay in a heap. Her eyes slowly opened as he bent over her.

"*B'nago,*" she whispered in greeting. "You must not be staying here. There is too much that you are having, na, to worry on."

"Get a doctor!" Ngebin shouted at his men. Two of them disappeared. Another, spotting Marika, pulled off his brown shirt and stepped forward to hand it to her. She nodded in thanks and turned her back to slip it on; the tail reached halfway to her knees. When she turned back again, Ngebin had stood up.

"Go on!" Florence was saying hoarsely to him. "I'm not dying without you to see, hey? Go now."

Men rushed by the crowd in the corridor, heading somewhere, to another crisis. Ngebin smiled at Florence. His head, leonine with its new growth of hair, rested on his shoulders a little stooped, as if he balanced a load on his back. Marika thought he would leave them then, without noticing her, but before he turned away he stepped forward quickly, as if without looking he knew exactly where she stood, and gripped her slim hand with his large bony one. "I am grateful to see you," he said, resting tired eyes on hers. "We shall talk soon. No more harm can come to you. It is over."

She could not speak but held Ngebin's hand a moment after he would have withdrawn it, as if through that clutch there passed volts of healing energy that burned away her scars and her sores, that shot clean through to whatever frail thing was seeking its life in her womb. Then she saw the flicker of impatience cross his face, and she let him go.

# Chapter 23

The crowd that attended Ngebin's march from the harbor pier to the Homeland Bridge swelled the streets with reckless cheering, waving miniature flags and shouting for Ngebin and the river forever. At the head of the column, half-pushed and half-swallowed by the mass, Marika stumbled barefoot over the uneven streets, dressed in the guerrilla's long shirt and blinking continually in the sun, so much brighter even than the blinding corridors of the prison. There seemed to be nowhere else to go but where Ngebin led, nowhere else to stand but behind him.

He led to the Parambo. New in its water but old in its course, it shot under the bridge and skimmed out to sea. The shantytown that had grown up on the lip of its bed was gone; a small amount of wreckage floated with the current, the level of the river still far from its highest point. Out of sight far above them, at the dam, men were reining it in, holding tons of water in the reserves, locking what gates were left to control the inundation. The untrained water lapped eagerly at the dry shore as if kissing it, and carried its crust of brown mud along to turn the river a rich acorn hue. Ngebin stopped and stood at the center of the bridge, and Marika found herself near him. Above them, the cables creaked and swayed.

"*Liberté!*" the people on shore shouted. "Ngebin! *Dai!*"

He lifted his hand, and the shouting quieted until they could hear the burble of the river flushing out its course.

"My people!" he announced to them, his rich voice carrying just past the crumbling wharf where they gathered. "The hour of freedom has come to Yumana!"

They cheered, a roar echoed by the crowd that stood at the other bank, the entrance to the western hills. When he had held his hand aloft for a long while and they had grown quiet again, he went on. "No one must live with fear in their hearts. We have not come to take away. We give back, first our precious water, then our hope!"

Marika lost herself in the shouting that welled up after this. In a wave of nausea, she leaned back on the old railing of the bridge and wished for a moment that she were in the hospital where they had taken Florence, in a crowded bright room that could have been a stepping stone to this roar of energy, this throng. Fandella had remained there in the overflowing care unit, tending to Florence and to others around her who lay thrashing with fever or open wounds, as if she had been building her strength for this honor through all the months of prison. Marika would have stayed, too, but that one of Ngebin's lieutenants had taken her elbow and said quietly, "He is wanting you should come with him," and there had seemed no choice left to her.

So she had taken leave of Florence, unconscious and—evident under the hospital's fluorescent lights—her generous body wasted to gauntness, the hip gangrened, her skin the color of smoke. There were two Nebo doctors weaving their way among the beds, bidding each one to be patient, the surgery room was occupied, they were taking cases in order of crisis. Beds lined the halls as Marika had found her way out. And she had followed Ngebin, propelled by the crowd as by a vast engine, to the bridge.

He finished his short speech and began to retrace his steps. Ahead of him, his coterie parted the mob; but as he passed Marika, he touched her shoulder and she stepped up to him. She was acutely aware of the bird's nest that passed for her hair, of the grime filling her long sharp fingernails, but mostly of the tan shirt that hung on her like a loose sail down to her pale legs and that the wind blew back against her skin to reveal an infinitesimal change in her shape, of which she was preternaturally certain Ngebin would guess the cause. But he studied only her face, oblivious to the wrecked body on which it rode.

"You need rest," he said, "and we here have only work ahead of us."

"Send me back to the hospital. Let me help there."

"No. You have people anxious, expecting you."

"Tell me first," she said, stepping quickly to keep pace with him, "where James Aholo Biswandi is now."

"Dead." His impassive face moved ahead of her.

"And Mayume?"

"Gone from the country. He will not try coming back."

"Oh, yes." She remembered his trip planned for Israel and Paris, his small snippy French wife.

"McGrath also," he volunteered, "is dead."

The word dropped like a stone in a pool. She heard satisfaction in Ngebin's voice and remembered Florence's saying, *Yet he will be doing violence, this one. It is outside himself. He must bring himself to it.* "And Curtis Lovell?" she asked. Strange to count Curtis among her enemies, his round face smiling, wheedling her to play his hand.

"That one," Ngebin answered, "was an accident." He

heard her sharp intake of breath and slowed his pace. "Unavoidable, tragic. He planted himself in the way."

Still more softly, she put her last question, held to the end. "What of his wife?"

"Ah, she!" In a sudden switch, walking faster, he threw back his long head and let out a bark of a laugh. "She is waiting for you, Marika, and you are welcome to her!"

She smiled for the first time in weeks, picturing Claire in the life of the *dai* camp. "Is she the one expecting me?"

"Not only she. Come, we'll keep it a surprise until you find your way to them."

They had reached the street, lined with jeeps confiscated from Biswandi's scattered army. Ngebin waved over the man who had given Marika his shirt and spoke to him quickly in Nebo. Jumping into a vehicle, the man started the motor and swung around to where they stood. Ngebin helped Marika in. "We may not have time," he said, "to meet again before you leave Yumana." The face turned up to her was filled with determined expectation—calm around the almond eyes and rose mouth but tensed at the jaw for days and nights of ceaseless work, building a government out of air. "I hope you will return to us when we have set it all right, here."

"Am I," she asked, speaking to hold him there a moment while the life growing in her struggled to declare itself to him, "of no more use, then?"

"You would be of immense use. But we have given you suffering enough for a lifetime. You were not born to this battle, you should not have to choose it. *B'nago b'maradi.*"

The mysterious life lay quiescent, knowing this to be the wrong time, as she placed one hand on her belly and returned Ngebin's firm, lingering clasp with the other.

The jeep edged away. As she thought of the baby, Marika recalled the other mystery, the one she had come to Yumana to solve: Richard's death. "What happened," she called to Ngebin before he had quite turned to go back to his people, "to Seki?"

"Who is that, Seki?" he answered, a tired smile on his face.

"The woman who said she killed my husband! They brought her to testify!"

"Don't know of her!"

"She used to work for us! She said Richard—"

She broke off as she saw Ngebin waving her on, the crowd closing between, cutting off her words. Ngebin knew nothing of Seki, or would pretend he knew nothing. The mystery remained.

The bare-chested, olive-skinned Nebo squinted over the wheel and gave brief, incessant honks of the horn to clear swarming bodies from their path. Marika looked back until she perceived the heads of the crowd rise over the head of Ngebin, and the cries of *Freedom, liberté! Dai, Ngebin!* died away in the distance.

She examined her feet. They were swollen but tough, bleeding from a splinter in one side; hard pebbles stuck in the calluses of her heels. With the streets littered by glass, she could count herself lucky. A fine dust had silted between her toes and crusted there like paint. When she reached down to touch them, she felt she was handling foot-shaped rocks attached to her ankles; the idea of wrapping these wedges in shoes gave her a peculiar feeling of disembodiment, as if she were to dress an old and ragged doll.

The crowds had dispersed. The streets through which the Nebo drove, heading toward the terraced hills where Marika had lived with Richard, looked not merely deserted but abandoned, the debris of households and shops trailing from doorways that hung ajar in the bright sun and still air that locked in after the fall harmattan. Graffiti blazed across bare white stucco walls. Twice they pulled the jeep over to make way for a screaming ambulance galloping through the wreckage to the hospital.

"All week long," the Nebo volunteered in French, "fighting here. Curfew all finished. People fighting night and day, fires everywhere."

As he said it, they passed the burnt shell of a building, bare wisps of smoke rising into the air, and Marika spied two boys picking things out of the ashes. "The *dai* fought Biswandi's army here, in the city?" she asked, thinking how deathly quiet it had been, below ground.

"No, lady! All people fighting—because no food, because dying people coming into the city from Parambo sickness, because so many shot, you know, and disappearing into the night. And they know, now, the *dai* are coming, and the dam will come down. So they start to fight police, to fight each other, they cannot help themself."

The wind mingled the fresh scent of the new river with the acrid smoke of fires and gunpowder. Here and there a lone looter scurried through the street, his scavenged goods piled on his back or bundled clumsily under his arm. The jeep might have been invisible, it attracted so little notice. The cloudless sky had assumed a gray cast from the ashes that rose up from all parts of the city.

"So bad you be in prison," the Nebo said as he turned out of the city's heart to cross the causeway. "All will come changed now."

"You think so?" Marika asked, sniffing the burnt air.

"Yah, sure. Now *he*"—a nod toward downtown—"be in charge of things. The Lethe fish again like before, hey? They got their river back!"

"And Nebo?"

"Nebo live safe and quiet. No more curfew! No more favors for police, for army boys!"

"How," Marika asked slowly, "did General Biswandi die?"

"Oh, that one! Hee hee!" The Nebo did a little wriggle in his driver's seat. "It was as the water started to run, yes? So blue and pretty, and then sure enough they all come, this army, rolling up from the harbor. The general gets out of his jeep and is demanding for everything—surrender, guns, men—in this little horn they give him to use. So *he* answers back, we are now the people's government of Yumana, there is no army, this general has no right to be arresting nobody. So Biswandi, he is standing out on a precipice with the dam before him all busted open and the river below, yes? And he tells to his men, start firing, so they go down on knees and go with machine guns at the plant where are the *dai*. He is swinging his right arm like a lash, I see him my own eyes. We warn them—*he* warns them, Stop, they are in mutiny against the new government of Yumana, but General Biswandi is laughing, so, and waving his arm. He says fire again. So then this place where he is standing—hee hee!—it blows up!"

"Blows up?"

"Just like so! A mine there, they have not before used it, and away goes the precipice and the general like a rock from a slingshot, you know? Up in the air and over and over, parts of him flying away, then down to the river. Oh, we cheer!"

Marika laid her arms over the place in her belly where the nausea had set in, as if covering the ears of the child that it might not hear how James Biswandi had met his end.

They had swung out of the city and into the hills familiar to her, their smooth streets and lush vegetation like an island adrift just outside but unreachable from Revenir. Often in the early days, before curfews and night squads circumscribed their movements, she and Richard had walked these roads and breathed in the jasmine and oleander planted there for the delight of foreigners. Justin, too, had been with her here, and he had prompted her to sing as they walked—simple folk tunes or snatches from musicals, her voice clear as running water. She swallowed now, the parchment of her throat pressing in and releasing with pain. Only to sing again, to soften her feet back into human shapes, to move her limbs through the free air, would suffice—and yet what would not suffice, would never suffice again, were the flowers and the hollow talk, the imaginary sustenance taken of a man who was gone from her life.

The jeep stopped before a house that Marika recognized as the Lovells', though three men with yellow armbands guarded the door and all the front windows had been knocked out. Someone had run through Claire's rose garden in front. A scrawl of graffiti defaced the white stucco by the porch.

"Some," said the Nebo, the sun pointing up a scar on his shoulder as he helped Marika down, "became carried away, in the fighting. All calm now, all ended."

Her legs weak, she leaned on his arm as they approached the door and passed through the guards. There inside, moving toward her in a flowing black robe as if Marika had come for a late brandy, was Claire.

"Darling," she said, but the affectation in her voice had vanished. "They told us you would come, but I didn't believe them!"

Redolent as always of lilac, she enveloped Marika in her wide robe. Marika shrank away. "Don't get yourself filthy," she said. "I smell."

"Good God, she's months being tortured in prison and

all she can say is she smells." Claire pulled back to regard her at arm's length, then wrapped her in her arms again. "I never thought," she said, beginning to give way to tears, "I would see you alive again, you poor creature."

"About Curtis—" Marika began.

"Don't." A sliver of pain cut Claire's face. "Not yet, at any rate. I loved him, Marika. The world may not miss him, but I will. Now come get clean, there's someone to see you."

She kept an arm around Marika as one might to steer a child and led her upstairs through the room she had slept in as a guest, to the bath where she had first spread out the sheets of stolen architectural plans for the dam that Ngebin had now exploded. The bath was already running, milky hot water driving out of the faucet and erupting into steam on contact, mesmerizing to Marika as the room gradually filled up with the steam and the scent of hot coconut. She allowed Claire to unbutton and remove the khaki shirt and return it to the driver waiting below. Slipping herself from the dingy pair of nylon panties that had somehow remained intact, almost caked to her body, she straightened up, holding in her stomach. As Claire, like a nurse, eyed her up and down, the soft mound of her abdomen sneaked by the inspection.

"There's oil in the bath," Claire said, "and soap, shampoo, a razor. You'll be all right?"

"Fine," said Marika, standing still as Claire shut off the water and vapors rose from the surface of the filled tub. "Takes some getting used to, is all." But then as Claire turned to leave her alone in the room, she clutched suddenly. "Claire?"

"Yes, anything?" Claire answered quickly.

"Would you help me into it? I'm afraid I'll fall."

So Claire guided her by the elbows, settling her into the hot liquid and handing her a washcloth, much as Marika had done for her mother when Katya once sprained her hip and was fearful of slipping.

"Mama," Marika said to herself as Claire gently shut the door and left her alone. "I'm coming home."

It was like being drunk to emerge, her skin bright with long soaking in the tub, softened with layers of cream, her hair brushed away from her face, to the hallway with its plush white carpet as deep and untrodden as ever. Her mouth ached from brushing her teeth, her gums throbbing as they bled. Her feet, too, throbbed in the sandals that had rested under the bed where she left them; she had pumiced the calluses until the blackened outer layer rubbed off in quick little rolls. The cotton shirt and slacks she wore caressed her skin with their clean starch, though the waist pinched and made her take shallow breaths. She steadied herself on the banister. From the window of her room, she had seen the *dai* soldiers pacing in front of the house, smoking cigarettes. Otherwise, there was no change. The house stood deathly still; no gunfire echoed up from the city, and the dam's noise, or now the sound of the river, was cut off from this portion of the hills.

Her legs shook under her as she took the steps, one at a time, to see who was waiting for her below. Grateful as she was for the soft impress of the carpet under her new feet, and for the brandy and cashews that Claire had left for her in the room upstairs and that were now filling her with a pleasant buttery glow and no intimations of nausea, she wanted more than anything to get back to the sweltering hospital and find Florence. Whoever waited for her downstairs could wait. And who was it, waiting? Seki, ready to tell the truth? No, Ngebin would have known Seki's name, then. Could it be Katya, come from the States to find her darling girl? Marika's heart beat fast, from the brandy and the unaccustomed heat of the bath, and from anxiety that was greater, now that she walked free, than any she had known being brought a captive before General Biswandi.

Once downstairs, she heard the murmur of voices from the sitting room at the back of the house, and she approached gingerly across the wide polished floors. They were on the other side of the wavy glass that separated the still-pristine living room from the back of the house. She saw them, talking together like two old friends, as she stood on the other side of the glass. As she let out her long-held breath, the glass steamed before her eyes.

It was Justin Kilroy who had come to Yumana to find her. He spotted her even before Claire did, though Claire was facing the glass door and his back was to it. He raised himself up from the reclining chair and turned, as if Marika had made a sound, joy spreading like light over his face even before he had her in full view.

"Don't just stand there like a pumpkin!" he cried, getting up. "Time to join the party!"

She stood with her fingers on the door handle. With the glass between them, he rose before her like a spectre. Almost imperceptibly she shook her head. She had not sought Justin Kilroy; his was too many worlds away. But he stepped forward and pushed at the door handle, and she gave way.

"Hey, lady," he said, flashing his straight teeth at her but softening his voice, "we kinda wondered if we'd see you next in a concrete slab."

At that he put his muscled arms around her and enfolded her, and for the first time since she had grieved in this house for Richard, she gave way to tears. Sobs racked her body as he pressed her to his hard chest, each fit of weeping paving the way for the next until the tears were spent and she only heaved drily, held upright by Justin Kilroy of all people, her knees gone to jelly. He let her cry and beat her fists against him; finally he walked her over to a small divan, where she pushed him away and buried her head in her knees.

"Justin. *Justin*," she repeated, not looking at him, as she recovered herself. "Christ. The last one I'd have expected."

"Well, hey! It's nice to provoke such a strong reaction. You've given me one whale of a time hunting you down!"

"How long have you been here?"

"In this stinkhole of a country? About three weeks. I finally snooped my way to your freedom-fighting friends, and they had wind of where you were. A helluva different tale from the official story, by the way. They had me figuring you'd been extradited to Cuba. Not that I believed *that* one."

"What—what made you come to Yumana?"

"I told you I'd haunt you."

"But you didn't know where I'd gone."

"Someone smuggled a message out to me." He glanced sideways at Claire, who sat slim and quiet, her hands folded on her black-draped knees.

"Why, in God's name—" Marika began to Claire.

"Look, darling," she said with a hard edge she had lacked before, "I wasn't so sure our friends in the jungle were going to bring this little revolution off. *Or* that they'd bring it off in time for *you*. Someone had to be got hold of."

"But how did you know—*him?*"

"A person has to wonder what you were doing with all

those paintings around your house, dearie. And I had a talk with poor Richard, years ago, when we were all younger and had our guards down. He dropped a little hint—*you* know Richard, so subtle it was maddening—but just a suggestion of this bohemian life you'd led. Well, it wasn't hard to track down a famous artist. Your friend Gabin—"

"Ngebin," Marika corrected.

"Well, he had a wire, and I cabled a museum in New York. After that I don't know what happened. They didn't let me come down to the house until last night."

"When Curtis—?" Marika began.

"Curtis was dead two days by then." The muscles in Claire's neck jumped, but her voice stayed steady. Had she given way yet, Marika wondered, or would she, too, wait for grief to track her down? Or was there no grieving from the moment Mayume had mutilated her, when she had run from her husband faster than from the knife itself?

"Meantime, I'm staying in this fleabag downtown getting visits from every honky in the place," said Justin. "They got maps and timetables of where you were last seen, they ask for my telegram from Claire here, they claim they're hot on the trail of these *dai* guys who've got you both stashed in a cave somewhere. Hey, I know what a fish smells like. I keep snooping around asking questions, like how come is it these communists would want you cluttering up the works in the first place, till I almost get myself locked up for being abroad after hours. Finally these guys blow up the dam and come ripping into town, and next thing I know a couple guerrillas come asking for me. And took me to this lovely lady here." He nodded at Claire.

"It was good of you," said Marika, "to try to find me."

"Good, hell. It was selfish." Self-deprecating, his grin showed the disarming space between his front teeth. "You see, I remember recently this old friend showed up to surprise me, and how I practically threw her out on her ear, which got us off to a pretty lousy second start. I wouldn't want someone to pull that with me. So I figured to pull off a rescue and scotch the situation. But this rebel guy beat me to it."

"What *is* the situation, down there?" Marika spoke to Claire but kept her eyes on Justin. The sight of him, his torso charged with energy, his limbs restlessly akimbo on the immaculate couch, his black hair straggling down his bronzed neck, the snap of his eyes, drugged her with pleasure. Soon this dream would end, and she would wake again, nauseous and hungry, on the hard floor next to Florence, around them the incessant moaning of the wakeful women like trees bending in the night, above them the inexorable menace of Biswandi.

"They tell me the army's declared allegiance to Ngebin," Claire said. "All I know is that caravans of people were leaving the city for three days, and today they started coming back."

"I want to get to the hospital," Marika said, "and see Florence."

"You'll do nothing of the kind. You're practically ready for a hospital yourself, and you haven't had a decent meal."

"Who's Florence?" asked Justin, his eyes fixed as intensely on Marika as hers were on him.

"Just this nice African woman who was in prison with Marika," Claire explained.

"She's dying," said Marika.

"Well, all *right*, dear, if you feel up to it, then we can see if the coast is clear and get a jeep. I'll just leave you two lovebirds alone a minute while I check with our watchdogs out here."

Smiling beneficently, but with a strained downward turning at the corners of her mouth, Claire exited the room, and Marika was left facing the flesh-and-blood Justin.

"How is she taking the news," she asked him, "about Curtis?"

"Hell, I don't know. I only met the lady twenty-four hours ago. Seems she bears her sorrow okay. I take it he was one coldhearted bastard."

"He was"—Marika turned her palms up like the Lethe, searching for the right word—"in power."

"Well, some of us like to be that way." He crossed the room to where she sat on the divan. As he joined her, she remained still as a statue, her numbed nerves, awakened by the bath and the flow of conversation, at war with one another. "Where are you, my little Rika?" he asked gently, searching her face.

"I'm here."

"No. You're not the same. They took part of you away, down there, and I'm going to get it back."

"Why? You let me go before."

"I haven't painted since you left. I haven't even *thought* about painting. You crowded it all out of my head. If I'd come over here and found you dead, I think I would've hit the bottle and not stopped till they ran out of grain to make the stuff with."

"But I'm alive." She let her fingers stray over to his knee, her blood quickening at the touch. All the horror of the past weeks seemed to fall away, in the bright sunny room, like dead skins.

"And I'm not letting you go again. You're catching the next helicopter out of here with me and coming back to New York to have my baby."

"To have—" Marika's hand flew up from his knee to make a fist at her mouth.

"Hell, at least to try. You blew me away, saying that back in the spring. But I wouldn't mind another chance. At the whole caboodle."

"Oh, Justin." She felt the flowering of the seed already planted within her. It would be a horror to him, to all of them. "Don't—don't bring up the past."

"You cruel boy, you're about to make her cry," said Claire, mercifully appearing at the door. "They say you can get a lift to the hospital, but to hurry. One of them's been called back to the city right now. Seems all's not so quiet down there, my pretties. You sure you want to do this?"

"I'm sure," said Marika, rising. She glanced down at Justin; he nodded, releasing her. When he turned his face up to her, she thought only, *I had forgotten such beauty.*

She found Florence at the hospital at the end of a long corridor of stretchers, cots, and mats laid on the floor. On these slabs lay creatures screaming at their limbs hanging right-angled, clutching their torsos to stem tides of blood that welled up from destroyed ribcages, or utterly silent in unnatural positions, like marionettes dropped carelessly from a far height. Among those worrying the corridor with their rolls of bandages and bottles of pain-killing pills was a figure Marika recognized, tending a young boy who had been knifed in the thigh. Catching the young woman's arm as she straightened up, Marika said to her, "Olanda."

"Who—?" The girl looked up; unlike Ngebin, her head was still smoothly shaved in mourning for Amet. "Oh, Missis Hooper, go quick. She's calling for you, na, thinking you be dead. They going into operating soon now."

She pointed to where Florence lay, naked, covered with a white sheet. Looking mistily at Marika through drugged eyes, Florence parted her lips in the ghost of a smile. "You looking so pretty," she said. "Like a woman in love."

Marika touched her hand to Florence's forehead; the fever still raged. "I'll wait here until you come out," she said. "Maybe we can find a better place for you to go, after."

"Don't be talking to me of better places. Sound like a Christian priest, scaring me!"

"Nothing scares you, Florence."

"You be wanting those herbs we speak of before? Hey?"

"I—might," Marika said, hesitating. "If it's not too late."

"We talking more when I get made into this peg-leg," Florence said as two men in masks approached the stretcher.

"Don't talk like that! They're just going to put a pin or something in your hip. Aren't you?" Marika asked the two, who had straightened the sheet around Florence and made ready to bear her away. They looked but made no answer.

"Not to worry." Florence's hand reached out suddenly and caught Marika's wrist like a grappling hook. "We Kikuyu put our bad spirits down into our legs. Lose one, and you lose only devils."

They lifted her then, and she let go.

Marika backed away down the corridor. The stench of the place would have been overpowering had she not spent many weeks in the cells by the harbor. When she found Olanda again she asked, "Why so many? I thought the army had spoken for Ngebin. I thought the *dai* had cleared the way for the river without hurting anyone. Where are these people coming from?"

"Army, yes. Police, no. They know who's going to be tried, na, for all the killings that happened before. They don't want our man to say, 'Do this, do that.' They going to want the state themselves. They pushing for Biswandi before, and now he's dead, they going to push for themselves. I think it's not so good you be here, Missis Hooper."

"I've been other places," Marika said. "Give me a roll of bandages."

"No, no, better you leave. You push too hard, you be ill."

But she handed over the bandages and antiseptic when Marika put out her hand for them, and with little reluctance showed her where the buckets of hot water were left standing. Together, speaking little, they went from one injured to the next. Marika worked through fatigue that grew thick as a blanket around her. She thought vaguely of Justin, up on the hill, waiting to take her home and give her the life she had hankered for, so many years. But what she had said to him months ago held true: he was gone from her mind, and she could revive him only as one might recall a painting, vivid in its colors but voiceless, bloodless. Yet he had crossed, at last, an ocean to find her.

From outside they heard gunfire, close and then distant. The injured poured in. When she could stand on her feet no longer, Marika found the operating room door down another corridor and waited there on her haunches, resting against a wall. When at last they brought Florence out, she followed the stretcher eagerly until they laid it down in another wing, among other still, white-sheeted victims of the surgeons' quick knives and hurried stitches. Unconscious, Florence's face was the color of dried mud, marked by large bones that had once gone unnoticed in her fleshy cheeks. Over her right hip, the sheet bulged and then dropped away to the smooth flatness of the thin pad beneath.

"Is she going to recover?" Marika asked the intern on his way out.

"Don't know." He glanced back at Florence and shrugged; each one was a gamble to him.

Marika leaned against the wall, the tubular light humming and crackling over her head. Unlike the rest of the hospital, this room was quiet with recovery and with death.

Crowded together, the injured bodies breathed as one, shallowly, with a slight shudder at the exhale. They had said, outside, that the rioting had been quelled, that Ngebin had taken firm command and was enforcing a new curfew. He had promised his people their hour of freedom, and yet in the next hour she had heard him say of Curtis Lovell, *He planted himself in the way.* A dread crept over Marika like cold sweat in the stillness of the recovery room.

They would continue to pour in here, Sacatra and Lethe and Nebo, African against African. She had no more strength to stay and help. Her legs wavered under her. With a sigh, she sank to the floor, and the dark closed in.

Justin and Claire revived her together, shaking her by the shoulder and whispering loudly, "Come on, Marika, up. They say we've got to go. There's a plane for us. Come on."

Waking, she had thought herself in her cell, the odor of human flesh around her, the cold unyielding wall and floor. The white light hitting her eyes brought her back to where she lay, and she struggled to get to her feet. "Florence," she said. "She's here somewhere. In that cot? Is she there? Is she alive?"

She pushed past Justin, who was holding her by both arms, and reached the narrow bed in which Florence had lain. Under the white sheet was a lean Lethe man, his head heavy with bandages. "She was right here," Marika said, pointing.

"Maybe they moved her, dearie," said Claire. She was dressed in a black linen suit that made her skin look white and troubled as the moon's surface.

"We've got to look. Somewhere else in the room. Or

maybe they took her out with the rest. How long was I asleep? We can't let something happen to her."

"We can't exactly stop it, Rika," said Justin, coming up to where she stood among the cots, peering across the row. "We've been combing this joint for you for over an hour, and you left Claire's eight hours back. There's a plane waiting for us. Now hop along, this is no place for political jailbirds."

"Why? What's happened? Did they get Ngebin?" Marika's talk came wild and breathy; her thoughts flew in fragments around the room.

"Hell, no. He's the one says we've got to go. Now, *I'm* not arguing with that, and *Claire's* not arguing, so we figured we'd come get you and hop this puddlejumper that's leaving for civilization."

"Not till we find Florence." Marika headed out the swinging door of the recovery room, into the festering corridor. A doctor rushed by her, and she caught his sleeve. "Do you know Florence 'wa Mthongo," she asked, "who was in there?" She nodded at the door.

"No, lady. If she has been in there and she is not now, she is most probably dead." He shook himself free and went on.

"Come on, Marika," Claire said as they followed her through the halls. "Whether she's dead or not, we have to catch a plane before one of us *is*. You're not well, dearie. You need a good doctor in London."

The hospital wards were the same as the hallways, packed with the casualties of two days' fighting, frantic and unclean. Marika heard Justin's and Claire's voices like echoes, calling that she'd never find Florence, never never; they had to leave, there was a plane to take them away, away. Still she looked, her eyes running over every miserable body waiting for attention, her throat constricted. Finally she saw Olanda and cried out.

"Missis Hooper!" said Florence's daughter, turning away from a patient. "There are these men outside, waiting for you and your friends!"

"Where's your mother, Olanda? She's gone from the room they took her to. Is she—"

"No, Missis, not dead. I take her out myself, to another room, far in back. I am—nervous. Not from the fighting outside so much as here. We are taking all in now, police and soldiers and *dai*, Lethe and Sacatra. Not everyone is going to be my mother's friend. So I hide her a little."

"Can I see her?"

"Christ, Marika," cried Claire, exasperated. "The woman's *alive*. Now can't you find her when the country's stable? We are getting *out*."

Marika turned to face them, her self-appointed companions. Their faces were eager and alarmed. They knew nothing of the prison, the pails of water and bowls of guava paste, of the herbs Florence had offered her. They knew nothing of the child within her.

"My mother is asleep," Olanda offered. "She would not be knowing you, anyhow."

Marika touched Olanda's mahogany cheek, then turned to the two Americans. "You want to go to the airport," she heard herself say weakly.

"Give the lady a gold star," muttered Justin under his breath as he propelled her the rest of the way out of the steamy hospital. Indeed, the car was waiting outside, not an army car but an inconspicuous Renault, and it wove its way dangerously through the teeming streets. Everywhere lay signs of destruction, broken windows and smoking wings of buildings, refuse scattered over the street, toddlers wandering by themselves and screaming. Marika was silent as they pulled away from the city and reached the open road that led to the airport.

So many times she had come this way to commune with Justin. Now he sat beside her, drumming his fingers on the back of the front seat where Claire sat with the driver. Marika looked at him as she might regard a stranger and pitied his anxiety.

Once past the city and away from the river, the car slowed, and the scenes that went by them seemed little changed by the revolution they were leaving behind. There were the boys still selling baobab trunks, the old men selling beads. There were the fields of maize, the groves of cacao. Now and then they passed a confiscated army jeep, filled with *dai,* waving and shouting at them as they drove on. The harmattan had dried the roads into maps of cracked mud, the dust lifting over the wheels of the car. Over the undulating land that sloped to the sea, the sun hung low and flat like a deflated ball of helium, and its elongated rays glazed the parched land. Justin talked incessantly, as if he knew they needed words for humor. He joked with the driver; he gave a comic-strip account of looking for Marika through the maze of the State Department and the officials in Revenir; he asked questions, which Claire answered with forced brightness while Marika kept silent, staring out the square window of the Renault. She felt sure, despite what Olanda had said, that Florence was dying. The face above the white sheet had looked too dull and vacant of life to be opening its eyes in another room. And Ngebin? Who was to say he would not violently follow Florence, leaving nothing more than a river running free?

As she dwelled on the river, Marika's eyes filled with tears that she blinked steadily back. The Parambo was what she had come for, and she was leaving with barely a glimpse of it. Barely a glimpse had she had, too, of the mystery in Richard's death. No one could tell her where the girl Seki was. She would need to search the corners of the city for her and wrest the truth from her, because Biswandi was dead, and Curtis and McGrath with him, and who else would know? Ngebin had taken Marika's vengeance for her, if vengeance on those who were dead was what she had sought. What she had not sought, not here, was the child in her belly, the child she had come to see as a commingling of the comfort and the horror, a baffling child engendered in love and in violence, nurtured with delight and malice.

*—It's not that I want the baby,* she said silently to Justin as he tossed questions at Claire. *It's that I have to finish this out.*

"Hola!" cried Justin as they drew up to the airport. "Will you look at that beautiful bird!"

It was a small jet, poised on the runway, pointing north. Its white metal glistened like snow in the hot sun. Inside, the terminal was filled with Americans and Europeans, loaded down with hastily packed suitcases. Marika spotted Jeremy and Suzanne among the crowd, waving at them.

THIS PLANE IS EMBARKING FOR LONDON IN FIFTEEN MINUTES, a loudspeaker was broadcasting. TICKETS ARE COURTESY OF THE FREE REPUBLIC OF YUMANA, AND ARE BEING HELD BY RESERVATION AT THE COUNTER. PLEASE HAVE YOUR BOARDING PASS READY. CET AVION DEPART POUR LONDRES DANS QUATORZE MINUTES . . .

"I wanted to say, earlier, I'm sorry about Curtis," Marika said to Claire as they took their place in the line for the counter.

"Don't say what you don't mean, dearie. We were both sorry about Richard. Leave it there."

"Do you know where he—is?"

"In Washington already." Claire's eyes were dry; little creases ran around them, as if stitches had been taken out. "The people who—were responsible—arranged at least for that."

"Do you wish you could stay?" Marika was looking out the glass wall of the terminal that faced the runway and the rainforest beyond. The sun was almost down, the dust that drifted through the air had gone to taupe.

"Stay? Hah!" Claire tossed back her head. "Darling, I think the only one gladder than *I* to be getting out of this madness is *you*."

"I don't know about that," Marika said pensively.

"Rika, when we get to New York," Justin said, pulling her up with him, "I want you to see this pal of mine who's *the* hotshot on African diseases. God knows what you got floating around in that place they threw you."

"I'm all right."

"All right, nothing. You're a *case*. And listen, Rika." He drew her close, his mouth tight. "I can understand why you're stiff-arming. I know they did things to you, in there."

"Did *things?*"

"I can tell by your eyes. How you look at *me*. But we'll put it together as we go along. I'm not pushing."

They had reached the clerk giving out tickets. "Lovell," he said in a monotone. "Hooper. Kilroy."

"Hallelujah," said Claire, taking up all three and handing them out. "If my feet never touch this soil again, it will be too soon."

She turned away with Justin, but Marika stayed, staring at the orange ticket as though it contained a message in a code she could not decipher. The ground seemed to move beneath her, not from nausea, but as if she were standing on a barge in the river and had to keep balance as it traveled. Finally, as the next tickets were being handed out, the clerk calling, "Andersen, Reilly," she cut into the line and faced him.

"I won't be using mine," she said, laying it gently on the counter.

"Marika, come *on*." Claire had turned back for her and nudged her elbow, but then she saw the flat orange rectangle. "You've got to be kidding," she said.

"What the hell's the problem?" said Justin, joining them. Claire pointed to the ticket.

"I need to stay here awhile," said Marika. She stepped away from the counter and clasped her hands in front of her as if she were about to pray. "I'll catch the next plane, or the one after. You two go ahead."

"But your guerrilla pal *told* us to get lost," said Justin, advancing on her. "You need medical help, Marika. You can't stay in this jungle."

"He won't mind if I stay. There are a few details—I need—to look after. If I flew back with you, I'd just turn around again in London."

"I'll stay with you, then!"

"No." Holding her ground, she placed one hand flat against his broad chest. His familiar geography made her fingers tremble. "It's between me and this country, here."

"Is it the guy who ordered us these tickets? You staying for him?"

If only it were so simple, to fall into obsession with the steely Ngebin and lose herself where he led. But power and his homeland, she had seen already, possessed him first, and if there were to be a love struggle, it would be between those two. Florence and the others had to trust Ngebin to break new and higher ground than Mayume or Otomo had trod; Marika had only to watch and hope.

Or simple, too, to chase Richard's ghost down the last corridor, to stay in Yumana so that she might put him to rest. Harder to admit that he was resting already in her heart, that whether Seki or the *dai* or Biswandi himself had fired the bullets mattered less than discovering who he was and why he had chanced death. To admit that in awakening her to love his death had been a cruel and priceless gift.

"No," she answered Justin. "It is no one, only something inside myself."

He frowned as she shook her head, caught by her own double meaning. Could it be true that she stayed in danger for an unborn, unknown child?

THIS PLANE IS NOW LEAVING FOR LONDON, the loudspeaker announced. THIS IS THE FINAL BOARDING CALL. PLEASE HAVE YOUR PASSES READY. EN CE MOMENT LE DEPART . . .

"You go, too." Marika leaned down and picked up Justin's knapsack—the same, she remembered in a flash, that he had taken seventeen years ago when they went together to the coast of Maine. "You go, and take up right where you left off. I'll find you in New York—in a while."

"What's a goddamn while?" he asked, backing as she pushed him gently toward the boarding zone. "Days? Weeks? Months?"

"I'll keep in touch. I'll let you know."

He stopped at the gate and dropped his bag. "That's not enough, my Rika," he said, taking her by the shoulders. "I may—I *will* let you get away again. I know when I'm beat. I don't fight. But you promise me"—he put a palm against her forehead, as if checking for fever—"that I'll live. In there. Where you said I'd disappeared. Keep me alive, Rika. Tell me you'll come back someday, for me to paint."

"I will keep you," she answered, "as alive as I am myself."

"And I'll paint you."

"Oh, you'll paint me. I'm sure of it."

"All right, then."

He touched her lips first with the tips of his fingers, then planted a kiss there like a blessing. His big arms encircled her again, and left an invisible bridle that glowed as she stood and watched him slowly walk away toward the impatient plane.

Night had fallen as it always did in harmattan, like a blanket thrown from the hills over the alluvial fan that spread outward from the river's mouth. When the plane had gone, Marika turned back to the empty terminal, yawning like her own hunger and fatigue. Far off, an amber pillow of light in the dark sky marked the city of Revenir. A cool southerly wind, moaning under its breath, was changing the air from salt to musk. If she could just find a ride down, she would rest somewhere, and then begin. Stepping out to the sparse gravel lot, Marika waved her arm at a car that was starting up. Its wheels turned, and it swung around to meet her.